Praise for Between

"There's just something about Jaclyn
me. I sank my teeth into this book and

- @books.with.shay

"Emotional roller coaster, spicy steamy sessions, lovers quarrel
and the shadow daddy himself are all things found in this book. I
couldn't put it down! I can't recommend this series enough,
anything Jaclyn touches turns to GOLD."
- @queenofvikings

"You know when you pick up a new book and you can instantly
tell it's going to be a new all-time favourite? That is this series for
me! It brings delicious tension, nail-biting action and excitement,
and devastating heartache that will leave you needing the next
book ASAP - what more could we ask for?"
- @promisevideo

"I didn't think I could be more obsessed with a book (or its
characters), then Jaclyn went ahead and wrote BSAM. She's
steamy, she's action packed, and she's a 10/10!"
- @vees.reads

"I could not put this book down!! Truly one of the best romantasy
books I've ever read.
P.S. Von is Daddy."
- @coralieslibrary

"This mesmerizing, fast paced fantasy romance series will easily
become a new favourite. Jaclyn's writing effortlessly transports
readers into a world you'll want to get lost in and will have you
greedily turning each page."
- @diemsbookshelf

"Between Sun and Moon is easily my favorite fantasy book of
2024. It's that amazing. I would happily live within this book
without a single complaint."
- @thealexisnielson

"This is a story about how a woman that was pushed to her knees
by her oppressor, rises again, and learns to push right back.
Intense, dark, addictive, and oh so steamy…"
- @onceuponafrida

THE PAST IS
COMING

BETWEEN
SUN
&
MOON

JACLYN KOT

Between Sun and Moon

Jaclyn Kot

Copyright ©2024 by Jaclyn Kot

Editing by Jessica McKelden

Proofreading by New Ink Editing and Veerie Edits

Cover design by Fantasy Cover Design

Formatting by Imagine Ink Designs

Intended for Mature Audiences

CONTENT
WARNING

This book is a dark fantasy romance that contains contents
that could be triggering.
Please visit www.jaclynkotbooks.com for more information.

*To those considering taking a bite of an apple,
be wary of those little, black seeds, won't you?*

EDENVALE

Whispering Pines Forest

Old Northoway

Mount Brimstone

Fisherman's Paradise

Lake Azura

Grasslands of Old Northoway

Old Man's River

Black Elk Forest

Grasslands of Old Westland

Old Westland

The Rift

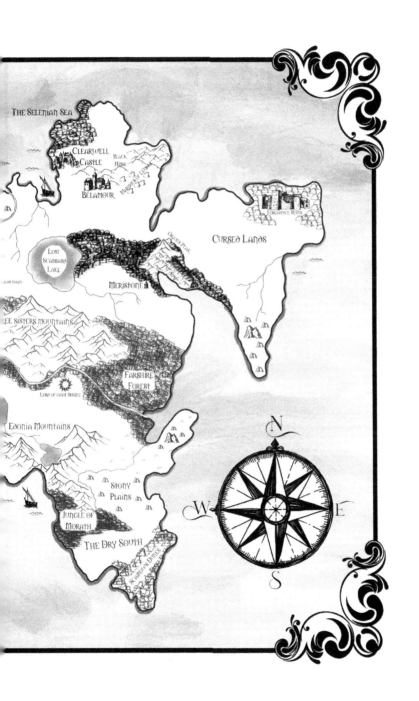

PROLOGUE

Age sixteen.

Sage

Ezra sat on a wood stump across from me, sorting through the bucket of chokecherries we had picked early that morning. She was looking for any leaves, stems, or bugs that might have gotten added into the mix, separating them from the perfectly ripe fruit.

While she did that, I sat cross-legged on the grass, a piece of cedar in one hand and a knife with a fixed, thin blade in the other. The handle was curved to fit comfortably in one's hand to prevent fatigue—perfect for whittling. Kaleb had traded five rabbit furs for the knife and gifted it to me after he caught me looking at it during one of our trips to the market. It was a steal of a deal considering the fine craftsmanship, but when he purchased it, guilt gnawed at my stomach. Kaleb could have used the rabbit furs to buy a month's worth of food, or something for himself—something he so rarely did. When I asked him why he didn't do just that, he bumped my shoulder playfully and said I needed to do something other than just train all the time. And so, I picked up whittling—something Ezra also did from time to time.

Carefully, I made long, sweeping cuts with the grain, working on the general shape. Apart from the delicious smell of cedar wood, the color of it was a deep red, perfect for the animal I was trying to carve—a fox. It was to be a birthday gift for my friend, Adelina.

Adelina and I first met seven summers ago when her father became deathly ill. Ezra and I had been at the market, selling tonics and salves, when Adelina's weary-eyed mother, Mrs. Westford, came up to our table and begged Ezra to come take a look at her ailing husband. Ezra agreed. After the market closed for the day, we went over to the Westfords' residence. While Ezra examined Mr. Westford, Adelina and I sat outside on the stairs. Adelina had been very worried about her father, so to help her get her mind off things, I struck up a conversation with her and asked, "What's your favorite animal?" With a big, toothy smile, she said it was a fox.

I glanced down at the wood carving and frowned. Rather than a sleek fox, it looked more like two blobs with lopsided ears. I grumbled and tossed it to the ground. Despite how hard I tried, the wood never spoke to me. Not like it did with Ezra.

Ezra quirked a graying brow. "What is wrong, child?"

"It doesn't even look remotely like a fox. It looks more like Old Man Winter's cat," I stated, annoyance clipping the words short.

"The one with the missing ear," Ezra agreed with a chuckle. She leaned forward, picked up the discarded wood, and then held her empty, purple-stained hand to me, gesturing for me to give her my knife. I did. She leaned back and began to whittle, skimming off thin pieces of curling wood. "There is a thin line between success and failure. Do you know what determines either outcome?" she asked.

I pondered her question, looking at the wood and then her—I had a feeling I knew the answer behind this lesson, but with Ezra, one could never be completely sure. "Not giving up on something?" I said, more questioning than not.

She worked on one ear, shaping it into a point, before she moved on to the other. "You are correct, child. It takes a great deal of self-discipline to see something all the way through, from beginning to end. We are not born with self-discipline. It's something we must choose for ourselves, something we must continuously work on."

I thought about her words while watching as she worked.

After she was finished with the ears and they were nearly perfect twins, she handed me the knife and the carving. "Go on, give it another go," she said.

I nodded, took the knife and the carving, and tried again.

Lungs heaving from my morning training session, I flopped down in the field of switchgrass and broken, decaying trees and looked up at the crisp, blue sky. Not a cloud in sight. I ran my fingers up a blade of vibrant green grass, stopping just below the delicate, feathery flowers which were beginning to go to seed. The color of their soft panicles hinted of autumn— a rich burgundy.

"Sage?" shouted a familiar female voice in the distance.

"Over here," I warmly called back.

A few moments later, I saw the top of a head covered in dark-brown hair appear just over the tops of the swaying grass. Next, a big, warm smile, mirroring my own.

"There you are," Adelina said as she stepped through the grass. A small braid crowned her head, a lilac-colored ribbon threaded throughout. She flipped her skirt, more patches than original fabric, to the side and sat down. "You aren't in your usual training spot," she observed, glancing around.

"I decided to give this spot a try today." I rolled onto my side and propped my head up with my hand, my elbow digging into the ground beneath me. "There's a lot of fallen trees here. They make for good obstacles and help with my footwork."

"That makes sense," she replied, her earthy brown eyes shifting to mine. "Must have been some wind to take them all out like that."

I nodded in agreement. "It could have been a plough wind, or a tornado that briefly touched down, or—" I smirked. "It could have been someone with the Curse of Air."

"That's a lot of fallen trees for a Cursed to take out on their own. If magic was involved, it would have to be someone much more powerful." She paused, pondering for a moment. "If anything," she cracked a smile, "I'd say one of the gods did it."

I chuckled at that. We both did.

I decided to play along. "Which god do you think it was?" I asked, feeling the gentle breeze chase the scorching caress of the sun from my skin.

"Well, there is one god well known for his ability to control the wind—more so than any other god." She dropped her voice to a whisper, serious eyes meeting mine. "The God of Death."

My stomach knotted, but I heeded it little mind. I whispered back, "Okay, let's say it was him. Why would he demolish a bunch of trees?"

She shrugged one shoulder. "I mean, he's the God of Death. Does he need a reason?"

"I feel like there's always a reason why gods do what they do," I said.

"Alright, I'll bite. Then what would give the *God of Death*—" she whispered his name, "—reason to destroy a bunch of trees?"

I pursed my lips and swished them from side to side, thinking for a moment. A flicker of a thought invaded my mind with such potency that I blurted out, "A lover's quarrel."

Adelina shook her head. "No way. The God of Death was a ruthless king. According to the books I've read, he doesn't possess the ability to love, because he doesn't have a heart."

And it was the strangest thing, because even though I knew next to nothing about the gods—especially the Old Gods—I felt tempted to argue with Adelina. But I shook it off, deciding it was pointless, since again, I knew pretty much zero about the gods and Adelina had made herself the self-proclaimed expert on the subject.

Adelina started, "It's a pity, too, because the pictures I've seen of him?" She fanned herself. "He is on an entirely different level of delicious handsomeness."

"Really?" I said, this bit of info piquing the interest of my sixteen-year-old mind.

"Oh, yes. He's ridiculously handsome," she exclaimed. "All I can say is if *that* is what waits for me on the other side, then sign me up for a one-way trip."

I snorted out a laugh, the sound mirroring hers.

Adelina's mother referred to us as two peas in a pod, and for the most part, she was right. There was a sisterhood between us, and it wasn't just because we were both Cursed, although like a hammer to heated iron, that had been the main element that originally forged our friendship.

"Speaking of handsome men, how are things going with Oliver?" I asked. For a girl who used to gush daily about the things he did with his tongue in her mouth, she had been awfully quiet about him the last two times we had seen one another.

"They're not." She let out a sigh and waved her hand over a spot of barren ground. Her brow furrowed as she concentrated. A few seconds later, a small plant sprouted, two drooping leaves unfurling from it. She pulled her hand away, a frown on her lips as she observed her struggling creation.

"I thought everything was going well with your courtship?" I asked as I placed my hand over top and conjured my Curse. Droplets of water emitted from my palm, raining down on the plant. Before long, the leaves stiffened up.

Adelina smiled in thanks. Her hand returned beside mine as she used her Curse to help the plant grow some more, while

I continued to water it. As we did this, she continued, "It was. Oliver is great. He has prospects and I think we could have a great life together. But . . ." She trailed off.

"It's the Curse, isn't it?" I asked, knowing the feeling all too well—it was the main reason why I never planned to get married. I wasn't about to risk my neck, quite literally, for a husband.

She nodded. "It is. I know my Earth Curse isn't very strong, but it's still a part of me. I can't imagine hiding it from my spouse for the rest of my life. That would be like hiding my true self." She nibbled on her bottom lip, her voice growing softer. "I've been debating telling him—"

"No!" I shouted. My voice was stern to the point that I reminded myself of Kaleb. "Adelina, you *can't* tell him."

"But what if he's not like the others?"

"But what if he *is*?" I shook my head. "If you want to tell him, then tell him when you are old and gray, and you've lived a full life, but do not tell him now, when you have an entire life to live. It is not worth the risk." My eyes flickered between hers, pleading with her not to do such a foolish thing.

Her knitted brows softened. "I understand your concern. Truly, I do. I'm well aware of the risk."

"So then say you won't tell him," I urged her.

"I won't promise you that, Sage. It would be a lie. And I'm tired of the lies," she said as she stood, her hands dusting off the back of her skirt.

I leapt up. "Adelina—"

She cut me off. "I'll see you at my birthday tomorrow, yes? Mom's going to make a whole chicken. You know it's my favorite and we don't get it very often, especially not since

Mrs. Chesterfield raised our rent." Adelina sighed. "That bitter old woman is something else. She's always barging in, unexpected."

"Yes, of course I'll be there," I said quickly, eager to get back to what we had been discussing, regardless of her attempt to change the topic. "Just wait. We need to talk about this."

"We did talk about it," she replied softly, not a hint of anger in her voice.

Mine didn't fare so well. "Not really. You more or less told me that you are debating telling Oliver about your Curse, something no good can possibly come from. If you tell him, you won't be wearing some pretty white gown. You'll be wearing a cheap piece of cloth and an iron collar around your neck as they drag you to the pyre, not the fucking altar," I spouted like a teapot hitting its boiling point.

"Then I guess I'll get that one-way trip to the Spirit Realm that much faster," she replied sarcastically before she turned and stomped away.

I huffed at her, too stubborn to go after her.

I regretted our fight that happened yesterday, regretted not going after her and making things right. Perhaps if I hadn't been so abrasive, she would have given me a chance to talk things out with her. But instead, I'd jumped on the don't-do-it-wagon, and it made her shut down.

I glanced down at the red cedar fox, collared with a large red ribbon tied in a bow. The carving wasn't perfect, but it wasn't half bad either, and in some small way, I was proud of it. I'd paid for the piece with sweat and blood—the multitude of cuts on my fingers attesting to the latter.

Hopefully, the gift, accompanied by my apology, would be enough to earn her forgiveness.

My knuckles rasped against the plank door. The bottom was broken and cracked to the extent that I could fit my shoe underneath it in some places.

The door swung open.

An elderly woman—Mrs. Chesterfield, the owner of the property—peered up at me like a vulture sizing up a chunk of meat. I had seen her before, but usually she was on the other side of the door—nearly beating it down as she demanded the Westfords pay their monthly rent. She'd kicked the door a few times, which certainly didn't help its poor, dilapidated state. In fact, that might be the very reason it was in such poor condition.

"What do you want?" she grouched at me—sprigs of gray hair shooting out from underneath her bonnet.

"Is Adelina here?" I asked, eyes shifting beyond her, into the house. I didn't see Adelina, nor her mother or her three siblings. And when I took a deep breath, all I smelled was the summer air—not a whiff of savory, cooked chicken.

"Who?" she asked, turning her ear towards me.

"Adelina Westford," I said, much louder, remembering that she was hard of hearing.

The woman's eyes flared wide and then she spat on the ground. "How dare you mention that Cursed trash. She'll get what she deserves if she hasn't already."

"What?" I shook my head. "What are you talking about?"

"Yesterday, I found the witch trying to grow magical plants in the backyard, so I reported her. Not too long ago, the soldiers dragged her out and took her to the pyre to be Cleansed. Filthy, vile creature that girl. And living under my roof. Would you imagine that." She spat on the ground again. "I'll be kicking the rest of her disgusting family out when they return from the Cleansing. One can never be too sure how many more of them might be Cur—"

I didn't hear another word as I took off towards the village square, my heart leaping into my ears. I had to hope that I could make it to the pyre before they did. That I could save my friend.

But when I arrived, all that I found was the king's blood-colored banners flickering under the gaze of the sun and a small mound of smoldering ash.

CHAPTER 1

Sage

Von was alive.

Those three words were my unraveling.

Like a string pulled from a constrictive corset, my lungs suddenly filled with air. My first real breath in weeks—*in months*. I breathed again, fearful that this newfound capacity might escape me. Fearful that I had found myself in another dream, waiting for it to turn into a nightmare where everyone I loved was ripped away from me. Because that was where I had been these past few weeks—caught in a nightmare.

Except that nightmare *was* my reality.

"But I saw him take his final breath," I whispered to Kaleb, who was kneeling in front of me—returned to me from the Spirit Realm. "I felt him . . ." I looked down at my hands, the memory of him disintegrating into ash replaying in my mind. The phantom corset returned, and the air fled from my lungs. "I felt him fade from existence," I choked out.

Kaleb took my hands in his, cradling them gently as he spoke. "What you felt was real—he *was* fading, but he did not go . . . not completely."

My brows pinched. "What do you mean?"

"When he returned to the Spirit Realm, he was not himself—it was like the life was being leached out of him. After he saw to the destruction of the Crown of Thorns, he entered a sleep-like state." Kaleb paused. "He remains that way to this day."

"I have to go to him." I shot off the bed and turned towards Kaleb, desperation carved into my voice. "You must take me to him."

Kaleb stood, his expression as flat as the stone walls of this room Arkyn had imprisoned me in, here, in Clearwell Castle, home to the horrible King of Edenvale. Despite the warm, crackling fireplace and ornate matching furniture—all made from white rosewood—this room had felt like a cold, empty dungeon to me over the past few weeks.

It was a world without color.

But now? Now that I knew Von wasn't truly gone, the color was starting to return.

Slowly, Kaleb said, "I can't take you to the Spirit Realm, Sage."

"Why not?" I asked, pacing back and forth, the lace hem of my nightgown sweeping the floor.

"I cannot transport the *living* to the Spirit Realm."

"That seems like something we can easily remedy," I countered a little too easily—being locked up in a room against your will could have that effect on a person. Add on everything else that had transpired over the past month and I had probably lost more than just a *few* marbles.

Kaleb crossed his arms over his chest, his white tunic stretching over his biceps. He had packed a bit more muscle onto his lean figure. It looked good on him. "Says the mortal who is actually an immortal goddess. You can't die like a mortal can, remember?"

I sighed. In all honesty, I had forgotten about that one not-so-tiny detail—

Later, I would think about *that* later.

"There has to be a way I can go to the Spirit Realm," I said, plucking at my bottom lip, racking my scattered thoughts—permanently mussed by the wind of Von. I turned to Kaleb. "How does Von travel back and forth? Between the realms?"

He offered a one-shoulder shrug. "He shadow walks."

I was an idiot—of course that was how Von passed from realm to realm. Unfortunately, for me, shadow walking was an ability I didn't have—or at least . . . I didn't think I had.

"How do *you* travel back and forth?" I asked.

"I have to be in my raven form to pass through to the Spirit Realm."

I quirked a brow. "What do you *pass* through?"

"I can't explain it." He combed his fingers through his blond hair, gray-blue eyes flickering back and forth as he searched for the right words. "It's not a physical barrier or anything like that. I can just *feel it* and then I pass through."

"What does it feel like?" I asked—searching for a needle of understanding in a haystack of unknowns.

"When I come to the Living Realm, it feels cold. Lonely." Kaleb fumbled for a moment, like he didn't really want to tell me the next part. "But when I'm returning to the Spirit Realm, it feels warm. It feels like . . . home. What the cottage felt like."

I understood Kaleb's hesitancy in telling me. Hearing that the Spirit Realm felt like home to him was . . . strange. It reminded me that our lives would never return to normal, at least not like they used to be.

I paced some more.

The bed groaned, snapping me out of my thoughts, as Kaleb sat down. His voice fell soft. "There's something else."

Unease sank low in my belly. "What?"

"Von's wound isn't healing."

My pacing slowed.

If Von was still wounded because of the sword Soren forced me to make, forced me to thrust through him while I was unconscious . . . my presence would only make it worse. Realization turned my feet to lead, and my pacing came to a quick stop.

I couldn't go to him.

My heartbeat thundered in my ears, my temples—*ba-dump, ba-dump, ba-dump.*

"There's more," Kaleb said, shoulders rising as he took a deep breath. "Some of the healers believe that Von's body has entered a self-preserving state so that the wound won't kill him in the immortal way. But the wound won't heal because it was part of the deal—to give his life in exchange for the Crown of Thorns . . . his life for yours."

"Meaning Von won't ever wake up." I tried not to choke on the bitter words.

Kaleb's lips thinned. "Not unless the deal is broken."

I didn't understand. "I thought deals were set in stone—that they were binding." I regurgitated the same words Harper had once spoken to me. "How does one break them?"

"No one seems to know—not even the Old Gods in the Spirit Realm. Von was the one who coined tattooed bargains, so if anyone knew, it would be him. Unfortunately, with his current state, it's not like we can just up and ask him."

I let out an aggravated sigh before I picked up my pacing once more.

My thoughts drifted back to that day in the kitchen when Harper explained what tattooed bargains were. She said they weren't like a piece of paper that could just be torn up. She made them sound like they were impossible to break, and Von hadn't said anything to make me think otherwise.

So how could I break something that could not be broken?

. . . I couldn't.

I glanced down at the tattoo on my arm, my fingers tracing the vines, searching for answers. And that's when it hit me—maybe I didn't need to break the deal. Maybe I needed to make a new one . . .

Could I make a new deal with Arkyn to trump the one he made with Von?

Was that even possible? And if it were, what did I have to offer Arkyn that would be tempting enough for him to end his deal with Von?

There was only one thing I could think of—

"I don't like that." Kaleb's eyes were fixed on mine.

"What?" I asked on reflex, my thoughts galaxies away.

"That look in your eye. It's the one you get when you are about to do something really dumb—like use your Curse on a village-worth of trained soldiers to try to save your brother."

I was transported back to that day—the day Kaleb was conscripted for the war. I remembered standing there, watching him tap the spot over his heart, eyes pleading with mine not to do anything. In that moment, I was given a choice. I could stand down, or I could fight for him. The answer had come easily. Now, I was faced with a similar choice—stand down or fight for someone I loved. Again, the choice was an easy one.

Kaleb sighed. "The look has returned."

"Hear me out," I said as I plopped beside him on the bed, tucking one foot underneath me. "After we thought Von had passed, Arkyn took me to the Endless Mist. He said something about seeing if it would grant us passage this time around. When it refused me, he seemed almost . . . beside himself. I don't know why he wants to get through it so badly, nor do I really care, but maybe I can make a deal with him. Passage through the Endless Mist in exchange for ending Von's deal with him."

It wasn't the best plan, but it was still a plan. As soon as Arkyn returned from his travels, something he said would take about a week's time, I would ask him about it.

Kaleb rubbed his jaw, rough fingertips sounding against a few days' growth of blond stubble. "It's not a bad idea, but how are you going to grant him passage? You said it yourself—the Endless Mist refused you last time."

"It did, but that doesn't mean it always will. I know I'm tethered to it—I just don't know how. I think the answer lies in my lost memories." I sighed, not liking the next part of my plan.

Kaleb bumped his shoulder against mine. "Don't worry, we'll figure it out together."

A moment passed before he pushed off the bed and rose to his full six-foot height. "Okay, so thoughts on how we're going to break you out of here? There are guards posted on the other side of the door." He nodded towards it.

As much as I wanted to leave this place, to return to the cottage or go to the Cursed Lands, I knew I couldn't. "I have to stay here . . . for now."

The line between Kaleb's shoulders grew ramrod straight. "What? Why?"

"I'm going to ask Soren to aid in recovering my memories." I paused briefly before I tacked on the rest. "I'm sure he's still here in the castle."

It was the only place that made sense for him to be. After he had betrayed me, I couldn't see him going back to the Cursed Lands out of fear of them finding out what he had done. That was if they didn't know already. The Cursed Lands were the only home Soren had, so he had nowhere else to go.

"Soren?" Kaleb hissed his name with such distaste that I wondered how I ever related the two. "Soren is the reason you're here. The reason why Von almost lost his immortal life." He threw his hand to the side in anger. "He messed with your mind that day, he convinced you there was a fire, and there was *nothing* I could do to stop you from going inside the cottage—that's how much control he had over you. *That* is

who you are going to trust to retrieve your lost memories?"
He shook his head in disbelief.

I took a deep breath. Kaleb's anger was visceral, and I could feel it working its way through me—knocking on a door I was trying so desperately to keep closed. If I opened it, my own anger would come pouring out of me. And right now, anger would solve nothing.

"I know how it sounds, but it's the best option currently available to me." I paused, his words repeating in my mind— *There was nothing I could do to stop you from going inside the cottage.* My gaze lifted, meeting his, understanding dawning. "You were there . . . that day, in raven form."

Kaleb nodded. "I was, but I was too much of a novice at that time to shift into human form, or even speak for that matter." His fists were clenched so tightly that the bones in his knuckles looked like they might pop through the taut flesh. "I had never felt so useless as I watched you charge into the cottage—knowing you were walking right past a sea of soldiers, into a trap."

The dream I had months ago flared before me. Kaleb and I were running, trying to get to Ezra. When I reached her, it was my body that became strapped to the pyre in place of hers. Even though some parts of that dream were off, most of it came true, in one way or another.

But it wasn't just a dream, was it? That dream was a vision, courtesy of my Dream Curse. Sure, I could try to harness the power of my Dream Curse to find my memories, but learning how to properly use it could take months, or worse, *years*—time I did not have.

Kaleb sat beside me, the bed dipping. Firmly, he said, "I don't trust Soren. And neither should you."

"I don't trust him either," I confirmed with a sigh, "but it's the best option I have right now."

"I don't like it."

"Neither do I."

Kaleb sighed, his neck arching and Adam's apple protruding as he looked to the stone ceiling for guidance. "You know you are in the enemies' hands, right?"

"I'm well aware." And I was—the iron collar wrapped around my throat served as a permanent reminder that I was a prisoner here, that I had been cut off from my Curse.

Kaleb's gaze leveled with mine. "You know that the king is lurking somewhere outside this room right now, and he would probably like nothing more than to torch your Cursed, immortal ass, right?" A hint of a smile touched the corners of his lips.

I grinned. "Not if I torch his old, mortal ass first."

Kaleb chuckled at that. We both did. And damn it felt good.

He glanced towards the balcony doors and his smile faded. "I hate the thought of leaving you here."

"I'll be fine," I reassured him before I tacked on playfully, "Immortal, remember?"

He gave me a half smile, but his eyes were dimly lit. "Just because you are immortal, that doesn't mean you can't get hurt."

"No, I suppose it doesn't." I looked down at my hands.

His words served as a stark reminder of everything I had gone through. Especially these past few months. I had experienced what so many of the Cursed had gone through—the destruction of my family.

Sure, Arkyn and Soren had played their parts, but there was one person I placed the blame with more than anyone else—

The king.

Something ugly swelled inside of me, a potent mixture of hatred and disgust, and it seeped into my veins. It was the exact same feeling I had felt on the day Adelina died.

The king's laws and his complete disregard for human life had led to so many pointless deaths. He could rule differently than his forefathers had—he could choose peace instead of war. But no, he followed in his father's footsteps, and his grandfather's before him, and so forth. And this was the result of it. Because of one family's bias, they'd destroyed *thousands* of lives.

How many more would have to die? When would the raping and pillaging and complete disregard for human life end?

I knew the answer—over the past few weeks, while the castle slept, it was all I could think about, and like a brush fire on a windy day, it consumed me.

A deep sigh fell from Kaleb's mouth, pulling me from my thoughts. "There *is* another reason you want to stay, isn't there?"

I could lie to him—it would make what I planned to do a lot easier, as I imagined he would try to talk me out of it. But maybe I needed to say it out loud. Maybe I needed to voice it, to hear it, to pledge it.

I decided to tell him the truth. "There is."

"What is it?" he asked, scrubbing at his temples as if he sensed a headache coming on.

"I'm finally in a position where I can do something to end the suffering," I said. I took a breath, the words that had echoed inside my mind these past few weeks assembled on my tongue. My heartbeat rang in my ears like a bell, growing louder and louder with each strike—urging me on, urging me to say those six powerful words.

And then I did.

"I'm going to kill the king."

CHAPTER 2

Sage

Kaleb just sat there, staring at me—*gawking* at me, like he was seeing me for the first time. And when I was certain his eyes were about to fall out of his head, he seemed to snap out of it, and he opened his mouth. I waited on bated breath, mentally preparing for the tongue-lashing coming my way. But before his tongue could form a single word, his mouth sprung closed like a bear trap snapped shut.

He rose from the bed. This time, it was his turn to pace—his feet carrying him back and forth. Back and forth. And back and forth.

Finally, I said, "You are going to wear a hole in the floor. Just spit it out."

Kaleb ran his fingers through his hair as his gray-blue eyes lifted to mine. He let out a withheld breath. "When I was a boy, I used to ask Ezra why she trained you so much, why she had no interest in training me . . . One day she finally told me." He shook his head in astonishment. "Sage, she told me that one day, you were going to kill the king."

Now, it was my turn to be speechless.

Despite her hokey-pokey nature, Ezra knew things, things that most people did not. To hear that she had told Kaleb that . . . it felt like reassurance, confirming that this was the path I was destined to take.

He spoke softly. "You do this on one condition, Sage." He held up a single finger, furthering his point. "You let me help you."

I nodded. "I can agree to that."

"Good." Kaleb crossed and uncrossed his arms repeatedly. It was like he wasn't sure what to do with them, or rather, what to do with this new agreement between the two of us—what to do with the fact that we were going to kill the king.

To be honest, I wasn't exactly sure what to do with it either.

For the next little while, we fell into our private thoughts—with me on the bed and Kaleb leaning against the wall.

I didn't consider myself a murderer, nor did I know how I was going to do it.

All I knew was that the destruction of innocent lives needed to end, and there was only one way I could see that happening: by cutting off the proverbial head of the snake and hoping that the body would fall after—the body being those who followed the king.

Kaleb jerked his head up, his tone urgent. "I have to go."

My heart thundered wildly. "Is it something to do with Von?"

"No." He shook his head. "I have to collect a soul."

Collect *a soul?*

That was going to take some getting used to.

Curiously, I asked, "How do you know?"

"I can feel them when they are close to passing," he answered as he crossed the floor towards me. He gave me a quick hug. "I'll return as soon as I can. Keep your head down until then. Okay?"

I offered him a closed-lip grin. "Me? Keep my head down?"

"Sage, please," he groaned.

"Fine, fine, I'll try to keep to myself."

. . . I was a filthy liar.

"Good," Kaleb replied, before he started towards the balcony doors. When he reached them, he opened one and spoke over his shoulder. "And Sage?"

"Hmm?"

Cast in moonlight, his lips curved into a mischievous grin. "For the love of the gods and for the sake of us all—take a bath. You smell worse than a drunk who pissed himself and passed out in an onion patch."

Before I could reply or throw something at him, there came a flash of blinding, vivid light—so bright, it rivaled the stars. I sheltered my eyes.

When I uncovered them, Kaleb was gone.

A caw sounded, in place of goodbye.

To my surprise, the door that led to the rest of the castle was not locked. I could tell as soon as my thumb pressed on the latch and no resistance was met. I opened the door just enough to peer out into the wide hallway.

Candle sconces and paintings alternated with one another. The lit sconces bathed the hallway in a soft, honey glow, illuminating the stretch of crimson rugs that lined the floor, that same color echoed in the banners that hung from the ceiling.

Metal screeched as a guard stepped in front of the door and the king's royal emblem, etched on the chest plate, was planted in my line of view.

"Do you need something?" the guard asked abrasively, his voice about as gentle as sandpaper on a bare ass.

I nearly told him as much, but instead, I placated my tone with kindness and said, "I would like to have a wash."

He grumbled. "At this hour?"

"Yes," I confirmed, thinking he'd move a little faster if he caught a whiff of me through the crack in the door. My Curse might be shackled by the iron collar, but that didn't mean I was without power—all I had to do was lift one arm and *Pow!* Right in the sniffer.

"I will summon your ladies-in-waiting." He sounded annoyed, as if my late-night request was the last thing he wanted to deal with.

"Ladies-in-wai—"

The door was pulled out of my grasp and slammed shut. Jingling keys sounded seconds after. The jerk *locked* me in.

If there was another guard outside the door, I doubt he would have locked it, which meant he was the only one on duty tonight. I wondered if that was the case every night, something I would make sure to pay attention to.

I pressed my ear to the door, listening to the sound of his fading footsteps and screeching, stiff armor. No wonder he sounded like he had a twig lodged up his ass—I'd be grouchy, too, if I had to wear that ridiculous armor.

I chuckled to myself and plopped into the wingback chair, waiting for the guard to return.

But my smile was swept away as my thoughts turned to Von—a visceral ache forming in my heart. I tucked my legs against my chest and dropped my chin on my knees, wishing he were here. Wishing his arms were wrapped around me.

Keys chattered briefly from the other side of the door before it swung open, birthing two young women adorned in fancy, expensive-looking dresses. Their hair fell in long, loose curls, silk ribbons tied at the ends. Delicately, as if they were made of glass, they stepped into the room, their hands clasped, and their heads bowed in subservience.

The guard, who I had decided to nickname Grouchy, emerged behind them. He tossed his head, his face hidden beneath his helmet, towards them. "These are your ladies-in-waiting."

"Greetings, milady," they chimed in perfect, rehearsed unison. Neither of them lifted their heads to look at me.

The collar around my neck suddenly felt a lot tighter.

"Hello," I greeted them, pleasantly enough.

Grouchy cut in. "Due to this ungodly hour, most of the staff are asleep, so we cannot have the bath brought to your room. You will have to attend the shared bathing chambers for tonight."

"That's fine." I motioned to the door, a false smile painting my lips. "Lead the way."

His gauntlet shifted, settling over the pommel of his sword. "You first."

I raised a questioning brow. "I don't know the way."

"You first," he reiterated, grating out the two words between clenched teeth, like I was seconds away from stepping on his last nerve—that was, if I hadn't already.

"Yeesh, alright, alright," I said, throwing my hands up defensively before I walked past the girls and out the door. I didn't miss how they shied away from me, taking a step back as I passed in front of them—like I was a disease that they wanted no part of.

I refused to let it bother me. I couldn't erase whatever lies they had been told. All I could do was show them my truth—that apart from my Curse, I was no different from them. Well, sort of.

I glanced over my shoulder, my bare feet enjoying the soft feel of the rug, a welcome change from the stone floors of the room I was kept in, and asked, "Where to?"

"To your left," Grouchy responded, the ladies-in-waiting stepping behind him.

"Alright." I followed his direction.

After a few sets of winding staircases, three incredibly long hallways, and six short ones, I found myself standing before a giant pool of steaming water. Its perimeter, shaped like the sun, was bedecked with glinting gemstones—brilliant yellows, glittering oranges, and vibrant reds. Elegant marble benches stretched along the sides of the pool. Above it, a twin sun was carved out of the roof—replaced with seamless colored glass. In the dark, the glass read a deep orange, but during the day, when it was under the gaze of the sun, I imagined it would be lighter—gold, perhaps.

The bathing room boasted of unbelievable wealth—enough to feed all the people of Edenvale for the rest of their lives.

And then some.

Apart from myself, the ladies-in-waiting, and Grouchy, no one else was here. And despite it being nighttime, the cavernous room glowed with candlelight, likely due to the wealth of candle sconces positioned throughout.

"Well, are you just going to stare at the roof, or are you going to take your bath?" Grouchy barked at me, his voice echoing amongst the towering stone walls, skittering off the surface of the slumbering waters.

I pulled my gaze from the ceiling, leveling it on him. "I'd like some privacy."

"No can do," Grouchy said, the ire in his voice lifting, replaced with . . . intrigue.

I stifled a gag—the pig was looking forward to seeing me bathe. Goddesses above, I wanted to throttle him right between his tin legs.

"I don't think the king's advisor will be too happy to hear that you saw me naked," I said, hoping he might bite on the lie I was using as bait.

"Lord Arkyn has told me to keep *my eyes on you*. And that's exactly what I plan to do."

"Pig," I muttered.

"What was that?" he growled.

Don't say it, Sage. Don't say it. I chanted the mantra.

But when I looked at the guard trying to assert his male asshole-ness over me, my self-restraint dissolved like sugar on a tongue, and I answered him honestly. "Pig." The word spread like gossip amongst the stone walls, chattering back at us, over and over again.

The ladies-in-waiting let out a shocked sound, like I had just said the dirtiest word their clean, little virgin ears had ever heard. I tried not to roll my eyes—the hypocrisy of it all.

Despite his age, Grouchy moved fast. He lunged towards me. I ducked underneath his grasp, a laugh escaping my lips—admittedly, this was the most fun I had had in days. He twirled around, lunging for me again, but even in my laid-in-bed-for-two-weeks sorry-ass state, I was too quick for him. We continued our little dance, his anger growing with each failed attempt. I swore that if he took his helmet off, his face would be as red as the banners that hung above—

Come to think of it, it might do his withered brain cells some good to have a little fresh air. Perhaps I should take it off for him.

So I did just that when he charged me again—I stole his helmet.

As he raced past me, I glanced down at the shiny metal, scuffed with a few battle scars. Suddenly, it felt like a scalding hot potato in my hands. Eager to get rid of it, I yeeted it into the pool.

A loud *plunk* sounded, followed by a ripple of protest—the water disturbed from its peaceful, dormant state.

All four of us paused, watching as it sank down, down, down. My gut followed its lead.

My head swiveled to his. That was the first time I got a good look at his face. Crow's feet shot out like cobwebs from his eyes, and deep wrinkles etched around his mouth—and they weren't of the smiling kind.

"You are going to pay for that!" he bellowed at me. His hand flew to his sword, the metal singing as he withdrew it from its scabbard.

Apparently, I had struck a nerve.

Although I wanted nothing more than to take the sword from him and ram it up his pompous ass, I did not think the king, nor Arkyn, would take kindly to me killing one of the guards—self-defense or not. And the last thing I needed was to draw attention from the king.

"Look," I started, my hands raised in defense. "I think we got off on the wrong foot."

But he wasn't in the mood to listen—no, he was locked on me like a bull locked on a matador's red cape, steam coming out of his flared nostrils.

"What's going on here?" demanded a male voice behind me—a voice gilded in regality and splendor. Poised and clipped and heavily accented.

Immediately, the ladies-in-waiting dropped into a respectful, elegant bow.

"Your Royal Highness," Grouchy sputtered like a toddler stringing together the alphabet. Dropping his sword, it clamored against the stone floor as he fell onto bended knee, his head drooping, metal screeching.

Slowly, I turned, my gaze lifting. Lifting . . . to meet *his*.

It was as if the Creator had taken liquid gold, sprinkled it with stardust, and poured it into his eyes. They were the most beautiful eyes I had ever seen. Undoubtedly.

But it was not his eyes that made my mouth fall open, it was the color of his hair—as white as winter's first kiss of snow.

The very same color as my own.

CHAPTER 3

Sage

"I apologize, Your Royal Highness, I—"

The regal male raised his hand, silencing the guard immediately.

As he watched me, I watched him, my gaze shifting, taking all of him in.

Gold robes clung to his tall, lean-muscled frame. They did very little to hide the masculine form that dwelled beneath. His hair was unbound, the long, wintery strands spun of fine silk and woven with thin, gold chains that were connected to a finely crafted crown. The crown was not boasting in riches, even though it was undoubtedly a priceless piece. It was the careful detailing, the delicate architecture, the slender, steady arches that made it seem—

Ethereal.

A crown befitting its owner.

Surely, on the day of his creation, the Creator had decided to take their time, to ensure every line, every contour, and every dip was painstakingly carved to perfection. He rivaled the sun.

No. He *was* the sun.

From the way he held himself to the way he looked—my body could not help but grow weak in the knees. Like it was begging me to bow to *my king.*

Who was he? And why did he possess the same rare hair color as my own? Were we related somehow?

No, we were not kin. *That* was a truth I could feel in my soul.

"Leave us," he commanded the other three, his voice severing me from my private thoughts.

Without so much as another word, they hurried quickly out of the room, their departure leaving me alone with the angelic, beautiful man—if he could even be called a man. The word felt too lackluster to describe him.

I had no doubt that he was royalty—the crown he wore, the title the guard addressed him with, and the way he held himself stated as much. But I knew he wasn't the king because the king was in his sixties—unlike the male standing before me, who appeared to be around my age, perhaps a bit older.

"What happened?" the golden-eyed male asked in that enchanting voice, the type that poets wrote sonnets about. Even though his words were posed as a question, it didn't really feel like one—it felt like a soft demand—an escapable one at that.

"I asked the guard to bring me for a bath, but he refused to let me do so without him watching," I answered as politely as I could, all things considered—a piggish guard being the *all things considered* part.

"Ah," the male replied softly, regally, his gaze shifting briefly to the bathing pool. "And that is why you threw his helmet in the water?"

. . . I didn't realize he saw that.

My throat suddenly felt like a barb of foxtail was stuck in it. I cleared it, then said, "Things sort of escalated between the two of us."

His long, white lashes lowered, his gaze dipping to the collar wrapped around my throat. The hairs on the back of my neck raised as he surveyed it with knowing eyes. Every fiber of my being screamed at me to run—to do *something*—but my useless feet were locked in place. So, I waited on bated breath, waited to see what he would say.

His golden eyes shifted to the sword still laying on the floor and a smile touched the corners of his lips. "Well then, I am happy I could de-escalate the matter before one of you got hurt."

His smile. His voice. It was an intoxicating combination, one I could drown in. It felt like this male was to me what bourbon was to Von—my own personal brand of alcohol. And if the past had taught me anything at all, there was probably a reason for my body's response to him.

The question now being . . . *what* was it?

"I have to confess, I was also coming down to bathe," he said, as he gracefully walked away from me, towards the benches. "Would you care to join me?"

Despite how enchanting he made that offer sound, I bristled. "Oh no, Your Royal Highness, I wouldn't want to impose."

"You would refuse me your company?" he asked softly, long, adept fingers loosening his golden robes.

Yes—

"No," I lied cautiously. "I presumed since you came to bathe at such a late hour, you must wish to be alone."

"I was looking forward to being alone, but—" The robes fell to the ground, a puddle of gold pooling at his feet, rendering him *naked*. His skin was immaculate—there were no scars, no markings, only smooth silk wrapped around steely muscle. He glanced over his broad shoulder, that illustrious smile adorning his lips once more, the chains of his crown shimmering. "—that was, until I saw you."

Heat blossomed across my cheeks, licking down my neck. I looked away, silently cursing the traitorous response of my body.

"It is not a sin to look at me," he teased, a soft laugh following after. I heard the gentle splashing of water, a beckoning call to me, as he walked down a set of stairs and into the bathing pool. "You came here to bathe, yes?"

I glanced his way, thanking the Creator that his lower half was now hidden beneath the dancing, twinkling waters.

"I did," I replied.

"Then join me," he insisted playfully.

Three little words had never sounded so . . . *enticing*. It was like the casting of a spell.

I nearly took a step forward, nearly pulled off my nightgown and let him gaze upon my naked flesh—*I nearly joined him.*

But . . . despite the strength of that intense pull, the one I had with Von was stronger.

"I can't."

If my refusal bothered him, he didn't let on.

"Are you married?" he inquired, that grin only seeming to grow wider as he backed further into the embrace of the water. It was just over his navel, wetting the tips of his white hair, wetting his sleek, chiseled abdomen.

What a random question, I thought to myself.

"No, I'm not," I answered with a hint of caution.

"Are you sure about that?" he chuckled, his rich laughter wrapping around me like a fur coat—tailored specially for me.

Mentally, I shook it off and shot him a funny look. "I'm quite sure."

His brows raised slightly as if he were skeptical of my answer. "Are you betrothed then?"

"No."

He chuckled again, the sound decadent. "Then you have no reason to refuse *your* future king."

Future king? That would make him . . .

The Golden Prince, the heir of Edenvale.

I took one sweeping look at him, adorned in all his splendor, and I was surprised I hadn't realized it before.

How many times had I heard his illustrious title praised on the lips of the villagers back in Meristone? Too many to count, surely.

Every year, during midsummer, all of Edenvale held a week-long celebration for him, leading up to the summer solstice—the day of the year when the sun graced the sky for the longest period, and the night was at its shortest. This day was the day of the Golden Prince's birth. It was already considered a sacred day because it was the same day as the creation of the sun—the same day that the Lord of Light had been born on. The people took it as a good omen that the Golden Prince was born on such a sacred day—that the gods were showing favor to him and his future reign.

Part of me felt an ounce of relief that I had figured out who he was, but when I reminded myself that he was the *king's son*, and he wanted *me* to take a *bath* with *him*, my unease quickly returned.

"I think it's best I leave." I slid one foot back. Then another.

His lips thinned, a slight growl weaved into his royal voice when he said, "I do not permit it."

Permit it? Prince or not, no one *permitted* me to do anything—especially a man. I needed to leave before I told him as much.

I performed a quick, sloppy bow. "Enjoy your night, Your Royal Highness."

Turning, I took a step forward and walked straight into a wall of stone.

Except it wasn't a wall at all—it was a *wet, naked, prince.*

I stumbled backwards, which was a huge mistake, because now I could see more of him—too much of him. Hooked by the perfect "V" of his lower torso, my gaze was directed to the weapon between his legs—great divine, it looked to be gifted by the gods.

And it was most definitely aroused.

I gasped, embarrassment chasing away the cool complexion of my cheeks. "How did you . . ." I stammered, rearing back, trying to understand how he could be in the pool one second, and behind me the next. Only Von could do that. Which meant—

"You can shadow walk!"

His hand shot out faster than a viper. Gripping my arm, he pulled me into him—against him, his body making my nightgown wet. "No, Moonbeam, *we* light walk."

"What do you mean *we*?" *And did he just call me Moonbeam?*

"I think it's rather self-explanatory," he said, his grasp forged from iron itself.

Self-explanatory? Sure, the concept was easy enough to understand, but that didn't make it any easier to grasp. As it currently stood, I couldn't shadow walk—light walk, whatever—although, perhaps, in the past I could . . .

I tucked that thought in my back pocket and focused on trying to pull my arm away from him, but no matter how hard I tried, his grip was unbreakable—his strength beyond that of any *mere* mortal. I blinked, looking at his hand and then at him, feeling like I was seeing, truly seeing him this time—he who was cloaked in divine glory. No wonder my body felt so compelled to be wrapped up against his . . .

Like called to like. Why hadn't I seen it before?

"You're a Demi God," I blurted out.

He laughed at that. "You insult me, *goddess.*"

Everything in me ground to a sudden, heavy halt. Like a pebble thrown into a lake, down, down, down, I sunk.

"How do you know what I am?"

"Because you and I are one and the same." He lowered his face, his voice dropping an octave as he spoke softly in my ear. "Just as my body yearns for yours, yours does for mine."

I trembled at the cadence in his voice, my body going limp—dormant—just like the time that snake bit me in the woods. That same sort of paralysis had struck me again, and as much as I was screaming at myself to move, to do something—*anything*—I could not stop staring into those beautiful, golden eyes.

"What are you?" I asked breathlessly, even though I already held the answer.

"You know what I am," he whispered, a breath away from my lips.

And then he kissed me.

CHAPTER 4

Sage

I took a page out of Von's book, and I bit him—I bit him *hard*.

He jerked back, tearing his bottom lip from my clenched teeth, shoving me away from him with his immortal strength. I stumbled backwards, catching myself before I fell, my hand shooting out to a pillar to help stabilize myself.

My expression twisted—I could taste his blood on my tongue, but in place of copper, I tasted the *sweetest, richest honey*. It trickled through me, reaching every cell, every nerve ending. Instantly, my body became hot and needy. Lit with the flame of desire.

I smothered that fucker out, cleared my throat, and spat on the ground—wishing I had a shot of bourbon to drown the prince's taste out. I looked up at him, my chest heaving, adrenaline pounding in my ears like the beat of a thunderous drum.

He casually pressed the back of his hand against his lip, blotting it—blotting the thick, golden liquid that seeped from the gruesome tear in his otherwise perfect lip.

Ichor . . . The blood of the Gods.

No better than an overheated teapot, I sputtered, "You bleed gold."

"All of the New Gods' ichor is that color," he said, his hand flicking to the side, splattering the gray stone with droplets of gold. He raised his head, the wound in his lip completely healed—the evidence of my bite gone.

My brows furrowed. "I don't."

"You will." He smiled seditiously, before he started to walk towards me—still very much naked, the weapon between his legs harder than ever.

I reared back, eyeing the discarded, forgotten sword, the metal blade shimmering upon the ground—it was not far to my right.

"Don't even think about it," he warned with a soft growl.

Oh, but I wasn't just thinking about it.

My feet slammed against the ground, the muscles in my legs launching me towards the sword. I wrapped my hand around the hilt at the same moment his foot fell over the blade—trapping it to the ground.

I looked up, snarling.

He snarled back, the two of us warring for dominance.

"You have taken my ichor," he growled. "And for that, I will have yours in return."

"Like I said, I don't bleed gold," I said, tugging on the sword. It felt like a mountain had fallen on top of it. Foolishly, I tugged some more, not ready to give up.

"Like *I* said—" His fingers wrapped around my arm, and he hauled me to my feet as if I weighed no more than a feather. I tried to take the sword with me, but it remained trapped under his foot. "You will."

With one hand, he dragged me towards the bathing pool while I struggled against him, my feet skittering to keep myself upright. My fingernails bit into his perfect skin, chewing into his flesh.

Skillfully, he twirled me so I was facing him and my back was positioned towards the bath. His hands slid to my waist, and he hoisted me into the air.

"Don't you dare," I growled, my jaw aching from how tightly I clenched my teeth.

I slapped and clawed at him, trying to break his impossible hold. He looked unimpressed, as if he regarded my strength similar to that of a child's.

Without a word of warning, he threw me over the edge.

Midair, I caught sight of the pleased smile he wore—the satisfactory twist of his lips as he watched me fall in. But just before I went under, I flipped my middle finger at him.

Feeling the warm water encase my body was a blessing in itself, especially because the iron collar cut me off from my Curse. I took a moment, allowing myself to sink as if I were back home, back in my lake.

How greatly I had missed my connection with the element of water.

But like so many things in my life, that moment of peace was snatched away.

I felt the water shudder, breaking out into waves—a silent whisper that *he* was coming for me. Heeding its warning, I pressed my heels down, my feet searching for purchase. When I found it, I pressed them into the smooth rock and mortar bottom and jerked myself upright, breaking through the surface. I inhaled a deep breath, my hands sweeping hurriedly across my face, clearing the water and my hair before my eyelids sprung open.

"Don't—" his voice was in my ear, the warmth of his body a sudden caress against my back, "—move."

And to my horror, I couldn't. I was frozen in place, my traitorous body obeying his order. *What in the Spirit Realm was this?*

"We have rules, goddess. Allow me to remind you of them," he said, coiling my hair and roping it around his forearm, cinching his hold. The roots of my hair were pulled taut, causing a pinch of pain at my scalp, just enough to make me uncomfortable.

Mentally, I was still at war with those two words—*Don't move.*

"I'm sure you've heard the saying—an eye for an eye?" His free arm cinched around my waist, locking my frame against his.

An eye for an eye? Panic rode me hard, taking over the reins, but it was just the thing I needed to burst through his command that rendered my body his prisoner. I threw my elbow back and planted it into his iron-crafted ribs.

He didn't even wince.

As for me? It felt like I'd shattered my elbow.

"In this case, it is ichor for ichor." His tongue collected a bead of water from my neck before it could slip under the collar. "Because you gave me no pleasure when you took mine, I will return the favor. Perhaps it will help you remember what you are to me." Forcefully, he yanked my head to the side.

"Wait!" I yelled, my voice echoing back at me, bouncing around the walls of the vast room. Like me, it had nowhere to go.

But there was no waiting. There was only feeling as he plunged his teeth into my neck, just above the iron collar. I could feel his incisors, feel them grow erect as they sunk deeper and deeper into my flesh—reminding me of the time the snake bit me in the woods.

But this? This hurt much—*much*—worse.

His jaw clamped down even tighter and pain pumped into me—bolting through every nerve ending, making me feral and wild, like an animal prepared to chew off its own leg to free itself from a trap. Right now, I'd claw my neck from my body, just to make the pain stop. My hands tried, but he captured my wrists and locked them against my chest.

It was agony, and it just continued to build and build and build like an orgasm—but instead of the language of pleasure, all it spoke of was immense, scarring pain. The kind you never forget.

Beyond my screaming, I could hear him drinking from me—the slurping as he pulled my blood from my body, into his mouth, drinking me down.

With each swallow, my fight grew weaker.

With each passing second, my eyelids felt heavier.

I held out as long as I could until I finally gave in—and it hit me like a tidal wave, dragging me under. I handed myself over to the murky depths with one last thought on my mind—when I hit the bottom, would Von be there waiting for me?

Von . . .

CHAPTER 5

Von

Morons.

As I had lain on the cement slab over the past so many weeks, forced to listen to the conversations taking place around me, *that* was what I had determined. I had surrounded myself with morons. They blathered on and on and on, their incessant ramblings grating against my frayed patience.

Granted, they were trying to figure out a way to wake me up from the chokehold of my eternal slumber—something only I could do, because I was the one who had put myself in this self-preserving state. Without doing so, my existence would have ceased, and unfortunately for Sage, she wasn't about to be rid of me that easily. And so, I supposed I could find it somewhere within me not to throw the whole lot of morons in the Da'Nu when I awakened.

Although the thought was tempting.

My body had been poked and prodded and cut into countless times as the healers conducted their tests with their enchanted tools—it took a special blade to cut into my steel-derived flesh. Regardless of what they did, I could not feel a damn thing. I was just . . . there, my body asleep, but my mind very much awake. I was stuck between comatose and what came beyond the end of my immortality.

All because of the deal I made with the royal ass licker.

I was the one who had created tattooed bargains and now, ironically, I was stuck like this because of it. In the early days of the realms, when things were far less . . . civil, mankind lacked the ability to uphold their end of the bargain when they tried to make deals with one another. And so, I created the bargain, but instead of using chiseled stone—paper did not exist during that time—it was forged in the skin.

There were three ways for a tattooed bargain to end—if the deal was completed, if both parties agreed to end it, or if one of the parties died of natural causes.

But as I was a sly fucker, I left *myself* a loophole and told only my siblings—should I ever find myself in a situation such as this.

The problem? It required an item I no longer had in my possession, an item that was lost to the decades—the Blade of Moram.

In truth, I preferred the blade stayed lost.

The blade had been forged by a trio of sisters, powerful females that did not belong to either Old Gods or New. Their creation went beyond the concept of time. They were known as the Three Spinners—Fate, Destiny, and Free Will. Each one cut a thread from their being and set it in the mold. They'd poured lava overtop, creating the blade and handle. When it hardened, it turned to obsidian, locking a fragment of each goddesses insurmountable power within.

On the day of my coronation, they gave it to me.

And on the day that I was stripped of the Living and Immortal Realms, they took it back.

I didn't realize they had taken it until I walked into my study and found the glass case that I displayed it in empty. One could imagine the cataclysmic anger I felt when I saw it had been regifted to the new king—my severely lacking, much-less-handsome replacement.

But that emotion soon left me when I saw what he held in his arms . . .

The Goddess of Life.

Divinely made as a full-grown woman, woven from the joining of the Selenian Sea and Luna. Ecstasy written in the female form, every bit of her built to conquer—lands, men, women, whatever she wanted.

Creator above, she was a lovely creature. Enchanting, really.

The embodiment of her given title—*the Lady of Light.*

I had lived for thousands of years in darkness, days coming and going, with a natural, unnoticeable rhythm to them. Just like breathing, they all tended to blur together. But that day would forever be imprinted on my mind, my flesh, like a red-hot brand seared into my skin—

The day I first saw *her.*

The day she burrowed into me so deeply, whether I wished to admit it back then or not, I knew I would never get her out.

She stood behind him and peered at me over his shoulder with those wide, blue eyes of hers, effervescent and ice-cold, regarding me like the monster her instincts told her I was—the villain in her story, come to destroy her life.

She was not wrong.

I could feel the fear rolling off of her—off of him—as they wondered what I would do next. But all I wanted was to feel my wind in her hair, to touch her skin and find out for myself if it was truly as silky as it looked. Creator above, when I thought of tasting her, of the ichor that coursed through her veins, of the sweetness between her legs, it nearly brought me to my knees.

My emotions had never felt so . . . unknown.

With one terrified glance, the azure-eyed goddess had bewitched me.

That was the first time I felt *it*—that strange, incessant impulse, that fierce need to *claim* her. To make her *mine*.

Suddenly, there was nothing more I wanted than to take her.

So, that's exactly what I did.

I stole her from the God of Life.

"Get out," grated a voice, coming from the doorway—effectively pulling me from my thoughts. "All of you, out." The sound of bootheels striking the glass floor approached me, while a dozen feet scattered towards and out the door, closing it behind them, taking their suddenly hushed voices with them.

I would have breathed a sigh of relief if my lungs weren't stuck in a frozen state.

"Hello, brother. You look—" Folkoln paused. I didn't need to see to know that he was standing beside me, looking over my useless shell of a body. "The same."

A glass cup sounded against the cement slab, followed by the *pop* of a cork and the *glug* of a bottle as some of its contents were poured into the glass. The bottle clinked softly as it was set down, the cup making nary a whisper as it was picked up.

"This might just be one of the finest batches yet." He took a heady sip. "It's a shame you're stuck in this situation, but I suppose that just means more for me."

He sat down, the click that sounded in his bending left knee—an old war wound that even his immortal body could not properly heal—telling me as much. The boots that thudded, one over top of another, just off to the side of my head as he put his feet up, confirmed it.

There were very few people I allowed to get away with such behavior, but I had a soft spot for my insolent brother, so I let him do—mostly—as he pleased. Besides, what else could one expect from the God of Chaos? Keeping him contained and not wreaking havoc on the rest of the realms was hard enough.

Folkoln drew out a sigh. "I just got back from seeing Saphira. She has expressed zero interest in helping me search for the Blade of Moram, although knowing her, she's probably already searching for it just to spite you. If you hadn't taken her wings and exiled her, I imagine she would be a lot more helpful. You know my stance on this . . . you should not have taken them in the first place."

Despite his bleeding heart for our sister, Saphira did not deserve to have her wings back. But I had never told Folkoln the entire story, of what had been expected of me . . .

After I gave up the Living and Immortal Realms and withdrew from the Immortal War, Saphira started to question my rule—question me. She staged a coup and *tried* to have me overthrown, believing she was fit to rule the Spirit Realm, that she was powerful enough to take back the other realms on her own. Even though her rebellion eventually failed, her actions began to incite the possibility of another one. I heard the whispers her rebellion stirred, passing from mouth to mouth, spreading like a disease—that perhaps the Goddess of War was right that the God of Death was not fit to lead.

After days of debate regarding how to quell the rumors, my council decided that to regain control over the Spirit Realm, I needed to show the realm that I would not take her betrayal lightly—I needed to make an example of her. They wanted me to end her immortal life, to be the means to an end that they so often rumored me to be. And for the most part, as the God of Death, I lived up to that expectation.

But I disagreed.

I told them that taking her immortal life would acknowledge that she had reason to make her claims—worse, it would make me look as though *I* feared *her*. Before my council could argue any further with me, I had my guards bring her from the dungeon to my throne room, full of hundreds of witnesses. There, I made a spectacle for all to see—of what happened to those who betrayed me. I chained her arms above her head and her feet to the floor, and then, with my bare hands, I tore her wings from her back. As I walked out of that room, her lifeless, ichor-coated wings dragging behind me, I delivered my final blow. I told my sobbing sister that she was exiled from the Spirit Realm, forcing her to live among the humans she despised.

But my actions were a necessary evil—they allowed my sister to keep her life.

That was many, many decades ago.

As Sage would say, I was a bastard for it.

And truly, I was.

But at least I knew that about myself. I was not a good male, nor would I ever claim to be. I never attempted to hide that part of me, unlike so many others who hid their darkness behind a giant, fake smile. Those narcissistic assholes were much worse than I.

I drifted from my thoughts, returning to the sound of Folkoln pouring himself another glass and catching the last remnants of his sentence: "—and that's all I have to report on Sage."

—What about her?

My mind filled in the blanks, spewing out different ways his sentence could have begun—all of it enough to drive me mad, considering she was with *him*. A potent anger swirled within, ratcheting itself up inside of me. I had no way of letting it out. All I could do was drown in it, over and over and over again.

"By the way, her brother is a poor excuse for a reaper. Why you thought it was a good idea to give him the position I'll never understand." Folkoln chuckled. "I've never seen such messy landings in my immortal life." His laugh faded, but the amusement never left his voice. "Perhaps . . . I should take him under my wing. Turn that mess into something truly chaotic. He has the potential for it. All the boy needs is a bit of guidance."

That was the last thing I needed. Sage wouldn't just have my balls for letting Folkoln dig his talons into Kaleb—she'd water harpoon them off. And for what I had planned for Sage, I was definitely going to need my—

Two pricks of pain stabbed at my neck.

It lasted all of a second before it exploded into something so horrible that I wanted to crawl out of my own skin. It felt like two nails had simultaneously been driven into my neck, but that wasn't what hurt the most—it was the way it electrocuted the surrounding nerves, making them scream and blister with pain.

It was pure torture.

Then came the incessant pulling, like someone was drinking from me—pulling the blood from my veins without a care of thought for how much they took.

I had never felt pain such as that before, and I was the bringer of death.

But how could that be? The healers had hacked into my flesh and I could not feel anything. Which meant it could only be one thing . . .

White-hot adrenaline coursed through my veins as panic curdled my stomach.

Sage.

This immense pain *was happening to her*. From the location and the feel of it, it didn't take a genius to figure out that she was being bitten right now. And I was stuck here, unable to help her—to make it stop. It was more than I could stand, especially when I realized who was most likely on the other end of her suffering.

Internally, I roared.

His teeth had no place in *my* female's neck.

CHAPTER 6

Sage

Groggy and disoriented, I stirred from my slumber, uncertain if I had paid the Spirit Realm a visit or not. Not that I would know thanks to the iron collar. I guess if I was looking for a bright side, that would be it—the iron collar blocked all dreams and nightmares and anything in between, which meant I was actually able to sleep.

I opened one eyelid and peered up at the stone ceiling looming above me. I was back in my chambers. I could tell because if I looked hard enough while tilting my head slightly to the left, one of the stone's markings looked like an old woman's face, the nose predominant and bulbous. Over the past few weeks, as I'd stayed in my depressed state, grieving Von, I had stared at that spot in the ceiling more times than I cared to count. Now? I had it committed to memory.

Suddenly, the heavy oak door swung open.

I peered out from the protection of my soft furs, hoping the princely god with those horrible teeth or his redheaded henchman hadn't returned.

"Good morrow, my lady," a middle age woman said as she bustled into the room. Her hair was bound beneath a bonnet, despite a few loose gray strands that poked out at the base. She was far from thin, but despite her considerable girth, she moved quickly—*too quickly*. She grabbed hold of the deep-red drapes and flung them open, a billow of dust wafting into the air, emphasized by the scrutinizing rays of the sun. She coughed. "Oh my, I apologize, my lady. I'll notify the staff and have these taken outside for a good broom dusting before nightfall."

I didn't respond.

Curtain dust was the least of my worries—especially when my neck was still throbbing. I turned away from the bright light, onto my side. Delicately, I swept my finger over the bite marks, wincing even though my touch was faint.

When Von bit me, all I had felt was blissful pleasure.

When the Golden Prince did it, it was stitched with horrific pain.

She scuttled towards me, her hand retrieving the bed warmer pan from underneath my mattress. Efficiently, she walked over towards the fireplace and dumped out the remaining bits of ash and burnt-out embers. The bed warmer pan was new. I wiggled my toes, discovering that they were considerably warm.

Seconds later, she was back beside the bed. Her ruddy, plump cheeks lifted as she offered me a pleasant smile— clearly not worried that I was *Cursed*, no more than I was worried about her being a mortal. "My name is Brunhilde. I'm your new permanent lady's maid," she said sweetly. By way of an added greeting, her thick fingers grabbed hold of my fur blankets and she flung them back.

I shivered, the cool, morning air sinking beneath my nightgown and pricking my skin—reminding me of the Golden Prince's *teeth* as they sank into my neck. I swallowed the acidic lump that rose in the back of my throat and blocked the memory out.

Two women walked quietly into the room, the downward positioning of their heads gave them away—my *apparent* ladies-in-waiting. I rolled my eyes at the silly term. Waiting. Waiting for what? A big, strong man to carry them away?

. . . On second thought, that didn't sound so bad.

Where was Von when a girl needed him?

"From my understanding," Brunhilde said, "there was not a proper greeting done between you three. Allow me to do so now." She motioned to the shorter one with brown hair. "This is Naevia."

The girl performed a quick, efficient bow, her eyes fixed on the floor.

Brunhilde continued, "And this is Cataline."

The taller strawberry-blonde bowed, her head tilting up, a soft smile adorning her pleasant face. Although her eyes did not meet mine, the fact that she raised her head and offered a smile was a leap in itself.

Seeing the two girls standing there together reminded me a bit of Lyra and Harper, the difference in their height making the connection for me. My heart struck a heavy beat—oh, how I missed them. Ryker too. And Ezra. And Von. Always Von.

"Good morrow, my lady," they said pleasantly. Once again, they spoke in perfect, practiced unison.

I shifted to the side of the bed and greeted them in return, tacking on, "Please, call me Sage."

"That is most improper, my lady," Brunhilde gasped. She looked repulsed, as if I had hocked a loogie in her stew. "They will call you *my lady*, and that is that."

I didn't have it in me to argue, nor could I see any benefit in doing so, so I kept the ol' trap shut.

"Now, I also understand that you have not had a proper washing since your arrival. We shall see to that now." She turned to Naevia. "Dear, please tell them that we are ready for the bath, and then see that the dresses are brought up. And Cataline—" she turned to the other girl, "—go to the kitchen and find out what is taking so long with the breakfast tray. It should have been here a good five minutes ago."

Five minutes? Someone was a stickler for time.

The girls nodded, starting towards the door.

"Oh, and one more thing, Cataline, make sure it is just a light breakfast—His Royal Highness has arranged for the dressmaker to work with my lady today."

A wave of nausea trolled my stomach—the prince did what now? Why was he taking a sudden interest in what I wore? It didn't sit well with me, especially after what happened last night.

A hand pressed against my forehead, the unexpected touch causing me to jolt back.

"Apologies, I didn't mean to scare you. You looked unwell for a moment there. The color seemed chased from your cheeks," Brunhilde stated, her hands returning to her voluminous hips. "I was just checking to see if you were running a fever. You know how it is when winter comes—she brings all forms of nasty colds with her."

"I'm fine," I assured her. Although the pain in my neck and the nausea in my stomach was making me feel anything but fine.

"Well then," she patted my hand, softly, "we should get on with the day."

As if her words were a summoning, two men wearing servant's clothes carried an empty, wooden tub in. Brunhilde directed them to set the tub by the fireplace. After they left, a continuous line of young boys rolled in and out of my room, each one of them struggling with the heavy buckets as they waddled awkwardly towards the tub. I scrambled off the bed and hurried over to the youngest one, who looked not much older than six.

"Let me help you with that." I offered him a smile as I slipped my hand around the handle, and lifted, taking the heavy weight off his little legs. He offered me a toothy grin in thanks. It was a pleasant surprise. Apparently, not everyone hated the Cursed in this castle.

Brunhilde swatted at my hands. "Now you give the boy back his bucket, my lady. This is his job, not yours."

I let her have her way when it came to what the ladies-in-waiting were supposed to call me, but I wasn't about to let her have her way with this. Ignoring her, I helped the boy with his task, and then I turned to help another one. And then another.

Brunhilde didn't so much as make a peep, but I felt the scrutiny of her glare burrowing holes into my back as I helped the rest.

When the tub was three-quarters full and everyone else had left, Brunhilde motioned for me to get in.

Happily, I complied.

I shucked off my nightgown and tossed it to the side.

After working at the bathhouse, I had very little shame when it came to being undressed in front of other women—something the girl from the cottage would have never done. I dipped my toe into the steaming hot water, a smile gracing my lips as I lowered myself inside.

Heavenly.

Cataline returned with a heavy looking tray, her eyes rising, so very close to meeting mine—but not quite. Still, it was another step. Brunhilde pulled a small, round end table over beside the tub, motioning for Cataline to set the tray down there, which she quickly did.

The tray housed an expansive spread of breakfast foods. Fruits—no apples—boiled eggs, ham, toasted bread, and cheese. If this was what Brunhilde considered light, I could only imagine what a heavy breakfast would consist of—I doubted poor Cataline would be able to lift such a tray.

Leaning over the edge of the tub, I plucked a grape and popped it into my mouth, a sugary, slightly tart flavor bursting across my tongue.

Brunhilde set her hands in the voluptuous contour of her hips. "I apologize, my lady. This is an old part of the castle so there is no indoor plumbing here. The newer parts of the castle do have it though."

I nodded while filing that bit of information away—who knew what would be beneficial to my cause. Anything I could learn about the castle seemed like a good thing.

"Well, go on, eat up, my lady," Brunhilde said, gesturing for me to eat. She didn't have to tell me twice—I was famished.

Fishing the silver fork from beside the plate, I stuck the pronged end into the side of a plump, boiled egg. I brought it to my mouth and chomped part of it off.

"Oh, goodness. No, my lady, that is most improper," Brunhilde protested in dismay. "We do not eat boiled eggs like that. Here, let me teach you how it is properly done." Gently, she took the fork from me.

I chewed, watching as she cut the egg into tiny, bite-sized slivers—small enough that not even a toddler would choke on it. I gaped at the tiny pieces—I'd starve before I finished eating the egg.

"We take small, little bites. One at a time," she instructed slowly, searching my expression to see if it was sinking in—it wasn't. "And we keep our mouths closed when we chew." For emphasis, she clamped her mouth shut and pretended to chew—visually showing me how it was done—like a mother showing a baby how to eat.

I grumbled, closed mine, and did as I was told.

She teetered her head from side to side. "Well, it's a start." Sighing to herself, she turned and walked over to a bucket, full of various soaps and oils and scrubbers. When her back was turned, I shoveled the egg into my mouth and turned my face towards the fire so she couldn't see my stockpiled, chipmunk cheeks.

I heard Cataline giggle under her breath, and I couldn't help but smile at that—she probably thought I was some deranged, diseased, Cursed beast—the irony that I was actually a goddess followed by her king's chosen religion made it all the more satisfying.

I hadn't really thought about the whole goddess-y thing, to be honest, at least, not until now. But I was a goddess—*apparently*. Did I feel like one? *Not really.*

I felt like plain old Sage.

Apart from getting a droplet of my memories back from a sea of forgotten ones, there was nothing else that really seemed to change. Despite being classified as a New God, I still bled red—that was something I could be certain of after last night's debacle with the prince. I hadn't noticed any physical shifts within me in terms of power or healing abilities—then again, the iron collar could have something to do with that.

For the most part, I still felt mortal, even if I wasn't.

Being mortal felt more real than being the reincarnation of Lady Light, the Goddess of Life.

Goddess of Life? I rolled my eyes. Clearly the universe was not paying attention—I couldn't even keep a plant alive for more than a week without it shriveling up and dying on me. Even Ezra didn't bother to ask me to look after her plants, knowing it would be their demise. Especially not after I overwatered her garden when I was ten and killed two-thirds of the plants, something I had never heard the end of.

In a way, it felt like some sort of cosmic joke—one I wasn't privy to.

Then again, what in my life didn't feel like a joke lately? As I reached over the edge of the tub and snagged a slice of buttered bread, I considered the fact that I was taking a bath in my enemy's castle, feasting, while the most powerful god in the existence of all gods was stuck like some fairytale princess in an eternal slumber. And unlike the stories I read as a child, no, my kiss would not wake him up. In fact, it would probably be the final nail in his immortal coffin.

I sighed, crammed the rest of the bread into my mouth, and sank lower into the water—the steam no longer rolling off the surface like it had done before.

After I was scrubbed by Brunhilde—vigorously, meticulously, every nook and every cranny—and my fair skin was turned the same color as the banners hanging in the halls, Brunhilde yanked me from the embrace of the cooling waters. Her strength surprised me. I eyed her suspiciously as she dried me off with a towel—was she a goddess too? Something in me said *no, you are just being paranoid,* and I decided that was probably true. Still, I made a mental note to visit the castle's library and find some books on the gods and goddesses and start learning who was who—a topic I had blissfully ignored for the sum of my life. The divine were a topic Adelina had been passionate about . . . I should have paid more attention when she spoke of them. I regretted that I didn't. When it came to Adelina . . . there were a lot of things I regretted not doing.

A cacophony of bells sounded, chattering in different, striking tones and Brunhilde let out a flustered groan. "Oh, dear me, I let her sit in the water too long," she decreed to herself, as if I was a poached bird. Her little legs quickened in pace as she dragged me over to the bed, my hand knitting the ends of the towel together, keeping it tightly wound to my body.

"Hurry, my lady, pick one." She gestured to the three dresses draped over top of the bed, accompanied by their own sets of gloves. All three of the dresses were beautiful and elegant and so expensive looking it made me sick. People were starving in the streets, while the wealthy flounced around in clothing such as this. "So we can get you on your way," she finished.

"On my way?" I asked, looking them over, wondering when the dresses and Naevia, who was standing in the corner beside Cataline, head tucked down, had gotten back.

"Well, yes, to morning praise, of course!" Brunhilde exclaimed.

I shook my head, still not grasping why I was expected to attend a morning devotional to the New Gods. "Since I have been here, I have never attended morning praise. Why now?"

"Girls, come here and help me with this," she barked at my ladies-in-waiting, their hurried footsteps answering in quick reply. She didn't wait for me to pick out a dress, instead plucking the golden one, handing it to Cataline, and then shucking off my towel with a swipe of her hand. Preparing the first layer of skirts, she looked at me briefly and said, "Because His Royal Highness wishes it so. Now, arms up and be quick about it."

CHAPTER 7

Sage

There were two guards posted outside the door that led into the hallway. Because of their helmets, I couldn't see their faces, but I could tell right away that neither of them were Grouchy. The first one was a hulking beast, much too big to be him, and the second one was so small, I was certain Lyra could take him in a fistfight.

I wondered if they were as sour as Grouchy. I decided to dip a proverbial toe and test the infamous waters. Conjuring the actress from the bathhouse, I said in a sultry tone, "Top of the morning to you, boys."

The big one moved slightly, but that was it for a response.

I was beginning to wonder if the *asshole* persona was a requirement for them to be hired on as guards. I clamped my squirming tongue between my teeth, all too tempted to ask them if they could taste wood, because that's how far the stick had been shoved up their—

"Come now, my lady, you are already late." Brunhilde shooed me out of the doorway I was standing in, cutting the thought off before I could verbalize it.

Saved by the lady's maid, I thought before we started on our way.

Doing my best to gather the ridiculous amount of underskirts, I followed behind Brunhilde. Despite my grievances against the weighty dress, the pointed leather shoes I wore were remarkably easy to walk in. Who knew such luxury existed—my feet sure didn't. I made a mental note to swipe them when I made my getaway from the castle.

Cataline, Naevia, and the two guards followed behind me, Brunhilde taking the helm as she declared for the various castle servants to *make way, make way, make way!* Not to my surprise, they did—scrambling to the sides of the hallway before Brunhilde could barrel them down. For a short woman, she packed a surprising amount of authority.

I tried to map the castle as we walked. The sooner I got a layout of this place, the sooner I could figure out how I was going to kill the king.

Kill the king . . . the words were harsh. I had never taken a life before—at least, not in this lifetime—and even though the king was a monster, I wondered what that would mean for me if I achieved what I had vowed to do. Would it change me?

After a long, seemingly never-ending stretch of corridor, we reached a grand, winding staircase, the steps gradually widened towards the bottom level. I could hear singing—a plethora of angelic voices melding beautifully with one another. I gathered my skirts once more and began my descent, the singing growing closer with each step.

When I reached the bottom, my foot landed softly against a luxurious, thick carpet that spread from wall to wall, trailing down the length of the monstrosity of a hallway that stretched in front me. At the end of it, massive twin doors were swung open, revealing not just a room, but an entirely different building attached to the castle—a temple.

From floor to ceiling, it was made of meticulously polished white stone—the stone itself reflecting small bits of light wherever the sun shone on it. The roof was supported by two rows of giant columns, the size of them similar to ancient oaks. It reminded me a great deal of the Temple of Light, however this building had walls, something the airy Temple of Light did not.

"Cataline will show you where you are to sit," Brunhilde said, gesturing for me to walk through the giant doors.

I nodded and followed her in.

Rows upon rows of stone benches flagged each side, a sea of people dressed in their best attire filling them from end to end. I could not fathom how many people were here in attendance, but I suspected it was in the hundreds.

On the far end, a stretch of people stood upon a sprawling dais—the choir. They wore robes, the fabric a deep red, and each one of them exhibited straight, perfect posture, their blank expressions an injustice to the breathtaking sounds their voices crafted. Their sacred melody combined with the dancing colors shining through the stained windows was . . . *magical.*

I didn't realize I was staring, not until I felt a tug on my gloved hand. I glanced down and Cataline's wide eyes met mine—that was a first. She gestured to the open seat beside her. I blinked, realizing that while I stared at the choir, a good portion of the crowd was now staring at me. Quickly, I sat down on the stone bench, my movement less than graceful. My skirts were so thick that they puffed up in front of me, a mountain of fabric practically blocking my view. I pressed them down. How ridiculous.

On the right side of the dais, three golden thrones proudly stood, their seats wrapped in lush, crimson-colored velvet. The middle one was the largest and grandest, a gilded sun positioned at the very top, its rays chiseled into deadly looking spikes, sharp enough to prick your finger.

All together, the choir cut out, allowing for one young girl to step forward and sing, her angelic voice amplified by the acoustics of the sprawling temple. After a few beautifully sung lines, the rest of the sopranos joined in, their combined voices raising the melody to new heights. The altos and tenors weaved in next, building on the mighty sound.

The hairs on the back of my neck raised—a standing ovation for their incredible melody.

An older woman wearing a simple white garb and a gold headpiece with a bright, glittering ruby stepped out onto the dais. Her hands were hidden behind wide, cascading sleeves that stretched all the way down to the floor. As she walked up to a marble podium, she chanted in a foreign tongue. The language sounded harsh, the words spoken as if she had to clear her throat with each one. Her chanting stopped and her hand thrust forward, gesturing towards the back of the room.

Instantly, everyone stood and turned to face the indicated

direction as if this were a wedding and the bride was about to come down the aisle. I stood and turned as well, but I couldn't see past the rows of people who were packed densely in front of me, shoulder to shoulder. The choir started to sing again, their resonating harmonies coaxing tiny bumps to pebble my skin.

And then, in perfect unison, everyone bowed their heads. Okay, everyone but me. Lightly, Cataline swatted me. I followed her lead and dipped my head—*slightly*.

Through the tops of my lashes, I watched a man and a woman walk by, dressed in the finest clothes I had ever seen—silks and furs and vibrant colors. I couldn't even begin to fathom how much coin was spent on their attire. The man's hand, decorated with gaudy rings, was held out in front of him, his palm facing down. The woman who walked beside him positioned her hand a mere inch directly over top of his, not enough to touch. Both of them wore wigs, but the one the woman wore was something else. There was so much fake hair piled on top of her head, it was a wonder her neck could withstand the weight.

Recalling a conversation I had with Arkyn, I knew that the queen had to wear a wig because she suffered from the pox. That meant that the man and woman walking down the aisle were most likely the king and queen. This came as no surprise, considering everyone was bowing.

My brows raised as I took one good hard look at the king—this was my *first* time seeing him, other than on minted coins and in painted portraits, both of which portrayed a handsome king who looked *nothing* like he did in person.

Despite the fine, luxurious clothing he wore and the

carefully polished gold crown sitting upon his head, he was *just* a man—a man who had caused *nothing* but pain, suffering, and devastation. I wondered what gave him the right to lead a kingdom. What gave him the right to take lives, to destroy families—to destroy mine.

He had no right.

A white-haired prince caught my attention, quickly snuffing out my thoughts surrounding the king. In their place, the memory of teeth embedded in my neck surfaced and a sickly feeling washed over me, leaving my skin clammy and my stomach uneasy. The corset of my dress suddenly felt much tighter.

If he had noticed that I was standing there, he didn't let on. Instead, he kept his eyes fixed ahead as he walked behind the king and queen towards the dais. When they reached it, the king and queen parted, and the prince stepped between them.

As the three royals stood there, I realized that appearance-wise, the prince had absolutely nothing in common with his so-called parents. Physically, he was ethereal and enchanting, and they were nothing of the sort. I wondered if they were even related at all. Neither of his parents appeared to be divine—I felt almost certain of that.

Yet, he was a god. Undoubtedly.

I didn't know a whole lot about how things worked with the gods, but I did know that the joining of humans did not produce one, no more than two cats could produce a lion.

Only the Creator could make the divine.

That meant the prince wasn't actually their son.

A girl, not much older than twelve, stepped up onto the dais, her hands holding a golden bowl. The older woman, who

I gathered to be the priestess, dipped her thumb inside before she pressed her thumb to the prince's neck. After, she repeated the same action for the king and the queen, marking their throats with red paint. The action was fairly common in most temples, although I'd never devoted the time to learn the meaning behind it.

When she was finished, she bowed her head and the three royals departed for the thrones—the prince taking the middle one with the carved sun.

The choir finished, and the priestess began to speak again—this time, thankfully, in a language I could understand. "Today, in the thirty-fifth year of our king, we have gathered in the temple of the gods of new to praise them. On this day of worship, if any man, woman, or child has come with unnoble intentions, by the laws of the gods, or the laws of this realm, come forward now."

"We come with noble intentions to praise our beloved gods and goddesses," the crowd chanted back, their thunderous reply cracking like a whip across my back, causing me to jump. No wonder they forged the walls from stone and not wood—the mere force of so many voices would have shaken a wooden foundation to its knees.

The priestess bowed in reply before she walked towards an altar made of stone, her thick, heavy robes dragging behind her. "Let us begin with a prayer for King Hakred, Queen Melayna, and Prince Aurelius." The next part she continued in the foreign tongue. But even if she had spoken in English, I wouldn't have listened, because I was hooked straight through the lip by the reveal of the prince's first name, which I had never heard before. Despite all of Edenvale holding a weekly celebration for him, people *did not* call the prince by his first name—he was only ever referred to as the *Golden Prince*. To call him Prince Aurelius would be considered blasphemy.

Aurelius.

Aurelius.

The male equivalent to the name Arkyn had called me, the first given name of Lady Light—Aurelia.

So coincidentally, not only did we share the same hair color, and not only were we both immortal, our first names were unnervingly similar. But those *coincidences* were not the ones that hit me the hardest. No, it was that fact that not only did he have the same date of birth as the Lord of Light—he shared the same first name too

But those coincidences were not just coincidences, were they? *And* despite whatever little charade he was playing at, he wasn't some namesake for the Lord of Light—

He *was* the Lord of Light.

The God of Life.

The King of the New Gods.

And my . . .

Oh shit.

The conversation from last night emerged on the forefront of my mind, bludgeoning its way through like a battering ram.

"Are you married?"

"No, I'm not."

"Are you sure about that?"

Next, a memory with Arkyn wheedled its way in. When he took me to the Temple of Light, he'd asked, *"Will you be a good little wife?"*

The hinges in my jaw snapped open, my nostrils no longer able to supply the amount of air I needed—not when this cage of a corset was constricting my quick, frantic breaths.

"Are you alright?" Cataline whispered to me, her eyes gone wide.

No. No. *No!*

I shook my head while my eyes pleaded for help. A silent prayer formed on my trembling lips for someone to get me out of here, to rip the cage from my ribs.

"I get like this sometimes, too, where I can't breathe," she whispered softly, her hand grabbing mine. "Think about something else. Whatever it is, you need to get your mind off of it."

My clammy hands, slipping inside my gloves, squeezed hers back, and although her sudden concern was sweet, it did little to tame the building frenzy wrenching itself up inside of me.

"Think about something else. Listen to the priestess, focus on her voice," she whispered, her eyes pleading with me not to make a scene.

For her sake, and mine, I yanked my head up and forced myself to focus on the priestess. But then my gaze darted to Aurelius, and when his golden eyes met mine, I lost what was left of my composure.

I turned to Cataline and sputtered, "I can't do this."

My feet got trapped in the front of my skirts as I shot up from the bench. Without a shred of grace, I began the longest *going to fall—not going to fall* act of my life. And I'm sure it looked as awkward as it felt. When I was certain I was about to finally go down, instinctively, my hand shot out, landing on the shoulder of a man who sat on the other side of the aisle a few rows back.

I pulled my hand away faster than a bee sting. "Sorry," I stammered, my eyes as wide as the queen's fine saucers, no doubt.

He looked like he was about to say something pleasant, but when his eyes fell to my neck and he saw the iron wrapped around it, his expression forged into disgust. "How dare you touch me with your filthy Cursed hands!" he yelled, his voice echoing around us.

"I—I—" I didn't know what to say. I knew that some people hated the Cursed. I mean, that was what the Crown taught them to believe—that we were a disease, a danger to society, that we needed to be dealt with and cleansed from the lands to keep our plague at bay.

The woman beside him glared at me as she handed him a handkerchief. He grabbed it and began to scrub at the spot where I had touched him with my *gloved* hand.

I stood there, gaping. I had never been treated with such disdain.

When I realized that an entire room full of scowling faces were now glaring at me, with nothing but hatred written in their eyes, my world began to spin like I was a weathervane being pushed around and around, faster and faster as the storm continued its approach.

A hand gently grasped my wrist. The spinning stopped.

"Are you alright?" asked a decadent, masculine voice.

I glanced down at the hand that gingerly cuffed my wrist,

at the perfect, perfect skin. But when I saw that solid-gold ring shining on his elegant finger—knowing damn well what it signified—that moment of peace was lost.

"I can't." I tore my wrist from his hand and spun towards the exit. As fast as my quaking legs would carry me, I ran— like the hounds of the Spirit Realm, belonging to my slumbering lover, were nipping at my heels.

Like my past was finally catching up with me.

CHAPTER 8

Sage

I knew why I was running. I was running because my past was threatening to cut the last remaining thread of sanity I had left. But just because I knew why I was running, it did not mean I knew *where* I was running to.

But there was a time when I knew.

Once, I would have run home. To the lake. To Kaleb or Ezra. But then Kaleb had been taken and that all changed. My small, simple world had been torn straight out from underneath me—leaving me teetering.

So I adapted, but I hadn't done that alone. I had found something—some*one*—more secure than the setting sun. I had found Von. And not only did he become the person I could run to—*he became my home.*

But Von wasn't here—*my* home wasn't here.

So where was I running to as I grasped my skirts and ran

down the sprawling, unknown halls with two guards chasing after me, yelling at me to halt?

I didn't know. I didn't know where I was running to.

And I didn't know when I would stop.

I could see my breath in the cold morning air, small puffs born with each ragged exhale. I leaned over, my forearms pressed against my quaking thighs. My body was flushed with heat and slick with sweat—part of me felt sorry for whatever poor soul was going to have to scrub the pit stains out of this dress later.

Then again . . .

Pit stains were *the least* of the dress's concern.

I glanced down at what was left of it—the golden hem was tattered and torn from me stepping on it, and dirty, like I'd swept the castle's floor with it.

And then there were the ribs sewn into the corset—they were beyond repair. At some point, I had snapped them like they were made of peanut brittle rather than sturdy strips of metal. Mortal Sage would have never possessed the strength to do that—she might have been able to bend them, but never snap them. Which made me think that some slumbering part of my immortality was beginning to wake up.

Deep down, I knew the answer.

From the moment I left the temple to the moment I found myself outside, everything in between was a blur. It was like

I had drifted from my body, and I was looking down, watching myself just run and run and run, through long, never-ending corridors, turning this way and that.

Now, I was outside, standing in a sprawling courtyard filled with elaborate fountains, and beautiful statues, and a wide spread of trees and shrubs, most of them in dormancy, preserving themselves from winter's deadly caress.

Screeching armor sounded to my right—quickly approaching.

"You are not permitted to wander the castle unchaperoned, milady," decreed a young, male voice—loud and clear and barely a day over puberty, judging by the squeak at the end.

"I just needed some fresh air," I offered, watching as they approached. They were the same guards from earlier this morning.

"We must return you to your chambers at once," the young voice replied. It came from the smaller guard, which made sense—he probably wasn't even fully grown yet.

The fact that this young guard was working here struck me as odd. It was common knowledge that the king only kept highly trained guards at Clearwell Castle. He shipped the new recruits and younger ones to the Cursed Lands. So why was this young man here? Either his family had some sort of connection to the king, or those highly trained guards were somewhere else. The last thought didn't sit well with me.

"Come, milady, we will take you back," the young guard chirped, his head swiveling to the massive guard standing beside him in a silent plea for help.

But his comrade didn't say a single word. He merely

crossed his arms, his stance surprisingly casual, like he had all the time in the world—a feat in itself considering the stiff armor he wore. I didn't know if he did it on purpose, but I offered him a small, thankful smile anyway—my gaze widening when I saw what stood behind him, slightly to his left.

"Please, milady, we have to return," the young guard pleaded with me.

"In a moment," I said mindlessly, walking forward.

"Milady, where are you going?" he half barked, half squeaked.

I slipped off my gloves.

"Mila—"

His voice became lost to me. All I could hear was the beat of my heart, strumming in my ears as I reached out. My fingertips fell into the deep fissures as I lowered my forehead against the rough, thick, cool bark. I took a slow, deep breath, inhaling the earthy, woody scent—the smell of home. Not even winter's approach could conceal the smell of it.

I don't know how long I stood there, under the watchful gaze of that towering, ancient oak, but at last, I had found where I was running to.

CHAPTER 9

Sage

Footsteps, barely audible, approached me. I didn't need to look to know who it was. There were only two people I knew that could walk that quietly. One of them was locked in an eternal slumber and the other—

"Walk with me?" he asked.

I turned my head, pressing my cheek against the bark as I looked at the offered hand, at the telltale band wrapped around his ring finger.

Slowly, my gaze lifted, meeting his—meeting those incredible pools of molten gold.

I *should* be furious with him for last night, for causing me to feel pain so immense, the thought of it curdled my blood, and yet . . .

Something strange was happening inside of me. In particular, my heart.

As if it were a lute, it began to strum, faster and faster. It recognized *that* hand—*those* eyes. My mind was just having a hard time catching up between what happened the other night and a lifetime of forgotten memories.

And the combination of the two left me drowning in the middle—confused and unsure of what to do, of how to proceed forward without plunging myself back into the mind-shattering panic I had felt moments ago.

"Alright," I whispered softly, pulling away from the comforts of the oak and taking my first step into a world of unknowns.

I didn't take his hand, and if it made him feel some sort of way, he didn't show it. Instead, he gestured towards a winding path made of slabs of flagstone. Gravel surrounded the pale, flat stones, filling the small gaps between them. Neatly trimmed shrubs, their barren branches painted white with frost, bordered the path, allowing us just enough room to walk side by side.

"I apologize for how I treated you," he said as we walked, breaking the silence between us. Even though he was considerably taller than me, our paces matched rather well. "When I learned that Arkyn had brought you here, I planned to give you space, to give you time to adjust, but when I saw you last night and you didn't recognize me, I became overcome with emotions. And when you bit my lip, I reacted in the way of the gods but failed to remember that you do not recall those customs because you have spent this life living as a mortal." His broad chest expanded as he inhaled a deep breath. "I should have handled things more carefully, but instead, I let my emotions rule over me, and I acted like a brute. For that, I am sorry."

I wasn't sure what to do with his apology.

On the surface of what happened last night, I was attacked, but when I allowed myself to sink into the confusing, murky waters, I realized there was more depth to it than just that.

An eye for an eye. Those were the words he had said to me after I bit him, just before his teeth sliced into my neck. And although, yes, the act was barbaric, I knew enough about the saying to know that it had, in fact, originated from the gods. That was their way—their law. And he had acted according to it. Did that make it right or fair to me? No. It didn't. But a *small* part of me could understand why he reacted that way.

And then there was the catalyst—that kiss.

At the time, I believed a stranger was kissing me and so I acted in self-defense. But to him? The man wearing the golden ring? He wasn't kissing a stranger, he was kissing his—

I tripped up over that part—*that word*—acknowledging that it could complicate things a whole lot more. As I was fresh out of a panic attack, I had no desire to have another one, so I decided to leave that one alone for the time being.

Later—I would process *that* later. Or never. That seemed like a favorable option.

Eyes fixed on the flagstone path stretched before us, I said, "I appreciate your apology and I can understand that you were—" I paused, searching for the right word. "Conflicted. Still, that doesn't change that what you did to me was awful. However, for the sake of moving forward, I am willing to accept your apology."

"Thank you," he said softly.

I nodded and wrapped my arms around myself. The heat from my run had long since left me, and now all I felt was the creeping cold, its fingers digging deep, wrapping around my bones.

Something heavy and warm fell over my shoulders and the sweet and musky scent of saffron blossomed around me. I glanced down, my pace slowing—it was his robe, gold in color but trimmed with plush, white fur. I marveled at its softness as I pinched the front together, locking out the cold.

"Thank you." I glanced up at him. "But now you're going to be cold."

"I appreciate your concern, but it is unnecessary." An amused smile graced his full lips. "My body temperature burns hot enough that I do not feel the cold."

My eyes went wide, realization pulling them open.

"Because you were born of the sun," I whispered in awe. "And I—" My feet halted. "I was born of the moon."

That explained why I never felt the need to search for my biological parents. I wasn't a daughter of man and woman—no, the moon was my mother. That was why I had always felt drawn to her. Even as a little girl, I would sit beside my spot at the window, my arms propped against the sill as I peered up at the bright, vivid moon. Excitedly, I would exclaim to Ezra, *do you see my moon?* My heart warmed at the memory.

"Yes, you were knitted together in the womb of Luna, while I was forged from the stomach of Sol. That is why one of your given titles is the Lady of Light and mine the Lord of Light," he said, gesturing with his hand for us to continue along the path.

I resumed walking, we both did.

For a short while, we continued ahead in silence. The world around us was just as quiet, as if it were holding its breath.

"May I ask you something?"

"Please do," he answered.

"You are a god, so why are you pretending to be a prince?"

He bit back a laugh. "I have a few reasons, but my biggest motivator is because Edenvale needs a proper leader—a true king."

I didn't disagree. If the king had proven anything during his reign, it was that he was not fit to lead. But I wasn't satisfied with Aurelius's answer.

"But you are the King of the New Gods, the King of the Immortal Realm and the Living Realm." I paused. "I do not mean for this to come across as rude, but . . . why do you want to be the king of Edenvale? Isn't that a bit. . ." I shrugged. "Beneath you?"

Briefly, his steps slowed. "It is, but just like you, I'm stuck here. The Endless Mist prevents me from leaving. So I might as well do something that is beneficial for the people of Edenvale while I'm here."

I was all on board for doing something good for the people of Edenvale, but I found this new admission confusing. Von could shadow walk between here and the Spirit Realm, so—

"Why can't you light walk out of here?" I asked, finishing the thought out loud.

"I have tried. Many times. But I have never been able to get through the Endless Mist. It refuses to let me pass."

I mulled that over.

Why would the Endless Mist allow Von to pass but not Aurelius? Was shadow walking somehow more powerful than light walking? Or was it because shadow walking and the Endless Mist were born from the same type of magic?

I plucked at my bottom lip, feeling even further from the answer. "So you can't leave at all?"

"That is correct," he stated, ducking under a branch that dangled over the path. It narrowly missed the tallest spire of his ethereal crown. Knowing what I knew now, I highly doubted the crown had been forged by human hands—no, it was too perfect. I thought back to the ones that the king and queen wore, realizing Aurelius's crown made theirs seem rather lackluster. Just as he did himself when he was standing beside them this morning.

"And how do the queen and king fit into all of this?" I asked curiously. "I'm guessing they know that you are not their biological son."

"Oh, they are well aware." He catered a charming smile. "As I'm sure you've noticed, we don't have much in common, especially in terms of physical attributes."

"That, I have," I said as we stuck to the right side of the path, split by a giant willow tree, the long, slender branches bent over, reaching for the ground. "But they have other children. Why would they hand you the crown when they could give it to one of their true heirs instead?"

"Because they no longer possess a kingship to give."

I lifted a brow. "I don't quite follow."

"No, I would suppose not. That answer was a bit ambiguous after all," he chuckled, and I was amazed at how poised and perfect and regal even his laughter sounded. "Allow me to start from the beginning."

I nodded as we continued forward.

"Twenty-five years ago, on the day of the summer solstice, I reincarnated here in Edenvale. Arkyn brought my infant form to the king and queen, who were barren at the time, due to the Great Pox they suffer from. A highly esteemed priestess confirmed I was indeed who Arkyn told them I was. As they were, and still are, followers of the New Gods, they took me in." He paused for a brief moment. "When I was old enough and within some control of my ability to create life, the queen asked me to bless her unfruitful marriage with children. I told her I would, but in exchange, I would need the king to give me what he held dearest—his monarchy. Originally, the king was not willing to part with his crown, but when the queen reminded him that they had no children and the next in line was his estranged nephew, the heir of his deceased brother—a man the king viciously hated—the king was all too eager to accept my deal, and so he named me as his heir."

"So upon his death, the crown will transfer to you," I stated, piecing things together.

"Exactly." Aurelius nodded, his white, silky hair and thin gold chains catching on the rays of the late morning sun.

Questions spun abound.

Would Aurelius be a good king? Would he end the Cleansings? Or would he let them continue? The Cursed were the distant descendants of the Old Gods—the enemies of the

New Gods, which was what Aurelius and I both technically were. But I didn't consider the Cursed to be my enemies—in fact, for most of this life, that's exactly what I had believed I was. In truth, I still felt a bit like one of them. But Aurelius had grown up in this castle, under the rule of the king, so had that influenced his feelings surrounding the Cursed?

There was only one way to find out.

"When you become King . . . will you continue the Cleansings?" I dared a glance at him.

Softly, Aurelius shook his head. "As I told you before, I plan to do good for the people of Edenvale. Besides, the mortal kings have allowed the Cleansings to go on for far too long."

I didn't know exactly what it was—perhaps the brilliant gleam in his golden eyes or the warm smile he offered me— but I felt inclined to believe him.

His words filled me with hope. And they made me even more sure that I was on the right path. I decided to leave the rest of that conversation for another day, especially the part about me vowing to kill the king.

"And your memories? Your powers? How are they progressing so far?"

"Unfortunately, in this reincarnated form, I am just like you, Moonbeam—my memories from my past life are severely lacking. I know a bit about myself, and the basics of you and I—that we were wed and that we loved one another greatly, once upon a time."

Lead filled my belly. There it was again, *that* word.

I put it in a box and shoved off from it.

Aurelius continued, "Apart from my scattered memories,

my power is not even a fraction of what it once was. I can create life, yes, but my ability to control the elements is limited. I am no better than an un-nursed infant."

It was too bad that Aurelius's memories were as lacking as my own—if he remembered more, it might help me find my lost memories as well.

All of this was confusing.

"Can I ask you a question?"

His regal voice pulled me from my thoughts. With the number of questions I had, I was not sure if I was qualified to answer any of his. Still, I said, "Alright."

A white brow raised ever so slightly as he offered me a cheeky, lovely grin. "Have you read any good books lately?"

I smiled, thankful for the mundane question.

"I'm afraid not. It's been a while since I read."

"Well, we can't have that now, can we?" he said with playful charm. "The castle has an expansive library. Would you care to accompany me there sometime?"

I grinned. "I would like that."

"As would I."

"Are you a fan of literature?" I asked, curiously.

"Yes, I read and write frequently."

"What do you write?"

"I have a wide palate, so my writings vary. I've dabbled in a variety of things." He gestured to a stone and mortar bench tucked between twin winged statues—sister carvings carrying baskets of fruit. "Will you sit with me?"

"Sure," I said as I took a seat, my fatigued leg muscles aiding in my answer. I hadn't realized how out of shape I had become over the past few weeks.

He sat beside me and the scent of saffron renewed—rich like honey, but slightly bitter like metal on the tongue. It was masculine. Indulgent.

"I'll admit, some of the things I write are . . . less than noble." A whisper of a sensual smile graced his lips. "I recall having a naughty muse." Gold eyes met mine, as mesmerizing as the sun. "I blame her for tainting me."

I didn't need to ask who his muse was because I could physically feel the answer. A wealth of touches, kisses, and caresses washed over my skin. My cells remembered it all, even if my mind could not.

Heat licked at my cheeks, and I turned the other way.

Silence fell for a moment.

"There's something else I've been meaning to discuss with you," he said softly, seriously. "I am sorry about the collar. Although Arkyn was the one who put it there, I am the reason that it remains."

Instinctually, my hand roamed to the heavy weight fastened around my neck. Although it was thinner than the collar I had arrived in, the symbolism behind it remained the same—Cursed. Underneath the collar, my skin felt itchy and raw from the metal constantly rubbing against it.

"In all honesty, you did spend a great deal of time with my enemy—the God of Death. I cannot be certain what lies he might have crafted during your time with him or any poisoning he might have done. Add to the fact that you do not remember being wed to me, that I am essentially a stranger to you, and you are living in your enemy's castle, the collar feels necessary for now. At least, until I feel we trust one another."

Surface level—Aurelius was a dick for neutering me

from my Curses, something that was as essential as a limb.

Deeper down—I understood why he felt the collar was necessary. There was a lack of trust between us. That same lack of trust was why I hadn't told him my plans to kill the king.

So for now, that was how it would be between us—until I could convince him to trust me.

CHAPTER 10

Sage

After we left the courtyard gardens, Aurelius escorted me to my chambers, our conversation light and meaningless. It was a welcome change.

I couldn't help but notice how people responded to him as we passed by. Regardless of if they were nobles or servants, each of them exhibited the same response—they were completely and irrevocably spellbound, like their mortal souls unintentionally recognized the divinity emitting from him.

Sometimes, he stopped to speak with some of his subjects, and it was in those moments that I found myself somewhat in awe. I'd thought Arkyn was extremely charming when I first saw him at the bathhouse in Belamour, but now I realized that he paled in comparison when it came to Aurelius.

It was like comparing the fallen leaves of autumn with the blossoms of fresh spring—both were of seasons and charming in their own right, but spring, the season of rebirth, was far more enchanting.

When we approached the door that led into my chambers, the two guards waiting outside bowed to Aurelius, their armor squawking in the process. He heeded the guards little mind, his attention fixed on me.

I began to take off the robe he lent to me during our walk, but he raised a hand, gesturing for me to stop. "You may keep it."

Keep his cloak? *That* didn't sit right.

I shook my head. "I can't."

A curious brow raised. "And why *can't* you?"

Because couples shared clothes, and as far as my memory went right now, we were not a couple, regardless of the ring he wore on his finger. Von and I—we were a couple. Taking a cloak from another man felt like a sliver of betrayal poking its way in, something that was bound to get infected.

But instead of telling him that, I just handed him the cloak. "I just can't."

He folded it over his arm, his expression stoic.

Unspoken words and feelings dampened the air.

I took a breath. "Please understand that this—" I gestured to him and me, "—situation is all very new to me, and I need time to process. So for now, I would prefer it if we could just be friends."

He nodded. "It's alright. It's a lot. I know. I understand that you need time."

I smiled softly. "Thank you."

"You are most welcome. By the way, I was wondering, would you care to have dinner with me sometime?"

My mouth popped open—someone clearly did not understand the meaning of being friends.

"Aurelius, I—"

"No, not like that." Softly, he cut me off, a smile tugging at the corner of his lips. "I simply wish to be in your presence. If you are worried that having dinner with me alone is too intimate, then we can do so in a public setting instead—the dining hall, perhaps?"

My tightly strung shoulders relaxed as I thought over his request. I had heard about the grand feasts that were held in the king's dining hall before. In fact, it was something the villagers spoke of regularly—in particular, what it must be like to gaze upon tables so full of food, it was a wonder the legs didn't combust. Apart from the food-occupied minds of starving village folk, they also talked about the people who attended the illustrious dinners. Most notably—the *king,* himself.

Part of me felt excited, while the other part wondered if dining at the same table as someone you planned to kill was bad table manners. Regardless, it didn't really matter because declining an invitation to learn more about the king's everyday life seemed like a wasted opportunity.

I smiled at Aurelius. "I'd be happy to join."

"Wonderful," he said approvingly, smiling back at me with those straight, perfect whites.

After we bid one another good night, I opened the door and walked inside, unprepared for the red-faced fireball that waited on the other side.

CHAPTER 11

Sage

"Where have you been?" Brunhilde gruffed at me, her arms folded tightly over her abundant chest, one foot tapping the floor faster than two jackrabbits fucking in the woods.

Lightly, I closed the door as that walking-on-eggshells feeling washed over me. "I was in the courtyard gardens with Prince Aurelius?" I said, posing it as a question in case it was the wrong answer.

Her mouth was already halfway open before I finished, prepared to give me a tongue-lashing, but when she heard who I was with, she clamped it shut. She smiled wide, morphing into a ball of sweetness and pleasantness before my very eyes. "Did you have a nice time?"

"Yes," I said, drawing out the word, still wondering if it was safe to move. Spending your adolescent years with a woman like Ezra would do that—it would put the fear of older women into you. And rightfully so. They were a force to be reckoned with.

"That's wonderful to hear, my lady," she said, nodding. Her gaze dipped, surveying the sorry state of my gown and then her eyes went wide. Judging by the look on her face, she was correlating my time with the prince with the wreckage of my dress.

Heat scorched my cheeks. "We were just walking!" I exclaimed, tossing my hands in front of me in defense.

"Yes, of course, of course," she said, her words not meeting her eyes. She scuttled over to the armoire.

"I'm telling the truth," I snipped, somewhat annoyed she didn't believe me. I traipsed behind her, stopping a few feet away. My shoulder bit into the wall as I leaned against it, arms crossed.

"You were gone for quite some time," she argued as she plucked out another stuffy-looking dress. She held it up in front of me and poked her tongue out the side of her mouth, one eye closing. Shaking her head, she returned the dress to the armoire and pulled out another—this one even more cumbersome than the last.

"It was a long walk," I defended before I gestured to the dress. "Do I have to wear that?"

"You are welcome to pick out your own dress," she muttered as she ran her hand down the sleeve. She grasped the cuff and shook it lightly, weighing if she liked it or not while her head teetered from side to side in silent debate.

"What about a tunic and a pair of pants?" I asked, knowing it was a wishful thought.

She dropped the sleeve, her gaze jumping up to mine. And then she laughed, her laugh so boisterous, so infectious, I couldn't help but smile—even if she was laughing *at* me.

"Oh, my lady, you have quite the sense of humor," she said sweetly, shoving the dress back and selecting a third one. Just like the rest, she eyed it over before she gave it a satisfactory nod.

. . . I guessed the pants and tunic were a no-go then.

She placed the dress on the bed, then came over to me, gesturing for me to rotate.

I turned, saying at the same time, "There's something I've been meaning to ask you."

"Hmm?" she answered distantly, focusing on undoing the busted remains of my corset

"When the king's advisor brought me here, there was a young man who was with us. His name is Soren. I don't suppose you would happen to have any idea where I could find him?" I asked.

"Soren. Soren," she repeated as she worked, thinking it over. "Not that I recall, my lady, but I can inquire with some of the other servants and see if anyone else knows."

"Thank you, Brunhilde. That would be wonderful if you could."

I wasn't particularly looking forward to seeing Soren, but I needed to start working on getting some of my memories back.

"Of course, my lady. Alright now, arms up," she directed.

I lifted my arms and she peeled the dress over my head. The fabric was so tight, it felt like I was being born all over again. When I was finally free of it, my respite was short-lived because Brunhilde potato-sacked me with another one.

When I made it to the other side, she said, "I am happy to hear you and His Royal Highness were finally able to spend some time together. Unfortunately, now we are behind schedule." She gestured for me to hold on to one of the bedframe pillars.

My hands clasped the wood post and I braced myself as she laced up the corset so tight, it felt like my organs had packed their bags and taken up real estate in my throat.

"For what?" I wheezed.

"Your appointment with the dressmaker. We are almost three-quarters of an hour late." She clicked her tongue before she added, "As she is a very busy woman, I imagine she won't be very happy."

"Such insolence! Such disrespect! One hour of my precious time gone. And for what?" the petite, young female hissed as she folded the fabric at my hip and shoved a pin through it. I could feel the metal slide against my skin, stirring a shiver to spider-walk down my spine.

Despite her size, the royal dressmaker was not someone you wanted to piss off, and I obviously had. Ever since we arrived in her workshop, she'd put the fear of the Creator in me every time she picked up a pin and jammed it roughly into the folded fabric.

Her workshop, stationed in the castle, was a sizable room. It was stockpiled with so many different fabrics, she could give all the fabric vendors in the city of Cent a run for their coin. Rolls of fabric were haphazardly stacked on top of one another, some piles so tall it was a wonder they didn't topple over. Bamboo bowls, full of an array of various sewing supplies, sat on top of wood tables, no rhyme or reason to any of them. The room was far from tidy, but the dressmaker seemed to know where everything was regardless.

Gorgeous—that was the first word that had popped into my head when I first saw her. She had big, sweeping, dark-brown eyes paired with plush, full lips set in a long, oval face, her skin a warm, glowing copper. She wore a stroke of kohl along her eyelids that she had winged at the sides and continued past the inner corners, giving her eyes a feline effect. Her brown-black hair had tight, springy curls that she piled loosely on her head. A few untucked curls fell by her temples.

"Did you hear me?" she growled with a tug on the dress, causing the gold bangles she wore to chatter in response.

I had a clear view of her through the three-sided mirror that stood in front of me, but I glanced down, directly at her. The vantage point from the round, wood pedestal I was standing on made her look even smaller, but no less feral.

"We are very sorry for our tardiness," Brunhilde jumped in, apologizing for the umpteenth time. We both had taken turns apologizing over the last hour. It seemed to appease the dressmaker for a few minutes, but then she would start back up again.

Wash. Rinse. Repeat.

"It will *not* happen again," the dressmaker snipped as she reached for another pin, moving on to a different section.

Brunhilde and I nodded quickly, agreeing with her.

There was a saying back home, and it went something like *The Spirit Realm hath no fury like a woman scorned.* I understood it now. I didn't fear many people, but the dressmaker with the arsenal of never-ending pins?

She was definitely one.

CHAPTER 12

Sage

Colorful ribbons, ornamental hair combs, and a spread of other hair items were placed in an orderly fashion, laid out across the makeup vanity I sat in front of that morning. Brunhilde hummed to herself as she brushed my hair. Occasionally, the brush would get stuck in a tangle, courtesy of my fine hair strands and a night of tossing and turning— thanks to me missing Von. Brunhilde would press her hand against the back of my head and give it a good yank, her approach to detangling knots far from gentle. At one point, I yelped, feeling half-inclined to rip the brush from her hands and bonk her on the head with it. But I refrained and played the part of the empty-headed stooge this society so clearly wished for me to be. It was a small price to pay if I was to make good on my vow to kill the king, a small price to pay if I were to break the deal between Arkyn and Von and be reunited with him at last. Those were my two reasons for staying in this castle, for enduring this isolating world of theirs.

I lifted my gaze, catching on the reflection in the mirror. I knew that face. The slightly upturned nose, narrow-angled jawline, and almond-shaped eyes.

And yet . . .

Did I *really* know her?

Sadness drifted over me, rooting itself deeply. It was quick, and it was immense—to the point where my shoulders sagged and my eyes became cloudy.

I looked down to my hands, clamped tightly together. *Who was I?*

The back of the brush clicked upon the wood vanity as Brunhilde set it down, and I lifted my fallen gaze. Forcefully, I pulled myself from my thoughts, watching as Brunhilde's hand hovered over the ribbons until she finally picked one.

"This one will look lovely," she said, holding up the gold ribbon for me to see. "And I think the prince will like it, don't you agree?"

"It's very nice," I replied mindlessly.

Brunhilde nodded in satisfaction and began to weave it into my hair.

My gaze strolled across the vanity, catching on one ribbon in particular. It was thinner than the rest, but the color of it was what caught my eye—

Black.

My heart leapt a tick. It reminded me of Von.

I picked it up, and asked Brunhilde, "What about this one instead?"

"My apologies, my lady, I'm not sure how that one made it into the pile. Black is reserved for times of mourning." She continued to braid the gold ribbon into my hair.

"I know. I think it would look lovely." I raised it for her to take, lifting my gaze to meet hers in the mirror.

We stared each other down until finally, she huffed and said, "How about you wear both, my lady?"

"Alright," I sighed, meeting the stubborn housemaid halfway.

She snatched it from my fingers and began to work the black ribbon in, alongside the gold. I chalked it up as one small win.

A short while later, there came a knock at the door. Both Brunhilde and I turned towards it. Quickly, she tied the remainder of my braid and rushed over to the door. Swinging it open, she efficiently bowed and said, "Good morrow, Your Royal Highness."

"Good morrow," Aurelius's accented voice greeted her as he stepped into the room, his gaze swiftly meeting mine. Knee-high leather boots stretched up his strong, sturdy calves, sitting overtop of his fitted—and I mean *fitted*—breeches. He wore an unbuttoned leather jacket that was tailored to his mid-thigh, showing off the white tunic beneath. A gold livery collar was slung across his wide shoulders, the square bezels holding blue stones too light in color to be sapphires. He smiled at me with his perfect, white teeth. "You look lovely."

"Thank you," I said, standing up. I didn't know if I was to bow or not to bow or what was expected of me. All of this was still quite new.

"I was just wondering if you cared to take a walk with

me?" he asked.

I thought it over for a moment, deciding a walk wouldn't do much harm. Besides, I might be able to fish out some details about the king.

"Sure," I replied.

As we departed my chambers, Brunhilde said, in place of goodbye, "Don't forget, you have another appointment with the dressmaker at one o'clock."

Oh goody.

The stiff fabric of my underskirts brushed abrasively together as we walked down the length of a spacious corridor. Columns, chiseled from pale stone and about half of my height, checkered one another on either side of the room. There were dozens of them, each one housing a meticulously carved head.

I glanced at Aurelius. "Are we going somewhere?"

"We are," he answered with a hint of a dashing smile, his face set forward.

"Where?" My gaze caught on a sculpture that looked as though it had seen better days—in particular, the nose, which was missing.

"It's a secret," he said, a hint of mischief steeped into his perfect, proper tone.

I gave him a quick, questioning glance as we rounded the corner, but I didn't press any further. "It's nice to be without the guards," I mused happily—purposefully.

Me changing the topic was a bit calculated—the guards followed me whenever I left my chambers, which posed a bit of an issue with my plan to kill the king. If I could convince Aurelius to stop them from accompanying me everywhere, that would only help to further my cause.

Speaking of causes, it had been well over one week since Arkyn left. The longer he took to get back, the more anxious I felt. Like I wasn't doing enough to save Von.

"I apologize for them," Aurelius said. "I know it may not seem like it, but they are for your own protection."

"The first guard didn't exactly seem too keen on protecting me," I countered.

"He never should have been assigned as your guard. It was a lapse in judgment on Arkyn's part."

"And what if the other guards are similar to him?"

"I can assure you—" Aurelius smiled. "—these ones won't be."

Internally, I grumbled. This was not going like I had hoped it would.

I pressed a bit more, playing into what he was saying, regardless of if it was the truth or not. "I know they are for my protection, but are the guards really all that necessary? They make me feel as though I'm a prisoner." It wasn't a stretch from the truth. That's originally why I thought they had been stationed outside my door—to keep me locked up. Arkyn had not exactly brought me here in accordance with my own will, after all.

"You are not a prisoner," he stated as if it were a matter of fact. "And yes, they are necessary. In truth, I'd feel better having more positioned outside your chambers. You know yourself how deeply rooted some of the mortals' hatred runs for the Cursed, which they think you are. That's why the guards are necessary."

I didn't know what it was, but a part of me felt inclined to believe him.

I also understood what he wasn't saying—that people might do more than scoff or show disgust towards me. *Some* might take their hate one step further. I decided to drop the subject of the guards. For now, at least.

Aurelius gestured to a set of open doors positioned to my right, a few paces ahead. "We're here."

I had to do everything within my power to keep my jaw from dropping as I stepped through the double doors and took in the grand library, formed from one of the castle towers. Round in structure, the library was made of many, many, levels, each one filled with rows upon rows of dark shelves, chock-full of books. I tipped my head back, glancing up, up, up towards the ceiling.

In the middle of the main floor were a bunch of wood tables. Although there were a few stacks of books on some, none of them were occupied. I glanced around, noting a similar pattern. Positioned around the exterior, where there weren't any bookshelves, were various seating spaces, some centered around crackling fires.

I turned to Aurelius, finding his eyes on me. "Are we the only ones in here?"

He grinned softly. "We are. I had the library closed so you could explore it properly, completely unbothered."

"You didn't need to close the library." I paused. "But . . .

I appreciate the obscenely aggressive gesture, nonetheless." It wasn't a lie. What girl didn't dream of having an entire library to herself?

I began to walk forward, towards a small aisle, barely large enough for two people to pass through.

"I had a feeling you would," he mused as he followed silently behind me.

My fingers drifted over the leather spines and a light layer of dust slowly began to gather on them. Every once in a while, my gaze would snag on a title, but none intrigued me enough to pick out a book and explore it further.

"Are you looking for something in particular?" Aurelius casually asked, his voice coming from a short distance away. I glanced over my shoulder, noting that he was at the far end of the aisle, where I had first entered.

In particular? Yes. A book that could tell me how to break a tattooed bargain would be a great start. But if I said that, it might lead to questions, and I'd rather not contend with those. So, I needed to think of another way to find the information without giving away what I was actually looking for . . .

"Maybe a book about the gods and goddesses? I imagine I should start learning more about them. It might help my memories come back."

"Works about our kind are located on the third floor. If you continue forward and then turn to your left, you'll see a set of stairs that will take you there. Would you like me to show you?"

I shook my head. "I think I'll be okay. Thank you."

"You're quite welcome," he said with a warm smile. "I'll leave you to it then."

"Alright." I nodded and headed towards the indicated direction.

Two flights of stairs later, I found myself standing at the circular railing. Swirling, intricate, iron balusters propped up a thick, polished wood banister. I marveled at the wood, wondering how the architects had managed to get it to curve so perfectly. I glanced down, overlooking the main floor, my gaze pausing on Aurelius.

He was seated at one of the tables, the space before him bare. He reached forward and a quill appeared in his hand, as well as a bottle of ink and a stack of paper, placed before him.

As he started to write, he asked, his voice slightly elevated so I could hear him, "Are you staring at me, Moonbeam?"

Heat kissed my cheeks. "Just admiring the library."

"Mhm," he said teasingly.

I smirked as I pulled back from the railing and lost myself in the rows of books. I had never seen so many before. There were books upon books upon books.

After wandering aimlessly for a good half of an hour, I found the area I had been looking for, according to a wood sign, hung on a set of small chains. It read *Gods and Goddesses*.

I began to walk up and down the aisles, plucking any books that seemed of potential interest. When the stack nearly towered over my head, and my arms were growing weary with their weight, I walked over to a small table and dropped the books on top with a loud *thunk*.

I spread the books out on the table before me, debating which one to read first. One caught my attention. I ran my

fingers over the title stamped into the leather-bound cover—
The Dawn of the New Gods by Sir Antony Roberts.

I decided to start with it.

"Did you find what you were looking for?" Aurelius asked as
he half-sat on the table, one leg propped up, while the other
stayed on the ground, supporting his weight.

I closed the book and set it down, lacing my fingers
together over top of it. "Not quite," I said honestly. "But it is
an interesting read, nonetheless."

"That is good to hear." He smiled. "What is it about?"

"Ironically . . . it's mostly about you."

"Uh-oh," he teased. "Sounds like trouble."

A small smile caressed my lips. I picked up the book and
handed it to him. "Sir Antony Roberts must have been a big
fan of yours," I said as he looked over the cover.

Aurelius chuckled as he lifted his gaze, meeting mine.
He feigned seriousness. "But did he speak of my dashing
good looks?"

"In fact, he did," I said, blowing out a laughing breath
through my nose, fighting the temptation to roll my eyes.

"Oh good, good. That is a relief," he replied playfully. A
small dimple appeared in his left cheek. Oh yes, Sir Antony
Roberts had spoken of that too. And as much as I hated to
admit it, it was rather charming.

I lifted my gaze from his dimple. "Have you read it?"

A soft nod. "I did, quite a while ago."

"And did it help you regain any of your memories?"

"I can't say that it did," he sighed. He set the book down on the table. "And as much as I'm enjoying your company, I believe you have an appointment with the dressmaker in half an hour."

My brows shot up. "I hadn't realized so much time had passed."

"I figured as much," he said as he gracefully stood.

I glanced at the books scattered around the table, and started to clean them up. Aurelius helped.

When there was one book left, we reached for it at the same time, our fingers colliding. It felt like a bolt of lightning had struck my ring finger, traveling straight through to my heart.

I jerked my hand back and looked it over, trying to determine what had just happened.

"Are you alright?" His eyes darted between mine as if he would find the answer faster there.

"Did you feel that?" I asked breathlessly, my chest heaving.

"No, I can't say that I did." He continued to survey my expression, concern written clearly in his own. "Did you remember something?"

"No." I shook my head and forced myself to take a deep breath. "It was just a strange feeling."

"When we touched?" he asked.

"Yeah," I said, still a bit dumbfounded by what just happened. I took another breath, looking to the mountainous tower of books. "Can I take them to my chamber or—?" I trailed off, waiting for him to fill in the rest.

"Unfortunately," he pointed behind me, "they have to stay here."

I turned and read the large sign that hung on the far wall, stating that the books were not supposed to leave the library.

I sniffed at the sign and turned to Aurelius. "That seems like a rather silly rule."

"I concur. It is one of many things I plan to change when I become king," he said with a great deal of confidence. "Anyway, I suppose we best get you on your way. I know the dressmaker doesn't like to be left waiting."

I didn't disagree.

Following that day, it became routine for Aurelius to show up at my door in the mornings with a smile on his face and that damned dimple showing. Then, we would head off to the library. While he wrote, I read, continuing my search for any information that might help me in my quest to break the deal between Arkyn and Von. It gave me something to do, other than fret about how long it was taking for Arkyn to return. Afterward, Aurelius would escort me to the dressmaker's workshop, and each time she opened the door to let me in, the scowl on her face only seemed to deepen.

Aurelius had arranged for an entire wardrobe to be made for me—which made me uneasy for a few reasons. The first of my qualms was the dressmaker's increasingly sour mood—

she was definitely going to stick me with a pin one of these days. The second was because I was not in need of a wardrobe while existing under the king's roof—it was not like I had plans to stay.

In truth, daytime *here* was slightly tolerable. But during the night, the river of time slowed to a trickle. As the rest of the castle slept, I tossed and turned, thinking only of Von.

Sometimes, I'd catch a tall, shadow form walking at the foot of my bed, and I'd nearly beg for it to take me with it before it dissolved. To take me to it's master. Whether it was my mind, or the late hours, or something tethered to Von, I did not know.

No matter how much I promised myself that this separation between us was temporary, that we would be reunited again, it never dulled that visceral, raw ache of how much my soul yearned for his.

CHAPTER 13

Von

The Goddess of Storms threw a tantrum this morning.

Her howling, powerful winds battered the northwest side of my castle. Even though they were exceptionally strong, my castle was much, much stronger, because of what it was made from—flawless obsidian, the rare kind that did not possess any imperfections. It was one of the toughest natural materials in the Three Realms. The idea to use it came to me shortly after I was gifted the Blade of Moram—a testament to just how old this castle was . . . how old I was.

Why the goddess felt the need to take her anger out on my castle and the rest of the Spirit Realm this morning—when she should be directing it at her serial-cheating partner, the God of Lust—I did not know. And why the Creator thought it would be a good idea to pair someone as volatile as the Goddess of Storms with the God of Lust—an immortal physically built to feel and inspire desire—I also did not know.

And yet, here we were.

Here I was. Stuck.

I was stuck listening to the wind smash into my castle while Sage was out there. I was stuck lying on this cement slab, unable to protect her. There was so much she didn't remember about her past, about what I did to her—what I *took* from her.

The wind roared outside. This gust was the strongest one yet, by the sounds of it.

A low whistle emitted from the doorway.

"That's one pissed off goddess," mused my brother—the only soul in this realm who would be enjoying the winds—or rather, the fierce emotions that brewed behind them.

Bootheels struck the floor, counting down the seconds until the bottle and the glass hit the cement slab beside my head.

Clink. Clink.

Sure enough, there it was.

Although my brother was not known for being a creature of habit, this—him strolling in with a cup and a bottle of bourbon—was becoming a daily ritual.

"Nyko was at Hard Spirits last night, his arm wrapped around a foxy little redhead—who had been begging me for a job an hour before he showed up," Folkoln started as he poured himself one-third of a glass, something I didn't need to see to know. "I told him not to go home with her."

I waited, knowing full well that wasn't about to be the end of it. When Folkoln started a sentence that involved the God of Lust and Hard Spirits, Folkoln's tavern, trouble was guaranteed.

Folkoln chuckled. "I told him to go home with the twins instead. Low and behold, the idiot listened."

Of course, he did—Nyko was a brainless twit. And now, the Spirit Realm was paying for his infidelity.

Should I ever get out of this situation, I'd punt his sorry ass to the Living Realm, and if Sonya, the Goddess of Storms, wished to be with him, she could go live there instead—let the mortals deal with her blasted tantrums.

"I'm amazed how fast word traveled back to Sonya."

I didn't need my vision to see the dirty grin Folkoln wore—I could hear it in his words. Which told me he probably had something to do with Sonya finding out as well.

"Anyway, in other news, Sage is still as clueless as ever about her past. Little Bird says Kaleb plans to see her tomorrow, so she'll give me another update after he returns. And as expected, Aurelius is still playing the role of the Golden Prince." Folkoln chuckled. "I do wonder what his old followers in the Immortal Realm would think of that whole spectacle—their esteemed king playing prince, under the thumb of a mortal king. My, my, how far he has fallen."

I couldn't give two shits about Aurelius, so I didn't waste a single thought on him. Instead, I thought of *her*. I was relieved to hear that Kaleb was checking in on Sage. She would need him more than ever once more of her memories started to return . . .

"Also, I thought you might want to know—the Da'Nu is on the rise again, and just like the last time, it's mostly young women."

If I could have gritted my teeth, I would have—I figured

that would start happening again.

It wasn't uncommon for the Da'Nu to fluctuate, especially during times of mortal wars or when a plague was going around. But there was only one other time when the Da'Nu rose because of the sudden increase of young, female souls.

A memory stirred on the horizon of my mind.

I grabbed hold . . .

CHAPTER 14

Von

The Da'Nu was going to overflow any minute now.

Souls upon souls saturated the river. The deep current worked tirelessly, trying to sort which layer of the Spirit Realm the souls should be delivered to, to live out their afterlife.

Like the river, my ravens were also being pushed to their limits, collecting the freshly departed from the Living Realm. Over the past months, there had been so many of them—most of them women.

It was troubling.

But I was no longer the king of the Living Realm, and even if I was a bit tempted to find out what was going on, the visceral rawness of being stripped of two-thirds of my kingship had left me in a sour, bitter mood.

Right now, all I cared to do was lick my gaping wounds.

From my sprawling balcony, forged of smooth, volcanic

glass and etched in dark splendor, I looked over the Da'Nu, watching as a raven returned from the Living Realm. It dropped the glass orb into the river, and the glass shattered upon impact. From it, a soul was born anew—another girl, barely into her twenties. She drifted with the current, brown hair swirling around her. She would remain like that, in her slumbering state, until the river sorted her.

It was rare, but occasionally, an unsorted soul would wake. Even more rare were those who fought the current and found their way out of the tumultuous waters. The few who did make it out, I offered a place at my side, working as reapers.

"Those orgasms—" breathed the blonde mortal as she pressed herself into my side, snapping me from my private thoughts, "—were something else."

I glanced down at the curvy, naked vixen whose name was lost to me. I acknowledged her words with a flick of an arrogant, uninterested grin—gone as fast as it came. Her long, icy blonde hair fell over her ample breasts, her rosy, pink nipples poking through the silken strands.

Blonde . . . I had always been fond of the color, although if I could fade the gold from it, that would be preferable—an acquired personal taste with foreign origins.

Just this morning, I had spotted the pretty mortal in the throne room. I had never seen her before. Her big, doe eyes had shamelessly flirted with me—blatantly telling me her unnoble intentions. Before she had a chance to leave, I had caught her wrist, pulled her into me, and extended a private invitation to my chambers. When she arrived at my door an hour later, I pulled her inside and showed the little mortal what it was like to lie with a god.

For mortals, the act could be either extremely pleasurable or extremely painful—it all depended on the immortal they bedded and their particular . . . tastes.

The Creator designed mortal and immortal bodies differently. As a whole, immortals were crafted to be taller and larger than mortals. This transferred through to our reproductive systems as well. Mortal men were built smaller *than us gods, and the women had shorter canals than the goddesses.*

Most believed the Creator did this to prevent interbreeding between the two species.

Unfortunately, for me, I refused to bed any more goddesses—which was bad news for the bottom third of my length.

Why did I prefer sex with mortals? They didn't care about my status. They were more interested in the crown tucked behind my pants than the crown that sat upon my head.

Whenever I slept with another goddess, they always ended up wanting something more from me. Some of them plotted to use me as a means of raising their status. Some of them said they just wanted to give me an heir, something I had absolutely no interest in. I had no desire to raise a pup with a woman I barely knew. Any child of mine deserved more than that.

Children . . . A topic I didn't think about often. I had fathered none, something that was of my own choosing. I supposed that was the one benefit of being the God of Death— I could make any seed, including my own, null and void. My touch alone could wilt any flower. Speaking of . . .

I pulled away from the pretty little woman. "I have

business to attend to, but you can stay here for a while. Use the bathing room to clean up if you wish. All I ask is that you are not here when I return later tonight." My words were blunt but my tone was not unkind.

As I said before, I had no desire to form any type of connection with a female I took to bed.

I exited the balcony and walked through my chambers into the private bathing room, the doorway purposefully doorless as I saw no need in having one.

Who did I need privacy from in my own chambers— myself?

A large, oval-shaped bath was nestled in the middle of the stately bathing room. Steam curled from the surface of the heated waters, its reflection dancing on the ceiling above. Twin sinks sat on the same wall as the doorway, a long mirror hung over top.

Centuries ago, when I designed the layout of the bathroom, I possessed hope that one day, I would find my mate—that was why I put two sinks in. But it was a notion I had long since given up on. Over my eternal span of life, I had seen countless other gods and goddesses find their fated mates, but the Creator had chosen not to bless me with one. So, like a flame at the end of its wick, the hope I once possessed had long since burnt out.

"Wait, I thought you would drink from me? Isn't that how this works?" the blonde said, her bare feet padding against the floor as she scrambled behind me.

"Why would you think that?" I asked as I grabbed the top cloth from a pile of folded ones. A small stream of water rushed out from the faucet when I turned it on. I placed the

cloth underneath it, feeling the warmth of the water chase the coolness from my fingers. A few seconds later, I shut the tap off and gave the cloth a single-handed squeeze. I handed it to the girl, nodding to her sex. "To clean yourself with."

She looked dumbfounded, like she hadn't expected that. As she took the cloth, she started, "Because your sister—"

"What about my sister?" I snarled.

"She . . . she said you needed to feed, th-th-th-that you haven't since you were dethroned from the other two realms," she stuttered, her fingers shaking so badly she dropped the cloth on the ground.

I growled, my shadows snaking around me, beckoning for release.

The girl scrambled backwards until she bumped against the wall—the unexpected touch of it forcing her to yelp.

Reining my shadows back in, I scrubbed at my temple before I drew my hand down the length of my face. A sigh fell from my lips. "I'm not going to hurt you."

"You're not?" she whimpered, still cowering against the wall. She pressed her thighs together so tightly, it looked as though she were trying not to piss herself.

"I'm not," I reassured her. I conjured a thin, silk robe and offered it to her, my gaze snagging on the horizontal scar below her abdomen—a jagged white line of thick skin, running from hip to hip. Scars that remained on the soul's shell in the afterlife were usually an indicator of how they passed from the Living Realm.

Cautiously, she took the robe from me before she quickly put it on, covering herself.

I tipped my head to the side, curiosity getting the better of me. "I've never seen you before today. How long have you been in the Spirit Realm?"

"Just over a few weeks," she said, cinching the robe at her narrow waist.

"Your scar—" I nodded to it, but clipped my sentence short when she turned ghastly white.

"I'm sorry, my lord. I do not wish to speak of it," she stammered, and as if those were her parting words, she quickly scampered out of the bathing room, over to the bed, grabbed her clothes that were sitting on it, and then ran out the door, leaving one lonely sock behind.

I walked over to it, glanced at it, and then sent it to her. If she were to look down, she would find it neatly folded on her stack of clothes.

Where are you, Saphira? I growled through our private channel.

Seconds later, she strode into my room, shadow walking through the wall.

"I take it you didn't like the little snack I arranged for you?" she said in her clipped, arrogant tone. She ran a gloved hand over her black, velvet gown laced with silver, smoothing it. Her eyes fell below my waist, a grin touching her lips. "Okay, so you enjoyed her in other ways."

Unlike mortals, immortals didn't feel shame for their nakedness, even if it was in front of a sibling. That was due to a few reasons: the first being how long we lived—shame evaporated when you'd seen it all. The second was because we were not siblings in the same sense that mortals or immortal offspring were. Mortals were born from the union of a father and a mother, whereas immortals were forged in *batches at the great anvil, by the hand of the Creator.*

"Your insolence in the throne room this morning was one strike. Consider this your second. Do not push me, Saphira."

Her expression twisted, a scowl painting her ethereal features. *"And yet, I will, because I'm tired of watching you starve yourself. Tell me, brother, is it so impossible for you to believe that I care?"*

I threw my head back, laughing. *"You don't care. We both know that you do nothing unless it serves* you.*"* I narrowed in on her. *"What's your angle this time?"*

"What it has been since you *lost the realms,"* she said, stepping around me, circling like the vulture she was. *"I want to take back what is ours from those ridiculous abominations—those . . . those* New Gods.*"* She snarled the title like it had personally insulted her. *"I want war. You are the most powerful god and it will be you who wins the realms back for us. But if you don't eat, you will grow weak and then we'll never get back what has been lost."*

War. That was all she had talked about since the Creator stripped me of the other two realms. She had brought it up this morning, even though I told her not to. Continuously, she pushed against me—against my rule, seeding her wishes amongst my court as if she were its queen. Seeding them . . . in me.

She quit her circling, her defiant emerald eyes meeting mine. *"Just think of it—"*

"Saphira." My voice was a steel blade, cutting her off. *"We would not just be going to war against the New Gods, but also the Creator—we would be going against their wishes."*

"The Creator stole your birthright from you. You simply

would be taking back what is rightfully yours," she said, a wicked twist to her red lips. She brought her wrist to her mouth and sunk her teeth into her flesh. She raised it in offering to me, ichor pooling in the bitemarks.

Although I was tempted to drink, I didn't. I turned away from her, clothed myself in my leathers, and headed towards the door. "I will hear no more of this."

But, of course, that was not the end of it.

Because when Saphira wanted something, she did not stop.

CHAPTER 15

Sage

I was beginning to think agreeing to dinner was a bad idea, and it wasn't because there were *a lot* more people than I expected there to be—it was because of two other reasons: first, Aurelius was nowhere to be seen, and the second was because of the queen.

While everyone else was busy eating, chatting, laughing, and drinking their fill of wine and ale, the queen had not so much as glanced at her servant-dished plate—a fire-roasted dove, surrounded by a spread of cooked vegetables. I heard one of the nobles a few seats down murmur something about how eating a bird a day would lift oneself up, thus bringing them closer to the New Gods.

Little did he know that there was a goddess, *apparently*, seated at this very table, with an iron collar wrapped around her throat.

The hypocrisy of it all had my tongue sharpened and eager to take a swipe, but I sheathed my unspoken words and spared a quick glance towards the queen.

Her silk gown was stitched in finery, perfectly matching the ruby crown that shone brightly upon her head. A necklace, made from the same glinting gemstones, draped around her neck, distracting from the jowls forming under her chin, her body beginning to lose the battle against time. She had not touched her plate even though she had a fork in hand. Her fingers, covered in gaudy rings, strangled the metal handle with such intensity that it looked as though the bones in her knuckles might pop through the taut, thin skin.

One might think her sour mood was due to the Cursed filth—*yours truly*—sitting across from her, but her gray-blue eyes weren't shooting daggers at me, but rather, at the young, beautiful woman seated next to me—who shared similar physical traits to the dressmaker.

She looked to be around my age, maybe a few years my elder. The emerald color of her formal gown complemented her rich, copper skin tone and long, curly, dark hair. Slowly, she chewed her food, each bite smaller than the last as if she wanted to drag the meal out for as long as possible—the satisfactory setting of her lush, painted lips securing that motive.

Despite the building tension, the king seemed blissfully unaware. He sat at the head of the table, shoving his greasy fingers into his mouth and sucking on them loud enough for the entire room to hear—and it was no small room, by *any* means.

The hall was thrice as long as it was wide, a stretch of

tables placed directly in the middle, illuminated by the firelight coming from the torches hung along the walls and the iron chandeliers strung from the wooden beams above. At the far end, a gigantic fireplace stretched from wall to wall, its stone-framed mouth filled with a massive, crackling fire that brought forth a continuous roll of heat, chasing away winter's cold caress.

As I sat there, stealing small glances at the king and the queen—one whose table manners *I* even found repulsive, and the other, snarling like a beast—I was almost tempted to laugh.

These were the people leading Edenvale? The same people who sniffed their noses up at the Cursed, and sent them to the pyre because they labeled *us* a disease? Internally, I cringed.

"I do not see why she must eat with us, Hakred," the queen said as her gaze shot to the king with such force, it was a wonder it didn't knock him out of his chair.

The use of the king's first name nearly caused me to choke on the wine I was drinking. Sage from two months ago would never have believed where she was now. Dipping my head and pretending to be invested in the vegetables on my plate and not the court drama unraveling before me, I peeked at the king through the guise of my upper lashes.

"She sits with us because I wish it to be," he replied as he chewed with his mouth open.

"But she sits there, deliberately pecking at her food like a little bird. She does it just to annoy me." The queen jerked her head from side to side, mocking the woman, as she said, "Peck, peck, peck."

I hid my surprise at the queen's unqueenlike behavior.

"At least I do not eat like a sloppy, old sow," the woman beside me quipped confidently before she slipped a piece of cheese into her mouth.

My brow shot up as I eyed the king, particularly the ball of mashed-up food inside his mouth that made its debut every time he chewed. I was tempted to ask the female beside me if she meant the king rather than the queen, but kept my tongue trapped firmly between my teeth, lest it might slip free.

"A sow!" the queen wailed as she slammed her fist against the table, plates and cutlery chattering in startled response. "Are you implying that I, the queen of Edenvale, eat *like a sow*?"

The room fell deathly quiet.

"Well," the woman started, her voice controlled, unfeeling, yet sensual, "who else would I be talking about?"

I nearly fell over. She couldn't be serious. I didn't know who this girl was, but she had just insulted the second most powerful person in all of Edenvale, and worse, she had done it publicly . . . I decided I just might like her.

"You are a disgusting, dirty whore," the queen growled, her eyes nearly bulging out of her head.

Ah, and there it was, the missing piece to this whole puzzle—the woman was the king's mistress.

"Better to be a whore than an unwanted queen." The woman's sharp tongue was quick to strike again, continuing the queen's public lashing.

The king choked, his eyes going wide. He thumped his fist against his chest—trying to dislodge whatever he had sucked back. His face turned as red as the beets on his plate.

I couldn't help but notice that *not one* person jumped up to help him, not even the woman sitting beside me who clearly meant something to him. Just as I began to wonder if destiny was about to make good on my vow before I did, a chunk of half-chewed meat flew out with such force that it catapulted across the table.

I stared at it—*everyone* stared at it.

Quickly, a servant darted forward. Leaning over the table, they used a metal lid to sweep the saliva-coated meat chunk onto a silver platter. They closed the lid and then hurried out of the room, disposing of the evidence—too bad it was seared into my mind.

Unfazed by her husband's *almost* demise, the queen picked up her verbal sword and took aim at the woman beside me. "Someday, I will rid your filth from this castle."

Meanwhile, the king gasped for air like a fish out of water.

"Perhaps," the woman said, pausing as she reached across the table and plucked a cherry from a heaped fruit platter. "But even then, my scent will remain in the king's bed." She popped the cherry into her mouth, plucked the stem off, and flicked it onto the table towards the queen.

And that was when the queen of Edenvale grabbed a bread knife and hurtled it at the woman's head. The woman was quick to duck, a mischievous cackle leaving her lips. The knife ricocheted off of the wooden chair before it fell to the stone floor, clattering as metal struck stone.

"I'll kill you with my own hands!" the queen roared.

Having somewhat recovered, the king jerked upright, his chair shoved backwards. Panting, he said, "That is enough,

Melayna. You will silence your tongue. Sit down and eat. Or you can leave. The choice is yours."

The queen shot the king a withering glare, her fingers twitching. I wondered if she might reach for the goblet next and throw it at him. Instead, she wrangled her scowl into submission and lowered back into her chair.

The king nodded in satisfaction before he sat down, turning his attention back to his heaped plate.

I glanced at the woman beside me, who was casually swirling the wine in her goblet, a satisfied smirk twisting the corners of her red lips. She had come out of this battle completely unscathed, the king her knight in shining armor. The queen, however, looked unhappier than ever—even her meticulously styled wig looked out of sorts.

All those years ago, when the queen was taken by the Cursed rebels, the king had been desperate to save her—his Red Rose.

But now? If the Cursed rebels were to take her again, I doubted he'd ask for her back.

"I apologize for my tardiness," Aurelius's regal voice announced as he entered the dining hall, garnishing the attention of the room.

The rich, golden-red pelt he wore emphasized the breadth of his shoulders. Underneath it, a white tunic, the collar laced loosely and shaped in a "V" revealed a hint of the muscle that dwelled beneath. The sleeves were cuffed and perfectly made for the length of his long arms. Black leather pants and polished knee-high leather boots completed the outfit.

As he strode towards me, smiling with those perfect

white teeth, I was reminded that he was no mere prince. Aurelius *was* the king of kings. And whether the people around me knew of his divinity or not, I was sure their souls did, because simultaneously, each and every one of them rose from their chairs and they *all* bowed.

"Please, continue to eat," Aurelius said, his tone saturated in charm. He sat in the empty chair beside me. Leaning over, he said, "I'm sorry for being late." He flashed a playful, knowing grin. "Did I miss anything?"

"It's been . . ." I paused, trying to find the right words. "Entertaining, to say the least." I couldn't help but smile, my mind replaying the entire debacle that had just unraveled before my very eyes.

"As the mortals so often are," Aurelius whispered into my ear.

I chuckled, the sound produced from whatever divinity lived within—mortal Sage didn't bother to contribute. That part of me wondered when I had become part of the immortal group that joked about the humans, considering I believed myself to be just that—*human*—for the entirety of this life. I felt as though I had blinked and missed when that happened, and now I was at a precipice, teetering between two people— Sage and Aurelia.

One was home, the other a stranger.

My smile faded. Was I going to have to choose between one or the other?

"Is something wrong?" Aurelius asked, his platinum brow dipped, rooted in concern.

A servant placed a silver platter in front of him. With a gloved hand, they removed the lid and then quickly scuttled back, revealing a hot, steaming plate—the meat on it different from what the rest of us had been served.

"No," I said softly, the lie coming a little too easily. I nodded to his plate. "You should eat before it gets cold."

He glanced at it, then back at me, molten gold eyes meeting mine. "Your attempt to distract me has not gone unnoticed, but I will not pry into something you do not wish me to."

"Thank you," I said, genuinely meaning it.

"Of course." He reached for the goblet of wine sitting in front of him. Elegant, long fingers plucked it from the table, and he brought it to his mouth. The golden band wrapped around his ring finger shimmered dutifully, catching my eye as if it were purposefully trying to draw my attention to it. A mixture of feelings wormed their way into my belly—filling me with discomfort and something else I didn't care too much to dig into.

A man dressed in fancy clothes and somewhere in his forties sat on the other side of Aurelius. He leaned forward, clearing the phlegm from his throat before he inquired in a snobbish tone, "Might I have a word with you for a moment, Your Royal Highness?" He lengthened the syllables, as if it were an effort just to get them out—too good for the common tongue.

Trying not to roll my eyes, I pinned my gaze to my plate and focused on the crumbs I had purposefully left unharvested. Creator above, the foodie that lived within me made it damn hard to be a proper lady.

Aurelius nodded in reply, setting the goblet on the wood table without so much as a whisper of sound—a testament to his ethereal grace.

"Just yesterday, a carrier pigeon arrived from Old Northoway. It was a letter written by my younger brother, Lord Archibald. You remember him, yes? He visited in the fall," the man said.

"I remember him. How is his wife doing?" Aurelius asked, his fork slowly sliding into a piece of dark meat. With just enough pressure from his knife, he sawed a chunk off, the process itself graceful and elegant—the epitome of Brunhilde's proper table-manner dreams.

"Well, that is the thing, Your Royal Highness. My brother has written to inform me that she has become deathly ill, and he does not suspect she will make it to spring."

"What is she ill with?" Aurelius asked.

"The healers suspect it could be something to do with her condition," the man replied, his voice growing croaky, but not from emotion. He cleared it before he continued, "She is with child."

Aurelius's hands stilled momentarily, before resuming to cut another piece. "I am sorry to hear that she has fallen so unwell. Your brother must be beside himself." He took another bite, his lips wrapping around the fork.

"Oh, I can assure you he is, especially as he is desperate for an heir," the man said with an agreeing nod.

Aurelius finished chewing before he responded, "That, I can understand."

The man continued, "In his letter, he spoke of his wishes to come to court, so that he may begin the search for his new wife. As I said before, he *is* desperate for an heir."

Aurelius dabbed at his mouth with a cloth napkin before

he dropped it onto his plate—he'd barely eaten anything. He made eye contact with a servant and gestured for him to take his plate.

When the plate was removed, the man picked up the conversation once more. "Well, Your Royal Highness, what are your thoughts on the matter? Will you grant my brother time at court so that he might find another wife?"

Aurelius didn't answer right away. Finally, he said, "You may write to your brother and tell him that he can come to the castle, but tell him to bring his wife, as well, when he comes. Regardless of her condition. We have some wonderful healers here, and perhaps they can help her." Aurelius turned to the man, his tone edging with steel, but it was barely audible. "Would it not be worth his time to try to save his heir *and* wife, rather than looking for another one?"

The man's superior tone lost the confidence it portrayed before, as he stuttered, "Y-y-y-es, your grace. You are correct. I'll write to him at once and tell him to arrange his travels and to bring his wife with him." His tongue tripped up like two left feet, tangling over his words.

"Very good," Aurelius said with false praise. "And tell him not to dawdle, yes? From what I understand, her life hangs in the balance."

"Of course, Your Royal Highness," the man said with a respectful bow of his head.

I leaned towards Aurelius. "That's rather nice of you to extend hospice to his brother's ill wife."

Aurelius smiled, that lone, charming dimple forming in his cheek. "It was the least I could do."

I returned a soft smile, then said, "I've been meaning to

ask you something."

"Yes?" His attention lingered on my lips.

"Do you know when Arkyn will return?"

His eyes shifted to mine. "I apologize, but I don't. He is needed elsewhere for the time being. Why do you ask?"

I was asking because I needed to make a deal with Arkyn to save Von. Something I wasn't entirely sure Aurelius would want to hear, considering the bad blood between them. I wondered if Aurelius knew that Arkyn's deal hadn't quite worked and that Von was stuck in a catatonic state, still alive. Despite my curiosity, something within me told me to tread with caution and so I did.

"No big reason," I lied, pulling my gaze from his and reaching for my goblet. I tipped it towards me, noting it was empty. "I was just curious."

"Ah, well, I will let you know as soon as I receive word of his return," Aurelius responded pleasantly as he plucked a gilded wine jug up from the table.

"Thank you. I'd appreciate that."

"Of course. More wine?"

"Please." I reached forward, offering him my wine cup.

CHAPTER 16

Sage

Later that night, while the world slept, I was wide awake, thinking of Von.

In this lifetime, I had only ever spent one night with him in the same bed, and at the time, I had absolutely hated it. Von was a giver when it came to his tongue, but when it came to that night, he had been an absolute bed hog. His big, warrior body ate up the much-too-small bed, leaving me very little room. To make matters worse, he had snored.

I laughed softly. I had called it a windstorm of a snore, or something along those lines. Even though his snoring had kept me up, eventually, I fell asleep. Beside him.

That was the first night in a very long time where I didn't have any nightmares.

Now . . . I wondered if he was the reason for it.

I reached across the covers, my fingers curling at the

painful nothingness.

Tap. Tap. Screeeeech.

I blinked, my head jerking towards the balcony doors, where the strange sound had come from.

Whatever it was did it again.

There was *something* outside—that I was sure of.

The brave part of me wanted to go to the door and investigate, but the other part, the *one-too-many-bad-nightmares* part, wanted to go get the nightshift guards and make them look instead. I didn't think they would mind if I asked, especially considering neither of them were the guard I had nicknamed Grouchy.

In fact, I had not seen Grouchy in the rotation of guards since the night at the pool, but considering his abrasive asshole nature, I didn't waste a wink of sleep on it.

I decided to stay right where I was—under the safety of the covers and hope that whatever was out there decided it had the wrong door and found someone else to terrorize— preferably the king.

The tapping stopped.

Seconds passed and it was replaced by the sounds of a struggle. Whatever was out there sounded a lot bigger than before.

I jerked up from my blankets, eyes rounded at the corners, my fists white-knuckling the furs. Was it too late to notify the guards and send them out to be eaten first?

The door flew open, and Kaleb strode in—a sour expression on his face.

"Didn't you hear me knock?" he grouched as he chucked the door closed behind him.

"Creator's sake, you damn near gave me a heart attack," I seethed. My brow shot up. "*Knock*? All I heard was this constant creepy tapping. Wait a minute. . ." I offered him a closed-lipped grin. "You were tapping with your little beak, weren't you?"

He rolled his eyes at me.

I shot my foot out from underneath the covers, wiggling my toes. "And using your little chicken feet to claw at the door?"

"Chicken . . . chicken feet!" he sputtered, too insulted to string together any more words. Shaking his head, he walked over to the fireplace and crouched in front of it, placing his hands in front of the crackling fire.

I snickered, pulling my foot back underneath the covers. "I'm guessing it's cold outside," I said, watching him.

"It's freeeezing. I honestly don't know how people live here!" he exclaimed. "Also, it's snowing outside."

"Is it? It's so late this year." I flipped my covers back and scurried over to the window. I watched the fluffy snowflakes fall at a leisurely pace, tumbling through the abyss of night. "By the way, you lived here, in the Living Realm, for all of your life, might I remind you."

"Yeah, but that was *before*," he said, meaning nothing by it and yet—

I glanced down at the window ledge, forgetting about the snowflakes.

Before.

That one word reminded me that life would never go back to the way it was, and grappling with that fact wasn't easy. But for Kaleb, I would.

"What is it like?" I asked, picking up my fallen gaze.

Kaleb's footsteps sounded as he stepped beside me. "The Spirit Realm?" he asked.

I nodded. "Mhm."

"It's made up of nine different tiers, depending on how you conducted yourself in your past life, which determines which tier you belong in. People have the ability to move up or down levels, depending on their behavior. They can also request to be placed in another tier, but the process is a bit complicated. The top tier is reserved solely for the Old Gods and Reapers. The Spirit Realm was completely redesigned by Von after the Immortal War."

"Why did he redesign it?" I asked, curiously.

Kaleb shrugged. "Why does anyone redesign anything? To make things better, I imagine."

"I suppose that makes sense," I answered, thinking on the topic of the Immortal War.

It took place centuries ago, when the Old Gods, led by Von, and the New Gods, led by Aurelius—and *apparently* myself—fought for control over the Living and Immortal Realms. The last time it came up in conversation was with Von when we were back in Belamour.

Von . . . A pain formed in my chest.

"Have there been any changes with him?" I asked, watching the falling snowflakes move at their own leisurely pace, misting the canvas of night with sparkling white.

"Nothing," Kaleb sighed, his voice conjuring me from my hypnotized state. "How are things going with uncovering your past?"

My past? *That* was a complicated topic thanks to a

particular gold ring.

"They aren't. I inquired with my housemaid about Soren, but that was a dead end. Arkyn *still* hasn't returned." I let out a frustrated sigh. "Because he isn't here, I can't ask him about Soren or discuss striking a new deal. Apart from spending my days trying to gather whatever information about the king I can, I'm feeling stuck."

"We're going to figure it out," Kaleb offered reassuringly, giving my hand a gentle squeeze.

"There's something else."

"What is it?" he asked with a degree of concern.

"Part of my past is living in this castle." I took a breath and exhaled softly before I turned to him. "I know we weren't raised with much knowledge pertaining to the gods, but do you recall that the Lady of Light was once married?"

"Now that you mention it, I do—to the Lord of Light. Wait. Are you telling me that he *is here*?" Kaleb's blond brows drew together.

"He is."

Gray-blue eyes met mine. "So then . . . what does that mean for you and Von?"

"Well, as it stands, I don't really know. I . . . I don't think it means anything for us. I know that it is not uncommon for gods and goddesses to have a variety of spouses due to their longevity of life. Von told me that after the Immortal War, the two warring sides would be linked together through marriage—a marriage between him and I. But it never took place because I . . . died." That last word tasted strange on my tongue. Talking about my death, past tense, was . . . odd. But even worse was the nauseating feeling it left in my stomach.

Now it was Kaleb's turn to take a breath. "I'm not going to lie. It sounds like one Spirit Realm of a twisted tale."

I nodded in agreement.

"Have you tried talking to the Lord of Light? About your past?"

"I have, but his memories are as lacking as my own."

"Hmm," Kaleb said, thinking about it. "Well, I reiterate, we'll figure it out." He gave me a playful nudge. "Also, before I forget, Ezra has a message for you."

My brows shot up into my hairline. "Whoa, wait, you can talk to Ezra?"

He threw me a look. "You really have to ask that?"

He was right—the woman had full-on conversations with rocks. What was a little chat session with a bird?

"Where did you see her?" I grinned, eager to hear more.

"She is in the Cursed Lands in a town called Valenthia. Two girls were with her. One was a tall, smoking-hot brunette. And the other was smaller, a bit mousy. Come to think of it, she didn't say a single word."

My smile widened and my heart warmed—*they were together*.

"The brunette is Harper. And the smaller one is Lyra. Lyra is unable to speak, but I'm not entirely sure why. I spent a great deal of time with them, but I just never felt like it was my place to ask."

A sliver of regret poked its way in.

Did that make me a shitty friend for not asking? I'd rectify that someday—I'd learn Lyra's story, if she felt comfortable sharing it.

I looked at Kaleb. "What did Ezra want you to tell me?"

"Okay, how did it go?" Kaleb muttered to himself, his fingertips sounding against his blond stubble as he scrubbed his jaw. "Ezra wanted me to tell you to tell somebody by the name of Ryker not to hit on you, because, and I quote, *you have too many sprung logs in the fire, and you don't need another one added to it.* Also." Kaleb patted his pockets, producing a small, black rock. "She wanted me to give you this."

My face went slack as I held out my hand and he dropped the rock into my palm.

That was her message?

Why would she want me to tell Ryker that? Ryker was in the Cursed Lands with her so that made absolutely no sense. The log thing, however, made *perfect* sense, and I wanted to forget the image her choice of words evoked as soon as they *sprung* into my head.

Dirty old bird.

I turned to Kaleb. "Um, tell her thanks for the rock, I guess."

He snickered. "I will. She's got a stash of them waiting for you. Says it's your inheritance when she croaks."

I rolled my eyes, unable to fight my growing smile.

Great divine, I missed her.

Sprung logs and all.

CHAPTER 17

Sage

I took one good hard look, and I just knew . . . "It won't fit."

"It will," Aurelius reassured me, his eyes meeting mine.

"You can't be serious," I said, wondering if he was delusional. "I'm looking at the size of the hole, and what you are trying to put through it, and I'm telling you, it won't fit."

"It will, just trust me," he said in that rich, regal tone of his—even his voice was dipped in gold.

"Fine," I sighed, glancing at Brunhilde, who was also watching, her plump bosom held still on bated breath. I rolled my eyes at her dramatics—if it didn't fit, we could find a smaller one.

"Steady. Steady now. Take it slow," Aurelius commanded.

"Be careful. Don't break it!" Cataline chipped in, her hands wrung tightly together.

Aurelius and I both glanced at her, taken aback by the directiveness in her tone—like she was a general leading her soldiers to war.

When she noticed that the Golden Prince was looking at her, her cheeks bloomed a vibrant red. Quickly, she took a step back, dipped her head, and averted her eyes. The contrast between the girl from a few seconds ago to the girl now was as stark as day was to night.

I looked back at the door, watching as the armoire was slowly pushed through, its feet screeching across the floor in protest, like a child being dragged away from the new toy they desperately wanted.

When it was all the way through, I turned to Aurelius. "I guess you were right."

"I usually am," he said, the confidence exuding from him backing up his claim. He looked at the armoire as the two men moved it to its new home, beside the much smaller one. "Well, at least this will house some of your wardrobe for now."

"I think it should do the trick," I said as the two men who'd carried the armoire in walked up to Aurelius, bowed, and then started for the door.

"I, too, should be leaving for my morning meetings. By the way, I have news I think you would like to hear. Arkyn is expected back today," Aurelius said, watching the men as they walked out before his gaze slid to mine.

Excitement coursed through my veins. This was it. I was finally going to get a chance to speak with Arkyn and possibly find a way to save Von.

But that was just it, wasn't it? I had to *speak* with him.

A sense of dread filled my belly, the weight of it sloshing

from side to side. I was not looking forward to seeing him in person, not in the least. Especially after he tried to light me on fire. But it was a matter I had little choice in—I needed to talk to him about Soren and discuss striking a new deal. Despite how uncomfortable it made me feel, I would gladly do it for Von.

Aurelius's brows knitted. "Is something wrong?"

"No, not at all," I lied poorly. In an attempt to cover my elephant-sized tracks, I changed the subject and gestured to the door. "I'll walk you out."

He searched my face for a moment, before he said, "Alright."

I fell into step beside him, his knee-high leather boots as silent as my bare feet

"I won't be able to go to the library with you today, as I expect the meetings to be rather long. I will make it up to you though," he said as we reached the door.

I leaned against the frame of the doorway, looking up at him.

I would be a liar if I said feeling his gaze on me didn't conjure some type of feeling to my flesh, some type of yearning within. He was, after all, someone with whom I had been thoroughly intimate, once upon a lifetime.

As if on cue, a whisper of a forgotten kiss brushed across my lips.

Aurelius reached out, as if he were tempted to touch my cheek.

On reflex, I pulled back. I opened my mouth to speak, but he beat me to it.

"I know, I know. You can't," he said, dropping his hand.

If my reaction made him feel some sort of way, his schooled features did not let on. "I'll see you tomorrow."

I nodded. "Tomorrow then."

When he was gone, I closed the door softly and turned back inside.

Brunhilde was busy making the bed—that woman pulled the covers so tight, you could bounce a coin off of them. While she did that, she barked orders at Cataline and Naevia—something about going to see if some of my new dresses were ready.

I walked over to the window and looked out, surveying the foot of fresh snow on the balcony. I wondered if I carefully dusted off the top layer of snow, would I find little chicken tracks packed beneath?

I smirked to myself.

But my smile didn't last long when I spotted what sat on a canvas of white—a small, single, black feather. Even though it was small, the color reminded me of Von.

My stomach flopped. I felt homesick.

Not for Ezra or the cottage, but for the dark-haired male with the obsidian, starless eyes. What I wouldn't give to be back in his arms.

I pulled away from the window, a thought occurring. "How far is Belamour from here?" I asked Brunhilde.

"About an hour by carriage." She stopped fussing with the sheets and looked up at me. "Why?"

I leaned against the wall. "Would it be possible to go there?"

She gave me one good, hard look before she nodded, to my surprise. "I suppose a trip to the city wouldn't be a bad thing. Besides, I wouldn't mind paying my sister a visit. I'll have a carriage arranged to take us there."

Excitement swelled within me. I offered her a smile. "Thank you, Brunhilde."

"Of course, my lady," she replied kindly, before clapping her hands at the girls. "Alright, ladies, let's get a move on. The day is not about to look after itself, now, is it?"

CHAPTER 18

Sage

Clacking hooves and churning wheels sounded against the snow-packed road as the coachman clicked his tongue and the carriage pulled away, taking Brunhilde with it as she headed off to see her sister, while leaving me and the two guards behind, standing in front of the winding path that led up to the beautiful, gothic manor. Towering and powerful. A dark, ancient splendor.

I took a moment to take it in, letting the familiar memories of this place fall over my shoulders like that one trusty, old blanket that couldn't be thrown out—the one you turned to when you were sick or when you needed comfort.

Taking a deep, steady breath, and with the wind nudging my back, playing with the tips of my hair, I started towards the house.

When I reached the entrance, I expected to hear the

screeching of armor following me inside, but for some reason, the sound stopped at the door. I was thankful for that and didn't question why that was—why the guards were staying outside.

The manor was quiet, but it didn't bother me—I had come to walk with the ghosts of this place anyway. Even though I had lived here only weeks ago, it felt like a lifetime. The fireplace in the sitting room, just off from the foyer, was unlit, yet it was toasty warm inside. The heat of the air drifted over me, warming my face and chasing away the bitter, bitter cold.

And I knew it was *him*—his magic that I felt surrounding me. Even though he was a shadow in another realm, his power still reigned supreme. It was immense, welcoming, and it felt like home.

Home.

Remember, a feminine voice said. A voice from another life—*my voice*.

But when I tried, the canvas of my mind remained as blank as a starless night.

Gods, how badly I wanted to . . . to just remember it all. And yet, I could not.

When I'd first arrived here, Harper had told me to find something to wear for our first night working at the bathhouse. When I'd reached for an onyx-colored bit of lingerie that was hung in one of the armoires, a male voice had said to me, *Seeing you wear my colors . . . It makes me feral.* At the time, the voice was distorted, and I could not place it.

But now, I knew without a doubt who it belonged to—Von.

Had I lived here, in my past? Was the lingerie . . . *mine*?

Without realizing it, my feet had carried me to the kitchen. I walked past the obsidian island, my hand floating over top as I lost myself in the memories that were crafted here.

The food—Lyra's baking and cooking.

The victories—pounding back a cake with Harper after I made a deal with Arkyn, feeling like I was *finally* going to get Kaleb back.

My gaze fell to the empty, dark-stained wood stool two seats in from the left.

I had sat there while Von stood a breath away from me, our bodies so incredibly close, that unexplainable pull bringing us together. He had said we were bonded, but what did that mean?

Von's voice played in my mind when I asked him about his tattoos—*When I'm lost and out of my mind, and waiting for my light to return, they are the very thing that guides me through the darkness.*

That thin ice I walked on that kept me from fully understanding before began to crack, and when I fell through, I realized the truth—the weight behind his words.

Von was talking about me.

I was *his* light . . . the one he waited for.

And the way he looked after he said it—he had lifted the mask he so carefully kept in place and allowed me to see in. To see that visceral pain, the suffering, the breaking. The longing . . . for me.

My hand clasped over my thundering heart, a tremble working its way into my knees, across my bottom lip. *Oh,*

Von.

More than anything, I wished I could recover all of my lost memories, and then maybe I could begin to understand not just the little bits of our story, but all of it as a whole. I had a feeling I would only love him more.

Love?

Was that the right word for what I felt for him?

I rubbed at the spot over my heart, a noticeable ache there, and that was confirmation enough. Now it was I who was feeling that immense longing for him—the same feeling that woke me during the middle of the night. In my disorientation, I always reached across the bed for him, only to find it empty and cold.

I made my way upstairs, passing by the familiar wood door that led into my room and headed straight for Von's. I closed the door behind me and rested my back against it, my eyes closed. When I opened them, my exhale faltered as my breath became stitched to my lungs.

My memory must have been playing tricks on me because I . . .

I could see him.

His towering phantom was standing by the large chest at the end of the bed, taking off his chest plate, his furs. The apparition flickered and then it returned, but this time, his muscular arms were raised as he gathered his sleek black hair and tied it up. His beautiful onyx eyes met mine, teasing me, lapping at me, silently asking if I was enjoying the view.

And then he turned, his phantom prowling towards me on silent, deadly feet, so careful as to not startle me to run. His shadows reached for me—*he* reached for me. A finger curled under my chin, that familiar feeling of his cool metal rings pressed against my skin.

Tilting my face upwards, he asked in that signature bourbon tone, "Have you forgotten me, Little Goddess?"

"I could never," I said breathlessly, knitting my hands into his black tunic, amazed by how real he felt, at the tangible heat radiating from his broad, sturdy chest, washing over me in heavy, undiluted waves.

"I'm holding you to that," he murmured as he leaned down and kissed my lips.

I closed my eyes and allowed myself to fall into him. I did not care if this wasn't real. I would take this male in any form I could get him, even if it was just a phantom my mind had conjured up.

Von's kiss was the striking of a match—lighting me on fire, burning me alive. His hand, the one that said *king*, cupped the back of my thigh and he tugged it up, angling me so that my core was pinned against his thick, muscular leg. He pressed into me, anchoring me to the door. I groaned in response to the added friction, but the sound barely passed my lips because he swallowed that too.

This male would devour me, just as he had promised. And I would let him.

But first, I needed him here with me, physically. I pulled back, my head pressing against the door, Von's steel frame locked against my front.

He growled in displeasure as I stole my lips from his—as if he had been stumbling in the barren, sandy desert for months and I was the lake he so desperately needed to drink from.

"How do I save you?" I asked, my pleading eyes darting between his.

"You cannot." His fingers drifted from my chin to the collar, his eyes narrowing into slits, a black storm brewing inside.

I shook my head, refusing to believe that. "What if I make a new deal with Arkyn?"

The muscle in his jaw ticked so hard it was a wonder it didn't burst through his tanned skin. "You will do no such thing."

"If it means saving you, then I will do anything," I argued back, the space between my brows crinkling.

"You say that now, Kitten, but . . ." His eyes shifted down, a fan of thick, black lashes feathering his cheeks for a second before they raised back up. Gingerly, tenderly, he cupped my cheek. "Once you start getting your memories back, you will feel differently about me. For a time."

"I know that we were enemies in our past, but I don't care," I said, desperate to convince him. I tipped my face further into his warm touch, my hand falling over his. Creator above, it felt so good to be reunited with him. There was a missing part of me, which I had never known existed, at least not until I had met Von. Now, here in his presence, I was whole. Complete.

He lowered his forehead against mine, his voice—the tone, it was heartbreakingly gentle. "You don't know what I did to you. Of the monster I was to you back then."

"Then tell me now," I pleaded softly. "Help me understand."

"Our story spans decades, little darling. It would take

more time than I have right now for me to tell you everything that happened between us."

"Then tell me how I can save you," I begged, "and then we can tackle our past together."

He studied me for a moment, before he answered, "You cannot save me from this."

"I don't believe that." Desperately, I clutched his tunic, his broad, warrior-derived chest bracing my forearms. "There must be something I can do."

Von sighed as he lifted his forehead from mine. "There is an object that possesses the power to break the deal, but it has been lost for many years . . . It might not even exist anymore."

"What is it?" I asked, my eyes flickering desperately between his.

That telling muscle flexed once more in his jaw. "It is called the Blade of Moram."

"What does it look like?"

"The blade is made of obsidian. It can shift from dagger to sword, depending on what form its wielder wishes for it to be." He captured a lock of my hair and ran it between his thumb and forefinger, until he reached the ends.

"Do you have any idea where it might be? When was it last seen?" I asked.

Von's gaze darkened.

I gave him a moment to respond, and when it became clear he wasn't going to, I pressed on with a hiss. "What is it about this blade that has you so . . . conflicted? What aren't you telling me?"

"Because . . ." His voice dropped an octave as he released the lock of hair. "I'd prefer the blade stayed lost."

My brows knitted. "Why?"

He caressed my cheek. "Because, like everything with us, even though the blade would bring my salvation, if it fell into the wrong hands, it could mean your demise."

I cupped his wrist, feeling the powerful veins and hard muscles beneath. "Is the blade like the Crown of Thorns? Is it a weakness to me?"

"No and yes. The Crown of Thorns was a threat to your life, but the Blade of Moram is not, at least not directly. It is who the blade is linked to that makes it your weakness." His phantom flickered, the bits of shadow that forged it breaking off. For a brief second, I could no longer feel his warmth.

"What's happening?" I peered up at him, frantic to keep him here with me.

"I can't hold this form much longer." His tone struck like whiskey rather than smooth bourbon. "Sage, there's something else you need to know, and I *really* need you to listen to me. The God of Life, you must not trust him. And for Creator's sake, *do not* drink his ichor." Von sounded desperate. I had never heard him like that before.

"What do you mean?" My hands fisted firmly in his tunic, desperately trying to keep him here with me.

"I mean exactly what I said. Do not trust him and do not drink from him. And above all else—" He kissed me once more, and when he pulled back, he growled predatorily. "Do not forget who you belong with, Kitten."

And then his phantom was gone.

A short while later, I discarded my coat on the leather chair, grabbed the black tunic that had been tossed carelessly on the corner of his canopy bed, and put it on. His tunic ended at my knees, emphasizing the difference in our heights, and I was not short by any means. I gathered the fabric at the unlaced neckline and brought it to my nose, inhaling deeply. It still smelled of him, of his amber and sandalwood scent.

I snagged the bottle of bourbon from Von's desk, popped the cork, and brought the cool glass to my lips. Tears pricked my eyes as I drank down a heady amount, the smooth burn awakening the taste buds on my tongue.

If I buried myself in his scent, if I drowned myself in his bourbon, would my beloved Death come back to claim me?

One could only hope.

CHAPTER 19

Sage

"Are you drunk?" asked a familiar voice—chock-full of arrogance and swagger.

I yanked my head up from the plush pillow and squinted at the door, squinted at the hulking guard that stood just outside of it—the one I had never heard speak, until now. His voice sounded a lot like . . .

No.

How could that be possible?

Either Von's bourbon could give Ezra's tonic a run for its coin, or . . .

"*Ryker?*" I asked the beast wrapped in metal.

He took his helmet off, revealing rich brown eyes and that signature cocky grin.

"Hey, beautiful," he drawled in his chest-rumbling tone.

I sat up quickly—*too quickly*. My head started to spin. I

was a few too many swallows past buzzed, but not nearly enough to be staggering drunk.

He nodded to the bottle sitting on the bed stand. "You going to finish that without me?"

"Nope," I said, having a little too much liquor-induced fun as I popped the *p*. I crawled over to the side of the bed, grabbed the bottle by the neck, and extended my arm towards him while seating myself and patting the spot beside me. "How?" I shook my head slowly, narrowing in on the armor he was wearing—on the king's emblem displayed across his broad chest. "And why?"

He tossed his gauntlets onto the bed, snagged the bottle, and sat beside me, his stiff metal armor making the task more difficult than it should be. "I'm just going to start from the beginning," he said.

I nodded, waiting.

"After our search for Soren turned up empty, we traveled back to the Cursed Lands to speak with the Elders and Ezra, to try to figure out what our next step was. Ultimately, we decided that if Soren was alive, then he was probably at Clearwell Castle." Ryker paused, taking a deep pull from the bottle before he continued. "While deliberating on how to get Soren back, we received word that the king had been hiring and training mass amounts of new guards and bringing them directly to the castle. As you can imagine, it didn't sit well with the Elders, nor any of us." He lengthened his arm and peered at the amber liquid inside the bottle, studying it as if he were looking at an old friend he hadn't seen for a while. "But since I've been here, I've noticed that the castle guards are sorely lacking—it's like anyone with any experience is gone, like they've been shipped off somewhere."

"Shipped off to where?" I wondered out loud, a sense of unease pooling in my belly, warring with the relaxed feeling the bourbon had given me.

"That's the question, isn't it?" Ryker retorted. "And there's more . . . The king is conscripting healers and young women, but no one knows where they are taking them." He shook his head, took another swig, and then offered me the bottle, the rich, caramel-colored liquid sloshing around inside.

I raised my hand, gesturing I didn't want anymore. "I wonder where the king is sending them."

"I plan to find out," Ryker answered with that incredible determination of his—something I admired.

"I'll help," I said with a nod. I turned towards him, tucking one foot underneath me. "How did you become a guard?"

Ryker smirked, the expression boasting of male confidence. "It wasn't that hard. Since the king has been hiring new guards, all it took was a few forged papers and I was in. There are a few more rebels here as well, also working as guards."

Just then, something small scurried across the expanse of my mind—a shadow mouse. It was the first time I had felt him since *that* day.

Soren.

Time had not made his intrusion into my mind any less jarring, and yet, I needed the betrayer.

Soren? I asked inside my mind. *I need to talk to you.*

He gave no response. Of course, he didn't. The coward.

"What's that look about?" Ryker asked, noting the sudden shift in my mood.

I glanced down, not sure where to begin. I exhaled a deep

breath. "Do you know . . . about Soren?"

"I do." Ryker's grip tightened on the bottle. "I searched for him up until the day I saw that redheaded prick bringing you into the castle. Soren was following behind, no chains, no collar. It became pretty clear whose freedom he had traded for his own. I could have snapped his neck right there, but I knew I wouldn't be any help to you then. So I did the only thing I could think of— I started working towards getting placed as your guard."

I felt an ounce of relief that Ryker already knew. I didn't really feel like living through *that* whole ordeal again, nor having to explain just how badly Soren had betrayed me—that cut was deep enough and talking about it right now would feel a bit like pouring salt into a wound. My brows pinched. "That day in the courtyard gardens, that was you, wasn't it? All this time, why didn't you say anything?"

"Because the boy-turned-guard is always with me. He's young and eager to please and wants to move up the ranks. If he found out we were connected, he'd turn me in. It was another risk I couldn't take. I was going to slip you a note, but then today happened and it provided the perfect opportunity. I convinced him to let you wander around inside, knowing you'd take your sweet time. After a while, I told him I was just coming in to check on you and for him to wait outside." Ryker smiled softly. "Luckily, the young pup listens well."

That made sense. If Ryker had revealed who he was, or even so much as spoken to me, I would have caught on right away and I don't know how I would have reacted in the moment—I wasn't exactly known for my poker face. "It's probably a good thing you waited until now."

"Mhm," he rumbled. "So, are you going to tell me why

you're still playing palace princess?"

Realizing I was going to need another drink for this, I snagged the bottle and took a long, heady sip, feeling its smooth bite all the way down. I returned the bottle to him. "First, I have to ask, do you know what Von really is? . . . *What* I am?"

He gave a soft nod. "When I was a young boy, Von looked the same as he does now—that sort of tipped me off that he wasn't *just* Cursed, but it took a few years of prodding before I got confirmation out of him." His gaze met mine. "I know *who* you are, as well."

I sat with that for a moment, unsure how to feel about it.

Then, I said, "I'm guessing that means that Harper and the others know as well."

"They do—well, everyone but Soren. Von asked us not to tell him. He never quite trusted him, and looking back now, I can see why that was. Although now that Soren has access to your thoughts, I imagine he knows who you truly are." Ryker's expression twisted painfully as if an old wound were being cut open. He took another swig.

I knew full well that the topic of Soren and what he did to me when he broke the unconscious mind barrier was hard for Ryker—especially after everything that had transpired with the woman he had once loved.

I let Ryker sit with his thoughts for a moment before picking up our prior conversation. "You asked me a question— why am I still at the castle?"

"I did." He nodded. "So . . . why are you?"

"That's a loaded one," I said as I took a deep breath. Then I began.

I told him everything—everything that had happened after

Kaleb's death, from the moment Von and I left for Meristone, leading up until right now.

When I told him about my vow to kill the king, just like Kaleb, he made me promise to let him help me, which I agreed to. I told him that Kaleb was alive—well, sort of—and a reaper now. When I opened that festering wound back up and told him exactly what had happened with Soren, Ryker's knuckles turned bone white.

But when I got to Von and Arkyn's deal, when I had to tell Ryker that Von was stuck in a comatose state and unable to wake up, well, it was not easy for either of us.

The bottle of bourbon didn't last through that part.

Later that night, on our way back to Clearwell Castle, I figured out where my old guard ended up. Or, I guess I should say, I figured out where *part* of him ended up.

Surrounding the castle were towering stone walls with sharp wooden pikes sticking out of them. Occupying the pikes were heads—belonging to anyone who went against the crown, I presumed.

That was where I found my old guard.

His head had been severed and shoved grotesquely onto one of the pikes, the flesh picked clean by the ravens circling up above, waiting for their next meal.

And where his eyes used to be, all that was left were bloody, vacant holes.

CHAPTER 20

Von

When the Creator placed the makings of my being on their great anvil, they hammered the power to direct, to command, to dominate into my flesh, forging those traits into my immortal bones. That's why the Creator made me the first king of kings.

I was built to lead—to control.

But there was a balance to it. With control, one must know its brother—restraint. You could not possess one without the other, despite their similarities.

But when it came to her . . . my control and my restraint were always being tested.

After Kaleb's death, that day in the woods, she would have happily given herself to me. Creator above, how badly I wanted her. All I could feel was a visceral, raw need to claim her—her body and her soul. But I didn't, and it had taken every ounce of my immortal strength to turn her down. I had my reasons.

The first was because I wanted to take my time with her, to give her mortal-acting body time to adjust for mine. The second was because her brother had just died, and I knew my impulsive female and the way she used sex as a tool to feel when she was facing hardships, or when she felt numb. How many times had she slept with another male, only to regret it the next day?

No, I wasn't like other men, and I would not be something she regretted.

Sage wasn't just any other female—she was my soul's other half, my mate, *my bonded.*

The bond was an ancient magic that tethered two souls together, well past the limits of eternity. When two mates found each other, the bond gave them a connection unlike any other. It made it so we could feel what one another was feeling, while giving us a private channel to speak on. The bond could happen among any species, but it was most prevalent among the Old Gods, while it was almost non-existent among the New Gods.

Some speculated that the Creator chose to get rid of the bond when they created the New Gods. That was because there was a downside to it—it could turn well-mannered gods into rabid animals. It could drive them to insanity, making them obsess over protecting their mates—willing to do anything to keep them safe, even if it meant locking their mates away from the rest of the world, never to be seen again.

I'd be a liar if I said that thought hadn't crossed my mind—spawned forth by the beast that lived inside. Oh yes, I felt that animal within, the one the Three Spinners called

Nockrythiam—the Ender of Realms. But I did everything I could to keep that nasty demon under lock and key. I had warred with that part of me since the dawn of my creation.

When I felt her presence in the manor in Belamour, I had felt her soul calling out for mine. My restraint had snapped like a frayed rope stretched beyond its means, and although I knew it just might kill me . . .

I *needed* to see her.

So I'd used my shadows to conjure a phantom version of myself and sent it to her.

For a time, I was able to breathe her in, feel her warm, little body mold so perfectly against my own. I held that form for as long as I could, but the unhealing wound in my stomach was like a black hole, constantly swallowing my power.

Now that my shadows had returned, and my remaining stores of power were depleted even more, I could feel unconsciousness calling for me.

Water was an incredible force. When given time, one persistent little stream could carve through ground and stone, forging itself into a mighty river. Although I considered my sister more blazing inferno than calm water, Saphira, apparently, had taken note of this, because her persistence had strengthened over the past so many months.

Constantly, she was in my ear, in my council's ear, demanding we go to war against the New Gods and take back the Living and Immortal Realms, using the consistent increase of young women's deaths to pour a little extra cyanide on the fire she had so carefully stoked. But I knew my sister—she was the last of the divine to care about mortal lives.

She just wanted war.

The worst part of it all? I was starting to entertain the thought.

Which was why I was here, in the realm of the living, standing at the base of Mount Kilangor, its peak hidden above a blanket of clouds. The mountain, forged from bedrock, was too steep for anything to grow on it, rendering it a deathly gray.

My power was useless here, the wards of the Three Spinners making it so, which meant that I couldn't just shadow walk up the mountainside.

However, I wasn't about to walk . . .

I unfurled my wings and stretched them out, releasing the tension and stiffness from being cramped up for so long, a soft groan emitting from my throat.

With one mighty slap of my wings, I shot up from the ground. The natural wind was powerful, but my wings were stronger—they carried me up, through the white clouds, until I made it to the other side, to the never-ending stretch of azure. There, I flew to a small, flat clearing a few hundred feet below the mountain's sharp peak. My wings flexed once before they snapped shut and disappeared.

The mouth of a cave yawned before me, ancient runes carved around its opening, the magic potent, old, and strange. Strong magic always had a taste to it, but when it came to the Three Spinners' magic, it had the ability to cauterize the taste *buds on one's tongue. And despite the intensity of their magic, my mouth tasted of nothing.*

Ducking my head, I walked into the dark abyss. The tunnel was small and narrow, and if I hadn't tucked my wings away, I never would have fit. The tunnel broke off into different paths, creating a labyrinth of sorts—a maze one could get lost in for the rest of their life if they took a wrong turn, which explained why there were so many skeletons.

*This was not my first time visiting the Three Spinners, nor did I imagine it would be my last. I knew my way around the innards of the mountain almost as well as I knew the nine tiers of the Spirit Realm. I knew to always—*always*—stick to the main path, even though the labyrinth could easily persuade you to try another.*

No matter how deep I ventured into the mountain, the dripping of water was ever present. It sounded no better than a male with an enlarged prostate trying to take a leak—pissing out an inconsistent flow. Sometimes it was a light dribble, and other times, a sputtering stream.

A pulsating, luminescent orange glowed at the end of the tunnel. The closer I got, the hotter the temperature became, until it was enough to make my own blood feel like it was boiling in my veins. Reaching the end, I stepped out into the vast expanse that roared before me, peering at the twisted path that snaked ahead. An ocean of lava bubbled on either side of it, striking itself against it as if the two sides were trying to reunite with one another, but the path was in its way. With each strike, droplets of lava were tossed up into the air, landing on the path, pebbling it in the slippery, blazing-hot substance.

I glanced down at the boots I'd had a sorceress enchant prior to coming here, hoping that these ones lasted longer than the last pair. Considering there was only one way to find out, I continued ahead. Lava smashed against the sides of the path, spraying onto me, burning through my clothes, sinking well past my skin. Before the lava had a chance to cool, my immortal cells pushed it out and healed the bloodless holes. This process repeated over and over again as I forged on.

By the time I reached the end, overall, I was quite impressed with how well my boots held up against the lava. Normally, the flesh from my feet would have been long gone by now. Next time, I would get the sorceress to enchant my clothes as well.

A round dais was raised before me. On it, three towering, empty thrones sat side by side. Behind them, spanning from floor to ceiling, was a stretch of never-ending shelves chock-full of yarn-filled spools—one for every soul. The Wall of Weavings.

I glanced to the left of the thrones, finding one of the sisters sitting at one of the spinning wheels.

The Goddess of Fate.

Her bony, curled fingers worked tirelessly as she spun the glowing fibers by hand—spinning a life story for the soul she was working on. She wore her wiry, gray hair braided, an array of reds and purples streaked throughout it. Matching her hair, her clothing consisted of similar colors, resembling the berries she adored so much.

"Well hello, handsome. It's been a while." *Her stormy-gray eyes met mine.*

"Fate," *I greeted her.*

Knowing full well why I had come, she said, "Let me lay eyes upon the little treasures."

I slipped my hand into my pocket and took out a small bundle of cloth. Slowly, I unraveled it, feeling her greedy eyes watching my every move. I tilted my hand, allowing her to see the five tiny seeds.

Like my leather boots, I'd had them enchanted— enchanted to survive in even the most unfathomable conditions—like here, in the belly of the mountain's blazing inferno. With these seeds, she could begin propagating plants down here, something she had never been able to do before.

She quit her spinning. Quickly, she extended her purple-stained fingers towards me, gesturing for me to hand them over.

I gave her a devilish grin. "Not until you tell me what I have come to hear. If I wage war on the New Gods, will I win?"

She sucked on her yellow, cracked teeth, mulling my request over. Then she nodded. Waving her hand, a spool full of glowing, black yarn was pulled from one of the shelves, floating over to us. It dropped into her hand. She began to unravel it, her eyes scanning the threads every so often as if she were thumbing through a novel and just reading the chapter titles. It took her a while to find what she was searching for, but when she did, she stopped and began to concentrate on the portion she held between her hands. She brought it closer to her face as she inspected the yarn.

After a moment, her brows raised. Slowly, her hands lowered to her lap, the yarn still taut. Her expression seemed almost . . . surprised.

"Well?" I asked in soft demand, taking a step forward.

"The Goddess of Free Will has granted you a choice in the matter." She looked up at me, curiosity swarming in the pits of her gray eyes. "When the time comes, whether you take the Living and Immortal Realms will be up to you."

That vague answer was not what I had come here for and I knew the Three Spinners well enough to be cautious of murky answers. "If I am going to give you these seeds, Fate, I am going to need more clarity than that."

Her gaze bounced between my fist which held the seeds and the yarn in her hands—a decision standing before her. She clicked her tongue, her tell that her mind was made up. "Then ask specifically what it is you wish to know."

"If I declare war on the New Gods, will I win?"

"If you were to go to war now, you would lose," she said, not bothering to look back at the yarn. "But if you seed discord among the New Gods and give it time to grow, then you shall win."

"How long must I wait?"

"Many, many, many years," she answered as she began to roll the yarn back up.

Saphira was not going to be pleased about that, but I held no qualms about it. My patience was eternal. If I had to wait a while to get my realms back, then that was exactly what I would do.

When she was finished, she snapped her fingers and the spool disappeared. She rose from her wooden stool, which squeaked with relief. She walked towards me, her shoulders permanently sagged from spending her immortal life hunched over a spinning wheel.

"Now, let me see the pretties." She extended her hand.

I let her take them, and she snagged them so fast it was a wonder she didn't take my hand off. She unraveled the cloth quickly, brought them to her nose, and took a nostril-flaring sniff, inhaling them. She blew out a satisfied breath, a massive smile flaring on her weathered face.

"I am pleased with the seeds, so much so that I would like to offer you one more glimpse of your future." She rolled her wrist and the seeds disappeared. In their place, a dagger with a crooked blade materialized. She rolled her wrist towards me, her palm facing upwards. *"Give me your hand."*

I placed my large mitt in her tiny, fruit-stained palm.

Her fingers turned claw-like, sinking into my skin as she tugged my hand towards her. "After the war is over, you will face a much larger challenge. Except it does not come in the form of kingly matters, but rather . . . matters of the heart." *She ran the tip of the dagger against my palm, slitting the flesh open, but no blood filled the wound.* "When the war ends, you will find your mate. You will know it is her because she will be the one to make you bleed." *She let go of my hand, the two of us watching as the wound began to stitch itself back together.*

"A mate?" I said, unable to believe what I was hearing.

"Yes, a mate." The goddess nodded, a soft hum falling from her lips. She looked up at me, breaking off the sound. In a cautionary tone, she said, "But heed this warning, and heed it well—your mate's life is linked with the very male she is destined to kill."

Her warning did not sit well with me.

CHAPTER 21

Sage

"You saw Von's phantom?" Kaleb asked as he stood beside the fireplace, his frame outlined with a red-orange glow. He had arrived at my balcony doors moments ago, a map of Clearwell Castle in his hand and the cold night air biting at his back.

"I did," I replied as I hid the map underneath my mattress—something I was quite excited about Kaleb finding. I would look at it first thing tomorrow, but right now, I needed to speak with Kaleb about what Von had told me. "He said there is an item that can break the deal between him and Arkyn. It's called the Blade of Moram. Have you ever heard of it?"

"I can't say that I have," Kaleb said as he rubbed the back of his neck, his elbow pointed to the stone ceiling. "But I'll talk to Fal about it. She has been a reaper much longer than I have, and has more connections. Maybe she'll be able to speak with the higher ups and see if they know anything about it."

I joined him at the fireplace, the wood crackling and popping as the flames gnawed away at the split timber. "That sounds like a good plan. Let me know if she learns anything."

"I will," Kaleb said. "I'll ask her first thing when I get back to the Spirit Realm."

"Alright." I nodded. "By the way, how are things *going* with her?"

I glanced at him just in time to catch the hint of a smile.

"Things are going really well." His voice was lighter, his expression matching. "I doubt I could have made the transition from the Living Realm to the Spirit Realm without her. She's been good for me, Sage, in ways I didn't know I needed. I've never felt this way for anyone else before."

"Then . . . I'm happy for you," I answered warmly. And truly, I was.

If anyone deserved a slice of happiness, it was Kaleb.

The next morning, I woke well before the sun had a chance to claim the horizon—well before Brunhilde charged in to mold me into a *perfect* lady. I took the map of Clearwell Castle out from underneath my mattress, grabbed a quill and a bottle of ink from my dresser, and sat cross-legged on the cool, stone floor.

During the day, the king was surrounded by an entourage of people and guards, which meant it would be hard to slip a dagger into his back without being noticed. But during the night, I doubted his entourage watched over him as he slept. Sure, he might have a few guards posted outside his door, but if I could find a way in while he slept, that might grant me an opportunity to make good on my vow.

The question was . . . where were the king's chambers?

I didn't expect the map to blatantly state *king's chambers here* with a great big arrow, or anything like that. My plan was to use the map to mark down the areas I had been to and figure out which areas I needed to explore. Through the process of elimination, I would be able to figure out roughly where the so-called king slumbered.

Dipping my quill into the bottle of ink, I began ticking off the places I had been.

As I worked, I started noticing that every so often, there was a double line along some of the walls—particularly in the wing I was in, which Brunhilde once said was the older part of the castle. In fact, almost all of the hallways in this wing were drawn with double lines.

My brows drew together as I leaned in closer.

Why? Was it something structural? It was possible, but this was a map, not an architectural print, so why would the artist bother to document something that was structural?

. . . They wouldn't.

I swirled the tip of the feather against my chin, thinking. And then it hit me.

"Well, I'll be damned," I whispered in awe. "There are hidden hallways."

And judging by the spacing used for the other hallways, these ones were incredibly thin—so thin two people would not be able to walk side by side. During my time here, I had not once traveled down a hallway that small, which made me wonder if they were even in use anymore.

And if they weren't in use, if they had been forgotten about, I could use them to move about undetected.

I smiled to myself—the universe had finally granted me a boon.

My finger slid along the paper as I familiarized myself with the hidden hallway closest to me. It led to a large, round area, bigger than the castle's smallest wing. I leaned in, trying to read what was written in the middle of the circle, but the writing was smeared and impossible to make out. I traced another slender hallway, finding that it, too, led to the same space. I did another. Again, the same thing. I repeated this process for the next ten minutes—each time ending up at the same place.

"Why do they all lead there?" I wondered out loud, fully ensnared by figuring out the mysteries of the map.

A startling knock sounded at the door, and I nearly knocked the ink over in the process. I grabbed it with both hands before it could topple over.

"One moment!" I called out. Scrambling, I slipped the map under the bed, grabbed my robe, and put it on as I walked to the door and opened it.

When I saw who stood on the other side, I was tempted to close it, but then I remembered I needed him.

"Arkyn," I said, forcing myself to try to be pleasant.

"May I come in?"

Fuck off. That's what I wanted to say. But I didn't.

"Sure." I swung the door open, allowing him in.

He was dressed in his typical fine clothing, a gold livery collar draped lavishly around his broad shoulders, his attire as stiff as a washed blanket left out to dry in the clutch of winter.

"I was pleased to hear that your spirits have improved," he stated, the heels of his meticulously polished boots sounding against the floor as he entered.

"I'm sure," I mumbled, tossing the door closed with a little more force than I intended.

"It is the truth, Aurelia. You should know by now that my tongue cannot produce a lie." He walked over to the exact spot where I had been sitting on the floor only moments ago. He glanced down. "It is a bit odd that you have a bottle of ink and a quill sitting here, in the middle of the floor, without any paper."

I opened my mouth, but he held up his hand, stopping me. "Save your lies. They are like daggers in my ears," he groaned, his thumb and forefinger pinching the bridge of his nose.

Daggers in his ears?

His tongue couldn't produce a lie?

At one point, my gullible little mind would have brushed him off as being dramatic, but now . . .

"Why can't you tell a lie? And why do mine bother you?"

"Although I am a Demi God, I was born with the unique ability to tell when someone is lying. It is one of the reasons I have been bestowed the title of God of Truth."

I pondered for a moment. It made sense. Arkyn always had an uncanny ability to sense my lies—something I could trace all the way back to when I first met him at the bathhouse.

"Wait." A laugh bubbled on my lips as I realized the irony of it all. "I truth poisoned the God of Truth?"

Unimpressed, he nodded. "Why is that so funny?"

Great divine, I didn't know why. It just seemed so ridiculous now that I couldn't help but laugh. And the more I thought about it, the funnier it was.

I had truth bombed the truth God.

Arkyn let out a sigh as he crossed his arms over his chest.

When I finally reined in my laughter, I said, "I wasn't aware there was a God of Truth."

He shrugged. "They don't write about Demi Gods very often."

I didn't reply, my mind stuck on one not-so-little detail . . .

Demi Gods were the ancestors of the Cursed. By Arkyn serving the king, he was killing his distant relatives.

My eyes flickered from the floor to him, my lips thinning. "How do you live with yourself?" It was a genuine question.

He shoved his hand in his pocket, his stance annoyingly casual. "I'm going to need more than that, Aurelia, if you expect me to form a proper response."

I took a step forward, anger driving my movement. "How do you serve a king who cleanses—*murders*—your own kin?" I spat the word *murder* at him because that is exactly what it was. Fuck the crown and their terms they made up to sugarcoat what they were doing.

"I was born from the union of a New God and a mortal, so the Cursed are not my kin. And—" He thundered towards me, stopping an arm's swipe away, "—even if they *were* my distant relatives, I would still end their lives if that is what our king told me to do."

He could throw his weight all he wanted, but he didn't scare me.

I closed the distance between us, a condescending purr on my lips. "What a good *little* doggy you are, Arkyn, following *your* king's orders."

Arkyn's nostrils flared, his honey-brown eyes turning to liquid fire. And just when I was certain he might try to rip my throat out with his teeth, he turned around and strode towards the balcony doors. He threw them open and walked outside, into the golden rays of the sun, the rubies of his livery collar glistening in response.

Satisfied, I couldn't help but grin as I reveled in this small victory. But as soon as I remembered that I needed Arkyn to save Von, the upward twists of my lips fell flat.

Damnit. Now I've done it.

And it wasn't like I could go out there and apologize and say I didn't want to fight, because he would know it was a lie.

I gave him a few minutes to simmer before I slipped on my shoes, tucked my robe tighter, and followed him outside.

This side of the castle backed a long stretch of cliff, the ground below so sharply carved that it looked like it had been chopped off by the Creator's mighty ax. The Selenian Sea yawned before me, extending her deep-blue claim beyond the horizon. She was full of contradictions—beautiful and dangerous, wild and calm, patient and demanding.

Contradictions. That was something we both had in common.

I turned to Arkyn, my breath painting the crisp morning air. "Perhaps we should try this again. Just because we don't get along doesn't mean we can't be civil."

He looked at me. "I would hope that we could be more than just civil with one another. As I said before, we were once good friends."

I thought I sensed a hint of longing in his voice. I could work with that.

"It's hard for me to grasp that we were friends because I don't have any memories of those times." I waited a moment, purposefully letting that little teabag of truth fully soak before I served him the whole cup. "If I could *somehow* get my memories back, it would make things a lot easier. I could use my Dream Curse to try to channel them, but—" I pointed to the collar, grinning, "—I can't because I've been neutered."

"You don't have balls, Aurelia," Arkyn replied, his face as straight as an arrow. My attempt to joke with the God of Truth fell flat.

Aborting my original plan to get him to think it was his idea, I decided to skip ahead to one that used blatant honesty instead—that was a language Arkyn could understand.

I smiled sweetly as I said, "No, *I* don't have balls, but you know who has *teeny tiny* ones?"

He sighed. "I don't know why I'm entertaining this, but go on."

"Soren does!" I exclaimed. "Look, I'm going to be honest with you, I'm tired of not remembering. Soren can help me with that. He already has access to my thoughts, so I just need him to show them to me. I've thought it through and it's the best option I have available to me."

Arkyn was quiet for a while. Finally, he said, "I'll agree to it, but I have two conditions."

I nodded, hardly able to believe it was that easy. "Alright, what are they?"

"The first is that I'm in the room with you when he does it. He betrayed you once, and I wouldn't put it past him to do it again."

I was tempted to remind Arkyn that they *both* had betrayed me, so his offer to be in the room at the same time as Soren gave me little comfort, but I didn't.

"And the second?" I waited for his answer.

"You come to praise again."

I had avoided going to the temple ever since *that* day, where I was publicly looked down upon. It was the last place I wanted to return to, but if that's what it took to get me a brain session with the betrayer and the observing betrayer, then so be it.

I smirked. Channeling Von, I said, "You have yourself a deal."

And with a bit of luck, it wouldn't be the only one.

CHAPTER 22

Sage

The king was snoring. And no one seemed to mind . . . except for me.

No sooner than he plopped down on his throne had he started performing head bobs. A few moments later and he was fast asleep—not even the choir's singing could wake him, or the priestess's boisterous voice.

That was the feared king?

That was him?

The same king that painted Edenvale in bloodshed and killed hundreds if not thousands of people? I was not only having a hard time believing it, but it felt like I had been smacked upside the head—the idea seemed preposterous. Even more preposterous when I noticed there was a string of drool dangling from his chin. With each snore, it got sucked back up, and with each exhale, it dropped closer to his expensive fur robes.

I tipped my head to the ceiling. *Creator above, I think you made a mistake thinking this male was fit to lead.*

Softly, Cataline swatted my thigh. She was sitting on my right, and Arkyn was on my left.

Ah right, I was *supposed* to be listening.

I returned my attention to the priestess who stood behind the stone altar that was large enough to lay on. The altar was covered with a white, cotton cloth, a language I could not read stitched into the part that spilled down the front. Sitting on top of the altar was a large bowl and a slender pitcher, both of them solid gold.

"His Royal Highness has requested this week's praise be devoted to Lady Light, our pure and illustrious goddess. Let us start by worshipping her name," the priestess's voice echoed amongst the temple walls.

Wide eyed, I glanced at Aurelius, his golden eyes meeting mine, a slight smirk toying at his lips.

I looked away—not quite sure what to do with *that*, with us.

Von had warned me about Aurelius, but he had not been afforded the time to tell me why. Because I trusted Von, I would heed his warning—for now. I would keep Aurelius at an arm's length. At least, until I knew more.

The priestess began to give praise, her words spoken in the same harsh foreign tongue she has used before. Although I couldn't understand what she was saying, I could *feel* it, a gentle caress against my sleeping flesh, stirring *her* awake— the slumbering goddess. She stretched, her joints like rusty hinges, her bones aching and stiff. Her lips were cracked and dry, but the priestess's praise was like a few droplets of rain falling against them. Even though it wasn't nearly enough to hydrate her, it was enough to wet her lips, and it was exactly what she needed.

It was empowering in the sense that it reminded her of what she had been missing. And the feel of it, it was seductive—something my mortal body did not understand, but the immortal side of me?

She licked her lips, hungry for more.

When the praise ended, I felt dizzy, my mind swirling, my body confused.

What in the Spirit Realm was that?

The priestess raised her hands above her head, reaching towards the arched ceiling. She began speaking in her foreign tongue as she cupped her hands in front of her chest and a sun made of flame suddenly appeared, floating above her hands.

A waft of magic tinged the air.

My brows shot up—*she was Fire Cursed*. No different than any other Fire Cursed, and yet she was a *high priestess* in *the king's* temple. It reeked of hypocrisy. I tried not to make a sour face.

I leaned over, whispering to Arkyn, "A bit of a double standard, no?"

"The priestess using fire magic?" he whispered back.

I nodded.

"It is, but the people see what the king and queen tell them to see. It's how it has been for centuries. To the people, she isn't Cursed—she has been *gifted* magic by the New Gods, and that makes all the difference," he replied.

I snorted and rolled my eyes.

The priestess continued, her words lost to me, but her actions were not. She waved her hands above her head and the flaming sun turned into a heart. Lowering her arms, she placed the heart in the bowl. Then she picked up the pitcher and poured a clear liquid over the heart. She waited for a moment, then she raised her wet hands above her head for all to see.

In them, she held a crescent-shaped moon carved from crystal quartz.

And although I couldn't understand what she was saying, something about the sun and the heart and the moon connected with me.

Was that . . . how I was made?

"Did I do something wrong?" Aurelius asked as we stepped into the quiet library a few days later.

"I'm not sure what you mean," I lied, keeping a few paces ahead of him so he couldn't see my sorry attempt at a poker face. No, he hadn't done anything wrong, per se, but Von had warned me to stay away from him, and so that's exactly what I had been doing—or at least, trying to do.

"It's just that . . . you hardly say a word to me lately. I can't help but wonder if I have done something wrong or offended you in some way?" His long legs easily caught up with mine.

I took a deep breath. I couldn't exactly tell him the whole

truth, but that didn't mean I couldn't tell him *some* truth. Turning to him, I said, "It's nothing you have done. It's just this situation between us—" I gestured to us both, "—is a lot." I paused and took a deep breath. "I'm just trying to figure things out."

"Can I help you? In some way?"

I shook my head, opened my mouth to say *no*, but then stopped myself. There was something I had been wondering about.

"I know your memories are lacking, but do you remember how I was made?" I asked, my eyes flicking back and forth before they lifted to his.

He nodded. "I do. That was one of the first memories that came back to me. Which I can understand, as it was one of the happiest days of my long life." He gestured to a seating area beside a crackling fireplace. A continuous roll of heat emitted from the fire. "Shall we sit?"

"Alright," I told him as we walked over to two cream-colored settees, sitting adjacent to one another, a large bear hide spread across the floor in front of them. A small, oval table was centered between them, the edges worn from years of use. The table was spotless—not a book or piece of paper to be seen on it—a reminder that this public space was not a home. Something that could be said for the remainder of the castle.

When we were seated, Aurelius started, "Prior to your creation, I ruled alone for a great number of centuries. Although I was surrounded by many people, I never felt that anyone truly understood me, or really loved me, for that matter. Throughout the centuries, I courted a number of goddesses, but I found that I was always incompatible with them. I went to the Creator, and I asked them to give me a proper partner, someone I could share the rest of eternity with. And so they made you. However, it came at a cost, as these things always do."

My brows dipped, my tone lowering. "What did it cost you?"

Golden eyes met mine. "It cost me this." He placed a hand on the left side of his chest.

My heart hammered heavily, striking my ribs.

And suddenly, I could feel it—the visceral pain of being torn from somewhere that was safe and placed in something that was unknown and . . . new.

"I was to cut out my heart and give it to them. And so, that's what I did. Once they had it, they dipped it into the Selenian Sea and then buried it in the moon. From that, you were born as a fully made woman, a goddess in your own right."

Suddenly, I felt dizzy.

Blackness licked at the edge of my vision, but this time, I wouldn't fight it.

I wouldn't fight the memory bubbling up—I would embrace it.

This time, I would allow it to drag me under.

CHAPTER 23

Sage

Everything was cold. So very, very, very cold. Without feeling.

Until it wasn't.

Suddenly, everything was warm. So very, very, very warm. And all I could do was feel.

I felt the rocky ground beneath me, etching its imprint into my naked, newly created flesh.

I felt the expansion of my chest as breath filled my lungs for the very first time.

I felt the warm droplets that came from up above, shattering against my face.

Warm weight lowered overtop of me, encasing my body in a safe, protective cage. It felt like home, like I was tucked safely in the womb of the moon, safely behind the sun's iron ribs.

"Open your eyes, Moonbeam," said a male voice.

My—our—heart leapt at the familiar sound, quickening its trot into a constant, palpitating gallop. Slowly, I opened my eyes, peering up into his. They were lovely, spun from gold and glistening with sunlight. Tears rimmed his eyes, wetting his white lashes, clumping the long wisps together.

He was so incredibly lovely—perfection given male form.

A soft frown creased my brows, pulling the edges of my lips down. "Why do you weep, my love?" I wiped at his tears, my long, elegant fingers catching my attention.

This was . . . my hand. I glanced down at my naked frame, forged by a gently rolling landscape with supple peaks and curious valleys. Wrapped in soft, pale silk. I was a woman.

A goddess in my own right.

Gently, he kissed my forehead. "Because you are everything to me."

His body lifted from mine, and he gathered me in his arms, cradling me with such care, as if I were made of glass. He walked on a steady incline, out of the crater I had been forged in.

I believed him—I was his everything.

Just as he was mine.

"Where are we going?" I asked, my fingers weaving into his beautiful white hair—the twin to my own. But where his skin was kissed by the sun, mine was painted by the moon.

"We are going home," he said, his hold tightening around me, telling me that he would never let me go.

I hummed softly. "That sounds lovely."

He smiled down at me, casting me in his warmth.

"What will we do when we get home?" I asked, basking in his sun.

"We will do what we were made to do—we will create life. Together."

"Together," I repeated, smiling to myself as I laid my head upon his chest, listening to the absence that was there, knowing the sacrifice he had made for me. I owed my existence to him.

I looked up at him—beautiful, enchanting him—my golden king. Our heart would never beat for another. It belonged to him . . . forever.

A sudden burst of pure joy and love overtook me, my body resonating. Before I exploded like a star running out of life, I threw my arms around his neck, my laughter ringing out into the night.

His laughter married with mine as he pulled me closer. "Your beauty is astounding. Everything about you calls to me. You were perfectly designed for me, Moonbeam." His lips brushed against my ear as he whispered, "Would you think me barbaric if I took you right here?"

"No," I answered honestly. I felt that same need swell within me. I wanted to be joined with him just as we were designed to be, but . . . "I do not know how," I admitted, heat radiating from my cheeks.

"I will show you." He sealed the promise with a deep kiss that ended far too soon. He pulled away, his eyes flickering between mine, gauging my reaction.

My fingers brushed over my lips—so that was what it felt like to be kissed. My hand fell, drifting to my heart, feeling the way that it hammered within my breast, beating with such ferocity—with such . . . life.

"Again," I said as I wrapped my arms around his neck and hauled my mouth against his. We kissed. And we kissed. And we kissed. Our hands were constantly moving, roaming over each other—learning each other as our mouths spoke a language that was entirely of their own design. I opened my mouth to him, and his tongue slid inside, tangling with mine and I—

"I've never been so turned off in my entire life, and I'm old as fuck," interrupted a deep voice, bathed in dominance and dripping with unbridled arrogance.

One second, I was in my beloved's arms, kissing him, and the next, I was standing, tucked behind him.

"What are you doing here?" Aurelius growled, the regal authority in his voice making me weak in the knees. That ache continued to build, begging me to kneel for my king. The Creator designed us to be this way, our immortal bodies forged to obey the order of our divine hierarchy. "You are exiled from the Living Realm."

"I was coming here to bestow a blessing upon the little goddess. But now I'm trying not to lose my dinner," the male stated, his tone holding no softness. It was impenetrable leather and heavy, heavy smoke.

Whoever this male was, Aurelius's command seemed to hold no dominion over him. Which meant he was more powerful than Aurelius. My mouth popped open, a sense of dread pitting itself in my stomach.

Standing on the tips of my toes, I peered over top of Aurelius's shoulder. And that was when I saw him—the angel of darkness. His massive, raven-like wings spread out behind him, a black crown made of flame and bone floating above his head.

I knew him. I had felt him surround me while I was being forged in Mother Luna.

The God of Death.

And he was so incredibly beautiful. Devastatingly so.

He tucked his wings in, and his lips curved into a wicked grin, those black, soulless eyes narrowing in on me. "Well, well, well, you certainly are a divine little thing, aren't you? Why do you cower from me like a kitten? Perhaps you should step away from your captor and let me drink my fill of you."

"Shut your vile mouth," Aurelius growled, the air crackling with his infinite power—the power of the sun.

My knees wobbled once more, outright demanding that I bow this time. I fought the urge, gripping Aurelius's shoulder tightly. "Please, let's just go, my love," I whispered.

"Go?" The dark god chuckled, shaking his head as if that simply would not do. "But I traveled all this way. The least you could do is take my gift."

"We do not want anything from you," Aurelius decreed, the disdain in his voice ringing as clear as a tolling bell.

"You will not receive anything from me. Her, however . . ." Obsidian eyes met mine and that sinister smile returned. "She will accept my gift."

I paled, a sense of foreboding churning my stomach.

Aurelius's hand fell to the back of my thigh, clutching me to him, needing to feel me against him as if I might disappear at any moment. "She does not want it," he snarled.

"Is that true?" the God of Death asked me.

"Yes," I replied, my voice just barely above a whisper.

"Oh, Little Goddess, how can you say that? You don't even know what it is," he purred, the cadence in his voice seductive, his gaze matching.

I averted mine.

"Enough," Aurelius commanded, his mighty voice crackling amongst the stars with such veracity that they quit twinkling—fearful that the sun had come to chase them away.

Shadows swirled around the God of Death as he said, "No, young god, with me, it will never be enough. You stole my realms from me. For that, I'll take everything from you. Starting with the very thing you planned to gain from her."

In a fractured second, he disappeared.

"No!" Aurelius yelled, turning towards me. He reached out, but it was too late—a shadow wrapped its hand around my neck, and I was dragged into the darkness.

A flash of starlight erupted around me, gone as quickly as it came.

Then we were in a grand, private chamber that functioned as a bedroom, a private bar, and a library. From floor to wall to the ceiling, all of it was black, even the bulky furniture positioned throughout. The fireplace roared as it devoured the logs piled within, basking the sprawling room in a luxurious honey-colored glow and scenting the chambers with the smell of wintergreen. But that wasn't the only scent that painted the room. There was something else, and it was much, much more . . . masculine.

"Have a seat, princess," Death said as he discarded me carelessly on the massive bed, large enough that he could sleep with his wings flared out.

I scrambled to my knees, gathering the black silk sheet in front of me to cover my nakedness. Pulling it with me, I backed myself against the headboard, as far away as I could get from him.

He looked at me, a powerful muscle feathering his steel-cut jaw. He tore his gaze from mine and strode over to a large, wood desk, one tattooed hand plucking a cup by its lip and the neck of a bottle in one quick swoop. Creator above, he had huge hands.

. . . All the better to wrap around my neck and squeeze the life from me with.

"Where are we?" I asked, stiffening my bottom lip, refusing to let it tremble. I would not give him the satisfaction of seeing me quiver.

"We are at my mansion in the city of Ruhanne, in the Living Realm," he replied flatly. The fact that he answered my question at all surprised me, but it did little to ease my frantic nerves.

All nearly seven feet of him dropped into a large, leather chair. He poured two fingers' worth of the amber liquid in the cup—his fingers that is. For mine, it would have equated to four. He set the bottle on the floor beside him, his arm long enough that he didn't even have to bend to the side. He raised the cup to me, and then tipped the glass back and drank it straight down.

"Why did you bring me here?" I asked.

He eyed the empty glass. "Because I felt like it."

"I want to go back."

Black eyes met mine. "Then you best start walking."

My lips parted in disbelief. He brought me all the way

here just to make me walk back—to the moon? How, for the love of the Creator, was I to do that? Then again, I'd rather walk back to the moon than be stuck in here with him.

"Fine," I said, dragging the sheet off the bed with me. The length of it cascaded like a train behind me, my gown spun of Death's black silk.

I weaved around him, giving him as wide of a berth as possible, and headed straight for the door. His leather boot slammed down on the end of the sheet, and the fabric suddenly became like a chain, his foot the anchor, stopping me from going any further. This, coupled with my walking speed, caused the sheet to nearly rip right out of my hands.

I turned, a scowl painting my face as I stared down the menacing god whose power was said to be unrivaled. Catastrophic. I hissed, "Are you a child?"

"Asks the newborn goddess," he stated with mirth, those wicked, wicked eyes laughing at me—laughing at the title, suggesting I didn't deserve it.

Ignoring him, I tugged on the fabric with all the might of my right hand, my left curled at my chest, bunching the fabric there. But the sheet wouldn't budge, not even a hairsbreadth, no matter how hard I wrenched on the damned thing. It didn't even rip—what was it made from, steel-spun thread? I gave up with a huff, catching the look of pleasure flash in his black, soulless eyes—clearly already celebrating his premature victory.

He thought he had won? Wrong. I didn't need a sheet to walk out of here.

Without further consideration, I dropped it. Stepping over the pooled silk, I headed straight for the room's exit. I didn't know what came over me, but I slapped my ass, signifying what he could kiss. Just before I reached the door, a gust of air and magic flew past me, and the door slammed shut.

I grabbed the handle, jiggled it. Nothing.

I swirled, my eyes hurling daggers at him. A wealth of power was building inside of me, churning, begging for release. "You said I could leave."

"Did I?" he teased. His gaze leisurely roamed over my curves before they shifted up to my face, a feral black fire burning in those onyx-colored eyes. Before I could determine what had lit the flame, he snuffed it out and replaced it with an empty void.

I wrapped one arm over my breasts, my free hand shooting down to cover myself below. "You are such a . . ."

"A what?" A smile tugged at his lips.

"Bastard," I said hatefully.

"A bastard, am I?" Carelessly, he tossed his cup over his shoulder, the glass shattering as it struck the ground. He grinned, and it was terrifying and breathtaking all at the same time. "Shall I show you what a bastard I can be?"

Faster than I could comprehend, he moved. I turned to run, but his hand grabbed the back of my neck, locking me in place. Utilizing his hold on my neck, he steered me back towards him, my naked front smashing into his.

"Let me go!" I screamed, my hands shooting out like vipers, aiming for his face.

Large hands caught my wrists, shackling them. He tugged my arms behind my back, securing them with his one hand. His fingers pinched my chin, and he jerked my head up *so that I had no choice but to meet his gaze. "I don't think I will."*

I struggled against his iron hold, reaching for my powers. But right now, they were bowing to his, making them as immobile as my wrists.

"Now, about that gift." Slowly, ringed fingers drifted down my neck, between my breasts, stopping when they reached the flat of my stomach. They spread apart, his large hand spanning the full width. "I bestow my touch of death upon you."

"No," I stuttered, my hands growing more frantic to break his hold.

"Oh, yes," he chuckled, although his expression was flat. "I curse you, Goddess of Life, to never be able to do the very thing the Creator designed you to do."

And then I felt it. A shifting inside—a flower kissed by frost. The petals were starting to wither . . . to die.

"No, please," I cried out, my legs shaking uncontrollably.

"I curse you to never be able to forge life." His lips twisted into a cruel smile. He leaned in, whispering in my ear, "Unless it is my *seed that you sow."*

I screamed in anguish. Not only could I feel the curse taking hold, but I could see it taking hold, see him—Death—taking hold, his coldness seeping into my bones. His shadows plunged beneath my flesh, burrowing in deep. They ribboned themselves around my goddesshood and my womanhood, wrapping tightly, squeezing the ability to create life from me.

There was nothing I could do as the God of Death took everything from me.

When the curse was complete, he let go of me. My knees buckled and I fell to the floor, sobbing.

I would never be able to grow trees or bushes or flowers. I would never be able to give Aurelius what he wanted—to create life with me . . . I would never see him hold our children.

That last thought didn't just shatter me, it destroyed me.

"Why?" I wailed, knowing that I would forever be a barren goddess. Tears brimmed in my eyes, pooling in the corners before they spilled over.

"Because . . ." Death knelt down in front of me, a smile on his lips that did not match the lifelessness in his eyes. "I am a bastard."

"I hate you!" I screamed.

His ringed fingers swept over my cheek, mapping my river of tears. I pulled away from his touch and he grinned. He brought his finger to his lips, tasting my sorrow. "For now, yes. But I know you creation goddesses. When you lot come into season, you are a wild and feral breed, driven to madness with fever. When that happens, you will tiptoe from his bed and scamper into mine with a plea on your pretty, little lips— to give you what your body needs. What it demands. And like the bastard I am, I'll be more than happy to comply."

I lost it.

Roaring, I leapt at him, my hands aiming for his throat. I'd claw the bastard's jugular out with my nails if that was what it took. He caught my wrists before they could connect, but I still managed to knock him onto his back.

I straddled him, fighting with him, warring for dominance.

Somewhere, amongst the struggle, my rage began to dissipate. Somewhere, I realized how completely naked I was. Judging by the look on the God of Death's face, he had realized it as well. Our struggle took a pregnant pause.

Closing his eyes, he dropped his head against the ground, a groan coming from his lips as if he had been defeated.

I used the moment to fight his grasp, twisting my hips for leverage.

"You really should not wiggle like that," he said, his voice a mixture of a groan and a growl.

"Then let me go, you prick," I hissed, pulling with all my goddess might.

"As you wish, Kitten." He released his hold.

My equilibrium was lost and I fell backwards—ass over teakettle. I landed with a thud, whacking the back of my head against the ground, half of my body still atop his. I reached up, rubbing the hurt.

"Well, as fun as this was, I've grown bored," he said, a broad hand pressing against my leg as he shoved the rest of my body off of him. He rose to his full towering height, leaving me feeling so incredibly small as I laid there on the ground, looking up at the wild beast looming above.

He parted his lips, as if he were about to say something, but then he closed them. A muscle kicked in his jaw. And then he turned, starting for the door. "You are free to leave."

"Wait." I scrambled onto all fours. "How do I get back to Aurelius?"

He stopped, his head turning as he spoke over his shoulder, his mouth twisted in wickedness. "You're a goddess, are you not? You can find your own way back to your precious husband."

Warmth permeated my skin, the indulgent scent of saffron gently stirring me awake. Something hard and firm was pressed against my left side, that same hardness supporting my back and scooped under the crook of my legs. My feet ticked with a soft rhythm, swaying from side to side. When I opened my eyes, the God of Life was there—Aurelius was there—carrying me through the castle halls.

When we made it back to my chambers, he tenderly set me down on the plush fur blankets that covered the bed. Gingerly, his hand cupped my cheek. "Are you alright?"

Tears pricked my eyes, and when I opened my mouth to say *no*, a guttural sob tore out instead.

Aurelius swept me into his arms, holding me tightly to his chest.

For hours, he held me like that, as my world caved in on itself.

CHAPTER 24

Sage

Five painfully slow days had passed since I'd regained *that* memory.

If I thought my nights were sleepless before, now they were even worse. My eyes were puffy and swollen and red, and my head ached from the ferocity of my crying. Food tasted like ash on my tongue, lumped into an unpalatable ball that was even harder to swallow down. I rarely left the confines of my room, and I was lucky to make it out of bed some days. I had been reverted back into the lifeless soul that I was when I first arrived here.

And it was all because of him.

Von had been so wrapped up in his vendetta against Aurelius that he took away my ability to create—the very core of my divinity. He'd *stolen* it from me. Worse, he'd stolen it from us—me and Aurelius, who I seemed to have loved very deeply during that time.

It felt like I was looking at two entirely different versions of Von—the one I knew in this life and the one from my past, the contrast between the two as stark as black and white. Physically, he looked the same, his characteristics were the same.

But how he treated me . . .

Realms apart.

He'd vowed to take *everything* from Aurelius. I glanced down at the vine tattoo on my arm . . . *Everything*, the same thing I had once promised him when we were kissing. I thumbed my bottom lip as I paced across my chamber's stone floors—what if Von had never given up on that pledge? What if he was just faking an interest in me, using me to get to Aurelius? Just as he had done in my past life.

My heart felt like shattered glass, the pieces too jagged and broken to pick up. But still, I wanted to try. Because the laughing Von who walked with me in the woods with the basket leisurely thrown over his shoulder—I couldn't imagine a world without him.

I refused to believe that that version of him wasn't real. If the Von I knew in this life didn't exist, how could I?

A light knock sounded at the door.

Shucking my thoughts to the side, I trudged over to the door and opened it.

I never knew how much self-control I had until that moment, as I came face to face with Soren, my gaze unable to meet his. Glancing past his shoulder, I felt an ounce of relief seeing that Ryker wasn't on duty—I couldn't imagine what he might do if he were standing behind Soren right now. He'd probably do the very thing I wanted to do—slay the traitor right where he stood.

But I fought that part of me, stepped back, and allowed him inside.

We didn't greet one another—we didn't so much as look at one another.

His betrayal was like a blade, severing the friendship we used to have. And now, all that was left was two strangers, at best. Enemies, at worst.

True to his word, Arkyn joined us.

"You sure about this?" he asked as he walked in.

"I am," I said.

And truly, I was. Yes, that last memory was horrible, but sitting here in no-man's land and not knowing the rest of the story was even worse.

I was tired of not knowing.

Arkyn nodded in reply before he seated himself at the small table, his honey orbs watching us, observing. He was wearing his usual attire, steeped in wealth and luxury. I noted that Soren's clothing also looked like his status had been kicked up a few notches—apparently, someone was making a name for themselves, serving the enemy. *How noble.*

I laid down on the bed, as that seemed like something someone should do if they were about to have their memories rummaged through. I stared up at the ceiling, replaying the memory I had of Von when he stole my ability to create, showing it to the shadow mouse that lived inside my mind.

When the memory was finished, I said coldly, "Show me the next one I have with the God of Death."

"Alright." Soren's voice cracked, breaking the word in

half, just like he'd done with the trust I had once placed in him.

I'm sorry, Sage, his shadow mouse said.

"You don't get to apologize," I said out loud, refusing to carry on a conversation with him inside my head. I closed my eyes and took a breath. "Just show me the memory I requested." I didn't bother to hide the ice in my tone.

"Alright," he choked out softly. He scampered back to his hole as an oncoming storm approached—a storm ripe with lost memories.

I took a deep breath—I had a feeling this was going to hurt like a bitch.

The howling wind outside was no match for the piercing cry that ripped out of me—loud enough to bring mortal kingdoms to their knees.

Fire licked across my skin, scorching every nerve ending, embedding itself in my flesh until all I could feel was pain.

Pain. It was the only thing I had felt this past month— marking it as the longest month of my immortal life. Time had seemed to still, like it, too, was holding its breath, waiting to see if I survived this or not.

"Do something for her," Aurelius grated, his jaw clenched tightly enough to turn his molars to dust. He had rarely left my side since the sickness burrowed into me. My suffering was increased tenfold in him, a truth I could see in

his weary eyes every time they met mine. That lovely golden glow was barely there anymore.

"There's nothing we can do, Your Maj—"

Another scream tore out of my throat, swallowing up the rest of the healer's sentence.

"Give her more dwale then!" Aurelius yelled, the backs of his boots striking the ground as he strode towards the healer.

The healer shrunk away from the instruments he was cleaning. My ichor was all over them from the bloodletting treatment I had just undergone—the sixth one this week. Facing Aurelius, he whimpered, "We have already given her more than is safe, even for an immortal."

I heard the sound of a hand striking flesh, but I was too delirious to care. All I could do was dig my nails into the soaked sheets beneath me, shredding them as another wave tore throughout my body.

"I am your king, and you will do as I say." Aurelius's voice was so fierce that it startled the maid beside me into action.

Quickly, she dabbed my slick brow with a cold cloth, but my temperature was so high that in a matter of seconds, it turned the white linen scalding hot. Before it singed her fingers, she dropped it quickly into a bucket of water, an audible hiss sounding. She grabbed another cloth and repeated the process, but it was of no use—one could not fight the inferno of a forest fire with a damp rag.

Nothing relieved the pain, the suffering. It was like my divinity was being torn from my bones and ripped through my flesh.

I rolled away from her, turning onto my side and curling into myself as a moment of relief drifted over my shaking body. I knew it would be short-lived, and mentally prepared myself for the next wave of torture to begin.

A gentle hand stroked my cheek. "Here, my love, drink this." Aurelius knelt by my side, a golden chalice in his hand. He was the only person who could touch me directly and withstand my body's immense heat.

I shook my head slightly, knowing full well what was in that cup.

"Moonbeam, please, I cannot stand to see you like this," he pleaded with me, his voice hoarse from shouting.

I could no longer stand to see the pain in his eyes knowing that I was the reason for it, and so, weakly, I nodded. He helped me onto my side, just enough so I could drink. He guided the cup against my mouth, and I drank the bitter herbs down, choking on their horrible taste.

"This will all be over soon," Aurelius whispered softly in my ear, his thumb rhythmically stroking my cheek. "And when it is, I will take you to that little cottage in the Living Realm you always talk about. Just like you wanted."

My heart strummed at that, his pledge like fingers plucking at its strings, making it sing.

Clicking heels approached the room, their pace quick— urgent. "My Lord, I apologize for the intrusion, but the God of Chaos is here," Bronwyn, a Demi God who looked after various castle matters, said as she approached.

"Please remind the God of Chaos that he is banned from my realms, and he is to return to the stinking hole he crawled out of," Aurelius stated in his regal tone as he gently stroked

my cheek, the chalice now gone.

"We tried, my lord, but . . . he grew angry and killed Everett and Samona. He said that he will continue to take more lives until you arrive. I believe he said . . ." Bronwyn swallowed. "One life per minute."

"The Old Gods are such heathens," Aurelius said with a sigh. "Very well, I will meet with him and remind him of his place." The direction of his voice changed. "Everyone else, please, go get something to eat, but return within the hour." He pressed a kiss to my forehead. "I'll be back soon, Moonbeam."

I think I nodded, but I wasn't sure.

The bed shifted and then multiple footsteps sounded, announcing their departure, leaving me alone with my heavy, heavy eyelids. Hardly wider than slits now, I could just barely make out the towering, dark shadow standing before me.

Icy metal bit into my skin as a hand captured my chin, and I stifled a moan because it felt blissfully good.

"Did you miss me, Little Goddess?" Death whispered in my ear.

And then the dwale dragged me under.

I groaned as I came to, my body slowly awakening to the blistering pain.

There came a screeching noise, but it wasn't from me. A chair was being dragged across the floor. It stopped, just beside me, and then it groaned as someone sat down on it.

"Compared to the last time I saw you, you look like shit. How's married life treating you, Kitten?" asked a purely male voice, but his words became lost amongst the fog clouding my mind. The dwale had not quite worn off yet.

My eyelids parted just enough to reveal my surroundings. I was lying on a faded rug in a living room—an incredibly small one at that, just barely big enough to fit a fireplace and few chairs. A few strides away from me was an equally small kitchen with a few humble cupboards. Empty shelves hung on the walls. Towards the back stood two open doors. Despite them being propped open, it was too dark to make out what existed past them, although I imagined they were chambers to sleep in. The walls consisted of logs stacked upon one another, the space between each one sealed with a great deal of mortar.

Realization dawned. I was in a cottage *in the Living Realm.*

Something I had always wanted to experience . . .

While Aurelius spent his time at court, I spent my time watching over the mortals. A growing part of me wondered what it must be like to be them—to live so humbly, in a home small enough you could see your spouse sitting in the chair across the room from you, rather than in a palace so large you could wander its halls aimlessly, sometimes going weeks without seeing the one whom you loved. How many times had I begged Aurelius to take some time away from court so that we could come to the Living Realm and stay in a cottage, much like this one? I had lost count.

A wave of fire and pain washed over me, and I clenched

my teeth together, trying to smother out the scream growing in my lungs. I turned my head to the side, my eyes rounding at the corners.

The God of Death was sitting before me, one leather-wrapped leg thrown leisurely over top of the other, his giant boot hanging in the air, bobbing rhythmically. The male didn't just take up space, he engulfed it.

"What do you want?" I croaked weakly, the words hard enough to get out without letting that building scream spring free. My skin pebbled with sweat, the droplets pooling together and slipping onto the densely woven fabric beneath me.

"Many, many things," he purred. "But for starters, I'd like to give you relief from my curse."

"Never," I choked, horrified by the thought of his seed taking root—I would rather die an immortal death.

He chuckled. "You do not need my heir in your belly to cull your fever." A sinister grin widened his lips. "Although, the thought of you swollen with my pup . . ." He trailed off.

Gross. I wanted to vomit.

"You make me sick," I snarled.

"Do I now?" He threw his head back and laughed, the masculine, rich sound taunting me.

But my disgust towards him was soon forgotten as the next wave hit, this one too powerful for me to bite down. I sunk my fingernails into the rug as it came ripping out of me, painting the air with my screams as I thrashed about, my body convulsing. During the entirety of it, the God of Death simply sat there and watched, watched as my agony reduced me to nothing, knowing full well he was the cause of it. When it was over, I lay there twitching, my eyes rolling in the back of my head.

The tip of a boot nudged against my arm. "Are you enjoying yourself, Kitten? Or would you like me to give you relief from this?"

I was too weak to respond. All I could do was look up at him—at the God of Death whom I hated with every fiber of my being.

A large red apple appeared in his hand, a dangerously sharp blade in the other, the edge of the metal glinting in the firelight. "You are sick because your body is at war with you. It demands to create life, but because of my curse, you are unable to," he said as he carved a slice from the apple, that knife sinking deeply into its crisp flesh. "And so, because I am a gracious king, I am willing to offer you a deal. I will give you an apple seed to plant." He lifted the slice, sitting on the flat of the blade, to his mouth and began to chew.

I could use the seed to create life . . . It would be enough to break my fever—

But at what cost?

"What do you want in return?" I rasped, my throat feeling as if a bag of rusty nails had been rammed down it, brought back up and then forced back down. Repeatedly.

He grinned. "I want you to plant the tree outside the window that looks out from the chambers you and your husband share."

"Why there?"

"It's quite simple, really . . . Every morning when your so-called king wakes up, he will look outside and see my tree growing there, sowed by the hands of his precious wife. It will

serve me on two counts. The first—a message, stating that even though he presides over my lands now, just like that tree and the ones that come after it, eventually, I will take my realms back. And the second is a reminder that he cannot give you what you need, but I can." He flashed his perfect white teeth, showing off those wicked incisors. "I do hope that knowledge eats him alive."

"You're demented." And truly, he was.

He shrugged. "Do you want the deal or not?"

"One seed will only sustain me for so long. What happens when the fever returns?" I asked, my voice so weak it was barely audible.

"Then I will give you another apple seed to plant and so forth, until a forest of green surrounds your quaint little Golden Palace." He leaned forward, offering me a slice of apple with one shiny, black seed. "Do we have a deal?"

I made the deal.

When I did, ink wove itself into my skin, over my bicep— a woman's hand, my hand, holding an apple with a snake coiled around it, its mouth unhinged and ready to strike. I didn't see if a matching one formed on the God of Death's arm because he left seconds after his departing goodbye, telling me, once again, that I could find my own way back to my husband. Not that I would have cared to see the matching tattoo—I could barely stand to look at the one on my own arm.

It would serve as a constant reminder, for all to see, that I made a deal with the king of the Spirit Realm, the enemy of my people, and for that, the weight of betrayal dropped my once proud shoulders.

I returned to the Immortal Realm crawling on my hands and knees, my body so sick with fever it was a miracle I made it back. A Demi God whose name I could not recall found me when I was certain I could not make it any further. He helped me the rest of the way back to the Golden Palace.

Later that day, Aurelius, my pillar of strength, knelt behind me, his body supporting mine as he guided my hand to cover the apple seed in rich, fertile soil outside our bedroom window. Within seconds, my fever broke and strength was returned to my body.

I turned and threw my arms around my husband, and for a moment, he seemed hesitant to hug me back.

I hated that.

But not as much as I hated the God of Death.

CHAPTER 25

Sage

The memory washed over me like a tsunami, leaving me choking and sobbing and gasping for air.

I jerked upright, my heart slamming itself against my ribs over and over again, as though it were set on destroying itself. Because that was what was happening to the rest of me—I was being destroyed.

Piece by brittle piece.

Kneeling beside the bed, Soren spoke softly, "Sage—"

"No," I cut him off. I didn't want his sympathy, nor did I want him to see me like this, or Arkyn for that matter.

Soren, Arkyn—I was surrounded by betrayers, but their crimes did not cut nearly as deeply as Von's—his was lethal.

I wanted to crawl into a hole, where I could be alone. To unravel. To shatter.

But I would not grant myself that courtesy—at least, not

until I knew the rest. I brushed away the waterfall of tears that tumbled over the cliffs of my lower lash line. Blurry-eyed and on the verge of a broken heart, I turned to Soren. "Show me the next one."

"Don't you think you should give yourself some time to . . . process?" he asked, his blond brows weaving in concern.

I was tempted to laugh, my sanity teetering. Where was his concern that day at the cottage? He didn't get to act like he had some now.

"Do as she says," Arkyn commanded, his voice like a whip, striking our attention, our heads swiveling towards him.

"Are you sure?" Soren asked, his eyes returning my way.

"No," I whispered honestly, lowering myself back down. I took a deep breath. "But I have to know. Show me the next one."

So, he did.

And then the next.

And the next after that.

Each one mirrored the last—I was sick with fever, Von took me to some undisclosed location in the Living Realm, gave me a seed, and told me to return on my own to my husband.

Eventually, I did not need to ask Soren to show me the next memory, because the barrier that held them at bay had started to decay, and like a landslide, thousands of repeat memories of Von handing me a seed to plant came thundering down—each of them sowed so deeply with hate for the God of Death that it was becoming impossible not to feel that now.

I was drowning in those memories. Suffocated by them.

And yet, I couldn't stop. Perhaps, a small part of me was

looking for another type of seed—one that gave me hope, that reassured me that the Von I knew in this lifetime was real and true.

But the further I dug into the memories of my past, the only thing I found was a repeat of a bitter truth—

Von had *never* loved me.

I was nothing more than a tool for him to use—to carve out his revenge.

And he did it with expert, knowing hands.

CHAPTER 26

Sage

In the deep hours of the night, after Soren and Arkyn had left, and the rest of the castle had given themselves to the realm of dreams, I walked out onto the balcony, welcoming the icy air into my lungs.

I breathed it in. I needed the stifling cold to remind me that I was alive, that I was more than my numbness. It was like my body had taken pause, my heart stuck mid-beat, the blood in my veins turning from liquid to stone. Perhaps my body was trying to preserve itself from its inevitable demise, just before the world caved in around me. I braced my hands against the railing, clutching on to it—just in case it did. Just in case the stone gave way beneath my feet, and everything came crashing down, losing itself in the sea sprawling before me.

I wondered, for a moment, what would happen if I leapt

off this balcony—if I returned to the embrace of the water and gave myself to her depths? Would she claim my immortal life forever?

I looked down, peering at the vine tattoo on my arm—yet one more reminder of Von's trickery.

Everything, my breathy voice played in my head.

I was a damned fool.

I had sold my soul to the God of Death for a damn kiss. And now the reminder of my stupidity would mark my arm—my soul—forever.

A warm hand slipped over mine, a golden band sparkling in the moonlight.

"We don't have to talk. I am here for you, if you need anything," Aurelius said, his beautiful, ethereal face directed towards the sea.

My heart took comfort in his presence . . . *I* took comfort in his presence. Just as I had in all of my memories with him. Back then, he was my pillar of strength, the one who cared for me, even in my darkest hours when I was sick with fever. His love had been so deeply sown that he'd helped me plant the seed of his enemy in his own lands, just so I could feel relief.

With each memory, Von's image tarnished while Aurelius's bloomed.

If there was one thing that I knew now it was that Aurelius's love for me was so deep, so vast, it rivaled the very sea before us.

And now. . .

When I looked down, when I took in the ring he wore on his finger—the one that signified what he once was to me—I questioned why I was fighting the only thing that I knew to be real. And yes, maybe part of my decision was because of the crippling numbness I felt, the need to feel something—to fill the immense void that Von had left behind—but I was past the point of caring, past the point of thinking.

Right now, I didn't want to think—I just wanted to feel.

I turned to the king of kings. "Aurelius?"

White lashes lowered as his gaze met mine. "Yes?"

"I don't want to be *just* friends anymore."

CHAPTER 27

Sage

His brows lifted slightly, like he was struggling to believe what I had just said.

Then the God of Life smiled, and that charming little dimple made its appearance. And it was the loveliest smile I had ever seen—like the morning sun rising on the horizon, chasing away the night.

Gently, he took my face in his hands, his rich, golden eyes darting between mine. "Are you sure?" he asked, his tone a smooth velvet—warm and inviting, something I wanted to wrap myself up in.

I rested my hands on his forearms, feeling the corded muscle, feeling the god in him summoning the goddess in me. For once, my mind was quiet. Without an ounce of hesitation, I nodded, and it was probably for all of the wrong reasons, but I didn't care.

I was beyond reason.

"I'm sure."

Not even a second had passed before his lips came crashing down on mine. My heart—*our* heart—thundered in my chest, building in tempo as our mouths moved, as we tasted one another, stole from one another, and gave to one another.

The God of Life sucked the oxygen from my lungs and replaced it with the fire he breathed into me.

I wanted it—him—everywhere.

I wanted to feel.

I wanted . . . to forget.

And part of me? She wanted revenge.

Von had done such a good job of convincing me that I had a place at his side, that my lips somehow belonged to him, and I'd eaten it all up. I mean, when I had kissed Arkyn back at the bathhouse, those emotions, that jealousy—sorry, *territorial* nature—of his seemed so incredibly real.

I'd believed it.

I'd believed him.

But it was all just a lie, wasn't it?

My numbness gave way to anger, rippling and roiling through me. I channeled it, forging it into kindling to flame passion into my kiss.

Aurelius growled approvingly against my lips, pulling me up into his arms, my legs winding around him. Slowly, he sank to his knees, taking me with him. With his lips still entangled with mine, he knelt forward, positioning me so that I was lying on my back on the biting, cold, stone floor. I didn't care if it froze my skin.

I was beyond caring anymore.

When he broke the kiss, my lips went chasing after his, but his hand pressed into my chest, gently guiding me backwards. He sank onto his haunches, his gaze drifting over my heated body, taking me in. His golden eyes lifted to mine, the heat in them enough to burn me alive. "Lift your skirts for me, my moon," he commanded.

Heat singed my skin, the authority in his voice equivalent to a finger rubbing that sensitive bundle of nerves. The result only served to turn me on more. I pressed my heels against the cold stones, lifted my hips, and slowly pulled up my skirts—feeling his eyes watching me.

"No underwear?" he asked, a slight smirk touching his lips.

I blushed, feeling his eyes very much *on* me. "No."

"I like you like this," he said. His eyes flickered to mine, catching my gaze as his fingertips settled on my ankles, softly, like a butterfly landing. Slowly, his featherlight touch moved higher, drifting over the sensitive skin of my inner thighs, stirring the nerves awake. All the while, he watched me, gauging my reaction.

"Without underwear?" I asked, my breath growing increasingly short the closer he came to my center.

"Yes." His fingers found that little bundle of nerves, swirling and teasing it. "Seeing you spread before me, in offering . . . I have waited so incredibly long to see you like this. It is criminal what I wish to do to you." His finger pressed into my core, sliding in until he was knuckle deep. "I don't want to give your body time to adjust," he said as he added a second finger, wrangling a husky groan from my lips. "I want to drive myself into you right now and force you to take every inch of me."

I felt dizzy, remembering just how big he was. How bad *that* would hurt. I started to think this was not such a good idea, but Gods, his fingers felt so good—

I licked my lips. "Alright."

His nostrils flared, a possession overtaking him. He withdrew his fingers, leaving me hollow and aching for more. He reached behind his back and tugged up his tunic, tossing it carelessly to the side, revealing the golden skin beneath.

Shirtless, the King of the New Gods was something to see. He radiated with such beauty, such masculinity—all chiseled abs and rock-hard pectorals. Every inch of him was as incredible as the last.

He stood, loosened his belt, and chucked it to the side before he pushed his pants down, causing his length to spring free.

Great divine.

I'd had sex before, but I had never been with a male of that size. It was . . . incredible and terrifying, all at once. I swallowed, my insecurities bubbling up the longer I looked at that divine length, wrapped in silk—fit for a queen.

Aurelius returned to his knees, and then he was crawling between my legs, over top of me—his eyes never leaving mine.

He slid his length over that sensitive bundle of nerves. Our heads both dipped down. Like this, I could gauge just how impossibly deep he would be when he sunk himself inside.

This didn't seem like just a bad idea anymore—it *was* a

bad idea.

That was not going to fit. No way, no fucking how.

I swallowed, my head jerking up. Before I could tell him that I was having second thoughts, he captured my mouth with his. His hand slid beneath our bodies, his two fingers slipping into me, while the heel of his palm rubbed that sensitive spot—reminding me why I had agreed to this.

Gods, his touch was unfathomable.

I moaned beneath the smother of his kiss.

He pulled his lips from mine, his canines elongating before my very eyes. I whimpered, the memory of the pain he'd caused with those teeth surfacing, reminding me that there was a time, not very long ago, when he had not been gentle with me.

"Aurelius, I don't know," I said, two very different feelings settling in. The first was unease, like lava in my gut, churning uncomfortably. And the second was anticipation, drumming in my heart. Where my body wasn't sure about this, my heart undoubtedly wanted it.

I was torn.

Which one should I trust?

Golden eyes held mine.

"Trust me," Aurelius spoke softly, reading my mind. His hand slid over my cheek, gently caressing it. His immense warmth seeped into me, comforting my uncertainty. He tugged his bottom lip into his mouth and ran one sharp tooth over it, slitting it on the side. He lowered his mouth to mine, golden ichor pooling in the cut. "Taste me. I promise, it will help."

Somewhere, deep down, the mortal part of me knew this

was probably a very bad idea, but the goddess in me was begging for a taste. And when I recalled that tasting Aurelius's ichor was something Von had warned me not to do, it made my decision that much easier.

I took his bottom lip into my mouth and sucked, feeling his divine nectar spread over my tongue. He tasted incredible—like rich honey, but without the sweetness so you could drink it forever and ever. It was quenching, fulfilling, and so incredibly . . .

"Oh," I moaned, the word drawn out across my tongue. My breasts became full, and my sex throbbed. My body was begging to be touched.

I didn't need to ask, because Aurelius immediately started tending to my needs, his fingers and the heel of his palm stimulating me. "Ichor can be used as an aphrodisiac," he said, kissing my lips. "It stimulates your sexual desire." He pressed a third finger inside—a pinch of pain sounding at my entrance.

I yelped, but all I wanted was more. I bucked my hips against his hand, feeling the power of his ichor take me in one sweeping wave—until I was wild with desire.

I caught his bottom lip between my teeth and sucked until my body rolled with pure ecstasy. I didn't need a specific memory to know that I had been deeply addicted to this once upon a time—that was a truth I could feel in my bones. I was an alcoholic that had gone years without a drink, but now I was taking my first sip.

I wanted more—*needed* more.

He withdrew his fingers from me, and, grabbing hold of his length, he positioned himself at my entrance. "Look up, princess," he commanded. "I want you to look in my eyes as I take you."

I met his gaze and my breath all but buckled in my chest.

Slowly, he pushed his hips forward, sinking himself inside me, inch by incredible inch. I squirmed beneath him—caught between my insatiable rapture and the wicked, sharp pains of being stretched beyond reason. Even losing my virginity had not hurt nearly this bad, but the taste of his ichor, it kept me there, enduring.

When Aurelius had nearly sunk himself to the hilt, I cried out.

He captured that cry with his mouth, kissing me, and giving me more of his ichor—using that orgasmic nectar to counteract the pain of being invaded so thoroughly.

He pulled himself out, and I physically felt my walls cave in—stuttering at the size and loss of him.

"Hold on to me, Aurelia," he commanded softly.

I wrapped my arms around him, my eyes going starry when he drove himself into me without giving me a chance to adjust.

With time, the pain began to subside, replaced with something I could only explain as pure, incredible bliss.

"Oh my gods," I rasped to the dark night sky.

"Are you praying to me?" He chuckled, nipping at my quivering lips.

Then he pulled out and expertly flipped me over, onto my knees. My skirts flipped up and he plunged back inside, picking right up from his fast tempo. He reached around and worked that spot that made my toes curl, while his cock struck the spot inside that made me moan with pleasure. His fingers dug beneath the collar, pulling on it tightly as he pounded into me. Over and over again.

The combination of his stroke and his ichor—it all became too much, and my orgasm overtook me. It was strong and sweeping, enough so that it made me feel as though I might collapse.

When I was finished, I became all too aware of how sensitive I was—how uncomfortable and swollen. With each thrust, it became even more sensitive until I was ready to squirm my way free—even the ichor he had given me couldn't chase away how utterly raw I felt. But Aurelius held me there and continued to buck as he chased after his own release.

When he came, the mighty god tipped his head back and bellowed at the twinkling stars above.

Warmth shot into me at the release of his seed. I could feel it dripping beneath me, pooling with my own.

After, he picked me up and carried my quivering frame inside.

"You are so incredibly beautiful, Aurelia," he whispered as he laid me on the bed, kissing me.

I nodded softly, but didn't respond.

Even though my body was thoroughly ravished and my heart was content, I couldn't help but feel the sting of betrayal for what I had just done.

But it wasn't nearly as visceral as the sting between my legs.

And that was something I could hold on to.

CHAPTER 28

Von

When I regained the use of my body, his cock would be the first thing to go.

But first?

I would have words with *my* mate.

CHAPTER 29

Sage

I woke up alone.

Alone and somewhat sore, and if I was being honest with myself, full of regret.

I didn't regret sleeping with Aurelius. I regretted the reason I did it—because I was angry and hurt by Von's actions, by his betrayal. *That* should not have been the fuel I used to take things to the next level with Aurelius, and yet, in my brashness, that was exactly what I had done.

. . . It's exactly what the old Sage would have done.

I turned over, frustrated with myself. I was supposed to be growing into my new self, not taking a step back and reverting into old habits. At this rate, the Endless Mist would never believe I knew who I was—

Realization hit me.

Did I still want to unlock the Endless Mist? The whole

reason I was going to was for Von, so that I could make a new deal with Arkyn—his passage in exchange for him ending the deal.

But now? I didn't know.

I wished Ezra were here—she'd know what to do.

My eyes turned blurry with tears. I brushed them away and slipped into the heavy winter robe that Aurelius had had made for me. I cinched the sash around my waist, shoved my feet into my slippers, and walked—a tad gingerly—out onto the balcony.

There, before me, frozen on the snow-packed stone floor, was a hint of gold and a tinge of red.

I shoved my robes open, finding a smear of the same colors painted on my inner thighs—no wonder it felt like I had been losing my virginity all over again. The blood was obviously mine, which meant . . . the gold was his seed.

Damnit.

I hadn't taken the herbs to prevent pregnancy since before I showed up here. In my past life, Von had stolen my ability to have children. Had that curse transferred over into this life? Did I still need to take the herbs?

My hand slipped over the flat of my stomach. What would it feel like to carry Aurelius's child within me?

Nope.

I dropped my hand and shoved off from that hot potato thought as fast as possible. A child was the last thing I needed to worry about bringing into the equation right now. Cursed by Von or not, I wasn't about to take any chances. I would visit a healer and ask for some herbs. As the old adage went—better safe than sorry.

My slipper-covered feet carried me over to the balcony's edge. I propped my forearms on the railing, leaning against it as I surveyed the horizon, ignoring the cool bite that transferred through the fabric.

The sprawling, deep-blue sea stretched before me, sparkling under the orange-red gaze of the sun. White caps formed on the waters, the powerful wind skimming the surface, pushing it around. Down below, it crashed against the rocks—a rhythmic sound of water smashing stone and the spray that came afterward. Birds chimed in, most singing their morning song, but every so often, a crow would caw, adding in its say.

From here, I couldn't see the Endless Mist, but I knew if I were to sail into the horizon, I would eventually find it

A gentle breeze tugged on the tips of my hair, pulling them towards the sea.

Look up, a feminine voice whispered inside me.

I did—towards the clear, azure sky, dolloped with cottony white clouds leisurely floating by. My gaze landed on a large, black feather—it was floating towards me, shifting from side to side as it lowered down, down, down.

Instinctively, I extended my arm and faced my palm upwards.

When the silky plume settled into my hand, Von's bourbon tone poured into my ears. *Have you forgotten who you belong to?*

A breath of wind swept it from my hands, taking it from me—snatching it back.

"Well, have you?" asked a deep, dark voice—steeped in anger.

My head jerked up, my eyes rounding at the corners.

Von's phantom leaned against the railing, just to my left, his ringed fingers twirling the quill. He wore his hair up, tucked into a braid that fell down his back, exposing the one side that was shaven. As always, his masculine, muscular form was wrapped in black leather. And as always, he *owned* the look. *Damn the bastard.*

"You're not here," I said, backing up a few paces, hoping it would bring my swirling mind clarity. This was the male that had stolen my ability to create, who'd actively hunted me, who'd made me sick with fever.

I hated him.

I hated him.

And yet . . . how badly I wanted to hear him whisper his pretty little lies in my ear.

I was a stupid, stupid girl.

"No?" he challenged, tossing the feather over his shoulder. The wind swept it away, carrying it off into the horizon, until I could no longer see it anymore. I had thought that the feathers had some sort of meaning, but now I was beginning to question that too.

Von's gaze drifted to the spot—to the evidence of my joining with Aurelius. His nostrils flared and his onyx eyes darted towards my thighs, undoubtedly seeing right past the fabric. I dropped my hands in front, as if that were enough to block his vision.

I doubted it was.

Damn him.

Again.

His eyes snapped to mine, and he bared his teeth—

growling *at me*. The growl was unlike anything I had ever heard before, there was nothing human about it. Like a bolt of lightning, he struck. He wrapped his massive hand around the base of my neck as he reared me back against the stone wall, a *thump* sounding upon impact. His body crushed mine as he pinned me there, snarling like some deranged beast. His rings sunk into my sensitive skin like biting teeth, his grip firm, but not enough to sever my air.

I wheezed, "Von, what are you—"

His eyes were so black, so bottomless, I froze.

"Once again, you have proven yourself to have terrible taste in men," he sneered, furiously.

Him. Furious. *With me?*

He had no right.

"You know nothing," I hissed, throwing the words at him like a hand striking a cheek. He deserved so much worse from me.

He blew out a disbelieving laugh. "I know that I would *never* need to sway you with my ichor to fuck me. What part of *stay away from him* didn't you understand?"

"What?" My tongue stumbled over the word—*how* did he know?

"I can smell him on you," he answered, his thumb and forefinger roughly snatching my chin, forcing me to look at him. "*In* you." He forced my face to the side, the action far from gentle. He lowered his face to my neck, his upper torso curving to make up for the vast difference in our heights. "I should drain every vein in your body, rip *his* scent from you, and replace it with *mine*." Heated breath feathered across my neck as his teeth scraped over the sensitive flesh. "You should *only* ever smell of me."

And just when I was certain his teeth were about to pierce my flesh, he placed a sinister, gentle kiss against my neck—marking the spot as something he would return for later.

A shiver rumbled across my skin, pebbling it.

Removing his lips from my neck, he pulled back just enough to meet my gaze. He growled in that predatory way of his. "I claim you. I will always claim you, *mate*. No matter if you fucking remember what we are or not. There is no escaping what you are to me. You are mine, Kitten. And I *do not* share what is *mine*."

I scoffed. *His?* After everything he'd put me through, he had the audacity to believe that he had a right to *claim* me?

Anger, potent and raw, pumped into my veins, boiling my blood. "I do *not* belong to you," I spewed venomously at him, shoving against his steel-derived chest.

His expression turned primal—like a wolf that had just killed a rabbit and had no intentions of sharing it with the rest of the pack.

He caught my wrists as he growled at me. "Oh yes, you most certainly do."

No better than an animal myself, I spat at him. He turned his head to the side and it struck his cheek.

I wasn't proud of myself, but it felt *so* damn good.

I wanted to hurt him, to fight with him, to shove his phantom right off this balcony and dust my hands off after I did it. Let the bastard sink into the dark, murky depths of the sea—where he belonged, right next to his crates, chock-full of secrets and lies.

He jerked me closer to him, shackling my gaze to his. One brow raised. "Is this your way of *claiming* me, mate? Should I pry your mouth open and return the favor?"

"Fuck you," I hissed, firing my knee at his most treasured *goods*.

Guarding himself, he blocked it with the heavy muscle of his outer thigh. Pain shot through my knee.

"The last time you tried to knee me there, you ended up on your back. We can perform this little dance again, but I assure you the end results will be the same." His words lacked their usual dark charm, but they still made an impact. Momentarily, I was taken back to the decrepit city of Norwood, to the night *I thought* I had first met him. The domineering male who stood in the kitchen, cooking, shirtless. He had been so at ease with everything—with a complete stranger passed out upstairs. But I wasn't a stranger to him, was I? And he had hid that knowledge from me. Just like he had hidden everything.

I snarled in frustration.

He let my wrists go and brushed away the saliva from his cheek. He inspected it, sucking on his teeth before his eyes shot to mine. "*This* wreaks of him."

"Well, I guess so. I did drink his ichor after all," I snipped, a shimmer of divinity seeping into my words, like the goddess part of me was proud to rub it in. "And as you clearly know, that's not *all* we did."

Von growled as he flicked the spittle to the ground and then snatched my face with his wet fingers. He squished my cheeks, making my lips pucker. "I'll have my shadows chain you to my bed as I fuck the idea of you *ever* sleeping with another male again right out of you. No matter how long it takes, I'll carve myself into you so thoroughly you'll be stuttering *my name* for months." He tossed my head to the side like he was done with me.

I stood there, confused, angry and . . . aroused.

Somewhere, a part of me—a very stupid part that should know better—still wanted him.

. . . I must be going insane.

How could I want the man who had tormented me? Who'd caused me so much pain and suffering? I didn't understand it. Couldn't understand it. I felt like I was being torn in two.

I looked up at Von, in all his menacing, hate-filled, towering glory. Corded in muscle, veins, and tattoos. Wrapped in leather and shadows and rage. Aurelius's ichor was an aphrodisiac, but Von *was* the aphrodisiac—every bit of him. And he was right, I didn't need his ichor to feel that intense lust for him—the kind that drove me wild with need. *That* came naturally.

He swished his pointer finger from side to side, gesturing between my legs. "When you weep with *my* seed, I'll mop it up with a cloth and then I'll ram it so far down the God of Life's throat that he will choke on the taste of you and me. And then I'll find a way to end his immortal life for thinking he could take what is *mine*."

Just like that, the spell that had so quickly washed over me was shattered . . .

It all came back to Von's hatred for Aurelius. That was what this was about. It was never about us—there *never* was an us.

I met his hardened obsidian gaze, preparing myself to ask the question I needed to ask, knowing very well that hearing the truth might completely destroy me. That's if the lying bastard bothered to give it to me.

I raised my head as I took a step forward, courage and potent anger driving my movement. "Is that all I am to you? A *tool* to get back at him?"

"At first?" He paused. "Yes."

I made a sour face as I swallowed that bitter, bitter truth.

He continued, "When I first saw you in his arms, I knew you were a weakness to him. I knew that I could use you to sow discord amongst his court, and so that's exactly what I did. But a part of me also felt sorry for you, knowing what you would be forced to endure as his wife, and so I found a way to hurt him, but also benefit you."

Endure as his wife? What in the Spirit Realm did that mean? Was Von just planting more lies? I was tempted to point out that while Von had left me to suffer in my past life, Aurelius had been the one picking up my broken pieces and caring for me, but then why should I bother to even explain that to Von? It wasn't like I owed him anything.

"Benefit me?" I choked out a laugh—born of disbelief. Yet another ridiculous lie.

He performed a single *I'm-a-prick-and-I'm-fine-with-it* nod. "The curse I gave you was also for your benefit."

I threw my hand to the side, my anger bubbling to the surface. "I fail to see how cursing me was for my benefit. It certainly didn't feel like that as my body was being shredded apart by the fever."

"Believe it or not, Kitten, it was," he said, his phantom

breaking apart—just like it did that time in Belamour, telling me that he couldn't hold this form much longer. He sighed through his nose. "This visit has nearly chewed through the last remnants of my power."

"Good," I snarled.

He rolled his eyes like he didn't believe me, then nodded to the door. "The *mate-fucker* is on his way. Ask him to remove the collar and see what he says. Or did you forget what you wear around your neck?" His gaze dropped pointedly to my lips. "Just like you forgot who those belong to." His eyes shifted lower. "That too."

I growled at him, covering myself, even though I was wearing a robe.

Von's phantom dissolved on the wind, his wicked smile the last thing I saw.

The door behind me opened.

"Good morning, princess," Aurelius said pleasantly. "I'm sorry I had to leave before you woke. I would have preferred to spend the morning with you, but unfortunately, duty calls."

"Morning," I said, turning to greet him, a soft smile replacing the downward turn of my lips. "It's alright. I was just getting some air." *And having my head messed with by a lying bastard.*

"How do you feel?" Aurelius asked as he took me in his arms, surveying my face.

"Fine. Mostly. Perhaps a bit . . . sore," I admitted sheepishly, my arms wrapping loosely around his torso.

"I can help you with that." He bit into his wrist, drawing a mouthful of ichor. Gently, he coaxed my mouth to open, pulling my lax jaw down with his hand. His lips pressed against mine as he released the divine nectar into my mouth.

I swallowed it down.

Seconds later, euphoria erupted.

He pulled his mouth away from mine, a light smile touching his lips. A glistening bead of ichor rolled over his chin. Standing on the tips of my toes, I licked it off. Savoring it, I closed my eyes. This feeling—it was so incredibly seductive. *Addictive.*

"What do you feel like now?" he asked.

I thought about it before I said, "Like I just achieved something insurmountable."

He chuckled. "Would you like to feel like this all the time?"

"I don't know what would be left of me if I felt this good all the time," I said with a grin, a gentle buzz licking at my skin, my vision.

"I like seeing you like this—feeling good and happy," he said, just before he kissed me. We became enraptured in one another's kiss. I felt movement around me, but when I opened my eyes, we were standing in the massive room that housed the bathing pool.

Light walking with Aurelius felt different than it did with Von—I didn't doubt that if I opened my eyes when he did it, we would have been surrounded by a bright-blue sky, rather than dancing, twinkling stars.

Aurelius captured the string on my robe, pulling on it, causing it to fall open. White lashes lowered, as he took in the swell of my breasts, the flat of my stomach, and the evidence of us between my thighs.

He grinned. "You are positively filthy." He extended his hand to me, backing towards the stairs that led into the water. "Come, let me clean you."

I glanced around, my vision slightly altered from his ichor. Even though no one else was in the bathing pool right now, that could change at any moment. "What if someone comes in? What if they see?"

"Then we will let them look," he said, his grin widening. "And then I shall pluck out their eyes after." He winked at me, but the playful nature of it fell a bit flat, the thought replaced by another—specifically a head on a pike with the eyes gouged out.

"Is that what you did to the night guard?" I asked, and even though I wanted it to come out more serious, the euphoric feeling drifting over me kept it soft, peaceful. As if I were asking him a simple question, like what he had for dessert last night.

Oh wait . . . *that was me.*

"I did. He wished to gaze upon *my wife,*" he answered, his golden eyes like liquid fire. "We gods are a jealous bunch."

My breath hitched, hearing him call me his wife—it did something to my heart, made it whole somehow. And yet, it made me . . . squeamish too. Irony dawned on me that I'd long hated the idea of being married, but little did I know that I already was.

I slipped my robe off and placed my hand in his, embracing this moment between us. He bowed, bringing my hand to his lips as he placed a kiss against it—the simple gesture causing my heart's two left feet to trip over one another.

I followed him into the waters.

In the center, under the glistening sun, he swept my body up, cradling me against him. I looped my arms around his neck, and for a time, we just stayed like that, staring into one another's eyes—that sweet euphoria making the moment even more magical.

I weaved my wet fingers into his, playing with them. My gaze fell to the spot over his heart—there was no scar there and yet . . .

"You gave me your heart," I whispered in awe.

"I did," he answered, his gaze drifting to my chest, looking beyond my flesh.

Softly, I pulled on his hand and placed it over my breast. My hand slid over top of his—the size difference between the two was drastic.

"Does it respond to my touch?" he asked, mesmerized.

"Yes, it is very reactive whenever you are near. It's been like that since I saw you that first night. I couldn't make sense of it then, but now, I understand."

"It reacts to me because it is still my heart. But—" his gaze lifted to mine, a soft smile toying at the corners of his lips, "—you are the keeper of it."

I could feel the unending love behind those words and it swallowed me whole, my body overcome with an intense radiating emotion. Searching for release, my lips found his, and I poured what I was feeling into my kiss.

He walked us towards the edge. The water drifted against my body, gliding smoothly over my skin as we moved. His hands clasped around my hips as he lifted me and set me on the pool's ledge.

The cool air kissed my skin, coaxing a series of shivers to stroll down the length of my spine, chasing after the water droplets as they rolled over my soft, feminine curves.

"I need to ask something of you," I said, looking up at him.

"Alright." His fingers played with the tips of my white hair.

"I want the collar removed."

On bated breath, I waited for his answer.

If he said no, then that would mean Von was right.

But if he said yes . . .

Aurelius nodded. "Of course, princess. I will see to it that we have it removed today."

I smiled, wrapping my arms around his neck and kissing him.

Von was wrong about Aurelius.

And I was done with his mind games.

CHAPTER 30

Sage

Sitting on top of a table with a thin mattress pad, I winced as the healer rubbed a pungent, musky-smelling salve on my neck. She focused on the raw flesh, the top layer of skin long rubbed off by the iron collar.

My gaze shifted from the aged face of the elderly healer who stood in front of me to the iron collar sitting on the small wood table to my right. Beside it sat the tin can which housed the salve she was applying to my neck—a new jar with three finger swipes ran through it. There was something poetic about seeing the collar and the salve sitting beside one another. One was used to repress, the other to heal.

Aurelius stood in the corner of the room with his arms crossed, his posture too perfect, too poised for him to be caught leaning against a wall. Unlike his typical regal clothes, today, he dressed more leisurely. He wore high-waisted button-up trousers—black—and a white, long-sleeved tunic with ruffled sleeves. His ruffled collar had a deep neckline, exposing his perfect, sun-kissed skin beneath, and the look was completed by a pair of knee-high leather boots. His long, white hair fell over his shoulder—no crown, or gold cuffs—in its natural, perfect state. He watched the healer work, but every so often, his gaze would meet mine and the slightest hint of a smile would play at his full lips, causing my heart to stumble a beat. He *was* something to look at.

I winced again.

"Sorry about that," the healer said, her skin crinkling at the corners of her eyes as she offered me a gummy smile—her teeth long gone. Without her teeth, her cheeks fell concave, the bottom half of her face looking as if it had sunken in on itself.

"It's okay," I said warmly, knowing she was trying to be as gentle as possible. I offered her a smile of my own.

She eyed it for a moment before she said, "You have very pretty teeth, ah." She lowered her hands, scooped up the bottom of her apron, and wiped the remaining salve on the stained cotton.

"Thank you," I said, watching as she screwed the lid back on to the tin. Her compliment didn't feel out of place or weird to me—I imagined that if I were her, I'd probably say the same thing to someone who still had a full set of chompers.

After all, it was human nature to want what we didn't have, wasn't it?

"You are quite welcome," she said, her curved shoulders bouncing from side to side as she waddled over towards a wall of shelves full of various salves, tinctures, ointments, tins, and vials—Ezra would have been in her glory.

Ezra. Oh, how I missed her. What would Aurelius think of her? What would she think of him? I imagined she'd have a few things to say about him living under the same roof as the king. I could only imagine how that would go.

I nibbled on my bottom lip. Had I jumped into this too fast?

Probably.

My heart punched at my ribcage, reminding me that Aurelius and I had been married in our past life. I should trust in that.

"Can I do anything else for you?" she asked.

"That is all," Aurelius said at the exact same time I said, "Yes."

His eyes met mine, a white brow raised. "Sorry, I didn't realize there was something else."

"It's alright," I said, looking to the healer as she wobbled her way back towards me.

"What is it dear?" she asked, her eyes regarding me with nothing but kindness.

I looked at Aurelius. "May we have a moment—alone?"

He opened his mouth to say something but then cut himself off. Respectfully, he tipped his head. "Of course. I'll be outside if you need anything."

When the door was closed, I turned to the healer. "I was wondering if I could get some herbs . . . to ward off pregnancy."

The healer nodded in understanding, knowing this was a sensitive subject. "You, too, ah? Sixth girl this week." She cackled. "I don't blame you lasses one bit." She waddled towards her shelves, her fingers dancing over a row of clear jars, their labels nearly worn off.

Her remarks struck me a bit odd.

"What do you mean by that?" I inquired, leaning forward, one hand propped on my leg.

"I've had a lot of younger women coming in lately to request the same thing as you," she said as she plucked a jar, a small square cloth, and a short piece of yarn from the shelves, then started back towards me, her feet set at a slow-paced shuffle. "They say they are fearful of the new plague going around, that it searches only for younger women that are with child."

"A plague?" I said, recalling the conversation the man at the dinner table had had with Aurelius—about his brother's pregnant wife and her worsening condition.

"That's what they say it is, but I know better. It's not a plague," she scoffed. "The Creator is angry with us, for killing—" she nodded to me, "—your kind." She began to dish a spoonful of herbs out onto a cloth. "I know saying that out loud is considered treasonous to the king because it looks like I'm siding with the Cursed, but I'm old and I don't really give a damn anymore."

Warmth bloomed in my chest. Since my time here, it had been hard to find someone who was not prejudiced against the Cursed, but every once in a while—I glanced at her—I'd find someone who wasn't and that gave me hope. Hope for a better future.

"I appreciate you saying that," I remarked softly, the sappy part of me fighting the bulge in my throat.

She scooped up my hand and placed the small cloth sack in it, gently closing my hand around it. "Steep a pinch in your tea, twice a week. Should be enough there to last you a little over a month. I'd give you more, but my stores are running a bit low, and I need to save some for the other girls."

I clasped my free hand over hers. "Thank you."

"You are quite welcome, dear," she said with a wink. "Besides, us women must look after one another, ah?"

"I need to discuss something with you," Aurelius said, breaking the silence that had settled between us since we left the healer's quarters. We were walking down a lengthy hallway, its walls filled with massive portraits of royals who had once ruled over these lands. "It's about your conversation with the healer, after you asked me to leave."

I became all too aware of the cloth sack I had shoved into my dress, and how uncomfortable it felt squished between my breasts—the living quarters for the girls wasn't exactly spacious, at least, not when Brunhilde was at the helm of tying a corset.

"Alright," I replied, my skirts rubbing against one another as we walked, the sound accompanied by the click of my heels. Aurelius's steps were silent, as per usual.

"I am aware you asked her for something to protect you from becoming pregnant," he said, lowering his tone as we walked by two young girls. They stopped immediately and bowed. When they were out of earshot, he continued, "I just wish you had spoken to me first."

Spoken to him first? The request struck a nerve.

"Aurelius, we've only just started working things out between us. It feels a bit early for you and me to have discussions about what I do with *my body*," I replied, not bothering to hide the annoyance I felt. "And how do you know what I spoke to her about?"

"I have good hearing."

"Good enough to hear through walls?"

"Yes."

I committed that little fact to memory. Next time, I'd tell the eavesdropper to go down the hall. Annoyed, I stalked forward.

His fingers slipped around my arm and he softly spun me towards him. "This isn't just about *your* body. We are talking about the possibility of *our* child—the future king."

I felt like I was going to be sick—I was nowhere near ready to have a child. That was . . . if I even could.

"I am not ready for that." I tugged my arm out of his grasp.

He let it go. "Not ready? When you told me that you no longer wanted to be friends, I took it that you were choosing us. *This* is part of *us*," he said, gesturing with his hand between him and me. "Making life is the very thing we were created to do, and now we might actually have a chance at that."

"I can't believe we are even discussing this," I scoffed, taking a much-needed step back from him.

"If not now, then when, Aurelia?" he said, a droplet of frustration swirling in his typically even tone.

I gaped. Pushing me on this was unbelievable. "Fine, if you want to do this now, then we will. Yes, we were married in our past life, but that is not *this* life. You call me Aurelia, but you forget that I am *also* Sage—that I have lived a separate life from you for nearly twenty-three years, and even though we were something to one another in the past, I hardly have any memories of those times. The relationship between us, to me, *is* new. So once again, I am not ready to even *discuss* the possibility of a child."

Aurelius looked like I had just smacked him across the face, not even bothering to hide the hurt in his eyes. And my heart nearly fractured at that. Immediately, I regretted what I'd said, even if it was the truth.

Calling me *wife* was one thing, but to bring a child into this chaotic mess of a so-called life? That was entirely another.

"Unbelievable. Despite everything, *he* still has a hold on you, doesn't he?" he said, his calm tone holding the slightest hint of a snarl. The line between his shoulders was strung taut, his posture more rigid than usual.

I didn't need to ask who *he* was. That part I knew. But what irked me more was the fact that he was using Von as a crutch in this disagreement while simultaneously ignoring what I'd just said.

"How dare you even ask me that," I fired at him. And for the first time in weeks, I felt my power swirl within me—I felt that well fill, my Curse coming back stronger than ever. Creator above, it was good to feel that vital part of me again.

"I think it's a reasonable question. You have spent a lot of time with him over the past so many months. I'm sure he filled your head with plenty of lies, just as he did before." His words stung like salt in a wound—Von *had* lied to me. And having it tossed in my face left me feeling like a rabid cornered animal with a hand reaching for it.

"Oh, I'm sorry," I snapped back. "I thought we were past that. Does this mean you are going to collar me again?" I stretched my neck, showing him the rawness of my flesh, shining with salve.

Aurelius took a step towards me. "You know why I had to do that."

"To protect *yourself*," I hissed.

He stormed to the other side of the hallway and slammed his palm into the stone wall as he roared, "Even in death, he plagues our marriage!"

My brows hooked low, lured on a moment of confusion. Then, it made sense.

Aurelius must think that Arkyn's deal had worked.

I took a deep breath. "He's not dead."

Aurelius swirled around, his golden eyes burning as hot as a forge.

That was the only warning I had before the world around me was engulfed in flames. And although the fire did not touch me, I could not say the same for the rest of the hallway.

The paintings melted, creating macabre portraits—stretched out eyes and screaming mouths—before the flames swallowed them whole. The arched stained-glass windows began to liquify, caving in on themselves. The colored liquid dribbled down the walls, pooling on the stone floor.

Suddenly, the flames wicked out, leaving the hallway bare-boned and dusted with soot.

Wide eyed, I looked at Aurelius, feeling every bit of his immense magic filling the air, the vibrant taste of it on my tongue.

Aurelius reached for me, his voice soft as he said, "Aurelia, I—"

"No," I said, slapping his hand away. I gestured to the rest of the hallway. "You did this. And you are damned lucky no one got hurt because of it."

"I lost my temper," he said, his expression somber.

"That is no excuse," I growled, shaking my head. Done with this conversation, I started down the hallway, my thunderous steps fed by my anger.

CHAPTER 31

Sage

My mind was stuck—stuck on my fight with Aurelius, stuck on what had happened in the hallway, and stuck on the quiet walk back to my chambers, where I stayed for the rest of the day. Now, nighttime had fallen, sweeping its black paint across the canvas of the sky.

Naevia's face glowed as orangey-red as the fire she knelt in front of. Using an iron shovel, she fished out chunks of coals to put in the bed warmer pan. Brunhilde stood over top of her, telling her which ones to select as if she were a jeweler selecting precious diamonds.

Meanwhile, Cataline unlaced me from that wicked contraption known as a corset. When it was off, I took a deep breath, reveling in the ability to breathe again. My fingers slid over my ribs, slipping into the red angry divots stamped into my flesh, the skin stinging.

"I'll come early tomorrow morning and get you dressed before Brunhilde comes," Cataline whispered behind me, low enough that Brunhilde, the expert organ squeezer, wouldn't hear. Truly, they should have given Brunhilde a job as a torturer rather than a housemaid.

"Thank you," I whispered back, her offer warming my heart. With each passing day, conversations with Cataline were becoming easier, but while Cataline warmed to me, Naevia had grown colder. Earlier tonight, when she arrived with Brunhilde and Cataline, her eyes went straight to my neck, noting what was no longer there. Her usual blank expression turned soggy with disgust. When she noticed that I had seen the face she made, she turned her head quickly to the side and hurried off to start her nightly tasks.

I knew the prejudice against the Cursed was bad, but growing up in the woods had kept me a bit sheltered from the extent of it. I realized that sounded a bit naive, considering I watched countless people be tortured and then burnt at the pyre all in the name of the king. But this . . . it was different. It wasn't as cut and dry as the Cleansings. For the most part, the crowd that gathered around during the Cleansings took no joy in seeing their fellow villagers burn. Although no one dared say it out loud, there was a sense of sorrow among the small community. But here, in the castle, it wasn't just the king and his guards that despised the Cursed, it was also most of the people who lived here—Naevia being one of them.

And sure, it felt a little unjust for her to judge me considering she knew next to nothing about my character, but in truth I felt sorry for her.

She hadn't grown up in the woods like me. She'd grown

up here, in this stifling environment full of rigid customs, fakery, and lies. Yes, the castle was massive in size, but the box the crown kept people in—that was tiny. The false information they sowed into their minds was even smaller.

For years now, the monarchy had told its citizens that the Cursed were unclean, a danger to society, and any voices who said otherwise were silenced. So naturally, if one message was repeated, like an unruly weed left unplucked, it would eventually take over.

I couldn't blame Naevia for acting the way she did—she was a product of this place.

Yet, somehow, someway, Cataline pushed past those boundaries. And that gave me hope.

"Well, I think that'll be all for tonight, my lady. There's a teapot sitting on the table, hot water only, as you requested. There's a tin full of chamomile and lavender beside it, should you decide it needs a bit of flavor," Brunhilde said, her hands falling into the crook of her voluminous hips. She wore a satisfied expression, a telltale sign that she was pleased with herself and her nightly duties. I didn't think anyone took their job as seriously as Brunhilde—not even the king.

"Thank you," I said to her. To all of them. I glanced at the teapot, steam drifting from its spout. Four matching cups sat beside it, along with a wooden spoon and the tin she spoke of.

Cataline touched my arm as she passed by. "See you tomorrow morning."

"Good night," I said to her.

"Good night, my lady," Naevia said, her expression as lifeless as her tone. She didn't make eye contact, but she dipped her head and then quickened towards the door.

Brunhilde and Cataline followed her out.

After they were gone, I sat cross-legged on the floor with the map of the castle spread out before me and the cup of steeped herbs—the herbs the healer had given me—in my hands. Its warmth seeped through the cup and into my fingers. Over the past few days, winter had finally staked her claim, plummeting the temperature into a vicious, vicious cold—the kind that stung your face within just a few seconds of being exposed to it. Even the fireplace in my room was having a hard time fighting winter's chokehold.

Something my heart could attest to . . .

Aurelius and I had not spoken since this morning.

In the wake of our fight, I had had time to revisit our disagreement, to play it over again and again in my mind. It wasn't my best moment, but hey, it wasn't exactly his either—he had torched an *entire* hallway.

From what I remembered of him in the past, Aurelius had been kind to me—tenderhearted. But when I met him the first night, when he'd sunk his teeth into my neck—that had been an entirely different version of him. He had wanted to hurt me then. And then what happened today? Not only did he think he had a right to say what I did with my body, but when he found out Von was alive, that calm demeanor had been reduced to ash, quite literally.

Which begged the question—who was the *real* Aurelius?

I rubbed at the spot over my heart, a considerable ache having formed there.

Despite what he had done, my heart held love for him. That much was clear. But then again, the heart beating in my chest—it wasn't entirely my own, was it? It came from

Aurelius himself, so it just made sense that it would feel love for him, because it was a *part* of him.

But what did that mean for me? It had once felt love for Von, as well, which made me think that it wasn't completely just Aurelius's heart, but perhaps part of it belonged to me too.

Did I feel genuine love for Aurelius, or was it because my physical heart had once belonged to him?

There came a knock at the balcony door.

Kaleb.

I set the cup down and hurried over to the door, greeted by one great big smile.

I beamed. Creator above, it was good to see him. Quickly, I let him in and closed the door against the howling, pushy wind, trying my best to keep out the crippling cold.

"Not a nice night for flying," he said, shaking off the snow that had accumulated on him. In doing so, he reminded me more of a playful puppy than a sleek, stealthy bird.

"No, it doesn't look like it," I replied warmly, walking back over to the map. I wanted to show him the hidden hallways and see if he could investigate them for me.

Kaleb tagged behind. "Because I know you're going to ask . . . no, there hasn't been any change in Von's condition."

I came to a sudden halt and turned around, my mouth flopping open like a fish out of water—where do I even start with this one? How do I tell him that we had been wrong about Von—that he had just used me? That he had lied about—

"How did you get rid of the collar?" Kaleb asked, his question catching me off guard, but effectively keeping my mind from spiraling.

"I think you'd better sit down. Much has changed since

we last spoke." I gestured to one of the chairs.

He pointed to the cup of tea. "Okay, but first can I get a cup of that? I'm freezing."

"I don't think you want what's in there," I chuckled. "I'll make you something else."

His gaze darted to the cup and then to me, a question forming on his parted lips, but he just shrugged and said, "Okay."

And that, right there, was why I loved Kaleb.

. . . *Take note, Aurelius*—that was how you respected a woman's privacy.

"I'm sorry, sister, but I don't buy what you're selling," Kaleb said. He sat in the chair across from me, his arms crossed over his chest, his posture casually defensive.

After I finished telling him *everything* that had transpired since I last saw him, we started hashing things out.

That was well over an hour ago now.

I let out an aggravated sigh. "Kaleb, it's the truth. I saw the memories—Von took away my ability to create and he did it to cause friction within my marriage. He used me as a tool to get back at Aurelius. That's *all* I was to him. His phantom more or less confirmed it."

"If that's all you were to him, then why would he be willing to trade his life for yours? Give up his realms for you?" Kaleb snipped, tossing the words back at me. He shook his head. "He wouldn't."

"Who knows why he did that. If there is one thing I've learned about Von, nothing he does is just cut and dry. There's always a motive behind his actions—"

"Exactly!" Kaleb cut me off as he leaned forward.

I took a deep breath, feeling my frustration quickly mounting. That wasn't where I had been going with my point. I fumbled for the right words, looking for the best way to articulate what I was trying to say.

"Look, I get it, Sage, you're dealing with a lot right now." Kaleb left his chair, and positioned himself in front of me, kneeling. He scooped my hands in his—a trait we had both picked up from Ezra. "You are essentially living two lives right now and trying to figure out who you are—mortal Sage or immortal Aurelia. And everything that was of comfort to you has, well—" He let out a withheld breath. "It's been taken away. Ezra's not here. I'm not—at least, not as much as you probably need me to be. Von is gone, and in his wake, all you have are these shitty memories returning of him. Nothing in your life is comfortable right now."

His words struck an emotional chord.

I tried to fight the tears I had been holding back, but one slipped out. And then another.

"Oh, Sage, this is okay. You can do this." He dabbed at a tear. "You can cry. It's okay not to be strong all the time. That's what makes you *human*."

In so many ways, that was exactly what I needed to hear. His words became my unraveling. Tears poured down my cheeks—the tap had sprung a leak and I had no interest in fixing it.

Kaleb hugged me tightly as I let it all out.

Knock. Knock. Knock.

I raised my head from Kaleb's soaked shoulder, our heads both swiveling to look towards the door—the balcony door.

"Damn, I didn't pick a good night to introduce you two," Kaleb muttered to himself as he pulled back.

"Sorry. What? Introduce us two?" I asked, brushing the dampness from my cheeks. I could almost guarantee my face was a puffy mess right now—my nose probably doubled in size, my eyelids definitely swollen.

"Yeah," Kaleb said as he strode over to the door that led outside. He opened it and a short, cloaked figure walked in.

Feminine hands reached up and slung the hood back, revealing the heart-shaped face of a woman who looked to be not much older than me. Long, nearly black hair framed her lovely features. She didn't wear any kohl or paint her lips—she didn't have to because she was naturally beautiful. Vibrant hazel eyes were framed in long, sweeping lashes. Angular cheekbones contoured her feminine features.

She swatted Kaleb's chest, knocking the wind out of him, as she smiled politely at me. "Well, are you going to introduce us properly or what?"

"Sage—" Kaleb rubbed the spot where she smacked him, a grin saddled on his lips, "—this is Fallon."

CHAPTER 32

Sage

"We sort of . . . met before. You were a raven though," I said, fluttering my fingers up and down as if they were wings.

Kaleb shot me an awkward look.

I stopped my fluttering and dropped my hands immediately, feeling every bit of the idiot I probably looked like. I hoped she didn't take offense.

Thankfully, her smile widened. "Yes, we met when I was collecting his soul." She made it sound romantic, but that could just be the way she spoke—she had a very sensual voice.

. . . his *little marble* soul, that was. I mentally snickered. I tucked my lips between my teeth, physically silencing myself and my big mouth before I could cut a joke that might not make for the best of first impressions.

"Yes, that's right," I said with a soft nod.

"Yes," she said, returning the nod.

And then the three of us just stood there stiffly, the conversation dying out. We exchanged a few smiles, our gazes bouncing off one another. Mine ricocheted off Kaleb and then landed on the teapot . . . that was it.

I gestured to it. "How does some tea sound?"

"Yes, please," they both chimed in, just as desperate for something to break the proverbial ice. They glanced at one another and chuckled.

That's when I saw it—it was in the way they looked at one another. She tilted her head just slightly, her expression softening and her eyes rounding at the corners with wide-eyed wonder for my . . . ding-a-ling brother.

Unable to help himself, his hand saddled up on the small of her back and he guided her closer to him. There was a gravitational pull between the two—like they needed to make physical contact with one another just as much as they needed to breathe.

I knew that feeling . . . I had once felt it with Von.

Although it was faint, my heart stumbled just a tick. I tried my best to ignore it and placed the kettle over the fire.

While I waited for it to boil, Kaleb and Fallon seated themselves.

"How did it go?" Kaleb asked Fallon, his voice tender—caring.

With my back facing them, I quirked a curious brow. I had never quite heard him sound like *that* before.

Fallon let out a deep breath before she answered, "Another one, the same wound in her stomach as the last."

"I don't understand. After they are sorted by the Da'Nu,

why doesn't the council talk to them and see what's going on?" Kaleb asked.

"It's like I've said before, the Spirit Realm is not in the business of looking after what's killing those in the Living Realm, despite how much it has increased its toll on us and the Da'Nu. The Living Realm belongs to the New Gods—it's their jurisdiction."

I turned, my brow lowering. "Do you mind me asking what you two are talking about?"

Kaleb and Fallon exchanged a silent conversation, one I clearly was not privy to, before he nodded. "There's been an uptick in deaths as of late. All women of childbearing age."

"I've heard about that," I said, lacing my arms loosely over my chest. "I spoke with a healer earlier this morning and she said people think it's a plague, but she doesn't think that's what it is."

I didn't bother to tack on that she figured it was because the Creator was mad at them for killing off the Cursed because my gut feeling told me that wasn't it—there was something else going on.

But what?

I thought back to the conversation I'd overheard at the dinner table, between Aurelius and that man. He'd said his brother's pregnant wife had become ill. If she was with child, that would put her in the right age group as the other women. Was she connected to this somehow, or was that purely coincidental?

"Plagues don't cut into abdomens," Fallon said, shaking her head. "Unfortunately, that's how a lot of the bodies are when we get to them."

"Why there?" I asked, my brows crinkling.

"We think they were pregnant," Kaleb said somberly.

Chills ran down my spine.

On the verge of blowing its lid, the teapot sputtered in protest. I grabbed a cloth, slid it around the handle, and carried the teapot over to the small, round table, setting it on the trivet. "Are any . . . with child when you find them?" I asked, this conversation not sitting well with me. And judging by the looks on their faces, it wasn't sitting well with them either.

"No," Fallon answered.

A pool of unease sloshed around in my gut, making me feel sick.

"And because we have only noticed an increase in young female souls—that means the infants are alive . . . somewhere," Kaleb sighed as he scrubbed at his jaw.

I placed a scoop of tea leaves into the teapot, put the lid back on, and let it steep. Doing something so mundane while having this conversation felt so incredibly wrong.

"Why don't you just ask the dead themselves what happened?" I inquired.

Fallon rested one leg over the other, suspending one ticking foot in the air. "We have customs in the Spirit Realm—it's extremely rude to ask souls what they died from at the end of their time in the Living Realm."

"That sounds ridiculous," I stated bluntly, unable to help myself.

"Sage," Kaleb scolded me under his breath.

I shrugged unapologetically. "If finding out why young women are dying helps to save the lives of others, wouldn't it be worth asking?"

"You are viewing things from a mortal's perspective, wrongly thinking that death is the end, but as you can see . . ." She gestured to Kaleb. "It isn't the end. The time humans spend in the Living Realm, in comparison to living out eternity in the Spirit Realm, is minuscule."

"That doesn't mean their time in the Living Realm isn't important," I replied, my tone a bit more aggressive than I intended for it to be.

Her foot quit ticking. "Don't put words in my mouth. I did not say that."

"Ladies, please," Kaleb interjected, his hands held up defensively.

I ignored him, narrowing in on Fallon. "No, but you refuse to ask the dead what happened to them because it might result in lives saved? Do explain that to me." I didn't bother to hide the sarcasm.

"I thought you were supposed to be a goddess—" she gave me a once over, the demeaning action landing its mark, "yet you act like a foolish, little girl."

"Fallon," Kaleb reprimanded her softly.

My temper flared. After my fight with Aurelius today, my nerves and patience were shot. Leaning forward, I placed my hands on the table and brought my face to the same level as hers. "And you act like a heartless bitch."

Faster than I could react, her fist collided dead center on my face, causing my eyes to instantly water as I reared back. My hands shot to my nose, checking to see if it was broken as blood came leaking out.

She could land a solid hit—I'd give her that.

Oh, but she wasn't done. She leapt from her chair, and it fell over backwards, clattering loudly against the ground. She came at me again—her balled-up fists flying towards me. I ducked out of the way, catching her hand in mine. I shoved against her, pushing her back from me. For Kaleb's sake, not mine, I didn't try to hit her back. Although, the thought was damn tempting—I'd like to return the favor for her nearly breaking my nose.

Kaleb jumped between us.

"Enough!" he yelled at the top of his lungs. It was loud enough that it made my ears ring—loud enough that it made both of us freeze. "You two are acting like children."

The door that led into the hallway suddenly swung open, its rusty hinges groaning in aggravated response. "Sage, are you al—" Ryker's sentence fell short.

I turned to look at him. We all did.

When the towering fire twin removed his helmet, his expression was that of pure shock—like he'd just watched a ghost peel itself from its earthly carcass.

"Fallon?" he rumbled in disbelief.

I turned to her, my hand still holding my leaking nose. Like Kaleb, my mouth was slung open.

"Hello, Ryker," she said, her voice cracking with emotion. "It's been a while."

CHAPTER 33

Sage

I wouldn't consider myself an expert on Ryker's facial expressions, even though we had spent a good deal of time around one another over the past so many months, however there was no mistaking the way he was looking at Fallon right now.

Surprised. Curious.

But most of all—hurt.

Then it clicked.

This Fallon was *the* Fallon. The one he'd told me about when we were traveling to Belamour—the Fallon who he'd been willing to sacrifice his Curse for, so that they could live a normal life together. On the day the Elders decided to break her unconscious mind barrier, she had disappeared, along with the Crown of Thorns. I shuddered at the thought of it. Ryker had said that Von broke her out.

But now . . . she was a reaper.

So what had happened between that day and now?

"I don't—" Ryker shook his head in disbelief. He raised a large arm, his stiff armor sounding as he ran his gauntleted fingers through his dark hair. His eyes shifted from some undisclosed spot on the floor to another, flickering back and forth as he processed. His gaze finally lifted, meeting Fallon's once more. "Where have you been all this time? Why didn't you . . . come to find me or reach out somehow?" Ryker glanced at me, looking for answers but finding more questions instead. His eyes narrowed in on my bludgeoned nose. "And what in the Spirit Realm happened to you?"

"I think you'd better take a seat," I answered with a sigh, gesturing to one of the chairs—the standing one, not the one that Fallon had knocked over in her haste to punch me.

My thoughts flashed back to that night, just before we reached Cent—*One of the best female fighters I've ever gone hand to hand with. I still have the scar to prove it.* Harper's voice replayed in my mind, an image of her tipping her chin up to show the discolored scar following seconds after. I tested a wiggle on my throbbing nose, double-checking to make sure it wasn't broken. Harper wasn't kidding—Fallon knew how to land a blow.

Ryker closed the door behind him, then turned back to us. "I don't have much time. The other guard just left to go to the kitchen for his meal break. He'll be back shortly."

I turned to Fallon, the slightest of snarls on my lips. "Then I guess you better get started."

When we were all seated—Kaleb and I on the bed while Fallon and Ryker sat on either side of the small table—I introduced Ryker and Kaleb to one another while I blotted my nose with a blood-soaked tea towel. I looked at Fallon, visually handing her the reins.

"It's good to see you again," she started, her fingers fiddling in her lap. For the first time since I'd met her a wee few hours ago, she looked unsure of herself. I noted that her right hand was beginning to show bruising around the knuckles.

I bit back a smirk. Apparently, I wasn't the only one leaving our battle unscathed.

Good.

"I can hardly believe I'm seeing you at all." Ryker's voice hit a sonorous low, the kind that comes from deep in the chest, like it was spoken more for himself than anyone else. "That night . . . what happened?"

She took a deep breath, her petite but leanly muscled shoulders rising in response. Upon her exhale, she began, "After we made our plan and you left to find the Crown of Thorns, a woman showed up. I had seen her with the people you referred to as the Elders and so I believed that she was one of them. She said something about things not moving fast enough, that they didn't have a week to waste. She had the guards open the cell door, then snarled at me that she was taking matters into her own hands. I realized she had come to break the unconscious mind barrier."

Ryker's fists clenched, a potent darkness swirling around him, making the fire twin appear menacing. The muscle in his jaw feathered so violently, it was a wonder it didn't pop out of his rich, brown skin.

She looked up from her hands but didn't stop wringing

them as she met Ryker's gaze. "You must understand that at that time, I had been raised to fear the Cursed. It's what had been ingrained in my mind since I was a child. Also, I had heard horrific stories of what happened to people who had the unconscious mind barrier broken. I feared what the Elders would do, of the information they would find inside my mind relating to the king and the rest of his army—my brethren. So . . . I made a choice—I would protect my people, even if it cost me my life."

The room was so quiet, you could have heard one of the dressmaker's pins strike the floor.

"I didn't think about it," Fallon continued. "Before she could sink her claws into my mind, I just . . . moved. I grabbed the dagger she had hanging on her belt and sacrificed myself for something I believed, at the time, was the greater good." Her gaze lifted. "Von was the one who collected my soul that night."

We all sat there in stunned silence. Even Kaleb, who had most likely heard this before, looked distraught.

As for Ryker? He looked beside himself.

"And now you are among those who walk in the Spirit Realm," Ryker said sorrowfully. "I never should have left you that night," he whispered, his voice cracking apart, a direct reflection of what was happening on the inside.

"No!" Fallon dismissed his claim. "That was *my* path that I was fated to walk. My time in the Living Realm was meant to end that day. And even though I didn't understand that at the time, unconsciously, I did. Despite what mortals believe, no one can outrun their fate. And that was mine. I have made peace with it, and I know it's a lot to hear, but I—"

her voice softened, "—I want you to do the same."

Ryker shook his head. "How am I supposed to make peace with the fact I was the one that abducted you, took you back to the Cursed Lands, and ultimately, it was my actions that cost you your life?"

I swallowed. Hard.

I understood Ryker's feelings because I had felt the same way when it came to Kaleb's death—I had blamed myself for what happened to him. I lowered the soaked rag and peered at the crimson that coated my fingers—my hands stained with blood.

The message was not lost on me.

"That was *my fate*, Ryker!" Fallon exclaimed. "It was spun by the goddess herself, and it was something neither you nor I could outrun. I have long since moved on from that day. Again, I ask you to do the same because it is not worth wasting breath on. What's done is done."

Ryker scoffed. "Not worth wasting breath on? *You died.* Because of *me*." He stood up, shaking his head. "I need a minute." Without another word, he walked towards the balcony and then out into the blistering cold, shutting the door behind him.

The cool air swept inside, nibbling at my skin, turning it to gooseflesh. I tugged my arms around myself and got up, about to go after him.

"I'll go," Fallon sighed. "It's between us anyway."

I didn't disagree, even though part of me wanted to comfort my friend. I nodded and watched her walk out after him, her departure causing the room to lower another degree.

I tossed the bloody rag on my bedstand and made my

way over to the fireplace. Looking down, I stared at the blackened carcass of a fire-chewed log—one touch from the tip of an iron poking stick and the log would crumble into a pile of ash and embers.

Busying himself, Kaleb grabbed a few logs from an open chest and began to place them in the fire—the action reminding me of old times.

A lump formed in my throat, realization dawning that those simple cottage days had come to pass. Like Fallon, Kaleb was no longer a part of this realm. And like Ryker, I, too, blamed myself for it.

"I'm sorry, Kaleb," I said, watching as he placed the last log on the fire. It didn't take long for the glowing bed of embers to chew into the wood and make it ignite.

He dusted his hands and turned from his squatted position to look up at me. A blond brow hung curiously low. "For what?"

"If I hadn't jumped up that day in such haste to get you to see me, you probably would still be here, in this realm," I said, crossing my arms loosely over my chest. I chewed on a part of my cheek. Blame had been my initial reaction after Kaleb's death. I had hated myself for what I had done. I had never really dealt with those emotions, I'd just put them in a box and tucked them away.

Kaleb shot me a look, like he couldn't believe what I had just said. "Are you kidding me? What else were you supposed to do? Sit in the shadows and wait for me to run back into the camp where my life was probably going to end anyway? If things had been reversed, I would have been frantic to get to you." He nodded his head. "I would have done the exact same thing, so don't you ever blame yourself for that."

I fell silent.

After a moment, he bumped his shoulder against mine. "Besides, you are not the asshat who fired that arrow."

His playful action accompanied by his word choice stirred a chuckle from me. "No, I suppose not." I paused, my smile fading. "Although I—"

"Sage," he cut me off, leveling my gaze. "You are *not* responsible for my death. No more than Ryker was for Fallon's. She's right. The Goddess of Fate weaves our paths, and we have no choice but to walk them."

"I don't completely agree with that."

"Which part?"

"That we have no choice but to go along with what the Goddess of Fate has decided is right for us."

"Says the Goddess of Life." Kaleb smirked at me.

I rolled my eyes.

The air shifted, the light laugh lines on Kaleb's face drifting away as his smile receded. He sighed through his nose. "Tonight didn't exactly go as I had planned."

I gestured to my busted nose, the blood on my face now dried and crusty. "Me either."

Kaleb chuckled. "You gotta admit, she can throw a punch."

I teetered my head from side to side, before I replied, "Yeah, okay, I'll give her that."

"I was hoping you two would get off to a better start, especially because I—" He took a hesitant pause, further garnishing my attention. "I was thinking of asking her to marry me. But now?" He glanced at the balcony doors, where

Ryker and Fallon were conversing in private, their history a tangled mess in deep need of brushing. "I don't know anymore."

I nibbled on my bottom lip, recalling the ring I had tucked away, hidden in the bottom drawer of the smaller armoire. The day Arkyn took me back to the cottage to grab a few things, I had grabbed it so that I could keep a part of Kaleb with me. Although I wasn't exactly Fallon's biggest fan, the timing of Kaleb's intended proposal accompanied by the memory of Ezra's words propelled me forward.

You keep it safe until you can return it, her voice said in my mind.

Like always, Ezra knew things she shouldn't. I decided to trust her on this.

"There's something I need to give to you," I told him.

A short few moments later, I retrieved the thin gold band with the glittering oval sapphire. I turned to Kaleb and handed him the ring. It looked so small, so dainty in his cracked palm.

He stared at it, eyes chock-full of wonder. "Why are you giving me this?"

"Because it's yours," I said softly. "It's your mother's engagement ring and she wanted you to have it." Then I told him the story Ezra had shared with me—about his mother.

CHAPTER 34

Von

*C*link. Clink.
Clink.

. . . That third clink was new. A second cup. But for who?

"Come on in, Little Bird, don't be shy," Folkoln toyed like a cat with a mouse. He sat down in the chair beside me. His usual spot.

Light footsteps sounded from the door, walking towards me.

"Can he hear me?" Fallon asked softly. Curiously.

"He can," my brother answered.

"But how do you know?"

"Come here." It was a soft command. His leather jacket crinkled as he raised his arm. "Take my hand and I will show you."

"Okay," she answered wearily.

Skin brushed upon skin.

"Good girl," he praised. "Now, tell your *king* what you *did* to his mate."

"Folkoln," she attested, her voice desperate.

"*Now*, Little Bird."

"Fine," she huffed. "Things got out of hand and I . . . I punched her in the face. But I don't think I broke her nose."

She did what?

Anger boiled in my bloodless veins.

Earlier, I had felt an outburst of anger and a flash of pain from my mate. Now I knew what—or rather *who*—had caused it.

"Holy fuck!" Fallon cried out. Bony knees struck the floor—one falling quickly after the other. "I am so sorry."

Folkoln chuckled. "See? Just as I said. He can hear us."

Fallon didn't reply, too busy groveling beside me. Her words fell on deaf ears. Not because I didn't care about her useless apologies—well, actually I didn't care—but because I could feel my brother latching on to the tasty meal I was currently serving him. I cut the tether to my anger.

He let out a sigh. "Well, that was short-lived. Anyway, tell him what else you told me."

I waited.

"That the God of Life removed her collar?" she asked, somewhat unsure.

"Bingo."

Of course, the prick had removed it.

And as always, he was as predictable as ever.

Despite how I made it appear when I planted the idea that Sage should ask Aurelius to remove it, I knew he wouldn't say no. If he did, it would make it look like he didn't trust her and that would be damaging to his princely charade.

So, he'd agreed.

Just like I knew he would.

Now that the iron collar was gone, Sage could harness her powers if she needed to. At least she wouldn't be completely unprotected.

Still, worry plagued me.

"Is he still angry with me?" Fallon asked my brother.

"Hard to say." A cork popped.

Fallon let out an aggravated groan.

The bottle glugged, paused, and then resumed. After, glass chattered against cement.

"Have a drink, Little Bird. It will ease your nerves." The smirk he wore saturated his words.

"Alright," she said, soft fingertips whispering against the glass. She took a sip.

"Earlier, you mentioned you wanted to speak to me about something. What is it?" Folkoln asked as he took the remaining cup from beside my head—the jackass.

"The Blade of Moram—"

He cut her off. "We've already discussed that."

"You barely told me anything about it."

"I have my reasons." Two gulps were all it took for him to down his glass—that fucker had a big mouth. Much like my own.

"But if it can help Von—"

"Fallon, you will stay out of this."

"But if you enlisted the aid of the reapers, had them help in your search—"

Folkoln laughed. "Tell hundreds of people that there is a weapon so powerful it can break an unbreakable deal forged by the God of Death himself? I'm sure that information would light a fire under their asses to look for it, but what would they do *if* they did find it? Sure, some of the loyal ones would use it to save Von, but not all of them would. Some would use it for their own means. So no, I will not be enlisting the help of the reapers."

"Then what do I tell Kaleb? He keeps bringing it up and I just keep pushing the topic off, saying I haven't gotten a chance to speak with you yet."

"*That* is not my problem," Folkoln said, the click in his knee sounding.

"Wait, where are you going?" Fallon padded after him.

His nearly silent steps stopped. "Well, since you are no longer on the menu, I'm going to find someone else who is."

"Folkoln, I know things have been—"

"Save it, Little Bird. We had an understanding between the two of us, yes? It was just sex, nothing more. I am not like your complicated mortal lovers, so don't try to make me out as one." His tone shifted from boredom to intrigue. "By the way, how *is* that going?"

Fallon drew out a long breath. "I don't know. I didn't expect to have feelings for Ryker anymore, but when I saw him . . . they were still there."

So the paths of the two old lovers had finally crossed. I had wondered when that would finally happen.

"Sounds messy." Folkoln chuckled. "Well, good luck with that."

And then he was gone, shadow walking out of the room.

Leaving me and one confused little reaper.

Years ago, after I'd brought Fallon's soul to the Spirit Realm, along with the Crown of Thorns, I'd told her many times that she should speak to Ryker, but she refused. Instead, she pushed her feelings to the side—acting as though they meant nothing.

Now, she was going to be forced to face them, whether she wanted to or not.

Just as I would have to face my sister, an altercation that would likely end in bloodshed, but what else could be expected when Saphira had betrayed me yet again? After all this time, *she* was the one who'd *stolen* the Crown of Thorns—the very thing that could end my mate's life—and knowingly delivered it right into my enemy's hands.

CHAPTER 35

Sage

If I didn't know any better, I would think a bear had wrapped its massive paws around my waist and now it was trying its damnedest to squeeze the very life from me. At least, that's what it felt like with Brunhilde at the helm, cinching me smaller with the constrictive corset, inch by breath-taking inch. Last night, before she left, Cataline said she would come early this morning so that she could tie the corset in place of Brunhilde—granting my poor rib cage a fraction of relief. Yet, she hadn't arrived this morning, which was unlike her.

"Is Cataline unwell?" I asked as I held on to the bed's corner pillar, my fingers locked tightly around it as I tried to hold my ground.

"I'm afraid Cataline won't be tending you anymore, my lady." Brunhilde grunted the last two words as she wrenched on the cord, sucking me in another inch.

"Oh?" That was news to me. My brows lifted. "Why is that?"

"Her family sent word that they wished for her to return to their estate, immediately," she answered with ease, as if we were discussing what she ate for breakfast. "From my understanding, she has already left."

I was a bit sad to hear that Cataline had left without saying goodbye. We weren't nearly as close as Harper and me, but I had believed that we were starting to form a friendship.

"But never fear, my lady, we'll find another lady's maid to tend to you," Brunhilde chattered on, before she started telling me what was planned for the day. While she did, I became lost in my own thoughts, processing last night.

Ryker and Fallon had spoken for hours while Kaleb and I waited inside. In the early hours of the morning, after Kaleb and Fallon left, I told the young, half-asleep guard that I thought I heard something coming from the balcony. As he inspected it, Ryker snuck out into the hallway.

I felt for Ryker. The revelations of last night were a . . . lot.

After years of wondering what had happened to the girl he loved, he finally had an answer. She was alive—well, sort of. I don't know what all they had spoken of while they were outside, but judging by the looks of Ryker's weary eyes when they returned inside, it had been a painful conversation.

And then there was Kaleb. He wanted to ask Fallon to marry him. But now that Ryker was thrown back into the mix, would that change things?

Brunhilde patted my hips, signaling she was finished. "All good, my lady. I suppose we should be on our way to morning praise. Naevia, please fetch my lady her shoes."

Morning praise—Aurelius would be there.

I hated how things had ended between us yesterday, and I needed to tell him as much.

Knock. Knock. Knock.

Was that him? My heart quickened.

I didn't wait for Brunhilde to get the door—I rushed to it, the stiff fabric of my skirts brushing against one another as I moved. When I opened it, my smile faltered.

"Aurelia," Arkyn said by way of greeting. Sunlight filtered in through the arched window at the end of the hallway, shining on Arkyn. For the briefest of moments, under the gaze of the sun, he almost looked like Aurelius. He produced a wax-sealed letter from an inside coat pocket and handed it to me. "Aurelius asked me to give you this."

I took it, cracked the golden seal, embossed with an elegant *A*, and unfolded the letter.

Aurelia,

First and foremost, please consider this my formal apology for inquiring about something I had no right to ask about. I am sorry, Moonbeam. Please forgive me.

Secondly, I have urgent business in the countryside, which means I will not be around for a little while. I would have preferred to say this all to you in person, but alas, time would not grant me that this morning.

Please do not do anything to infuriate the king while I am gone—my protection for you only goes so far with him.
I will see you upon my return.
Yours,
Aurelius

I crumpled the lackluster letter, frustration mounting. "That's how he wishes to leave things between us? A formal written apology?" I glared at Arkyn. "When is he going to be back?"

"If we can get away at a decent time today, then I imagine two to three weeks," he answered, dusting something off his pristine jacket.

"Two to three *weeks*?" I exclaimed, trying my best not to blow my top. He was going to leave things *like this* for two to three *weeks*?! I felt like breaking something. But before I could decide what, my racing mind backed itself up. "What do you mean *if we* can get away at a decent time?"

We implied Arkyn was leaving as well, and as Arkyn was still here, it meant that Aurelius hadn't left yet.

"I will be traveling with Aurelius. Soren will be coming along with us as well."

I shoved against his chest, trying to turn him around. "Take me to him."

His immortal bones turned to cement. "Aurelia, he is very busy and—"

"*Now*, Arkyn," I demanded, my voice echoing around me with sublime power.

We both exchanged knowing expressions—oh yes, that

command had come from the goddess within.

"Fine," he sighed as he turned, starting down the hallway.

I followed him, Brunhilde shouting behind me about my shoes. I ignored her and pressed on.

Half an hour later, we reached the castle's grand front entrance. A string of carriages and carts lined the snow-packed road, expanding into the horizon—I had never seen so many carriages before.

"Are the king and queen traveling as well?" I asked Arkyn, the snow-covered ground melting beneath my feet, making my lacy hose stick to it. I was beginning to regret my decision not to take the shoes Brunhilde had tried to chase me down with.

"No, they are not," he answered. "This trip is solely for—"

"Aurelia?" a regal voice asked from behind me, gilded in nobility but made of something so sensual it made my bones ache.

I turned, following the voice.

Golden eyes met mine. Dressed in regal clothes and looking every ounce of the king of the New Gods—Aurelius.

Despite my anger, my heart kicked wildly in my chest.

If the Creator had placed their brush in my hand and told me to paint the key to my heart, I would have painted him just as he looked right now.

Like the seeds of a dandelion kissed by the wind, my anger began to dissipate—piece by piece, it flew away. My clenched fist—the one holding his crumpled letter—slackened.

We walked towards one another, stopping but a breath away.

I lifted my hand, showing him the scrunched paper. "I got your letter."

"I see that," he said, his hands not moving from his sides, not reaching for me.

How I wished that they would.

"You were just going to leave?" I said, my neck bending so that I could look up at him. The sun, positioned directly behind his head, illuminated his ethereal handsomeness, making it seem like he was glowing. My eyes flickered between his, waiting for an answer.

"I was." He drew out the two words in his rich, noble tone. "I thought that is what you needed from me."

I shook my head. "What I needed from you was to come speak with me."

A mousy-looking man walked up to us. He etched a bow before he said, "Pardon me, Your Royal Highness, but we are ready to—"

Aurelius held up a hand, silencing him. "I do not have much time, but we can speak now, if you wish."

I glanced at the lineup of carriages and the coachmen standing beside them—all of them waiting to depart. All of them . . . waiting on us.

I let out a sigh. "It's alright." *It wasn't.* "We can speak when you return."

"I can clearly see that it is *not* alright." He snatched my hand and gave it a gentle tug, pulling me behind him.

"Aurelius, where are we going?" I asked, my frozen feet trying to keep up with his.

He glanced over his shoulder, his lips twisted sensually. "We're going to talk."

"But your trip—"

"Can wait. For the time being."

He led me back into the castle, charging for the closest door to us, throwing it open and pulling me inside.

I blinked.

Buckets, mops, wooden carts, and various other cleaning supplies littered the sizable storage room, as well as wood shelves that lined the walls. A wood table sat in the middle— mostly clean, other than a few wash rags and unlit brass candlesticks.

Two young maids looked up at us, gawking. They bowed immediately, addressing Aurelius by his princely title.

"Out," he commanded.

One word. That was all it took to send them scattering— much like the rats this castle was rumored to be infested with. A rumor I suspected to be exactly just that, considering I had yet to see one—well, apart from the king.

When the door swung closed and it was just me and Aurelius left, he removed his robe and draped it over the back of a wooden chair. The act was telling. Did he think we were going to be here for a while?

He turned to me, gestured to the quiet room. "The floor is yours."

CHAPTER 36

Sage

"I don't really know where to start," I replied honestly, my gaze shifting between two random inky splotches on the floor. Probably from some type of wood stain. If Brunhilde was a maid working out of this room, she'd have the floor scrubbed spotless.

"Then let me," Aurelius said, his long, powerful legs closing the distance between us. Gently, he clasped my face, his gaze a lure, catching mine. "I apologize for my actions."

"I hear your apology, but . . ." I took a breath.

"But what?"

Although I was tempted to reach for him, to wrap my hands around his sturdy forearms, I didn't. "You burned an entire hallway, Aurelius."

"I did," he acknowledged with a single nod.

"You are lucky that no one was hurt." My tone was firm.

"I don't think you can say that. My actions hurt *you*." One hand slipped from my face, settling over my left breast, above my heart. "My actions hurt *this*." He sighed through his nose. "My temper got the better of me, Moonbeam."

Yes, it sure had. But it wasn't the first time . . .

"Just like you lost it the night you bit me." Anger wove its way into my words.

He broke contact with me, taking a step back. "I thought we were past that?"

"I thought we were as well. But then you did this and—"

Rrrrip.

Aurelius tore the collar of his tunic, exposing his purely male neck and a peek of the muscle brooding beneath. Molten eyes met mine. "Then do as the goddess in you so clearly needs to do. Take back what I took from you."

"What?" I sputtered, sawing air. In and out. Whether my breathless state was because of the raw sexiness of seeing Aurelius rip his clothing or what he said, I didn't know. Regardless, if I knew one thing, it was that I was no longer thinking with my head . . .

"Bite me back," he demanded.

My *teeth* in his *neck*?

The thought was enough to get the goddess within to awaken from her slumber. And awaken she did. I heaved a deep breath, my chest swelling against the tight confines of my dress.

A hungry fire blazed in Aurelius's eyes. I wondered if he saw the same one that had suddenly been lit within my own.

"Well?" he asked, the word spoken in such a way that it could make an elite courtesan fall to her knees and beg for *it*.

"No," I answered, my breath shaky. Unsure.

"No?" he challenged.

Creator above, this male.

I pressed my thighs together, all too aware of the ache building there.

He guided me backward until the table chewed into the backs of my thighs. He stepped into me, securing me there, the iron tucked beneath his pants pressed into my stomach.

I glanced down. We both did.

He lowered his head, his heated breath skittering over my ear. "You are either going to sink your teeth into me, or—" he cupped my sex, "—I'm going to sink my cock into you." He pulled back, just enough so that I could see the sensual grin on his divine lips. "The choice is yours."

His words were like embers upon my skin—stirring a sickness to surface. A fever. And there was only one way to break it.

My hand dipped over top of his, tightening his hold.

"This," I said, my voice husky. Breathy. Needy.

"Very well, princess." He slid his hand from my sex to the neckline of my dress. He tore my clothes off like they were made of paper, shredding through the layers of fabric and steel-boned corset. He threw the torn remains of my dress to the side, leaving only the lacy, white hose on.

I started to remove them, but his hand fell over mine—stopping me from doing so—he lifted me onto the table. "Keep them on," he said with a hint of a smile.

I raised a curious brow but didn't ask why. Instead, I watched. Watched as his hand trailed between my breasts, down my torso, over the lace hose, stopping at the sensitive bundle of nerves. The length of his nail sharpened into a deadly, sharp point. He pressed it against me, and I let out a gasp at the strange, unexpected sensation—my nerves flaring alive with both panic and . . . excitement.

It was like having the tip of a knife pressed against me. It was an erotic sight, something so dangerous pressed against something so delicate. A dance of trust.

Slowly, precisely, he slid his finger down, tracing my slit while cutting the hose along the seam. The fabric curled back, exposing my core to him. Sinfully wet.

Those golden eyes had never looked so greedy. They flicked up to mine.

"You are flawless," he said, tearing off his already torn tunic, just as he had done with my dress, and discarded the cloth on the floor. He undid his belt, the metal rattling as he moved on to his pants, working on the buttons. His length erupted—hard and thick and huge. And ready.

I throbbed at the mere sight of him, clenching at nothing to the extent that it was almost painful. I needed him between my legs. I licked my lips.

"Do you want to taste me?"

I nodded.

He stroked himself, the muscles in his powerful forearm as taut as the silky skin wrapped around his cock. He took a step back. "Then come and taste."

I slid off the table, our heated gazes never leaving one another's as I lowered to my knees before him. My hands slid up his powerful thighs while his hand wove into my hair. He held himself, guiding it against my mouth. His broad tip traced my lips, leaving a bead of wetness on them. I licked it, tasting the salty-sweetness of him—the mere act had his hand tightening. He nudged against my mouth, and I opened for him, not entirely sure how *all of that* was going to fit, and yet, I was willing to try. Angling himself, he slid his sleek, thick length into my mouth—filling it, inch by inch until I choked, too full of him.

He pulled back, but not out.

"Breathe through your nose, princess," he commanded softly.

I did. I focused on directing the air through my nose, relaxing myself.

He used my hair as leverage as he pressed himself back in.

For other men I had been with, I would suck in my cheeks to tighten around them, but for Aurelius, I did *not* have to do that, because the immortal filled my mouth, and to answer my prior question—*no*, it definitely *was not* going to fit. Which meant I would need to bring the unattended part of him pleasure . . . in other ways.

I reached for the handful of length that wasn't inside my mouth, feeling his smooth shaft, corded in prominent veins, as he bobbed his hips at a leisurely pace. I raked my nails along it, stirring a powerful thrust from him that sent him deeper than before.

"That's it, *Little Goddess*, show me how *deep* you can take me," purred an unmistakable *voice*. Bourbon and smoke and leather.

Confusion and panic stretched my eyes wide. I looked up, past the vast expanse of chiseled, perfect abs and labyrinth of messy, inky tattoos, right into the endlessly black eyes of the male I had once promised everything to—

Von.

No. I was imagining things. I had to be.

I closed my eyes, willing the fake phantom to leave, focusing on the feel of Aurelius's length in my mouth—but even *that* felt bigger now.

"Such a good girl," Von rumbled, snapping my attention back up to him.

His towering, dark phantom was *still* there—a wicked smile curling the left side of his mouth. The epitome of cocky arrogance and elite dominance was written plainly on his face—a face that was devastatingly handsome and framed by untethered, long, black hair.

Warrior. Predator. Commander.

King.

His gaze dropped to my hands, wrapped around *his* incredible length.

"Tsk, tsk. *That* is cheating." Cold rings bit harshly into my wrists, his one hand cuffing them. He raised my hands above my head, the backs of my forearms pressing against the steely hardness of his abs. The position rendered me as a person of worship, kneeling on his dark altar, hands raised in subservience. Prickling pain stung the back of my head as he tightened his grasp on my hair. The length I had been holding on to started to disappear inside my mouth, and my moans turned inward.

Gods, he was *huge.*

Unfathomable.

And even though I hated the bastard, I could not deny how completely divine he felt in my mouth. And if I really was just imagining this, then what was the harm in proceeding anyway?

When he pulled back, I grazed my teeth along his shaft, coaxing a powerful growl from him. "Fuck, Sage."

Hearing him growl my name like that, it was all the encouragement I needed.

I did it again and again. Until he was roaring.

He slammed his hips forward and I swallowed every inch he forced me to take, accepting anything the God of Death would give me. He picked up speed—his strong, powerful hips bucking as he *claimed* my mouth, my throat. Animalistic sounds came out of us both.

My lungs rattled in my chest, my legs trembling beneath me. The air became charged, like a storm on the horizon. His pace was relentless, like cannon fire going off in my mouth—exploding my senses.

He grunted and pulled out, springing free from my mouth. A string of saliva stretched between us. It snapped, trailing down my chin and neck.

Greedily, I gulped down mouthfuls of air as he hauled me to my feet.

His grasp tightened in my hair, angling my head so that my neck was exposed to him. Dipping his head, his thick, wet tongue traced the string of saliva, licking it up in one, solid sweep, until his mouth was on mine.

The obscene act of him licking me *like that* resulted in a clash of tongue and teeth and hands. I grabbed at him while his massive hands latched on to my ass, squeezing it roughly—passionately.

There was no warring for dominance this time because

his mouth outright commanded mine, like he knew exactly how I needed to be kissed—not soft or sweet, but fast and rapturous. Like it was going to be our last one before the world fell in.

His tongue carved *his* black magic in my mouth.

Inking it in his colors.

Claiming it as his.

I panted as I tried to keep up with him—the dark god was a force to be reckoned with.

When he broke the kiss, when he stole his lips from mine, I whimpered like a helpless animal.

His voice was in my ear, whispering darkly, "Are you wet for me?" His hand dipped between our bodies, to the apex of my quaking thighs. His finger slid in, along with the cool, bulky metal of his skull ring. I cursed at the unreal feel of it—of him—*checking* my readiness.

He pulled his finger out, bringing the glistening digit up for both of us to see—coated in his answer.

"You're soaked, Kitten," he mused, before he licked his finger clean—ring and all—with that impossibly long, thick, muscular tongue. His eyes stayed fixed on mine the entire time.

Seeing him do that painted me ten shades of dizzy. My arms laced around his neck as he dragged me into him, sweeping my feet from the floor and wrapping my legs around him. His tongue invaded my mouth as he walked us over to the table. He set me on it—the cool, harsh wood pressing against my backside.

"I need to feel you inside of me." I reached for his abdomen, the ink dissolving as soon as my fingers touched

289

him.

"Then spread for me, wife," Aurelius said, his hips wedged between my thighs.

What the—

Aurelius's fingers swirled that sensitive bundle of nerves, coaxing a moan from me. He parted my lips, running his smooth crown along my sex. He positioned himself at my entrance—

"Eyes on me," Von snarled ruthlessly from behind me, his hand wrapping around my throat. He dragged me backwards so that I was lying on the table.

I blinked. Confused. Dazed. Out of my mind.

Von's cock stood proudly beside my head, thick veins protruding. Creator above, it was massive. Even by immortal standards. I doubted I could make my fingers touch if I were to wrap my hand around it.

"Open," Von commanded.

A bead of wetness formed on his crown, and I licked my lips, dying for another taste.

I opened my mouth for him.

"That's my good girl," he praised as he sunk himself into my mouth at the exact same time Aurelius pressed into my sex.

I cried out but the sound was smothered.

White fire burned at my entrance as I was stretched, forced to accommodate what was being pressed into me. I tried to look, but Von's massive hand wrapped around my neck kept me pinned to the table.

"The veil I've placed over us prevents him from seeing me or what I'm doing to you, but it cannot prevent what you feel. You might feel him fucking you—" Von growled, the blackness of his irises spreading like a bottle of spilt ink, "—but your attention stays on me."

His hand tightened around my throat as he pumped himself inside my mouth. All the while, my body felt the intruder down below, forcing it to widen.

Aurelius sunk himself so deeply that I squirmed, my body attempting to relieve the tight, full sensation. His hands turned crushing against my hips, keeping me there as he forced me to take what he was giving. He pulled out nearly to the hilt before he slammed himself back in again. He repeated this process, breaking me in. *Molding me for him.*

"Molding *you for him*?" Von chuckled, the sound snatching me from my thoughts. I looked up, meeting his gaze as he worked my mouth. He pressed himself further in—further than he had before—my eyes flaring wide. "If that's the case, I sure am going to enjoy breaking the mold."

A strange sound emitted from my throat—one I had no words for.

Dizzy, my eyes rolled back in my head as the two males stroked my body towards oblivion. One in my mouth. And one in my sex.

When I thought of what was happening to me, I nearly orgasmed.

Aurelius struck that feel-good spot inside of me while his thumb worked the feel-good spot on the outside—that sacred, incredible spot that had me threatening to visit the stars. If I could have praised his name, I would have—but with Von in my mouth, that was impossible.

"Do you know what I'm going to do for this betrayal,

Little Goddess?" Von asked as he released his hand from my throat, moving on to my breasts. His large hands swallowed them whole. "I'm going to ink these by hand," he said, voice like gravel as he pumped in and out of my mouth. "Force you to wear *my* markings on them."

Oh fuck. That had no right to sound as delicious as it did.

"And as for these?" He pinched a nipple, wrangling a deep, throaty sound from me. "I'll pierce them with my silver."

He was going to . . . *tattoo me by hand? . . . Pierce me? Fuck.*

"Now come *for me*, little betrayer," he rumbled in command.

My orgasm slammed into me at a cataclysmic speed— hurtling me over the edge. It took me in one sweeping wave, drowning me on the spot—leaving me sputtering and gasping for air.

Aurelius roared, his scalding-hot seed spurting inside of me as he came.

At the same time, Von pulled out from my mouth, a snarl on his lips.

I panted for air. My vision was speckled with stars.

Von's breath tickled my ear as he whispered, "As for that prick that's inside of you right now, do you know what I'm going to do with it?"

Half with it, I shook my head, my body trembling in the aftermath of my orgasm.

He chuckled darkly. "I'm going to cut it off and feed it to my hounds, darling. And while my beasts eat, I will have you bent over the railing that overlooks their domain, screaming my name as *I devour your cunt.*"

And then his phantom was gone.

After Aurelius and I said our goodbyes, I watched as the carriages pulled away, the horses' hooves clacking rhythmically. I tugged the fur shawl tighter around my shoulders, trying to keep the creeping cold from sinking into my bones. I was thankful for the leather shoes I was wearing, something Aurelius had instructed one of the maids to retrieve for me after our little rendezvous, along with the dress and shawl I wore.

Although my thoughts should be on the departure of Aurelius, they were not. They were stuck on *the bastard.*

Stuck on what he'd said he would do . . .

I'm going to ink these by hand. Force you to wear my markings on them. And as for these? I'll pierce them with my silver, his voice replayed in my mind. A shiver ran down the length of my back, as if a pair of knuckles—*his knuckles*—were being dragged along it.

I glanced over my shoulder, expecting to see his towering phantom standing behind me, but he wasn't there.

And I didn't know what infuriated me more—the fact that I was stupid enough to desire the male who had taken my ability to create, or the fact that the bastard wasn't here, making good on that claim of his.

My nipples strained against the tight confines of my

corset.

Ugh.

He shouldn't have this control over me.

I tromped back towards the castle, purposefully kicking a small rock in my path. It skittered pitifully to the side, increasing my frustration.

The wind howled with laughter.

CHAPTER 37

Von

Feeling your mate's emotions as she gets off because of another man was a type of torture I wouldn't wish upon anyone. I'd rather have my fingers hacked off inch by inch, starting at the tips than feel *that* emotion from her again.

Sure, I had drowned myself in bourbon when I felt her screwing some idiot from Meristone, but this time, I didn't have that option, and knowing that it was the God of Life she was willingly fucking made it that much worse. And the fact that she *chose* to do it, *without* his ichor swaying her this time? It struck a primal chord.

So, I went to her with one goal—*her pleasure* would *be mine*, even if it killed me.

In doing so, I had chewed through the last remnants of my power—meaning I had cut myself off from her completely.

I couldn't feel her emotions anymore, and my phantom

form was no longer something I could access. That meant I couldn't help her. The thought made my stomach cave in, because for the next little while, my mate would be completely on her own.

And she still had so much left to remember . . .

I leaned against the trunk of an apple tree, my bootheel kicked against it and my arms threaded loosely over my chest. My shadows drifted around me, cloaking me from the light of the full moon. A gentle breeze stirred the air, rustling the canopy of leaves that hung above me. In the distance, fox kits chattered with one another, their high-pitched barking and baby-like wails an eerie late-night melody. The piercing howl of a wolf lurking nearby silenced the young foxes within seconds.

My eyes were fixed on a set of arched windows on the second floor of the Golden Palace.

*I was waiting—*waiting*—to get a glimpse of her.*

Behind me, our *orchard spanned for miles, blanketing the land in a densely packed layer of apple trees. They served as my silent army, each one of them acting like a wooden soldier—fighting on my behalf, reclaiming* my *territory. They were born from the seeds I had given her over the decades and now their numbers were in the thousands.*

Seed discord among the New Gods, *the Goddess of Fate had once told me.* That *was what I needed to do to win the war.*

So, I'd done just that.

I'd taken away the very thing the King of the New Gods planned to do with the goddess he had made for himself. I'd taken away the Goddess of Life's ability to create—plants, animals . . . children.

I wasn't sorry for it.

Knowing what he did when she had her back turned, I'd saved her more than she would ever know. Like taking my sister's wings, this was also a necessary evil. What I took from her ensured her the ability to live a life, instead of being treated like a factory for it.

If he were to be honest with her about his side activities, I'm certain the fiery little temptress would not stand for it.

An unfamiliar feeling swelled within me at the mere thought of her. Despite how hard I tried, I did not have a name for it. It was an obsession, a fixation. A sickness of my own.

Had the parasite I planted within their lives turned around and burrowed into mine? I looked at the window in her room, waiting to see her. The fact that I was here confirmed what I already suspected—the parasite had clawed its way inside me too. I bit back a growl that threatened to dislodge from my chest.

How dare she bewitch me. I was the God of Death. I was supposed to be immune to poisonous things.

When this was all over, when I won the war, I would end this sickness she had planted within me. My nostrils flared. I would rid myself of her. Permanently.

At that moment, she came into view.

She held a section of her silk hair, the color of freshly

fallen snow, gently brushing it. Her porcelain skin glowed just as vividly as Luna above. I knew, from the times my fingers had grazed her skin, how luxurious it was . . . how soft—how easy it would be to sign my handprint on her ass. She wore a lacy, white nightgown that left little to the imagination—it held tightly to her supple curves, diving low between her breasts, the slit nearly reaching her belly button. The fabric was so thin, it wasn't hard to make out the fullness of her breasts, or the pink buds of her nipples pebbling through. They were divine as it were, but when I thought of stringing a chain between them and using it to pull her towards me . . . using it to lead her on her hands and knees towards my throne—

I stifled a groan.

Tension riddled my muscles, stitching them tight. I glanced down—that wasn't the only thing that was stitched tight. Damn pants.

I cracked my neck, but it did little to help. When it came to her, nothing helped.

She studied the sprawling orchard, a smile caressing her lovely little mouth. Great divine, that mouth—*the things I could do with it, to it. She did this every night—she came to the window while brushing her hair and looked at the sea of green, dotted with red fruit. She took pride in what she'd created—it was evident in the time she spent in the orchard during the day.*

Oh yes, I watched her during the day as well—without her knowing, of course.

I had never met a goddess who was so . . . hands on. Most would have just used their magic to tend the orchard, but not her—she was always so eager to get her hands dirty, just like a mortal would. Unlike the rest of the high and mighty pricks that walked around this place, acting like they didn't have shit balls stuck between their cheeks.

Her smile faded and she turned around, her back facing me.

I knew why she concealed her smile and the joy the orchard brought her—it was to spare her husband's precious feelings. I blew out a mocking breath of air, a smirk catching on my lips. As if he didn't know. She spent more time in the orchard than she did in the castle.

He entered the large frame of the window, giving me view of them both. He proved the limited brain cells he had when he didn't take the lovely little female in his arms—something I would have done if the roles had been reversed. I would have done so much more than just take her in my arms . . . I would have noticed how scantily she'd dressed herself tonight, shredded the clothes off her body with a snap of my teeth, twirled her around, and pleasured her against the window, overlooking the orchard we'd created.

But alas, the young god and I were not born of the same breed, that much was evident. I wondered if she ever questioned why he no longer had sex with her.

Suddenly, their body language changed. They both went stiff—like rigor mortis setting in. Whatever they were talking about had quickly gone awry. This wasn't uncommon with them. These days, all they seemed to do was fight.

I twirled my wrist, my palm facing skywards, conjuring a plump, juicy apple in my hand—a little snack for the upcoming spectacle.

Like my incredible eyesight, I could listen in on their conversation if I wanted to. But their squabbles were so petty lately, I no longer bothered.

My brows shot up as I watched her throw the brush at him. Without so much as a flick of his wrist, he knocked it off course and it flew past him, narrowly missing his head. He snarled at her.

I bit into the apple, chuckling to myself—oh, this was going to be good. She had never gotten physical with him before. Good for her.

With his fists clenched, he walked past the view of the window, disappearing behind gold brick walls. She charged after him. I looked to the next window, only to see the two of them sail past it, out of view.

Well—I peered down at the apple—that wasn't very much fun. *I took another bite, setting my poor attention span on the apple in my hands.*

When nothing but the core was left, I tossed it on the ground, leaving the chewed-up gift for her come morning— something I did frequently. I had a sneaking suspicion she knew it was me, although I had yet to confirm it. I was just about to turn, just about to shadow walk to the Spirit Realm when I felt the sudden release of immense power, the magic clogging my nostrils.

Eyes wide, I looked back at the window. It granted me just enough view to see her briefly as she was thrown backwards. Not even a second later, she was out of view.

I didn't see what happened next, but I damn well heard it.

I heard her smash into the wall behind her, her immortal

bones snapping so loud it was like lightning had struck a tree and blown it into smithereens. The birds that had been resting in the trees startled into flight, thousands of wings flapping into a steady, humming chatter.

My jaw cut steel—my molars ready to combust. Something potent swirled in my veins. Something menacing. Something that yearned for blood.

I didn't think. I didn't need to. On instinct, and instinct alone, I moved.

One second, I was standing in the orchard and the next I was standing in their grand, luxurious chambers—big enough to fit an arena in.

My nostrils flared when I saw her.

She was unconscious, her neck snapped awkwardly to the side, her arms and legs twisted and broken. Shattered bones jutted out of her porcelain skin, her gold ichor rising to the surface, running like streams of a river, and collecting in an ocean of divine blood that pooled beneath her.

A snapped neck and broken bones weren't nearly enough to kill an immortal, but that did not justify what he had done to her. Seeing her like that, it stirred something feral within me and—

"What are you doing here?" Aurelius snarled, his fists clenched at his sides, knuckle bones threatening to cut through the stretched skin.

I growled back, placing myself between him and her.

What in the fuck was I doing? Protecting her?

My magic was much older than his, but I was not a fool. I knew who the people had been praying to for years—him, not me. Their prayers fueled his powers exponentially.

Aurelius could very well be stronger than me. That was something I really did not wish to find out right now, although that day would eventually come. And so, I did what I'd done a hundred times before . . .

I stole her into the night, taking her to the Living Realm.

To the tiny little cottage surrounded by swaying oaks.

Normally, an immortal's body was able to fix broken bones all on its own, but after a week passed by and I saw no progress in her healing, I decided to do it myself. Manually.

But while I straightened her shattered limbs, I grew sick to my stomach to the point that I had to go outside and vomit in the woods—a first for me.

And after I was finished, I decided I never wanted to do it again.

I was the God of Death and bones were my currency, but when it came to hers—when it came to seeing them broken like that?

I could have reduced the realms to ash.

I was surprised by how slow her regeneration took. Three weeks had passed since I'd brought her here. Any other

immortal would have been fully healed by now.

But not her.

I had never met a deity so lacking in the ability to heal themselves. Everything about her I found juvenile . . . Some goddess she was.

She was pathetic, really, I thought to myself as I caressed a strand of her silky hair—so soft against my rough, calloused fingers. I let it slip away, caught in the act as her eyelids slowly opened.

Lurching upright, weakly, she moved away from me, towards the other side of the bed, which, considering its small size, didn't allow her to get very far. Her feeble movement was no better than a newborn fawn. I bit back my need to reprimand her for moving so hastily when she was still so incredibly weak.

"Get away from me," she hissed.

I was tempted to reach for her, but I steeled myself instead. I let a smirk twist my mouth as I purred, "Hello, Little Goddess."

"Why am I here?" she asked, her gaze falling to the grizzly fur draped over top of her. She raised a linen-wrapped arm and pressed the back of her wrist against her forehead. "I am not sick with fever," she murmured to herself at the same time she noticed the gauzy fabric I'd wrapped around her arm. She pulled her arm down and studied it.

My brow raised ever so slightly. "Do you not remember your husband tossing you across the room and snapping your neck?"

She looked at me, horror filling those enormous blue eyes, rimmed wide with white. "No," she argued, shaking her head, fighting the memory as it returned to her. "He would never do—"

"He did." I cut her off before her pretty, pretty lips could finish that useless lie.

She looked down, her eyes darting back and forth as she remembered what she was trying so desperately to block out. Tears brimmed on her lower lash line before one slipped forth, tumbling down her cheek. And then another. And another.

On pure impulse, I rose from the chair, leaned across the small mattress, and swept the back of my finger over the small stream of tears flowing down her cheeks. She did not jerk away from my touch—that was a first. And for the briefest of moments, her gaze met mine and I . . . I could have fallen to my knees.

She was devastating.

Unable to help myself, my fingers lowered. Gently, I traced her jawline. I watched her, waiting for her to push my hand away like she had done a thousand times before.

But for some reason, right now, she was letting me.

My fingers lowered to her delicate, ivory neck. The contrasts between us, in our skin tones, of how large my hand was in comparison to her purely female neck, it spoke to some territorial part of me.

"Why do your bones not correct themselves?" I asked, marveling at the buttery softness of her skin. Mortal men spent their lifetimes chasing after gold, but if they were to take my place right now, they would find the metal severely lacking. For there were no riches that could compete with her. And that bothered me more than I cared to let on.

"I don't know," she answered, still studying me just as much as I was studying her.

"You take a long time to heal, as well," I added on.

"Sometimes it varies. The healers say that my body acts almost more mortal than immortal at times." Her eyes widened ever so slightly, and she nervously began to chew on her bottom lip, her actions speaking loudly—she regretted telling me something that I could easily use against her.

I couldn't blame her. She was right to fear me.

An immortal's body acting mortal? There were only a handful who could do that.

"You are not the first of your kind," I said as my thumb pressed against the slight divot beneath her bottom lip, slowly I tugged it from her teeth, causing her wet, plump lip to spring free. I was tempted to take it between mine.

"What do you mean I'm not the first of my kind? The healers said no one has had such an ability before." Falling into old habits, she pulled back from me, yet when she spoke, her voice held no malice. Interesting.

"Then your healers are either imbeciles or liars. The Goddess of Free Will is able to make her body age just as a mortal's would. She lives a natural mortal life, dies at a time of her choosing, and then is reincarnated again. If you are indeed like her, I would suspect you are able to reincarnate as well."

"I've heard of her. She is one of the Three Spinners."

"She is," I confirmed with a slight, single nod.

She was quiet for a moment, the cogs in her mind turning so loud I could hear them. Then, she said, "If I wanted to talk to her . . . do you know where I could find her?"

"When she must work, she lives with her sisters. Their home is inside Mount Kilangor. But she's a bit of a nomad, so she typically isn't there," I rumbled—still transfixed on her pouty, pink lips.

Silence fell between us.

I took a step back, lowering my tall frame into the much-too-small wood chair—crafted for a man half my size. Like the rest of the cottage, this room felt tiny. Why I brought her here whenever she became sick with fever was beyond me. It was more so just a feeling I had—some internal voice that told me to bring her here.

"I watch over them," she said quietly.

I quirked a brow, my hands settling on my thighs. I don't know how I knew what she was talking about, but I did. "The humans?"

"Yes."

"Well, you are the Goddess of Life. Looking after living creatures seems like something that would come with the territory."

"No," she said, sky-blue eyes lifting to mine as she gently shook her head. "It's not like that. I just watch them, and I wonder . . . " She glanced around the room, her arms wrapping around herself. "What would it be like to live like them? In these tiny, cozy homes?"

I smirked. "Cozy?"

She blew out a laughing breath and the goddess actually smiled at me. "Well, that is what they are."

Cozy. *The word felt funny. Foreign. I glanced at her, amusement lightening my tone. "You live in a giant palace and yet you wonder what it would be like to live in a pile of sticks? Like the mortals do?"*

"I know it sounds strange," she said, fingers knitted in her lap. Did she find this conversation uncomfortable or was it my presence?

"It is *strange," I teased. "Indulge me. You have everything you could ever want. Why would you want to live like a mortal?"*

"Because they don't have . . . eternity. They have their short span of a life, and because of that, they make the most of it." She shrugged one shoulder. "They live.*"*

"So, in contrast, are you saying that we, as immortals, do not?"

"I think—" Thick lashes flickered, her azure eyes drifting to a thin gold band that wrapped around her finger—a sun etched into the metal. She fiddled with it. "We immortals tend to take things for granted."

I could see right through her. "Is that how you feel? Taken for granted?"

Her head jerked up. "That's not what I meant."

"Oh?" I challenged, my brows raising in question. "I think that's exactly what you meant, Kitten. You put yourself in his path, and he walks right on by. He doesn't see you like he should. He never has."

Her expression turned murderous. "And whose fault is that? You were the one who made me barren. All he had ever wanted was an heir, and you took that from us."

I sucked on my teeth, my gaze leveling hers. "Sorry, I didn't realize that your worth relied solely on your ability to produce offspring. No different than a broodmare, really. Tell me, Kitten, should I fetch a bridle and a bit from my stables for you?"

"You are such a bastard," she hissed, her hands fisting the fur blanket. "You know how vital it is for a king to have an heir, someone to pass his crown on to."

"I'm confused, goddess, am I talking to you or your husband? Besides, that *is a foolish mortal rule—immortals do not need heirs to rule."*

She scoffed, her tone dripping with venom. "Says the failed *king who no longer rules over the Living and Immortal Realms."*

I took that one square on the chin, the fight in her coaxing a twisted smile to my lips. "Has the kitten finally found her claws? I do hope so because you are going to need them."

"What are you talking about?" she seethed between clenched teeth.

I stood from the chair, my imposing frame leaning over the bed. I lowered my face to hers, cuffing her gaze to mine. "I want you to be the one, Kitten, to tell your pathetic husband what is coming for him." I leaned forward and handed her my most charming smile. "War."

"You'll lose," she grated with confidence.

I cocked my head to the side. "Will I?"

I saw the flicker in her eyes, the chink in her armor that told me she wasn't sure. And that was message enough.

Both sides were evenly stacked—but there was one thing I had that Aurelius did not. He might be born from flame and sun, but I was born of wind and night, and unlike him, I had a will of iron.

I would take back what was mine—just as death always did.

CHAPTER 38

Von

T*he Immortal Realm had fallen and the Living Realm was on the verge of doing the same.*

Everything had gone as planned. Better than planned.

I was surprised to find out how many people in the Living Realm still supported the Old Gods. They prayed for us to win the war, and it was those prayers that filled me and the other gods and goddesses of old with insurmountable power. Some of them had never left the faith of the Old Gods so naturally, they cheered for us to reclaim what was once ours.

But something else unexpected happened that really tipped the decade-long war in our favor—Aurelius's reign had depleted the Living Realm of females to such astronomically low numbers that most of the people who had once prayed for him no longer did. In fact, most of those in the Living Realm had grown to hate the God of Life, to spit upon the ground when they heard his name.

There was another group that emerged—the people who prayed solely for their prestigious Lady Light. A smile caressed my lips—she had quite the little following. Her time spent in the Living Realm, speaking with the mortals as she made her way back to the Immortal Realm, had served her well—something, in all honesty, she could thank me for. If I had not stolen her away all of those times and taken her to Living Realm, she would have never been able to experience it.

She was one of the last New Gods left standing, protecting the Living Realm.

"Get your filthy hands off of me!" Aurelius bellowed as my sentries dragged him into the throne room of the Golden Palace.

The throne room had only one throne, and judging by the gaudy sunbeam carved at the top, it was for Aurelius. I couldn't say that I was surprised—he was too much of a narcissist to grant his female a throne. He couldn't even grant her the title of queen, demanding that the people call her princess *instead.*

I glanced at the marble floor, to a worn spot beside the throne—how many times had she stood there, showing her loyalty and respect to him, when he did nothing of the sort for her? Unable to help myself, I snarled at the thought.

Aurelius's head snapped up, his usually perfect hair horribly disheveled. He bared his teeth at me. The charred and shattered remnants of his golden armor were lackluster in appearance. He was the strongest god I had ever faced in battle, and if we were to fight again, I was not incompetent enough to think I could win a second time around.

My unbreakable cuffs wound around his feet and his wrists, the chain that joined them snaked up to the collar around his neck. They were forged from the crystal formations that grew in the deep underbelly of the Spirit Realm. Prior to the war, I had tested them on myself, confirming that their diamond-like structure was stronger than I. After, I had dozens of them made—one for each god and goddess that served Aurelius.

There was one set left . . . I'm sure you could imagine whose sweet little wrists, ankles, and neck they were for.

I sat in Aurelius's gilded throne, my legs spread, filling up the seat better than he ever could. I had one elbow dropped on the armrest, a thumb tucked under my chin and my forefinger pressed against the iron of my cheek, supporting the side of my head. Casual arrogance radiated from me.

"How dare you sit in my throne!" Aurelius barked at me, his voice still holding enough strength to crack like thunder inside the grand, empty room.

"How dare I?" I chuckled, gesturing to the room. "You built this golden palace of yours upon my lands. Took my crown. And my realms. Who stole from whom?"

"The Creator removed your crown and created me to take your place. I have ruled the realms in ways you could have only ever dreamed of. And I do it so much better than you," Aurelius snarled, attempting to match my level of mind fuckery.

It was a wasted attempt.

Footsteps sounded as a tall male, dressed in black leather armor strode in through the door, a spear in his hand. The God of Famine. "We've located the Goddess of Life."

"*Where?*" *I asked, feigning uninterest despite the urgency that thrummed in my veins.*

"*They switched continents. She now fights with the army defending Marsallae,*" *he replied.*

I hid a smile. What a cunning little minx. That move was not one I had expected.

Aurelius's eyes flared wide, boiling with anger. He fought against the hold of my sentries as he growled, "If you touch my wife—"

"*If?*" *I cut him off with a wicked grin. "Oh, little king, didn't she tell you that last time I took her, she* let me *touch her?" I bit my bottom lip, scraping my teeth along it as I let it spring free. I tipped my head back, ever so slightly, asserting my dominance. "Tell me, have you ever noticed how soft her skin is? Truly, it's more luxurious than silk. And the color of her skin, it is as if she were painted by the moon. So soft, so delicate—how easy it will be to mark. I will enjoy leaving my handprints all over her—corrupting her with my touch. Perhaps . . . I'll let you watch."*

I left that parting gift with the fucker before I shadow walked to the Living Realm.

My wings stretched behind me, slicing the air as I soared amongst the clouds, over the battlefield. Like a hawk, I searched for her, my sweet little kitten.

There—the left side of my mouth pulled upwards into a sly grin—I'd found her. At last.

Her armor hugged dangerously close to her feminine curves. I imagined it had once been white and gold, but now it was painted in the colors of war—blood, mud, and gore.

A horse belonging to my army barreled into her, tossing her backwards. Her head smashed into a boulder, the sound of it louder than the cries of her brethren—it echoed in my ears. My eyes narrowed. I clenched my jaw, the sound grating on my nerves for a variety of reasons—some of which I preferred not to dabble in.

What a stupid little female—did she not understand that fighting the inevitable was futile? The New Gods had lost the war, just as this battle was about to be lost.

Perhaps . . . I should show her.

I tucked my wings in and dove towards the ground. At the last minute, I flared them out, catching myself and landing silently. Above me, massive white doves circled. Aurelius had sent them for her, just before I beat him in battle. It was his last set of reinforcements. Like her, they wouldn't last long.

Without so much as a whisper of a sound, I made my way through the clashing armies, walking straight for her. No one dared to touch me, even my own men scrambled back in fear. They could feel it in their bones, the power radiating from me. Like a rabid dog, I kept it on a loose leash, just enough to snap at them if they got too close.

I watched as she rolled over, her eyes threatening to roll into the back of her head from the pain she must be in. Yet, she pushed on. Deep down, part of me was proud of her fighting spirit. After all, it was what I enjoyed about her the most.

She spat out a tooth, a mixture of saliva and blood stringing in its wake, dribbling over her chin.

At that moment, I decided to make my presence known. I stepped forward, the backs of my boots scuffing the ground as I walked towards her. My boots entered her line of vision, but I didn't give her long to look at them. Unable to help myself, I crouched down and roughly grabbed her chin. My rings bit into her velvety soft skin as I forced her to look up at me. "Your blood sings for me, Little Goddess."

"Blood King," she grated between bared teeth. It was adorable, really. I was tempted to prop her mouth open and run my finger over the blunt little canines until I could coax them to match mine.

My incisors were permanently lengthened, but hers had the ability to retract—a trait the Creator had given the New Gods, something they believed to be an upgrade. I thought it rather pointless, really—why bother to hide what we were?

Her hand twitched, like it was searching for something— her sword, probably. I didn't doubt there was nothing more she would like to do than take her revenge on me, for all I had taken from her.

I grabbed her arm roughly and pulled her to her feet. Even with the thin armor she wore, my hand easily wrapped around her bicep. She was so much smaller than me. Her smallness, her femaleness—it played on my animalistic nature, like a potent drug seeping into my bloodless veins.

Protect. The word beat throughout me like a drum, each strike growing louder and louder. I ignored it.

"I've been searching for you," I said as I stroked her dirty cheek.

She reared back from my touch, like she was made of metal and I was the elements determined to corrode her. I tipped my head back and laughed. If only she knew how much I enjoyed tormenting her.

My wings unfurled as I pulled her little body against mine. She struggled, of course, tried to break the cage my arms forged around her, but it was a foolish plight. I had no plans of letting her go now. My wings cracked the sound barrier with one mighty slap, propelling us into the air, towards the clouds.

When the battlegrounds were well beneath us, I landed on a small, flat spot about halfway up the mountain. She looked over the edge, taking in the destruction unfolding below. From here, she could see it all—the inevitability of defeat that loomed on her army's doorstep.

Death. I had come for them all. Just as I'd said I would.

Devastation settled into her features, evident in the concerned knit of her brows and her heaving chest. Her blue eyes scanned the battleground below, flicking from spot to spot—finding the same answer over and over again. They were going to lose.

Her gaze met mine, molten fire corrupting those pretty blue eyes. "Is this why you brought me up here? To gloat over your victory? To make me watch as my loyal men die?" she screamed at me.

"Partly, yes. Although, your judgment paints you as a hypocrite," I mused as I pinched her chin, forcing her to look at me. "Tell me, when you murdered my men, when you bathed in the spray of their blood—" I flashed a wicked smile, "—how did that feel? Did it feel good, darling? Did you take

joy when you ended their lives and delivered them back to me? Because I think that rather strange. I would think that would counter the very point of your existence—" I let her see the demon in my eyes, the darkness that lived inside, *"—*Goddess of Life.*"*

She spat in my face. "You bastard. I did not take joy in it. I am the keeper of life. The guardian of the living. When you declared this war, you forced my hand. With every life you forced me to take with this war, it has served but one purpose—to build my hatred for you."

I clicked my tongue. I thought I wanted her to hate me, but hearing her say it out loud? It struck a dark nerve.

I lowered my face to hers, my tone threatening. "What a pity. I thought you were rather fond of me. After all, goddess, you swamp my realm with so many, many gifts. Continuously, you send them to me—second after second, day after day, year after year. So many beautiful, departed lives."

The fire in her eyes stamped out, my words finding their mark.

Wearing a sinister smile, I continued, "You see, I was beginning to think you were in love with me. I mean, you take such excellent care of my apple trees."

"You bastard. You know nothing of love," she seethed, glaring at me.

"And you do?" I challenged, her words plucking an angry note out of me. "You have never loved him, and you know that, but you are too stubborn to admit it."

She ground her teeth. "You are wrong. I do love him. Deeply. Just as I love my people and they love me. It is because of them, because of their prayers, that I am made strong." Her expression changed suddenly, the smallest glimmer of hope filling her eyes. It was spellbinding. "Strong enough to finally end this."

Her hands flew out to her side, her white hair flailing around her as she channeled the last remnant of her power. Such a stunning little female. She conjured a water blade that looked like glass and let out a battle cry as she drove the blade through my stomach, her hands clamped around the hilt as she twisted it in further.

I glanced down, uninterested at first, but then when I saw it . . .

Everything changed.

Blood. It was my *blood.*

But I was the God of Death . . . I did not bleed.

I swept my fingers along the glass blade, collecting a sample of my blood, amazed by the warmth of it against my skin. I brought the coppery-red substance closer to my face, still fighting with what exactly I was seeing.

When the war ends, you will find your mate. You will know it is her because she will be the one to make you bleed. *The Goddess of Fate's words answered in my mind.*

No . . . that couldn't be! She was the wife of my enemy.

This had to be more of her treachery. The little witch.

I looked at her. "What sort of illusion is this?"

"It is no illusion."

I did not believe her. "Tell the truth. You spoke with the Goddess of Fate and learned of the prophecy. You thought to use it against me."

"I have spoken to the goddess, but I do not know of whatever prophecy it is that you speak of," she replied. The

confusion on her face matched the way I felt inside. "So . . . the rumors are true then."

"Yes, they are true. I do not bleed—" I answered as I wrapped my hand around the hilt of her sword. My teeth clamped together as I pulled the blade out from my body. When it was out, I couldn't help myself—I laughed. It all made sense. The Creator had finally given me a mate, a mate whom I had tormented for centuries. And the wife of my enemy, no less. I inspected her beautifully crafted blade, coated in my blood—deciding I liked the looks of it a bit too much. So that was the obsession I had with her. She was meant to be mine. I looked up at her, that possessiveness I felt for her snapping permanently into place. MINE. "—Until now."

I threw the blade onto the rocky, barren ground—barren, just like I had made her—my mate. The horror of what I had done to her washed over me. I was the reason my mate fell sick with fever. I was the reason for the hate swirling in her eyes.

I was the villain in her story.

She would never accept our mating bond.

She doesn't need to accept it for you to have her, the monster purred within.

And Creator above, it was hard not to listen to him. My control was slipping.

Take her, the voice demanded again.

I strode towards her, ignoring the visceral pain I felt growing in my leaking abdomen the closer I got to her. But it was nothing compared to the pain I felt for all the different ways I had betrayed her.

She didn't move. And even though she was very much armed, she didn't release her blades.

When I was close enough to reach out to her, it took everything within me not to. I ignored that voice that wanted to take her and steal her into the protection of my night. I had already done enough damage. And although every fiber of my eternal being thrummed for me to collect her, I did not.

"I am calling the war off," I told her.

"And why would you do that?" she asked in disbelief.

I reached forward, my fingers caressing a wisp of her hair. The white, silken strands were impossible to see beneath the blood and mud that coated them. This was what I had done to her. It was my actions that had forced my mate *to fight in this war.*

For the first time in my very long life, I hated what I had done.

I looked at her, the other half of my soul. "Since the dawn of time, I have spent millennia searching for an answer to the empty void inside. And now, at last, I have it. How fitting that she should be the very thing that can kill me."

I let her hair fall to the side. I let her go.

And then I let my shadows take me.

CHAPTER 39

Von

The God of Death was fated—fated—to the Goddess of Life.

Surely, the cosmos were laughing.

But I wasn't. None of us were. Especially Saphira.

She had not stopped pacing since I told her I was calling the war off. One could imagine how that conversation went. Whoever made up the old saying "if looks could kill" clearly had never met my sister, because the daggers that shot forth from her eyes were lethal. Her black heels struck the polished, obsidian floors of my sprawling throne room, beating like a drum, pounding with annoying consistency as she walked from one side of the room to the other. Repeatedly.

Clack-clack. Clack-clack. Clack-clack.

My grip tightened, the throne's arms crumbling under my fingertips, tiny bits of igneous rock biting into my skin. My bloodless wounds quickly healed, but not before pushing the bits of stone out. From where I held, deep cracks formed like bolts of lightning, splintering their way through the rest of my massive throne—something I had carved by hand many years ago.

"Would you quit your incessant pacing?" I snarled.

The sound slowed, then stopped.

My fingers relaxed their crushing hold.

Saphira glared at me, one black-gloved hand moving to rest in the nook created by her cocked hip. "She will be your demise, Draevon."

That, I had no doubt of. In many ways, she already was.

It had been six weeks since I left her standing there on that cliff, overlooking the destruction of the war I had started. Six weeks since I discovered she was my mate. Six weeks I had spent trying to decide what to do about it . . . about her.

Six long weeks.

Since then, I had released the New Gods from their chains and ended the war, just as I'd said I would do. The only god I had yet to release was Aurelius. I had thrown him in the belly of my dungeon in the same cell I kept one of my bloodthirsty beasts in—Marishka.

Marishka was a thirty-foot-tall immortal spider that would make even the bravest of men shit their breeches. In appearance, she looked like a giant tarantula, but her body was covered in metal-like scales rather than hair. From underneath her scales, she oozed a foul type of pus that smelled like a rotting corpse that had been left marinating in a tiny little room during the heat of summer. Apart from the putrid smell, the greenish-yellow ooze clung to everything, and once you got it on you, good luck getting it off.

I kept Marishka in the darkest depths of my dungeon

because she detested daylight. She went mad with hysteria whenever she was exposed to it. Naturally, I thought she would make an exceptional cellmate for the Lord of Light.

I smirked to myself.

During the swell of the night, when the rest of the realm was mostly quiet, Aurelius's disgruntled roaring peaked—the god had a set of pipes on him. He kept a good portion of the Spirit Realm awake and the people were starting to grow weary of it—and in all honesty, I was too. My nights were sleepless enough with her running through my mind at all hours.

Not that I needed sleep.

It was something other gods and goddesses did when they were bored and wanted to pass the time. They could sleep for centuries if they wished to, a luxury I had never been afforded as king because I didn't trust anyone to run the realm as well as me.

Eventually, Aurelius would break free of his restraints— they could only imprison a god for so long. He was proving to be a problem and I wasn't sure what to do with him.

In truth? I didn't like the idea of his hands touching my mate—in any capacity, whether it be for pleasure or pain . . .

The memory of her delicate neck twisted unnaturally emerged on the forefront of my mind. An inferno of boiling anger crept along my skin, digging its poisonous claws in. My body had been doused in oil and lit aflame and the only thing that could put it out would be to take the life of the god that had caused her harm.

I growled—the damned bond was messing with my mind again, playing on my instincts to protect her, the very weapon sent *to end my immortal life.*

"Are you listening to me?" Saphira hissed like the venomous vipers we had created millennia ago. They may have gotten their deadly nature from me, but their aggressive, bite-first instincts came solely from her.

A young viper looped around her neck, its head hovering between her not-so-ample cleavage, the tail coiling at her throat. The dress Saphira wore was made of dyed black leather. Knowing her, it was probably made from the hide of some poor mortal man that happened to look at her the wrong way.

"Not really," I replied honestly.

"Folkoln, tell him that he is a fool for considering this bond at all," she said to our brother, who was sitting haphazardly in a chair.

A cast of moonlight flowed in from the window, shining on his boot, while one long leg stretched out before him, the other one tucked underneath the chair. Luna's glow caught on his facial piercings, reflecting bits of light. Like me, he was covered in inky markings from the deals he had made. Saphira possessed the ability, as well, but she sniffed at the idea of using it.

True to her warring nature, Saphira started up again. "The Creator wishes to destroy you. That can be the only explanation for this bond. Why would they choose the little bitch—"

I growled in warning, the veins in my neck threatening to break through my skin. How dare *she call my mate—*

I snapped the sound off and ran my fingers through my disheveled hair, my chest heaving. My crown, made of black flame and bone, floated above my head, the flame-like shadows breaking off, licking at my fingers like a loyal house cat showing its affection, attempting to comfort me. I waved them off.

What in the fuck was happening to me?

Aurelia was my enemy, and by her hand, she would take my immortal life—that *I had no doubt of.*

"It is plausible," Folkoln mused, balancing the point of a dagger, a giant emerald embedded in the pommel, on his knee, his index finger pressed against the tip of the hilt. His obsidian eyes, the twin to my own, raised to mine.

All of the old gods had been born with black irises. It wasn't until we found our mates that they would begin to fill with color. Likewise, the longer we were away from our mates, the more the color would begin to revert to black. Some females took an immense amount of pride in ensuring their mates had their irises constantly filled with color—it was a primal way of claiming them, of showing the outside world that their male was bonded, that he no longer hungered. The Old goddesses and New Gods were born with their permanent eye color.

I glanced at my sister, studying her rich, emerald eyes.

. . . Would mine be like hers? It was a question I had never wondered before. But now—

No. I ran my fingers through my hair once more. I wasn't going there.

"Considering the Creator wanted another god to replace you, that they turned their back on you, perhaps this is their way of finishing you off for good," Folkoln said, tapping the tip of the blade thoughtfully against his temple. "If so, it is

quite the diabolical plan."

My brother and sister were most likely right. Aurelia was an assassin in disguise, sent by the Creator to see to my demise. She appealed to my tastes—my senses. Everything about her I found addicting. It was the very reason I had stood in her apple orchard night after night, waiting for a glimpse of her.

I didn't just want her—I craved *her.*

And it was that craving that would most likely get me permanently killed. I might be prehistoric, but I still enjoyed being alive.

*The Goddess of Fate's voice played in my mind—*But heed this warning, and heed it well, your mate's life is linked with the very male she is destined to kill.

I hadn't told this little tidbit of information to my already skeptical brother and sister. It would send them into a frenzy, cementing their stance that Aurelia was sent to kill me. I knew how the Goddess of Fate's warning looked, and I had plausible reason to believe that the male Aurelia was destined to kill was most likely me. But what if it wasn't? Then who?

I let out a sigh.

By my own actions, I had single-handedly ensured that Aurelia hated me. Why she hadn't taken my immortal life that day on the cliff, why she'd hesitated . . . I would never know. If given another chance, I highly doubted she would hesitate again.

Something I didn't plan to find out.

If her life was tethered to mine, my death would mean the end of us both. So what was I to do? I tapped my fingers on the shattered remnants of my throne's arm, thinking.

Was there a way I could get her to forgive me?

I nearly laughed at myself. I had done the worst thing you could do to a goddess and a woman—I had taken her ability to create. No, there would be no redemption for me, and that was justifiably so.

I was left with one last option . . .

But did I have it in me to kill my mate?

The sickening, heavy lava that angrily rolled around in my stomach told me no. But what I was feeling, was it even real? Or was it the Creator's way of manipulating me? I detested the thought. I was not a game-piece to be positioned and used—I was the game maker. Bonded or not, I made the rules. If Aurelia was the Creator's attempt to end me, I wasn't about to roll over like a courtesan and just take it.

I looked at Saphira. "What do you suggest I do?"

A wicked smile spread across her lips. "End her first, before she has a chance to end you."

"How?" I asked.

"While you've been obsessing over this silly little bond, I have been looking into things," she replied. Her long legs carried her to the steep stairs that led up to my throne—a stretch of fifty risers. Her feline frame broke into shadow before she appeared directly before me. She rolled her wrist, showing me her palm, or rather, what was in it—a six-inch clipping of a delicate white vine armed with thin, sharp thorns. It moved in her hand as if it were searching for the plant it had been cut from. "She might be your weakness, but this I believe to be hers. It belongs to a tree that grows in the Golden Palace. Word has it that she cannot come within a hundred feet of it without it making her violently ill."

She handed it to me.

"What am I supposed to do with this?" I asked, looking at the vine, wondering how such a delicate, little thing like this could end an immortal's life. The metaphor was not lost on me. "If I kill the Goddess of Life now, there will be backlash—she has gained a strong following because of the war."

"In celebration of the war ending, there is a ball that will be taking place next week. I suggest you go to it. Ask for her hand in marriage. In exchange, lie and say you will give them the realms, that you will give their king back. She won't decline the offer. Bring her back here and end the bitch before she has a chance to end you. No one will ever know."

"With this?" I said, gesturing to the twisting vine. "What am I to do with it? Ground it up and have it served sprinkled over her food?"

Folkoln chuckled. I did too.

Saphira hissed at us both. "No, brother, forge it into a blade. Or better yet—" Saphira's sinister grin spread on her bloodstained lips, "—make a crown for her to wear. A pretty one. Befitting the queen of the dead."

CHAPTER 40

Sage

The Sky Palace was an architectural gem, arguably Aurelius's most lavish residence in the Immortal Realm. Nestled on a stretch of flat land hidden in the embrace of the Alonia Mountains, we were high above sea level, settled among the cottony clouds.

I leaned over the smooth sandstone banister, reached forward, and dipped my hand into a fluffy white cloud as it lazily drifted by. When I pulled back, my hand was covered with a kiss of sparkling dew. I made the tiny droplets rise from my skin, suspending them in the air. I swirled them as if they were dancing in tune with the grand orchestra's music, the lively, joyful song coming from inside the palace.

Tonight, I wore my hair up—just as Aurelius liked it to be. The gold, feather-shaped, diamond comb he gave to me was nestled in my pinned hair. A gentle breeze drifted across my skin, kissing the back of my neck, tugging a curl free—it felt intimate.

The slightest hint of magic tinged the air. Ancient and lethal.

I knew who it belonged to—the scent permanently ingrained in my mind. "Come out, you bastard," I whisper-growled through gritted teeth. I bid him to walk out from his shadows, to show himself to me.

"Please be careful, Lady Aurelia," said a familiar male voice. "You really shouldn't be out here alone."

I turned, my airy skirts, which were made up of several layers of tulle and sparkle netting, taking a moment to catch up with me, swaying with my movement. Gold beads, thousands of them, were hand-sewn into the front of the corset, giving the appearance of an ethereal chest plate, the rest of my gown a stark white. Sheer sleeves draped over my shoulders, wisping to the floor as if they were relaxed fairy wings. Under the moon, the gown sparkled like starlight, twinkling brilliantly whenever I moved.

"Arkyn." I smiled in greeting as I let out a soft breath. "Thank you for your concern. I just needed a moment to myself."

He dressed formally tonight, adorned in gold fabric, except for his cloak, which showed the slightest hint of white stitching right beneath the rim of golden fur. Black leather boots, buckled at the sides, stretched to his knees. The livery collar crafted from gold and rubies draped across his broad shoulders. It had been a gift from Aurelius, one Arkyn treasured so dearly, I wondered if he ever took it off.

Although I had never met Arkyn's mortal mother before

she passed, I didn't need to meet her to know that Arkyn took after his father. They both possessed that incredible charm— people simply wished to bask in their sun.

In mortal title, I was Arkyn's stepmother, but that dynamic never existed between the two of us. At the time of my creation, he was of similar age to me. We grew into our divinity together. We were just friends, although sometimes I suspected Arkyn held the slightest romantic feelings for me— something he would never admit out of loyalty to his father.

Those affections I never returned for him, because if there was one thing I did not want to lose it was my friendship with him.

My life was an isolated one. I didn't have anyone—other than Arkyn—that I was particularly close to, but that was not for lack of trying. I used to attend afternoon tea with the other gossipy goddesses, but they never took much interest in me. They preferred to talk about my marital relations with Aurelius, in particular our nighttime activities—which had fizzled out decades ago. When I discovered that quite a few of them had slept with Aurelius prior to my creation, I turned red with jealousy and nearly drowned the lot of them.

After that, I wasn't invited to any more teas.

Stirring from my thoughts, I reached for his hands. "It is good to see you. I take it everything went well with the king of Tershov?"

His gloved hands clasped mine. "As it is good to see you. You look lovely, Aurelia." He pressed a quick kiss against my cheek. "Yes, it went rather well. Any word yet on Aurelius?"

Softly, I shook my head. "I'm afraid not. The God of Death has not made any ransom demands for Aurelius's *release and the council refuses to let me enter the room as they deliberate on what to do. Perhaps you could go in and speak with them?"*

"Yes, tomorrow morning I will. It is a shame they do not wish to listen to you. I have no doubt they would learn a great deal." Arkyn cradled my cheek, the tenderness in his touch a dead giveaway of those hidden feelings he held for me. "We will get him back."

I nodded, my hand falling over his. "I know we will, it is just a question of when." I let out a sigh and plastered on my best fake smile. "But for tonight, we play the part for the sake of our guests, so that we can keep up the charade that everything is fine." I paused, looking to the grand ballroom. "I suppose we better get back in there. Would you care to be my dance partner for the night?"

"I would be honored." He offered me his arm and I took it.

We walked through one of the many double doors that were opened to the night sky, the white voile drapes twirling on the breeze.

The lavish ballroom thrummed with life. An orchestra played an enchanting melody, conducting the dancing pairs whisking across the floor. Everyone wore gold tonight, in honor of Aurelius and his victory over the Old Gods.

If only they knew the truth . . . that we didn't win *the war, that we would have lost it if the God of Death had not called it off. But they would never know because the council and the other gods and goddesses determined it was best to hide the truth, and so we lied to the people about all of it.*

Aurelius, the conqueror of the Old Gods and defender of

the Living and Immortal Realms. That was what would be written on the historic scrolls, along with tales of grand victories that never happened. They would write about me too. But they would not say that it was my army that held out the longest against the enemy—they would say that I was beside myself, pacing the castle floors, waiting for my beloved husband to return. A perfect, doting wife. An example for all women to aspire to be. I scowled at the thought.

The wall opposite the terrace was made almost entirely of stained glass, giving view to the clouds, the mountains, and the vivid crescent moon. My mother's light spilled over the marble floors, painting the room in a soft, moody glow.

When the song finished and the orchestra started on the next one, Arkyn and I walked onto the floor. Our entry was encouraged with clapping.

"I think they like you," Arkyn teased as we began to move, our steps guided by the musician's notes—the song merry and upbeat. A song befitting a grand victory. What a sham.

"Are you sure it's not your dazzling personality?" I asked, looking up at him.

"Mine?" Arkyn chuckled. "I think they are too busy salivating over the rare diamond in my arms to be concerned with me." He leaned in, his voice loud enough for only me to hear. "As they should be."

"You flatterer," I chuckled.

"With you, it comes easily," he said, that unspoken attraction tinting his words.

Suddenly, the wind outside began to howl like some deranged beast. The noise became louder and louder as a *gust of wind barreled into the side of the palace—so powerful in force that the floor shuttered beneath my feet.*

The dancing stopped. The music stopped.

But the wind did not.

It struck again.

Arkyn and I held on to one another as the palace trembled—as we all trembled. I looked up at the ceiling, the grand chandelier shaking violently, some of its crystals, the size of my fist, rattling loose. They hailed down, shattering like teardrops as they hit the polished marble floors. Arkyn raised his arm protectively over my head as we ran under the canopy created by the second floor.

The doors slammed shut like a row of falling dominoes, one set at a time, but the process itself took seconds.

Outside, the howling wind stopped, but the storm itself was now inside—ancient and violent and lethal and dressed in the finest leathers I had ever seen. And he was standing in front of me.

The God of Death.

"Hello, Little Goddess," he purred, his obsidian eyes roaming over my face, drifting down my neck.

I stifled an unexpected shiver that walked the length of my back. It wasn't born of fear, but rather something I had no right to feel. I had been warring with that feeling for decades now.

"You are not welcome here," Arkyn cut in, taking a gallant step forward. "What do you want?"

I grabbed his gloved hand and tried to pull him back.

The God of Death glanced at one of the servants, raising his tattooed hand and motioning for the server to come over.

The waiter stumbled towards him, his eyes propped so wide I could see the whites. The God of Death plucked a glass of sparkling wine off the server's silver tray. He took his sweet time inspecting the bubbling liquid, purposely leaving Arkyn's question hanging—a testament to his unparalleled power.

The God of Death answered to no one.

"What do I want?" he repeated finally. His carnal gaze lifted to mine—something sinister lurking inside. He had not even tasted the sparkling wine before he carelessly tossed the glass over his shoulder. It shattered against the floor.

The action stirred a few shocked responses from the crowd, but the majority remained stunned silent, their tongues imprisoned by their fear. All eyes were on us.

He offered his large hand to me, his black and silver rings reflecting sparks of moonlight. "I came for a dance."

"That will not be happening," Arkyn stated, his voice dripping with authority.

I touched his arm, my eyes pleading with him not to do anything foolish. "It's alright. One dance won't hurt anything," I said.

Arkyn's face twisted, an internal war raging inside, before he gave me a curt, agreeing nod.

"Please, everyone, all is well. Let us get back to the celebration," I said, my voice dripping in regality. Proper and poised. The epitome of the cultured, elegant woman I portrayed myself to be—if only they knew that deep down, I was nothing of the sort. I looked at the conductor. "Please, continue."

The conductor, an older fellow with a weary smile, spun his hand in grandeur as he bowed towards me. He straightened, flipped his coattails back, and then began to conduct. The orchestra started playing a sad, dark melody, unlike anything I had ever heard them play before . . . I wondered if the God of Death had something to do with it.

Eager to get this over with, I didn't wait for Death to take the lead. I walked onto the floor, the shattered chandelier crystals crunching beneath my heels. I gripped my skirts and turned towards him, finding him standing in the same spot.

His dark eyes were fixed on me, the left corner of his mouth twisted upwards into a smirk. He had one hand tucked leisurely in the pocket of his tight black breeches, the fabric stretching over his muscular thighs. He stood taller than any man in this room, but it wasn't his height that sucked the oxygen out of it—it was the immense power he exuded. His onyx hair was tugged up, half of the length braided, the other half spilling down his back. Every part of him looked lethal, just like the vicious wind he commanded.

And right now . . .

He was coming for me.

*The soles of his boots struck the floor as he sauntered towards me, the sound performing a sort of countdown as he closed the distance between us. My heartbeat roared in my ears—*run, run, run!

When he was just about to reach me, on instinct, I reared back.

His shadows broke around him, and suddenly, my back was pressing against a towering wall of male. Notes of amber and sandalwood washed over me—the smell of him unreasonably delicious. Large hands gently clasped my shoulders. Slowly, they slid down the length of my arms, the heat of them scalding against my skin. Cool air waked in his touch, the combination of hot and cold electrifying my sensitive nerves. His hand grabbed mine, his other one pressing against my lower back as he pushed me further away from him. Using our connected hands, he swirled me, pulling me back into him in one swift, skillful move. I landed with a thump against him, my hand smacking against his steel-packed chest.

I looked up to find him peering down at me.

Sharp, thick, black brows framed obsidian eyes, eyes that held the slightest hint of amusement and something else—something that made me feel as if I was standing naked before him, as if he could see right through me.

Flustered, I quickly moved my hand from his chest to his arm. With iron forged in my voice, I asked, "Shall we get this over with?"

A teasing smile played at his broad lips. "This will never be over between us."

"There is no us," I answered, extending a pointed toe while ignoring the last part of his sentence.

His hand pressed against the small of my back, spanning the width of it, keeping me tethered to him. He tipped his head to the side predatorily. "There might not be an us, but there is something between us. I know you feel it too."

Before I could argue, he whisked me into the dance. He led, acting as the puppeteer, his body the master and I the puppet, forced to move wherever he guided me to.

I had danced with hundreds of men before, but I had never danced with Death. Now, I understood the difference. Dancing with other males was stiff and formal.

But this?

It felt sensual. Intimate. Personal.

I didn't need to think, because he was the hand and I the brush, and together, we painted the floor.

Every pair of eyes in this ballroom was fixed on us. Watching. Judging the way he made me move as if we were doing more than just dancing, as if we were publicly consummating a marriage. And I hated the bastard for it because judging by the smirk on his lips, he damn well knew what he was doing.

"Tell me, Little Goddess, did he apologize for what he did to you? How did that conversation go exactly?" he asked, his voice a deep, dark rumble.

I met his gaze, reading the fuckery written within them. I wasn't about to play his game, but he could damn well play mine.

"Why haven't you released him?" I asked, ignoring what he said.

"Answer my question first."

"Yes, he apologized, and I have forgiven him."

"Liar," he purred in my ear.

I ignored his goading. "It is your turn to answer my question now."

"No."

The space between my brows crinkled in frustration. "You just said you would."

"I changed my mind."

Stupid insufferable male, *I thought to myself, all the while ignoring the way our bodies moved in perfect rhythm with one another's—as if we had done this hundreds of times before.*

"Why did you call the war off?" I asked, careful to keep my voice down.

"I did it for you," he said, the rich cadence of his voice striking a sensual low.

He dipped me, stretching my torso before him like his own private feast. I could feel his eyes roam over me, taking me in. The backs of his fingers grazed the length of my neck, sliding downwards. I shivered under his touch.

"What are you . . ." I trailed off.

Ringed, tattooed fingers dipped lower, brushing over the sensitive swell of my breasts that peaked out of the neckline of my dress. His hand, the one that said king *on the knuckles, continued its descent. Watching him touch me like this was provocative. My nipples pressed firmly against the interior of my dress—hardening for him.*

Creator above, have mercy on me.

"Amazing, isn't it?" he mused, black lashes shifting up as his gaze met mine. "How responsive you are to my touch."

"I don't know what you're talking about," I lied.

"I think you do." He pulled me back up, continuing the dance. The light stubble on his face brushed coarsely against the smoothness of my cheek. He whispered in my ear, "Does your body ache for his touch half as bad as it does for mine?"

My cheeks heated.

Ignoring my reaction to his words, I hissed, "I do not ache for you. That is ridiculous."

"You can lie to yourself all you want. But I feel your responsiveness to me. I can scent it, too, pooling between your legs." His low tone resonated deeply within me—settling in

parts it had no place settling. *"Tell me, sweetness, if I were to steal you from this ballroom, unlace your corset and remove your gown. If I were to lay you down on my bed, take your hips and pull them to the edge. If I were to kiss the tender places that he never bothered to. If I took my time with you, something I know he's never done. What would you do?"*

My tongue tangled but it was my feet that showed it. I tripped on the hem of my gown, but he caught me. He shifted us, making it appear as if the slip-up had been part of the dance . . . how easily he covered for me.

But that was just it, wasn't it?

Death was a man of trickery. He had tormented me for decades. Now, he was doing the same. And worse, I was letting him.

I forged a backbone from a melting spine. "If you were to try that—" I started sweetly, using my feminine wiles to taunt him, "—I would run my blade straight through your immortal heart." I leaned in. This time, it was me whispering in his ear, "And we both know what that would mean for you, Blood *King."*

Our dancing ended abruptly.

The amusement he'd possessed seconds ago was gone. In its wake was something terrifying.

He pulled away from me, raising his hands in grandeur, garnishing the room's attention. Instantly, the orchestra stopped playing.

"For those of you who are unaware—which is probably the lot of you gullible idiots—your precious God of Life is not away helping to restore the war-torn lands in the Living Realm." He paused for dramatics. *"He's rotting in my*

dungeon."

People gasped. Some began to weep.

I clenched my fists, but what could I do? There was no point in denying his claim.

He grinned devilishly, sharing an unspoken message with me—this was about to get a whole lot worse.

"But do not fear, good people. I have come to make a deal." He feigned concern. "I will give you your realms and your pitiful king back. In exchange . . ."

I braced myself.

His gaze landed on me, and he bit his bottom lip in anticipation, his lips twisting into a sly grin. He let it slip free and said, "I ask for the Goddess of Life to come to the Spirit Realm with me, not as a prisoner, but rather, my queen."

"No!" Arkyn bellowed as he rushed to my side.

My molars were ground so tight that not even a diamond could withstand the pressure. "And if I do not agree?" I snarled.

"Then I suppose I will have to find another way to dispose of the problem." He laughed, the sound bouncing off the hushed walls. "Ladies and gentlemen, the problem." He looked to his left, and suddenly, Aurelius appeared. His body, covered in a strange substance, was in a kneeling position. Bonds tethered his wrists and ankles, stretching up to his neck.

I rushed to his side and wrapped my arms around his shoulders. I glared up at the monster standing before me, despising the wicked gleam in his dark, merciless eyes as he regarded me back, watching the way I held Aurelius. His lip tugged into a snarl, but he quickly smoothed it into a sly grin.

"*Careful, darling, you are getting Marishka's ooze all over that pretty dress of yours.*"

"*Fuck you,*" I seethed.

You will, *his laughing eyes seemed to say.*

I bared my teeth at him.

It only made his smile broaden more.

After a short passing of time, he said, "*Well? Have you decided, Little Goddess? Will you exchange your freedom for his, your freedom for countless others'?*"

I grated my teeth, tears filling my eyes. Aurelius was the king of the realms. Without his protection, there was no telling what the God of Death would do. As it stood, I had no other option . . .

"*Fine. I'll take the deal.*"

"*Wonderful. Consider it done,*" *he said. His eyes drifted down the length of my torso.* "*I do hope you enjoy the placement of this one.*"

I didn't need to ask him to know what he meant—he was talking about the tattoo. My cheeks flared red both from embarrassment and something else I would rather not admit.

He turned, expressing those broad shoulders towards me, and walked towards the crowd. They scrambled out of his way, falling over top of one another in their haste. He called out, over his shoulder, "*I'll return within two weeks' time to collect you, my darling little bride.*"

"*Wait! What about the bonds?*" *I asked frantically as he walked away.*

"*Those are to ensure the mate-fucker keeps his hands off of what is* mine,*" the God of Death growled before he dissolved into shadow.*

CHAPTER 41

Sage

Morning light spilled through the eastward-facing windows in the dressmaker's shop, painting the charcoal-gray stone floor with evenly spaced strips of brilliant gold. Various sized dressers and shelves spanned along the stretch of walls, chock-full of different folded textiles—wool, fine linens, silk, hemp, cotton, leather, and so forth.

Sitting atop one of those dressers was a plant I had not recognized before, although it had been a few weeks since I'd last set foot in the dressmaker's shop, so it could be a new addition. The plant had broad heart-shaped leaves larger than my head. The leaves were peculiar—although they were sturdy in structure, they looked like they had been repeatedly cut from the edge to the middle. It reminded me of a shattered heart.

The dressmaker hadn't said so much as a single word to

me since my arrival, other than pointing to the pedestal I was to stand on—which I did obligingly. I hadn't seen her for a few weeks now, but our time apart had done very little to dampen her sour mood towards me.

Judging by the way her eyes had regarded me this morning when she opened her door—with daggers and poison—I was lucky looks couldn't kill.

The dressmaker disappeared through an open doorway leading into a back room, leaving me alone with my thoughts.

As I no longer had the iron collar suppressing my Curses, last night, I dreamt for the first time in weeks, but the contents of that dream felt more like a memory than a dream. I suspected that's because they were—a memory.

I had been in the Sky Palace celebrating the end of the war with Arkyn, who was—

Aurelius's son.

I didn't know why I hadn't put that together before— they shared similar traits. It was in the way they spoke, the way they moved, the way they could catch the attention of everyone in the room.

Of course, they were related. And yet, the topic had never come up with Aurelius. Why wouldn't he mention that to me? Surely, he must know.

On top of that, it was just as Arkyn had said—we had been friends once upon a time. From the small glimpse of what I remembered, he had been my *only* friend. I did not fit in with the other goddesses, that much was clear. And because Von made me barren, it wasn't like I had any family either.

Even now, I could feel that dissatisfied, lonely feeling I felt back then swell within my chest. It was familiar. Isolating.

I turned from the dreaded feel of it, shifting back to the memory.

Von had shown up, and while we danced, he said, *Tell me, Little Goddess, did he apologize for what he did to you?* He had been referring to Aurelius, but what did he mean by it? What had Aurelius done that required apologizing?

I plucked at my bottom lip.

On top of that, Von had made his demands—my hand in marriage in exchange for Aurelius's release and the realms. Something I seemed very opposed to at the time. That feeling returned, filling me with claustrophobia—like a hand locked around my throat, cutting off my air. I closed my eyes and took a deep breath, reminding myself that it was just a memory. It wasn't happening now. I was safe.

Creaaaaak. Bang!

I jumped, startled from my thoughts. It sounded like a bunch of shelves had come crashing down in the back room that the dressmaker was in.

"Are you alright?" I called out.

Her answer came as a pained, drawn-out moan.

I leapt down from the pedestal. On quick feet, I ran to the back of the shop. My hand anchored to the door frame, using it as leverage as I wrapped around the corner, my heartbeat leaping into my ears.

It was just as I suspected—a bunch of shelves had fallen to the floor, tossing the fabrics they held in every which way, but the dressmaker was nowhere to be seen. I heard a jangle of golden bracelets slapping against one another before the tip of something sharp bit into my back.

"Don't even think about trying anything, you filthy

Cursed bitch," the dressmaker hissed from behind me. "Or I will plunge this dagger straight into you."

I felt my Water Curse bubble to the surface, ready at any moment to defend its keeper, but I wasn't sure it would be necessary.

"Why are you doing this?" I asked, my voice steady, calm. I was not fearful of the dressmaker for a variety of reasons. The main one being that the dagger she held against my back was shaking so badly, I doubted she had the lady balls to go through with it. If she had chosen one of her pins to attack me with? That might have been a different story.

"You are tainting him!" she screamed at me, her voice frantic.

"What are you talking about? Tainting who?" I replied, keeping my voice controlled and steady like a stream of trickling water. The last thing I needed was to further escalate the situation.

"You are trying to spread your disease to the Golden Prince!" The dagger wobbled even more. At this rate, I wondered if it would fall out of her hands.

I knew people were passionate in their hatred for the Cursed. The message that we were diseased was rigorously pounded into their heads from the time of their birth to the time of their death. In their minds, we were no better than rats, and because of that misguided belief, I was not surprised that someone would take up arms against me. But something in my gut told me that this was *more* than that.

And so the question stood, what was it? What else would drive the dressmaker to lure me into a trap and prick a blade into my back?

"I am not trying to do anything," I offered softly. "Why don't you put the dagger down and we can talk about this so that I can understand?"

"Yes, you are!" she yelled at me. "And you don't need to understand anything."

Perhaps I needed to try another route to reason with her. To her, I was just a Cursed mortal. Could I use that to my advantage to reason with her? I decided to try.

"I don't think you've thought this through. If you kill me, how are you going to hide the evidence of what you've done? My housemaid knows I am with you. When I go missing, they will suspect it was you. There's a good chance you will be implicated for my murder. Is killing me really worth rotting in a cell?"

I waited to see if she would take the bait—because of my divinity, she wouldn't be able to kill me, but she didn't need to know that.

She choked out a bitter laugh. "You are Cursed. You really believe they would toss *me* in a cell for killing *you*?"

She had a point. But I wasn't just Cursed though.

I was the woman the Golden Prince chose to spend his time with, and clearly, she had a problem with that, otherwise she wouldn't be standing behind me with a blade in my back. Were her actions due to her devotion to the crown, or did they run deeper than that? Something was telling me it was the latter.

"I want you to walk towards the door over there," she instructed venomously.

I glanced at the door on the far end of the room, unsure of what awaited us on the other side, and decided I'd prefer not to, which left me limited time to figure out how I was going to handle this.

The king and queen turned a blind eye to the fact that I was Cursed, something I had no doubt Aurelius had a hand in. But Aurelius wasn't here right now, and I didn't know how far his protection extended over me—especially considering what he wrote in his letter. If I were to do something, like defend myself with my Curse, that could have a very poor outcome for me, which meant I needed to be very careful about how I handled this.

"Move!" she yelled as she pressed the blade in, the tip chewing painfully into my flesh, gold bangles chattering.

I winced, but my mind remained transfixed on the sound of those telling *gold* bangles.

Gold.

Aurelius's signature color.

Something he gifted to people who were important to him.

He had gifted the livery collar to Arkyn, the hair pin to me, and the bracelets . . .

I gasped. "He was your lover, wasn't he?"

"He was," she snarled, the sound guttural, pained. "Until you showed up. And now he has all but washed his hands of me."

Well, that certainly explained a lot, especially her sour mood towards me. Why Aurelius thought it was a good idea to get his past lover to make his new lover's dresses was beyond me. Clearly, it was a poor idea on his behalf. Did his immortality remove him so far from the humans that he did not realize they had feelings too? A large, unknown part of me said yes.

"Look, I'm sorry things went south between you two." I really wasn't. "Aurelius and I, there is a lot of history between us and—"

She pressed the blade deeper, cutting my sentence short as it chewed into my skin.

I hissed.

"You will silence your poisonous tongue. All you Cursed do is tell lies. We will be so much better off when you all are gone. Now get walking before I end you right here!" she yelled at me, her voice growing increasingly impatient.

I understood now that there would be no reasoning with her. She was committed to getting me into that room, one way or another. Which left me one last option.

I ran, the muscles in my legs propelling me forward.

"Come back here, you stupid wench!" she shouted as she chased after me, slashing the air behind me—she was a lot faster than I expected.

I knocked a roll of fabrics off a small wooden table they were pyramided on, throwing them behind me, into her path, hoping the obstacle would buy me an extra second. When I reached the end of the room, I realized it hadn't.

The dressmaker was behind me—damn, she was fast.

She raised the dagger and brought it down with a vicious, bloodcurdling scream—the very sound of pure hatred.

I ducked and rolled, narrowly missing the sharp, long blade as it went sailing on by my head. I scowled at how poor my reaction time had gotten since I had last trained—Ezra would have skinned my hide for it.

Having made it past Aurelius's crazy ex-lover, I jumped

up onto my feet and raced back out into the main part of the shop.

She came tearing after me.

Weaving my way through tables full of fabric and various workstations, I kept my sights on the exit door I needed to make it through to get out into the hallway. I doubted she'd try to slay me in front of other people.

A skitter of tangled feet sounded behind me, followed by the sound of a heavy potato sack being slammed against the floor, telling me something had fallen. I spared a quick glance behind me, but when I saw what happened, I came to an abrupt halt.

I twirled, my mouth falling open.

Blood pooled around her, staining her copper skin in crimson. She made a sort of gurgling sound, her horrified eyes locked on me. She had fallen, faced forward, and somehow managed to drive the blade right through her chest.

I darted back to her side, crouching, my hands flayed in front of me, unsure of what to do. She sputtered some more, like a flame at the end of its wick. How she had managed to impale herself on her own dagger was beyond—

That's when it hit me, just as she took her last dying breath . . .

She had done it on purpose.

She knew I was going to make it to the door, and so she did the only thing she thought she could do to protect Aurelius—frame me for her death.

As if matters could not get any worse, at that exact moment, in walked the courtesan I had seen during dinner, the one that had fought with the queen.

A horrific scream tore from her when she saw the woman lying dead on the floor. There was no mistaking the similarities between the two now. The long, oval, pretty face or the dark, curly hair, or the petite frame, wrapped in luxurious, copper skin.

The dressmaker and the courtesan were sisters.

I am so screwed.

As if Fate herself agreed with me, she sent the king of Edenvale in next, just to secure how screwed I really was.

He took his wailing lover into his arms as he looked at the body on the floor and then at me—positioned over top of her. His brows drew together, his expression turning hostile.

"Guards!" he bellowed at the top of his lungs. "Seize her!"

Oh, fuck.

CHAPTER 42

Sage

Guards spilled into the room, piling in one after another, like a pack of starved wolves hunting for game. They buried the king behind them, protecting him as they unsheathed their swords—a metal *shinggg* sounding, emitted from a dozen blades.

My heart struck a frustrated chord, and I gritted my teeth in anger. This was not how things were supposed to go down. One of the two reasons I had stayed in the castle, away from my loved ones, was so that I could end the king's reign and give the Cursed a chance to live free and without fear of being persecuted. Now, because of the actions of one love-struck dressmaker, she had single-handedly derailed my plans.

Now, I had no other choice but to fight.

I spread my feet apart and reached for my Water Curse. It answered swiftly, and water emerged from my fingertips, pooling from them. I forged it into a sword, the molecules packed tighter than that of a glistening diamond.

"Guard the king!" shouted a guard.

"Get her!" yelled another.

I stepped one foot over the other, quickly picking up speed when the first guard charged at me.

He withdrew his sword behind his head before he brought it down. I braced the flat part of my blade with one hand and the handle with the other as I blocked and absorbed his blow. Firing up my biceps, I shoved him back with the use of my sword, but just barely. As he stumbled back, I caught the glint of steel in my peripheral.

Twirling, my sword blocked another just before it could chew into my side. I sent my fist sailing into the second guard's head, knocking his helmet free. Before his helmet struck the ground, my blade found its mark—planting itself into his neck.

Wide, horrified, blue eyes met mine as I slid my sword free, his warm blood seeping out, painting it in the colors of his death. I didn't wait to see him fall as two more guards came after me. I scrambled away from them, onto a rectangle table full of rolls of fabric. I punted one of the rolls at one guard and used my free hand to water blast another. One guard grabbed hold of the hem of my gown, fisting it in his metal gauntlet. With both hands, I brought my blade down, aiming for the unprotected nook where his gauntlet and the rest of his armor was attached. Hitting its mark, my sword chewed into flesh and wood, pinning his arm to the table.

He screamed in agony as he tried to free his hand. I left my sword there, conjuring another.

Two guards crawled onto the far end of the table. The table groaned in warning before one of the legs snapped and then the other leg gave out, that side of the table crashing into the ground. I slid down its top—the tumbling rolls of fabric made it hard to keep my balance, but somehow, I managed. I leapt over top of the two guards that were trying to get back up, using one's back as a means of launching myself further. When I landed behind them, a sword nearly decapitated me, but I bent backwards, and it skimmed over my torso, cutting a small skiff of my hair off. Righting myself, I shot back up, deflecting another sword, and then another.

More and more guards pooled in around me, shouting and barking like rabid dogs as they tried to take me down. I sliced and blocked and conjured and kicked—I did whatever I had to do.

My lungs were burning, itching for air. They were not used to this amount of exertion or the tightness of my gown and how little breath it allowed me to take. I reached down, asking my inner goddess to help me out, fumbling for my Fire Curse, but neither would answer.

A metal-wrapped fist smashed into the side of my head, setting my cheek on fire and momentarily blurring my vision. I shook my head, trying to clear it as I focused on the guard ahead of me—his body breaking into two forms. I conjured a spear, but never got to throw it.

I cried out in pain as something razor-sharp pierced my flesh, embedding itself into my side, just beneath my ribs. Instantly, my powers wicked out and my sword evaporated. I looked down, peering with wide eyes—

A thin, wood shaft stuck out of my torso, the end

vibrating from the velocity of being launched and then suddenly stopped. Blood pooled around the arrow, soaking the fabric of the dress. The shaft was smaller in size, one not made to kill, but rather impair.

And impair it had.

I did not doubt that the point was made of iron, which would explain the sudden loss of my powers. I grabbed onto the thin shaft, about to rip it out when a blade pressed against the side of my throat, the cool metal threatening to chew into it.

"Don't even think about it," commanded the guard who wielded the sword.

Although I could not die, that didn't mean I would not suffer. And the thought of me lying on the ground with my neck slit wide open as my life essence pooled around me, staying like that for Creator only knows how long . . .

Wincing, I dropped my hand from my side and tipped my head in defeat.

CHAPTER 43

Sage

"I did not kill her!" I pleaded before the king and queen, who sat on their imposing thrones set on a grand dais. From floor to ceiling, a massive arched window towered behind them, its colored glass washing the room in a foreboding red.

The throne room was filled to the brim with people, the majority dressed in rags, their attire telling me that they were commoners and not the nobles and aristocrats who lived in the castle. The fact that the public had come to attend this trial didn't sit well with me, especially when I thought of the horrors that had taken place during the public Cleansings— how the soldiers liked to make a memorable spectacle of things. The crowd hurled insults at me, attacking my Curse or gender or both.

The king's courtesan was nowhere to be seen. But considering her sister had just died, I imagined she was beside herself with grief. As for the queen, what she made of all of this I could hardly tell—her expression was as stony as the floor beneath my feet.

My wrists were bound behind my back. Two guards stood beside me, their metal gauntlets cuffing my upper arms, clamped around them like a dog's locked jaw, refusing to let me free.

Prior to the guards dragging me into the throne room, they had slapped an iron collar around my neck and tore the arrow out. Why they bothered to remove it, I didn't know.

"Kneel before your king, wench," the guard who stood behind me said, his sharp sword biting into the side of my neck.

I heeded him little mind, focusing on the person he served.

"Please, your majesty, you must listen to me," I beseeched the king, struggling against the guards who held my arms.

"I said kneel," yelled the same guard. His bootheel came down on the back of my legs, kicking them forward. At that moment, the guards released their hold and I fell, my knees screaming in protest as they hit the unyielding stone floor.

"She did it to herself," I choked out to anyone who would listen.

The crowd heard me, but my statement only served to antagonize them more, their insults growing louder. One of them threw something, hitting the guard beside me. He growled, snapping his head back towards the crowd, looking for the perpetrator.

"Your majesty, may I begin?" said a middle-aged man,

finely dressed, standing to the king's right. I could barely hear his voice over the roar of the crowd.

The king slouched to the side of his throne, one elbow propped on its arm. He rested his chin on his outstretched thumb, his index finger snaking up the side of his face. His eyes shifted to the crowd, one hand rising.

One hand . . . that was all it took to silence the room.

There was no mistaking it now, despite how lacking I found him—he *was* the king of Edenvale and his power to rule was absolute.

"Please proceed, Alderman Jarl," the king said, audibly handing him the floor.

The room emitted a medley of hushed whispers, bearing no resemblance of the boisterous heckling from seconds ago.

The alderman, a tall, thin fellow with dappled skin, bowed to the king before he stepped down the dais and towards me.

The guards pressed down on my shoulders, anchoring me in place. I hissed in pain.

"Consider this your one and only chance to prove your innocence. Your claim is that the woman killed herself. Is this correct?" he asked, his voice rough as gravel.

"It is," I said from my forced position, craning my neck to look up at him.

"And why exactly would she do that?" he asked, eyeing me skeptically.

"Because she was in love with Aure—" Remembering where I was, I corrected myself. "—the prince."

"What does the woman's feelings with the prince have to do with her taking her own life?" the alderman asked, his arms knitting tightly over his narrow chest. I could tell he had already made up his mind about me because I could see the guilty verdict written in the crinkled plains of his stern, hate-filled face.

"She was . . . courting him before, but that ended when he started courting me. She became jealous and lured me into the back room of her shop where she tried to kill me, so I ran from her. When she realized that her plan wasn't going to work, she took her life instead, because she knew it would look like I killed her and that I would end up in this situation. It was the second-best way for her to remove me from the prince's life," I seethed angrily, frustrated I was even in this mess of a situation.

"You are telling me that our highly esteemed, respected and admired, Golden Prince would court someone *like you?*" He threw the last two words at me as if they were daggers, a further attempt to pin me in place even though I clearly already was. I knew what those last two words implied. The entire room did.

Cursed.

That's all they saw me as. The label they gave me . . . it made me *other*, not human, not one of them. In their willfully blind eyes, I was no more than a rabid animal in need of being put down.

I looked to the king and queen. "I dined with you at your very table. I sat beside Aurelius. *You know* that he was courting me," I said, hissing as the guard on my right shoved me further down.

"*She lies*," the queen stated for all to hear, her face and tone married in disgust. "We would never let any of the filthy

Cursed dine at our table." She shook her head and laughed. "How preposterous."

I sputtered.

Realization hit me that I was a fool. The king and queen would never admit to eating at the same table as someone they had taught their subjects to hate. Nor did they have to. Not when their rule was absolute, built on a mountain of lies and treachery.

On top of that, the commoners were not invited to eat at the king and queen's dining hall or walk the castle corridors, so how would they know who was telling the truth? It was their queen's word over someone they viewed as Cursed—of course they were going to believe her.

And as for the nobles and aristocrats who had seen Aurelius and I together, who in their right mind would speak up for me and go against the queen? What could that possibly gain them?

A trip to the guillotine, that's what.

So this was it. I had reached the bottom of the proverbial well. I had found where Aurelius's protection ran out. If he was here, I doubted this would have happened. But he wasn't, which meant I needed to figure out a way to get myself out of this situation. The last thing I wanted was to be subjected to another pyre. My toes shriveled at the thought.

"Do you all hear the lies the poisonous creature spins?" the alderman said to the crowd. His words seemed better suited for the lying queen, and yet he was talking about me.

Their whispers became less hushed.

"I imagine—" the alderman started, the crowd growing quiet once more, eager to hear what he had to say. "—you found out that the dressmaker was courting the prince—who you clearly are obsessed with—and so, in your *female* jealousy, you murdered her."

The crowd murmured in agreeance, eagerly chomping at his false narrative—something I suspected he was doing on purpose.

Female jealousy?

"Fuck you," I growled, struggling against my bonds and the hands that pressed me down. I'd show him something female alright—*my rage*. The guards tightened their grip and my collarbones screamed in pain. I screamed in anger.

The alderman's eyes glinted with victory as he continued, "The dressmaker was a good, noble woman. And you—" he pointed to the collar around my neck, "—are Cursed. Your word is worth nothing."

The crowd grew ravenous with their bloodlust, increasing their heckling to eardrum-bursting levels.

"Cut out her tongue!" one of them cried out.

"Take her hands first!" decreed another.

"Burn the filthy witch!" said another.

And another.

And another.

The statements spread like a rash, leaping from one mouth to another, until close to two hundred people taunted and jeered for my dismemberment . . . for my death.

A part of me, that was still very much human, began to crumble apart.

I might have had an iron backbone, but I was not unfeeling. And to hear so many strangers so eager to turn against me . . . to hunger for my death. It broke something inside of me.

I looked down at the floor.

"Does anyone believe this woman? Come forth if you do," the alderman shouted at the roaring crowd.

"I do!" one voice said.

To me, it was the loudest of them all.

I glanced over my shoulder, finding the owner of that voice. It belonged to the healer who had tended to me before.

The alderman said to her, "You seem to be the only one." He turned back to the crowd. "And how many of you disbelieve her?"

A deafening roar emerged, the crowd turning into an angry mob, their invisible pitchforks held at the ready, each one of them salivating for my blood.

The alderman turned to the king. "Your majesty, I believe you have your answer." He bowed his head and then returned to the spot beside the throne, his triumphant eyes set on me, a smug grin on his thin lips.

I took one look at the king, and I could tell he had already made up his mind about me. I was guilty in his eyes and no amount of pleading or begging would do any good. Because just like the others, when he looked at me, all he saw was Cursed.

The king rose from his throne and the crowd grew silent. His eyes met mine. "I find you guilty."

The people went wild, whooping and hollering and cheering as if they had just won some hard-fought battle.

The king continued, "Your hands will be struck clean from your body for taking the life of another, and after, you will be Cleansed at the pyre." He pointed at the healer. "And you, Curse sympathizer, you will also be subjected to the same fate."

"No!" I shouted.

Two guards grabbed her by the arms and dragged her away. Tears filled my eyes when I thought of the sweet woman, of her sentiment that us women needed to look out for one another.

"Please, don't do this," I pleaded with the king.

But the king disregarded me with uninterested eyes. "Take her to the Well," he ordered with a dismissive hand.

At that moment, it was fight or flight.

My fear kicked in and I struggled against the guards, becoming the rabid animal they all believed me to be. I snarled, snapping my teeth at them, trying anything to free myself of their hold. But the mortal confines of my body were not enough to win my freedom, not when my arms were tied and my Curse was collared.

Something hard cracked against the back of my head.

Splintering pain was the last thing I remembered before the world before me cleaved apart and caved into darkness.

CHAPTER 44

Sage

D*rip. Drip. Drip.*

I awoke, stirred from my unconscious state by the feel of something wet consistently striking my cheek. Whatever was dripping wasn't just dripping on my cheek, but also spontaneously around me. The sound reminded me of when I worked at the bathhouse. After the men left and the bathhouse was quiet, that was when you could hear the condensation falling from the ceiling and landing on the marble-tiled floor. That was the same sound I was hearing now.

Besides the constant dripping, people spoke in hushed tones, their voices echoing. There were so many, many voices. Somewhere in the distance, I could make out the faint sound of someone sobbing.

Eyes still closed, I inhaled a deep breath, the vulgar smell of piss and shit and vomit assaulting my nostrils. The smell was tinged with something else . . . something I couldn't quite make out.

Slowly, feeling drifted back into my sore, aching, body—bruised and wounded. I was positioned on my front, my face turned to the side. The flagstone beneath me was hard, cold, and wet.

Groaning, I rolled over, my fingers darting to the awful ache at the back of my head.

"You're alive," whisper-squeaked a young boy on the edge of puberty.

I parted my lids slightly, focusing on the boy squatted in front of me. His front tooth was missing, the one beside it broken in half. His chestnut hair was matted, his clothes torn and dirty, covered in blood—some of it still wet. He looked about thirteen.

I propped myself up on a shaky arm. "Where are we?"

"We are in the Well," replied the boy, his hands resting on his knees.

"The Well?" I asked, my gaze shifting, taking all of it in. It looked more like a massive dungeon rather than a tiny well. I noticed there was a slight curvature to the walls, and I wondered if I walked to the other end of it, the part that was nestled in shadow, if those walls would be similar as well. I imagined the gradual curve made one humongous circle—similar to a well.

Hence its name.

"That's what the guards call it," he whispered, an iron collar, smaller than mine, locked around his throat. It bothered me, seeing it there. No one deserved to have an iron collar placed around their neck, especially a child. "We are below

Clearwell Castle."

Like a lit wick, a memory flickered to life, of being in the king's throne room, with my hands tethered behind my back, the brutal crowd screaming for my death. Of the one person who said she believed me . . . the healer. They had dragged her off.

Was it possible she was here too?

"Were you here when they brought me in?" I asked the boy, working my way into a sitting position.

He nodded.

"Did they bring an older woman with me? She has gray hair. No teeth."

He shook his head. "They brought you in by yourself."

"What about before or after they brought me here? Did you see an elderly woman fitting that description?"

He shrugged his bony shoulders. "They bring a lot of people here. It's hard to remember them all."

Swallowing, I asked, "How long have you been here?"

"I don't know. It's hard to say. The days are the same as the nights." He paused, thinking it over. "A long time. Two years for sure. Maybe three?"

I glanced at his collar before I returned my eyes to his. "Are you Cursed?"

"Yes, I have the Earth Curse," he said, pushing his bottom lip up into the space where his broken tooth was. His cheeks looked hollow, his frame gaunt. I wondered how long it had been since he'd had a proper meal. "Everyone here is Cursed, or accused of being Cursed."

My gaze shifted, floating over the many, many faces—young, old, male, female, fair and dark-skinned. Each one of them wore an iron collar.

I looked at the boy. "How did you end up here?"

"My sister worked as a scullery maid, mostly in the royal kitchen, washing dishes. She loved to bake and decorate desserts, but she couldn't do that when the rest of the staff was there, so sometimes, she would stay late in the kitchen, when everyone had gone home, just so she could bake. There was this soldier, with an eyepatch, who would often come to the kitchen to see her. He wished to court her, but she turned him down. One night, when I was playing behind the curtain under the sink, he stumbled into the kitchen. He smelled of ale. He struck her and then he tried to force her to do something . . . something she did not want to do. She begged him not to. She was too scared to use her Curse for fear of what might happen to us. So I used mine. I knocked him out and we took off running, but his friends were waiting out in the hallway. Next thing I knew, they brought me down here." The boy swallowed so harshly, I heard it. Sadness filled his voice, his gaze falling to the floor. "I haven't seen her since . . . and I don't know what happened to her."

"I am so sorry," I said, at a loss for words. I took his hand. "Was she your only family?"

He nodded somberly.

I gave his hand a squeeze and did as Ezra would have done. "Well, kid, looks like I'm your family now."

He grinned softly and gave me a quick nod. Water dripped from above, landing just above his left brow. He wiped it away with the back of his sleeve, smearing it. But it wasn't thin or clear like water. It was thick and red, like blood.

I watched another droplet as it fell, tracing it to the

ground. I gasped.

The ground . . . it was covered in blood.

A torturous scream emitted from above, choked out through the thick floor, but still audible.

The room fell silent.

When the scream died out, there was a brief pause. And then there came another, just as bloodcurdling as the last. This same process repeated, over and over again.

The boy fell into the fetal position, his hands covering his ears, his eyes closed tight. I moved closer to him, my hand rubbing his trembling back as he lay on the bloody floor, rocking back and forth.

"It's going to be okay," I said, unsure about the words coming from my mouth, but saying them anyway. I continued to rub his back, continued to listen to the horrific sounds coming from above—the hair on the back of my neck stretching higher with each bloodcurdling scream.

As they persisted, the droplets of blood changed to a steady trickle. And then to a constant downpour.

The worst part? It was still warm.

Bile stung the back of my throat.

I crawled over to the wall, propped my forearm against it, and vomited.

A hand rubbed my back. I stole a quick glance over my shoulder to see who it was—it was the boy, conquering his terrors so that he could comfort me. If another wave of nausea hadn't overtaken me just then, I might have found it heartwarming.

When the screams finally stopped and I had nothing left to expel, a chorus of pounding boots descended a set of stairs.

Keys rattled before a large, iron door swung open.

I was wrong thinking the screams had stopped, because now they spread to the prisoners down here. Pure horror painted the air as the prisoners scattered like mice, scrambling away from the door, as two dozen guards filtered in.

One of them barked orders, pointing at one of the Cursed, a middle-aged man who was little more than bones and skin. Two guards grabbed him and dragged him, kicking and screaming, out the door and up the stairs. The one giving the orders set his sights on a little girl, no older than five, who was nestled in her mother's arms. With a flick of his head, he motioned for another guard to take her.

"No!" I screamed, my anger rippling through me, turning the blood in my veins to boiling lava.

The boy tugged my hand. "Don't make a scene or they'll take you too," he said, desperate eyes pleading with me. Goddess divine, those doe-like eyes looked familiar.

When one of the guards tried to grab the little girl, a man sprung forward, his fist colliding into the side of the guard's head. Another guard withdrew his sword and plunged it into the man's torso. Streams of blood rivered from the man's mouth, his head dropping as he looked at the blade now stuck unnaturally in his body.

"Anyone else?" the guard yelled, feeling every ounce of his power trip. He ripped the blade free, and the man crumpled to the ground.

The woman with the little girl let out a horrified scream, tears staining her cheeks as she tried to crawl over to the man while still holding her child. But she never made it to him because two guards stepped in, grabbed the man by his wrists, and began to drag him out. Another guard reached for the girl. Both child and mother screamed as they were pried from one another's arms.

I couldn't believe what I was seeing. Someone needed to do something—*anything*. I tugged my hand free from the boy's, pleading with my Curse to break free of its iron suppressor. But it did not answer. I begged the goddess part of me, but she was nowhere to be found. All I had right now was the limited abilities of my battered body.

It would have to be enough.

Leaving the boy behind, I moved as quickly as my black and blue legs would carry me, my hand pressed over my aching, wounded side as I chased after the guard who had taken the little girl. But the crowd didn't part for me like they did for him, making the gap between us wider with each passing moment. At this rate, I wouldn't make it. I needed to think of something to get his attention and fast.

At that exact moment, the tip of my shoe kicked a chunk of broken stone about the size of my fist.

That would do.

Hurriedly, I grabbed it, took aim above the door, and hurled it with all my might, the rock soaring over the prisoners.

"Hey!" I screamed at the top of my lungs as the stone smashed into the wall, bits of rock raining down. "Let her go!" I yelled, adrenaline stampeding through my veins, tamping down the pain I felt.

The guard turned towards me, the little girl kicking and screaming in his arms. "Grab the bitch!" he yelled at the others. "Her life ends today."

"No!" roared the guard who had been giving orders before. "She is to be publicly Cleansed. King's orders." He jerked his head to the door. "Let's go."

The guards listened and headed towards the exit.

When they were all out, the iron door swung behind them, the locking mechanism sounding in the stunned silence of the cavernous dungeon.

I dropped to my knees. She was just a little girl.

"Are you okay?" the boy asked as he ran up beside me.

"No. Not really," I answered honestly, fighting how angry I was with myself, and my uselessness—I was supposed to be the Goddess of Life, and I couldn't even protect one little girl.

CHAPTER 45

Sage

"When you woke, you asked about an elderly woman. We could go look for her if you'd like," the boy said. He was standing to the right of me, hands tucked behind his back as he rocked in place. It was amazing to see how quickly he recovered from what just happened—although I supposed living down here for two to three years would have that effect on a person.

I, however, was still slumped in my defeated position, an arm thrown across a bent knee as I leaned against the cold wall. I blinked, his words, or rather the task they created—a reason to continue forward—was enough to tug me out of my stupor.

I stood up, feeling every ache and pain in my body from the way the guards had handled me during the trial. And then there was the wound in my side from the arrow. It hurt viciously.

"Alright, let's go see if we can find her," I said.

He nodded.

"What's your name?" I asked the boy as we started walking, glancing over the faces of the prisoners, searching for the healer.

He gave me a funny look. "My *name*?"

"Yeah, your name."

He exhaled a soft breath. "Names don't exist down here."

"What do you mean they don't exist down here?" I asked, stepping around the body of an elderly male who was sleeping on the wet, cold floor.

"*People* have names. The second the guards shoved us down here, we stopped being people," he answered as he walked ahead.

"That's absurd." I lengthened my stride, catching up to him, the pace taking more effort than it should, but my body wasn't exactly in tip-top working order. Gently, I grasped his shoulder, turning him to me. "Whether you are in the Well or not, you are still a person."

"People don't live like this." He gestured for me to look to my left. "Animals do."

I glanced in the direction he had indicated, and my mouth fell wide open.

A man had pulled down his breeches and was hovering over a wood bucket. He was *going* to the bathroom, right in front of everyone—his rear on full display. The people sitting around him didn't even seem to bat an eye or care. This lack of privacy was normal for them—as well as the lack of sanitization.

I looked back at the boy, his eyes as dull as an overused bread knife. There was no spark there, no zest for life. And suddenly, I understood. He was no different than Vera, the girl who worked in the bathhouse. He became what he needed to become so that he could survive in this place. And survive he had.

"Alright then, you don't need to tell me your name right now. But on the day you feel you can be a person again, that is when I want you to tell me."

He nodded but didn't say a word more.

I ruffled his hair. "And so, for now, I shall call you Boy."

The further we went into the back of the Well, the less people there were. Light was also fleeting. When it became so dark it was hard to see and the voices were hard to hear, we decided to turn back—there was no one in this part of the dungeon.

No one alive, that was . . .

I stepped cautiously around the body of a woman who looked like she had died many years ago and her body had been left to rot. A few plump rats nibbled on her dehydrated carcass, her lidless eyes wide open.

Our search turned up empty.

I didn't know if I was relieved about that or not. I was happy the healer wasn't down here, but that also made me worry about where they might have taken her. I sent a quick prayer up to the Creator asking for the healer's safety. It helped. A little bit.

Boy had gone off somewhere, leaving me alone with my thoughts and my poor, aching body.

I sat slumped against the wall, close to the spot where I had awakened. I peeled my dirty-bottomed underskirts upwards so that I could inspect the backs of my legs. I could almost make out the perfect shape of the bottom of the guard's shoe, where he had kicked me. The flesh was stained an angry dark blue, the area slightly swollen. I didn't know what was more painful, that or the small arrow wound.

I shucked the bottom of my skirts back down, watching Boy as he approached—a stick in his hand, and a big smile on his face.

"Look what I have!" he exclaimed victoriously.

"A stick?" I asked, a bit perplexed at his excitement.

"Yup," he said, popping the *p*. "I didn't steal it either. I traded for it. Fair and square."

"Oh?" I said out loud, not entirely sure what to make of all of that. "What are you going to do with it?" I asked, a quizzical brow lifting.

He squatted beside me, shifting a small, broken piece of stone around with the stick. "Well, food is scarce, but the rats are in abundance down here. I'm going to see if I can use the stick to build a trap to catch one."

My stomach lurched and my lips curled back in disgust.

Boy chuckled. "Just you wait. Once you've been down here for a month with only a few breadcrumbs to eat, you'll be eyeing up the rats too."

"I hope not," I said, trying not to gag.

All he did was shrug, as if to say *we'll see about that*. "I've been meaning to ask," he started, his eyes dipping to the injury in my side. "What's that from?"

I'd gotten pretty good at ignoring the pain, but now that he brought it up, it was hard not to think about. "I got it from an arrow," I sighed.

He nodded. "One with a small head?"

"Yeah, how'd you know?" I asked.

"It's a newer weapon they've started using to subdue the Cursed. Some of the newcomers down here have the same wound as well. The soldiers always take the arrows out before they bring the people down here." He shrugged one shoulder. "I imagine they take them out because they probably don't want to give us prisoners anything sharp, in case we try to use it against them."

That made sense. And it explained why they had taken the arrow out of my side before bringing me here.

Boy withdrew a string from his pocket, something I imagined he'd traded for as well, and he started to tie it around the end of the stick.

While he focused on building his rat trap, I looked around, my gaze settling on the door. "Is that the only way to get in and out?" I asked him.

He paused what he was doing. "Yes. Why?"

Determination knitted my brow. "I'm going to get us out of here."

"How?" he asked.

"I'm not sure yet," I answered truthfully. "How often do the guards come down here?"

He scratched the back of his head, thinking about it. "Two to four times a day. Usually, it is to bring new people in, or take people out. Occasionally, they bring food, or they fill the water buckets." He nodded to one—it looked no different than the one I had seen the man relieving his bowels in. I shoved off the thought.

"That makes no sense. If they are taking people up there—" I pointed to the floor above us, "—to kill them, why would they bother to feed and water everyone down here?"

"They want us alive. I don't know why though." He shivered. "And I don't think I want to find out either."

Neither did I. Which was why I needed a plan. A weapon. Or something.

"What do they bring the food in?"

"Baskets."

"And the water?"

"They bring it in big wooden kegs, fill the buckets, and then they take them out with them when they leave."

"Hmm," I answered in reply, my mind drifting.

I could fit in a keg, as well as Boy, but getting in there without being detected was problematic, and the guards would surely notice the weight once they tried to take it out.

And—my gaze lifted, surveying the faces of the other prisoners, both young and old—how could I leave them all knowing that something horrible was waiting for them above?

There was no way I was going to leave them all to suffer whatever horrors waited upstairs. Which meant one thing . . .

If I was going to escape, we were *all* going to escape.

But it wouldn't be enough to just get them out of the Well—I would also need to ensure that they made it out of the castle too. During my time here, I had familiarized myself fairly well with the parts of the castle I was allowed access to, but I couldn't just walk a small village of prisoners out through the hallways.

I thought back to the map that Kaleb had brought me, my mind retracing the hidden passages. All of them had led to something that was shaped like a . . .

My eyes rounded at the corners as realization hit me square and center.

The passages *all* led to here.

I studied the stone walls, built strong enough to withstand cannon fire, noticing the odd patterns scattered every fifteen feet or so—arched doorways that had long been sealed off. I walked over to the closest one, my fingers running along the stone, tapping and feeling.

"What are you doing?" Boy asked curiously.

"I think there used to be hidden passages that all led to here," I answered as I rasped my knuckles against the stone. "And I think this was one of them."

"There are," Boy said.

I stopped, my gaze shifting to him. "What do you mean? You know of the hidden hallways?"

He nodded quickly. "I used to play hide and seek in them with the other kids."

Well, I'll be damned.

"How familiar are you with them? Would you be able to get us to one if I got us out of here?" I asked, urgently.

Another quick nod, his eyes twinkling for the first time since I had met him. "I know all of them. There's one not far from here. It's hidden behind a huge portrait of one of the past kings. The painting is on hinges, so it swings open like a door." He chuckled as he leaned in as if he were letting me in on a secret. He whispered, "We used to call it King Big Nose because the guy in the painting has a giant honker on him."

I laughed softly. "I think that's a great name."

He beamed at me.

I smiled, my mind already forging ahead in thought. I knew how I was going to get them through the castle, I just didn't know how I was going to get them out of the Well.

We had no weapons.

I scanned the area, chock-full of prisoners, searching for an answer. And as I looked from one to the other, and so on and so forth, an answer conjured in my mind.

I turned to him. "How many people do you think are down here?"

"Hundreds?" he guessed.

"That's right," I said proudly, my hands bracketing my hips. "Hundreds."

CHAPTER 46

Sage

I stood on an upturned water bucket, a dais befitting that of a cottage shrew—which I was. *Goddess of Life, my ass.* My arms were crossed over my chest as I listened to the prisoners squabble. This was not going like I'd planned.

"Don't listen to her! She's going to get all of us killed," shouted an old man above the rest.

"And what is the other option?" I retorted. "Wait patiently until the guards come back?"

"My time is limited anyway." He batted his hand at me dismissively. Slowly, he turned, his leg muscles so depleted that he could barely lift his feet off the floor as he shuffled away, swallowed up by the crowd. A few more people turned away and followed behind him.

I was losing them.

"How do we *fight* guards?" asked a man to my left.

"Yeah! We don't have any weapons!" exclaimed a woman who was standing beside him.

"We don't need weapons. We have the numbers. We can win," I said, my certainty resonating clearly in my tone. Weapons or not, two dozen guards were not enough to subdue hundreds of prisoners. It showed just how complacent the king had become.

"Say it works, say we break out of here . . . then what? The castle is full of guards. Don't you think they'll take notice of hundreds of prisoners walking through the halls?" someone in the crowd asked. I didn't see who it was. Their concern was supported vocally by a dozen others.

"Boy, here, grew up in the castle." I gestured to Boy, who was standing at my side. He wore a mixed expression—half excited and half ready to shit his pants. "There are hidden hallways, and he knows how to access them. With a bit of luck, we will all walk out undetected."

"I don't believe in luck!" shouted a younger girl, around fourteen.

I tried not to roll my eyes—of course, there *always* had to be one. A few more voices joined in on her claim.

Okay, *more* than one.

"I don't want any part of this," said another woman.

As if her statement were a rock tossed in water, within seconds, it rippled into waves—the crowd growing more boisterous with their disapproval of my plans.

I needed to get a handle on this before I lost them completely.

"Do none of you have something to fight for?" I yelled at the top of my lungs. My voice echoed, the message repeating, bouncing off the walls, amplifying for all to hear.

Mouths snapped shut, heads swiveling my way.

I tightened the proverbial fist, refusing to let the reins slip out of my hands now that I had them back, even if momentarily. Quickly, I continued, "Because if you don't, if you have nothing, then I understand why you won't fight." I paused, more and more faces shifting my way. "But if you have something—some*one*—then is this not worth the risk? I'm giving you a chance to see your loved ones again. And yes, nothing is guaranteed, but if we don't take a stand, if we yield, then you lose that chance to ever see them again." I took a brief pause. "When the guards come, I will fight for all of you, even if that means I must stand alone." I splayed my fingers over my chest, gesturing to myself. "I am willing to take that risk." I looked from face to face, my heart hammering. "Are you?"

Everyone fell silent.

On bated breath, I waited . . . Would my words be enough?

Footsteps sounded, carrying a man forward. He was probably in his early thirties, but the wrinkles that webbed around his eyes, and the bags that rippled beneath them wrote of his hardships, and it made him appear so much older. But even though his face was weathered, there was something about the way he proudly stood that made me think he wore his misfortunes like a badge of honor.

"I'm a farmer," he started, his voice gruff. "I'm used to working the fields so I don't know much about fighting, but I do know that I want to see my wife again and hold my baby boy." He gave me a nod. "I'll take the risk. I'm in."

An older woman with stiff, rigid posture came forth, her weary eyes meeting mine. "I want to see my daughter and my grandchildren again." She gave me a confirming nod.

Next, two burly men stepped forward. The dark-haired one spoke first. "My brother and I are pugilists. Grew up learning how to fight with leather bound around our fists. We might not have leather now, but we'll fight. For you, for everyone. For our parents in the Cursed Lands."

More and more stepped forward, declaring who they were fighting for—the torch of hope spreading from one to another, lighting a monstrous, burning flame.

And that was it—the thread that stitched a bunch of strangers together.

The shared hope of seeing loved ones again.

After I got down from the water bucket, the pugilist brothers and a few other brawny men began to break the buckets apart, creating a small pile of wood slats, as per my instruction.

While they did this, a group of kids came up to me, saying they were eager to help. So, I took a broken shard of flagstone and showed them how to sharpen the end of the wood into a small, hand-held spear—something Ezra had had me do frequently when I was a child, another part of my training.

Sometimes I had thought some of the things she taught me were useless, but now I'd praise the rock-loving woman's name.

As I worked with the kids, Boy led another group in searching the walls for rocks suitable for throwing—although the Well was a vast expanse of nothingness, we'd use whatever we could to win this battle.

Even though not everyone had volunteered to fight, the majority had—more than I'd expected. I didn't have time to train everyone, so anyone who showed any type of promise was automatically nominated as a member of our last-minute army.

For the next four days—time I judged by my rounds of sleep—we prepared.

We sent the elderly and the young to the far side, where the torchlight grew dim, keeping those who could not defend themselves further away from the battle.

A group of us stood with our backs pressed against the wall on either side of the door. I raised my fist and kept it clenched, signaling my collared warriors to hold their positions as the sound of boots striking the floor echoed down the stairwell—a foreboding sound that grew with each passing second.

My heartbeat thrummed in my ears, my hand clenched so tightly around the sharp-ended wood slat that it would surely leave an imprint.

Power in numbers, that's what we have, I repeated to

myself, used it to tamper that small, criticizing voice that feared wood slats and rocks were not enough to fight against real weapons.

The door swung open, and the guards strode in.

When they all were fully inside, I dropped my fist and we charged. A mighty roar emitted from my throat, shattering the nervous ticking of my heartbeat in my ears and replacing it with the song of a warrior.

My group charged to the door, sectioning it off and ensuring the guards didn't double back. We could not risk one escaping and warning the others.

The second group, led by the brothers, charged down the middle, separating the befuddled guards into two groups. The farmer's group charged in next, halving the guards again. Divide and conquer, we scattered them like mice. And then we closed in, releasing everything in our arsenal—rocks, spears, and fists.

The soldier closest to me turned, his blade glinting in the flame-lit chamber, striking the head clean off a fellow prisoner. I didn't allow my soft heart to take pause and mourn the loss of my newfound brethren, for there would be time for that later. Right now, I needed to focus—that was the only way I could ensure minimal casualties.

A female prisoner jumped on the guard's back, her arms clamping around the guard's neck. He stumbled back, unable to support both his weight and hers. He rammed his elbow into her, connecting with her ribs, and she fell to the floor.

Before he had a chance to turn on her, I was on him.

My fist groaned as I connected with the bottom of his jaw. He swung at another prisoner, his eyes held wide, frantic as he realized there were too many of us, and not enough of them.

Another prisoner caught his arm before the guard could deliver that fatal blow. Two more prisoners grabbed hold of him. And then another. And another. Until he was subdued.

We fought with our hand-sharpened spears, while they fought with their lethal swords. We fought in clothes drenched in blood, while they wore glistening armor. We fought for our loved ones, and they fought for their king.

And because of that final factor, this was a battle they would not win.

One by one, the guards fell. And when the battle was over, we raised our hand-sharpened spears and cried out in victory.

Hundreds of prisoners were on the move, and all of it was happening right under the king's pretentious nose.

It had been just as Boy said. There was a massive painting of an old king not far down from the top of the stairwell, propped on rickety, screeching hinges. He swung it open with a big, toothy grin, took a step to the side, and gestured to the dark passage, like he had just performed some sort of magic trick.

In truth, what he did was so much better than that, because in that moment, one young boy had just single-handedly gifted hundreds of people their path to freedom.

CHAPTER 47

Sage

I could deal with the tight confines of the hidden passageway, and the darkness that exuded from it, but the never-ending cobwebs, thick and sticky and consistently wrapping themselves around my head, my torso, and my arms, as if they had personally taken it upon themselves to clothe me in spider-weaved silk?

That was something I could do without.

Fortunately for those at the back, it was something they wouldn't have to contend with, not that I could say the same for those of us at the front.

I swiped at my face, trying to clean off the latest assailant. It tangled with my lashes, my hair. I sincerely hoped the spider that made it wasn't still in it. Not that spiders bothered me per se, it was just the idea of a bug crawling on me in the pitch black, unannounced, that gave me that creepy-crawling feeling.

In truth, the cobwebs were probably helping to ease some of the anxiousness that curdled my stomach. Although we were on the move, we still were not free. And we still had one major hurdle to jump.

"How much longer do you think?" I whispered to Boy as I walked behind him, my hand on the pommel of the sword I'd stolen from one of the guards. It was nested in its sheath, hitched to a belt that wrapped around my waist—another stolen piece.

"Not long," he answered, his voice as hushed as mine.

I nodded in the dark, nibbling on my bottom lip feverishly.

As the castle backed a cliff, there were only a few ways to get in and out of it, and one of those required swimming with the fish—something I doubted the majority of prisoners had the ability to do—which ruled that option out. That left two more: the front entrance—which had a steady hum of people coming and going through it—or the side door—reserved for guards and royal departures.

Both of them were garbage options.

But we didn't have a choice—it was one or the other. We picked the latter.

I bumped into Boy, who had come to an abrupt stop. My hands clasped his shoulders, my body reverberating from the impact.

"We're here," he said, his voice drifting into the dark void.

"How do you know?" I asked, squinting in the dark, unable to see anything.

"I know these halls like the back of my hand," he said. He pressed on something, and I heard the slightest protest of a squeak before a stream of light filtered in. Both Boy and I peeked through the crack into the much larger hallway which sat on the other side.

"I'll go first and scope things out," I whispered. "You stay with the others."

"But I want to come. I want to help—"

I cut him off. "And you will, but let me check things out first."

"Okay," he agreed softly. "Take the first hallway on your right, that leads to the entrance, but be careful."

"Alright," I said with a nod. I stepped around him and pressed my spread fingers to the door and gently pushed it open. I peeked my head outside, scanning the hall. Other than a plethora of old paintings staring suspiciously at me, this hallway was empty.

Now was my chance . . .

But before I stepped out, I felt a small tug on the back of my dress. "Just come back," Boy pleaded softly.

"I will," I reassured him, ruffling his hair before I snuck out into the hallway, closing the painting-turned-door behind me. The painted portrait was of a young queen with lovely auburn hair. She was watching me, her judgmental emerald eyes boring into me. I heeded her no mind, as I pressed my back against the wall and slowly inched along it, my senses alert and ready.

I knew my appearance was abhorrent. My dress—what was left of it—was in tatters. I was covered in crusted blood and I had the telltale iron collar looped around my neck—

declaring who I was for anyone who spotted me. And then there was my skin—littered with black and blue bruises, not to mention the wound in my side.

Reaching the end of the large, quiet hall, I craned my neck as I dared to look around the corner. The hallway before me was arched, and it was a short stretch, maybe ten paces before it ended, leading into a massive room, at least four times as large as the throne room. On the far end of the room, twin doors, which I presumed to be the exit, were swung closed.

My heart turned to stone as I surveyed what stood between the exit and me, row by armored row. There weren't just a few guards stationed there . . .

It was an army.

But something was off about them.

Even well-disciplined soldiers shifted or moved every once in a while. But these men? They were *perfectly* still.

I leaned in, studying their armor. Long gone was the clunky metal the king forced them to wear, replaced by armor that looked as light as a feather, and yet, it didn't seem weak—it looked the opposite of that. It gleamed brilliantly, trimmed with glistening gold—a sun embossed on each chest plate.

Footsteps sounded in the distance.

Damnit. Someone was coming.

I eyed the crimson banner that draped across the ceiling from wall to wall, the tails tumbling down to the floor on either side. The hooks in the ceiling held the fabric out just enough that I could hide behind it.

My heartbeat quickened as the sound grew closer,

accompanied by the sounds of metal screeching upon metal, telling me it was most likely a guard. When they had passed, I tugged the fabric back and snuck a peek.

My eyes widened—I'd know that mountainous build just about anywhere.

"Ryker," I whisper-shouted.

He came to an abrupt halt and turned to look my way.

I stepped out from behind the banner.

"Sage," he exclaimed softly, as he quickly walked towards me, the length of his long legs chewing up the distance in little time. His lips pressed into a flat line as he took in my sad physical state. Wild eyes flicking up to mine, he asked, "I've been looking for you everywhere. Are you okay?"

"I'm alright," I said, nodding softly. "I'm relieved to see you."

"As I am you. I wasn't at the trial, but when I heard what had happened, that you had been taken to the dungeon, I—" Ryker fumbled for words. "I'm so damn sorry I wasn't there to try to help you."

I shook my head. "There's nothing you could have done for me without putting yourself in danger."

"Putting myself in danger would have been the least of my concerns," he said, crossing his arms over his chest.

I understood that because I had felt that same way when Kaleb was taken. And if roles were reversed, and it was Ryker in my place, yes, I would have fought for him too. Whether that made us stupid or courageous, I didn't know. Perhaps it was a bit of both.

He unhooked a ring full of small brass keys from his belt.

"Let's get that thing off you, yes?" Ryker's eyes dropped to the collar around my throat.

My mouth popped open as I looked at the ring of keys.

"Where did you find those?" I asked, sweeping my matted hair back and tilting my chin up so he had more room to work.

"I stole them from the dungeon," he replied as he tried the first key. When it didn't work, he tossed it to the side—the metal key clanging upon its kin—and tried the next in line. "I bribed my way in, hoping to find you. But when I checked the cells in the dungeon, you weren't in any of them. Where were they keeping you?"

My brows shot towards my hairline. "Cells? There were no cells in the dungeon—it was just one cavernous circle."

Dark lashes lifted, his gaze meeting mine. "There must be two sets of dungeons then. I've worked here for weeks, and I've never heard so much as a peep about the other one." He looked back at the lock and tried another key. "I wonder why."

"Perhaps it's because they are doing something terrible to the people down there." I swallowed.

"What do you mean?" Ryker asked.

An audible click sounded. The left side of his mouth twisted upward in victory as the lock sprung free. He helped me out of the collar and tossed it behind the banner—covering our tracks.

I swallowed harshly. "I don't know exactly what they are doing to the prisoners. All I know is that the guards drag them from the Well, then shortly after, all you hear is . . . screaming." My gaze fell, fixating on the deep-red rug. "And then in some places, blood starts to rain from the ceiling."

Ryker said something, but whatever it was, I didn't hear it.

Because at that moment, all I could hear in my head were those horrific screams.

"Hey." Ryker stepped into me, his hand resting on my shoulder. "Look at me, Sage."

I did.

"You are free from there now."

I nodded, hanging on to his words.

There was something else he needed to know.

I took a breath. "There were hundreds of us down there. All Cursed or accused of being Cursed."

"Hundreds of Cursed?" Ryker repeated, his lip curling in anger.

"Yeah . . ." I placed a caring hand on the cool metal wrapped around his forearm. "But they aren't down there anymore."

"What do you mean?"

I pointed to the painting of the auburn-haired queen, just down the hallway from us. "They are behind there."

"Behind?" Ryker asked, quizzically. His expression shifted to concern—for me.

"I promise I haven't lost my mind," I stated with a chuckle. "There are hidden passageways that run throughout the castle. It's how we've all been able to move undetected. We were going to try to leave through this exit, but it's packed with soldiers."

Ryker thumbed over his shoulder, towards the room the soldiers were in. "That room was practically empty this morning, despite a few guards posted at the entrance." He dropped his hand, returning his arm to its crossed position. "I don't know what those things are, but they sure aren't soldiers. Soldiers move, but they don't."

I had noticed that as well.

Unease sifted, like winter's touch, into my bones.

"What do you think they are?" I asked, tempted to walk back and peer at them around the corner.

"Honestly, I have no idea. They look human, but I wouldn't be surprised if they are something else entirely."

I nodded in agreement. I felt the same way when I saw them too—something was definitely off about them.

"Do you think they would move if hundreds of prisoners were walking through them?" I asked jokingly.

"There's only one way to find out," Ryker said with a one-shoulder shrug, walking forward.

"What?" I said, following behind him. "Ryker, I was kidding."

We both peered around the corner, looking at the massive, perfectly still army—my skin turned to gooseflesh.

"Look. Their chests don't even rise," he pointed out.

A few seconds of watching confirmed he was right. "I see that."

He nodded. "It's like they aren't even alive."

"Then how are they standing there?"

Ryker shrugged a muscular shoulder, bulked up by his armor. "Creator above if I know."

My brows dipped. "Do you think they are under some type of spell or something?"

"Anything could be possible," he answered. "Stay here."

"Wait . . . what are you doing?"

"I'm going to test our theory out," he said with a confident smirk.

I was about to protest, but Ryker was already well on his way. He walked through the small hallway, then out into the other room.

I bit my bottom lip, watching as he strolled up to the soldier with a mind-boggling amount of confidence. I had to give it to the fire twin, most people would probably shit their pants if they were in his shoes, but not Ryker. He acted as though he were walking up to a baker on the street—not an army of frozen . . . whatever they were.

"Good day, soldier," Ryker said casually.

The soldier didn't say a word.

Ryker waved his gauntleted hand in front of the soldier's face, and I nearly fell over.

The soldier didn't even move.

Stepping in front of another, Ryker did the same thing and received the exact same response. He did it to two more. Again, nothing.

After he was done, he returned to the hallway.

"They didn't even respond to you!" I exclaimed as he walked up to me.

"No, they didn't," he confirmed. Those deep, brown eyes, nestled between lowered dark brows, shifted to mine. "I don't know what it is, but I have a really bad feeling about them, Sage."

I did too.

The sudden increase in women's deaths, the lack of military at the castle, and now this strange, unresponsive army? What exactly was going on? Was it all connected somehow? My gut told me it was.

I jerked my chin to the far end of the room, where the exit was. "Do you know how many guards will be posted out there, on the other side?"

"I can't see there being any more than ten out there. The castle is still lacking guards. In fact, their numbers are even more depleted right now as quite a few of them went with the Golden Prince." Ryker rolled his eyes at the term before he continued, "The ones on the ground won't be an issue. It's the archers in the towers that will be the problem, but I'll handle those."

"Okay, and what about the doors? They aren't exactly small. If we open them, that will alert the guards and we'll lose the element of surprise," I said, eyes flicking down the length of the hall, making sure no one was coming. When I confirmed that no one was, I looked back to Ryker.

"There's a smaller door that leads outside. It's what the guards use for shift change so they don't have to open those each time when they go in or out. We'll use those," Ryker supplied.

"That sounds like a good plan. I'll go gather some of the prisoners who can fight. They'll help us clear the grounds." I started to walk away, but Ryker gently caught my arm.

"Sage." He looked pointedly at my side, where the arrow wound was. "You are injured. Let me take it from here."

"Yes, I'm injured but I've been fighting ever since I was thrown in that awful place. And I'm not about to stop now, so don't ask me to." My tone was as solid as the stone floor beneath my feet, as unyielding as the goddess within me.

His eyes bounced between mine before he sighed, his

broad shoulders lowering on the exhale. Letting my arm go, he said, "Alright then, let's get those prisoners out of here."

I gave him a firm nod. "Let's get them out."

CHAPTER 48

Sage

Collars left behind and Curses at the ready, five of us filtered swiftly through the side door and into the outer court. The castle grounds were snow-packed and rimmed with mighty, tall walls. To my left was a long stretch of stables, the stalls vacant—I imagined the horses must also be with Aurelius in the countryside. A large pile of hay, pierced by a pitchfork, sat beside the stalls, as well as some water troughs. Straight ahead, a couple hundred feet away, stood an arched exit, the doors swung wide open—*freedom*. Twin towers flanked the exit, the stone and mortar behemoths shooting up into the azure sky, those damn crimson banners flicking like a serpent's tongue.

"What the—" a guard decreed, but his words were severed as Ryker's flame arrow buried itself in his chest with a sickening *thunk*. It reminded me of the sound I heard when

Kaleb died. My blood froze in my veins.

Focus, Sage, focus, I told myself.

My fingers stretched, conjuring the water molecules in the air, forging them with one another until my water blade emerged, edges as sharp as broken glass.

In the short span of time it took me to conjure my blade, Ryker took another guard down.

"Show off," I teased.

He chuckled. "That was nothing." His lips flattened as he looked to the towers.

"Go," I said, tracking his gaze, swinging my blade. "We'll handle the rest."

Ryker nodded as he turned to another prisoner. "You're with me."

"Right," the man replied, nocking an arrow in his magically crafted bow. The two of them took off towards the towers, leaving me and the pugilist brothers.

A guard leapt in front of me, his clean, polished sword itching for blood. He swung his blade and mine answered, sliding down the length of his. He retracted a step before he swung again. I ducked underneath his sword as it sailed over my head. His follow-through left him exposed. I took advantage of that and jabbed my sword forward, straight into his lower torso, where the armor didn't quite cover him.

Wide-eyed with horror, he sputtered, blood bubbling up on his lips. With a mighty heave and a bit of a grunt, I pulled my sword from him.

"Alert the other guar—"

The voice that came from behind me was cut off, replaced with the sounds of choking and sputtering instead.

Quickly, I turned.

A guard, a few strides from me, had a sword plunged through his torso. The pugilist brother, the brunet one, was standing behind him. He withdrew his blade and the guard crumpled to the ground. He gave me a quick nod, and I returned it.

The sound of clanging swords captured both of our attention.

Over by the stables, the brunet's brother had become entwined in battle with three guards. He reared back as they advanced, still managing to block their strikes even though he was outnumbered. Wasting no time, his brother and I ran for him, our entry into the fight evening the odds.

My sword tangled with one of the guards', our blades clanging against one another as we moved around the grounds. I grabbed hold of the post that held up the corner of the stable, using it to cantilever around the side, into one of the stalls. The guard barreled after me, chasing me down. I swirled, just in time to absorb his blow. His attack was so strong, he swept my sword from my hands.

But I didn't need a sword to fight—years of training with Ezra had taught me as much. And lucky for me, this guard wasn't fully armored.

I dropped to the ground and fired my foot into the guard's kneecap with every ounce of strength I had—wincing once more as pain enveloped my side where the injury was.

I heard a pop, and he yowled like a cat that had had its tail slammed in a door.

At that moment, Ryker returned, finishing the guard off. His eyes darted briefly to my hand, which I used to cover my throbbing, aching side. Meeting my gaze, he said, "The archers are down, but there's no telling when more might show up. We need to get everyone on the move. *Now.*"

I nodded as he helped me up. "Alright."

Walking through my enemy's eerie army with a few hundred Cursed prisoners had my jaw clenched so tightly, my molars felt ready to combust. I worried that at any moment, the soldiers would snap out of their catatonic state, withdraw their swords, and begin slaying everyone. It would be a blood bath.

I tensed at the thought. Tried not to think about it.

Boy, who was walking in front of me, stopped to stare at one. My hands fell over his shoulders, and I gently urged him forward, but not before sneaking a glance for myself.

Each time I looked at their unfamiliar, yet familiar faces, I found the same gut-wrenching message repeated.

Although they were not identical, they all shared similar traits to one person—

Aurelius.

Dread filled my stomach, weighing it down like I'd swallowed a cup of lead.

And even after we made it past the soldiers, past the outer court and into the world beyond Clearwell Castle, that feeling never went away.

What have you done, Aurelius?

CHAPTER 49

Sage

Even though the castle was half a day's walk away, and we were nestled deep in the embrace of the slumbering forest, fast asleep under winter's lullaby, my nerves were still on edge. Yes, we had made it out, but that didn't mean we were safe yet.

At any given moment, the king's soldiers could come for us.

I mean, it wouldn't be very hard to track us—a few hundred pairs of feet walking through a blanket of freshly fallen snow left a substantial trail. One that could not be covered, no matter how hard some of the kids tried.

The knee-deep snow created other challenges, especially for the elderly or the young children, or those without footwear. Most of the people were not dressed for the elements. Throw in the little bit of meat they had on their bones, and it was a bad combination.

The situation was not ideal, but the majority of us did our best to support each other.

People offered to help carry an infant when a parent started to lag behind—which was what I was doing now. Some offered their clothing, their shoes, their socks to one another. In truth, it was heartwarming to see—to see that despite the horrors they'd faced in the Well, they had not let it take their humanity.

As we walked, the keys Ryker had stolen made their rounds. Each time a collar was removed, a victorious cheer would come from the crowd.

It was a sound and a feeling I would never forget.

When night fell and the crescent moon reached her highest point, Ryker, who was aiding an elderly man with a lame leg, turned to me. "I think we should stop here for the night. It's getting harder and harder for some to keep up." His gaze dipped to my side where the arrow wound was. He nodded to the spot. "And you should let me take a look at that."

Ryker was right—the group's pace had slowed to a crawl.

As for my wound, he wasn't wrong about that, either, although I feared what he might find. Sanitary conditions in the Well were abhorrent, and I could only imagine what type of infection had crawled up into the open, untreated wound.

"Alright," I said with a nod, hoisting the shivering toddler higher on my hip. "We'll stop here for the night."

"I'll go to the front and tell the others," Ryker said as he helped the elderly man sit down on a fallen tree, dollops of white caught in every nook and cranny and nub.

"Okay," I replied, puffs of my breath painting the air. I rubbed the little girl's back in an attempt to chase away the cold, her arms twined tightly around my neck.

My brow furrowed as I looked over the crowd walking around me. I had thought that by getting them out of the Well, I would be giving them a chance at freedom, but now . . .

In the throes of winter's chokehold, I wondered if I had doomed them all.

As it turned out—I hadn't doomed them all.

Dozens of woodless fires, created by the Fire Cursed, dolloped the winter lands, bringing warmth to everyone. Rumbling tummies became quiet thanks to the Earth Cursed who used their abilities to track any game in the area. Although they hadn't found enough to feed everyone, they'd found enough to feed some, and that would be huge for aiding us in the journey ahead. If people were going to make it, they needed energy, and that required both sleep and food.

Boy and I sat beside each other in front of one of the many fires, along with eight other people, two of which were sleeping. Judging by the way their limbs were tangled up with one another, I presumed they were a couple.

I'd be a liar if I said it didn't make me feel a flicker of envy. There was a time I would have given anything for that to be Von—to feel his strong, sturdy arms wrapped around me. But then I'd learned the truth about our twisted past and it had driven me into Aurelius's arms instead. Now, after seeing the faces of those soldiers, I didn't know what to think.

"Would you like one?" asked a woman who walked in front of me. Her wilted torso and the bags under her eyes made her look much older than I suspected her to be. She carried a couple sticks in each hand, skewered with a few mouthfuls of steaming rabbit meat.

My mouth watered, but I ignored it. I shook my head and gestured to the others. "They need it more than I do."

The foodie in me might have died right there and then, but because of my immortality, I knew that I could not. And there were those—I glanced at Boy—who needed it more than I did.

The woman gave me a pleasant smile before she handed one to Boy, then moved on to the others. When she had no skewers left to hand out, she started back towards the fire where the game was being cooked, a few fires down from ours.

Boy licked his lips in anticipation, but just before he was about to dig in, he paused. Slowly, he lowered his hands until they rested on his lap.

"What's wrong?" I asked.

He took a moment to reply, but when he did, he spoke in a voice so small, I nearly missed what he said. "Graiyson."

The space between my brows crinkled. "Sorry?"

"That's my name," he said, looking up at me, tears brewing in his eyes like heavy-bottomed clouds on a summer night. "My name is Graiyson."

I couldn't help but become a bit misty-eyed myself as I

slung my arm over his shoulders and pulled him in, giving him a tight squeeze. "It's a great name," I told him.

And truly it was.

"Thank you. It was . . . my dad's name," he said slowly, dabbing at his eyes with the back of his sleeves.

"He would be very proud of you. Of all that you have survived," I said.

Boy nodded, and we sat like that for a moment. After a short while, he raised his kabob to me in offering.

I shook my head. "Eat up. You are going to need it."

"But you didn't get any," he said, threading his lip through his broken tooth.

"I'm alright. Besides—" I patted my stomach, "—I'm still full of that *bread*."

Bread. If it could even be classified as such.

Boy had brought it to me yesterday while I was chiseling one of the wood slat ends into a point. He'd looked as pleased as a house cat that had caught its very first mouse as he dropped the stale bread into my hands, exclaiming proudly that he'd gotten it for me. The bread had been rock-hard, but I had been desperate enough to eat it.

"You're lucky I fought the rat for it!" Boy beamed. "Little bugger almost made off with that piece."

My expression soured. "What? What *rat*?"

"When the guards dumped the bread off, a rat grabbed the—"

I held up a hand, stopping him from going any further. "I'd rather not know."

"Suit yourself." He shrugged his shoulders and turned his attention back to the kabob.

While he ate, I took in the night.

Apart from the crackling fires and steady, light conversation, things were quiet. Here, in the woods, there were no sounds of castle guards patrolling the halls or busy lady's maids chattering about dresses, gossip, or balls. It was just the light whisper of the breeze rattling the leafless branches of the trees and the odd animal who wanted to have their say. Every once in a while, I heard the raucous caw of a raven calling out.

I wondered if I were to track it down and speak to it, if it would be able to relay a message to Kaleb. To tell him to meet me in the Cursed Lands.

But the raven was probably just that—a raven.

I wondered if Kaleb had returned to my chambers since I last saw him—if he had found it empty and was now looking for me. His visits were always so sporadic, so it was hard to say if he had or not. There was also a possibility that he had no idea what was going on. Regardless of if he knew or not, he had made connections with Ezra in the Cursed Lands, and as that was where we were headed, if anything, I figured we would meet up there. Eventually.

Crunching snow and stiff armor sounded to the left of me.

I glanced up to the towering fire twin.

"Alright, let's take a look at that side of yours," Ryker said, two wooden bowls in his hands. I suspected one of the Earth Cursed had made them for him.

I patted Boy's back. "Enjoy that rabbit. I'll be back in a bit."

He nodded in reply, his mouth full.

Ryker and I walked to a private area in the woods, far enough away from the group to grant me some privacy, but close enough we could get back quickly if we needed to.

While I held onto a tree, Ryker unlaced the back of the corset of my dress, his fingers making quick work of the laces—something that didn't surprise me. When he was finished, I sat down on a stump beside the fire, my arm barred across my chest, keeping my dress from falling down.

Ryker crouched beside me. His hand emitted a white, heatless flame, something he used for light as he surveyed my side.

I had put off looking at my injury, reasoned there was nothing I could do for it anyway while I was in the Well. When the guards brought in the barrels of water, people drank from them with their hands—slurping it up eagerly. I reasoned that using the water everyone drank out of to clean the injury would do more harm than good, and so I had left it.

"Arrow wound?" he asked, more statement than question.

I nodded. "How'd you know?"

"Not the first one I've seen."

No, I would suppose not, considering he'd fought in his fair share of battles over the years, defending the Cursed from the king's soldiers.

"It doesn't look as infected as I expected it to, so that's a good sign. I suspect your divinity might have something to do with that. The entry point is fairly small, must not have been a very big arrowhead," Ryker stated, continuing his assessment. Dark-brown eyes met mine, a grin on his lips. "Still, I bet it hurt like a bitch."

"It did." I sighed, remembering that gut-churning feeling of the cold, sharp metal chewing into my torso. But the pain I felt then was not nearly as bad as when it was being pulled out of me. Now *that* hurt.

I heard the sound of water trickling before I felt something soft, spongy, and wet being lightly pressed against my wound. On reflex, I jerked away.

"Sorry," Ryker said with a lighthearted chuckle. "I should have given you a bit of warning."

"It's alright," I replied, easing back into his touch.

Tenderly, he began to clean the wound. As he did, he said, "A woman with the Earth Curse helped me find some moss. She revived it so it should help to disinfect the wound."

I glanced over my shoulder, peering down at the green, spongy mat he dabbed against my skin. I had seen Ezra do the exact same thing countless times before.

"Did you learn this from Ezra?" I asked.

"I did," he said in his chest-rumbling tone. "After my parents died, Harper and I bounced around different families for a few years, until eventually, Ezra took us in. She looked after me and Harper as much as she could. She taught us a great deal of things, but the one thing she pounded into my head, more than anything, was how to treat a wound."

A smile pulled at my lips. "That sounds like something Ezra would do. I'm happy she was there for you two."

"She did her best for us when she was around. Sometimes when she'd disappear, we'd wonder if she would ever come back again, but low and behold, she always did."

I tipped my head to the side, my brows raising slightly. "It's funny, Kaleb and I would wonder the exact same thing."

"Small world," Ryker drawled as he dropped the moss into the bowl. He picked up the other one. "Incoming."

I nodded, trying not to wince as he dabbed the sticky substance into my wound. The area was incredibly tender, but Ryker was surprisingly gentle.

"There's something I've been meaning to talk to you about," I said, glancing ahead, looking at the stark silhouette of the trees.

"Yes?" he rumbled.

"How are *you* doing?" I expanded a bit more, adding on, "After everything that happened with Fallon."

His hand paused for a moment, before continuing. "That's a loaded question. I suppose my answer depends on the day. Sometimes I feel anger towards myself, that I was the reason she lost her life. Sometimes I feel a bit numb to it all. And other times, I feel hurt. I spent a lot of years wondering what happened to her . . . a lot of sleepless nights too. She could have easily sought me out, but she never did. I guess she meant more to me than I meant to her."

My heart struck a heavy beat for my friend, at the way he said the last part, like a bit of his heart had broken off and stuck to the words.

"I think those are all normal ways to feel. I'm sure if I was in your shoes, I'd probably feel the same way too," I acknowledged softly. "What about your feelings towards Von? Knowing that he kept Fallon's death and her whereabouts from you all these years, I imagine that doesn't exactly sit well with you either."

"Yeah, that was a bit of a piss off too. He knew how torn up I was about her. But I've known Von long enough to know a little something about his character—when he genuinely gives his word, he means it. Fallon told me that she asked him not to tell me what happened, because she thought it would be easier for me that way. Figured the false hope of believing she was alive and somewhere out there was the kinder option than me learning that she had died. She said Von had agreed to respect her wishes, but that didn't mean he liked what he had agreed to."

"But he was your friend first," I countered. "Shouldn't that make him loyal to you?"

Ryker chuckled. "He *is* loyal to me. And he's loyal to his word too." He sat the bowl down in the snow, his eyes meeting mine. "I know you're mad at him right now, and knowing the bastard, he probably deserves your anger. But if there is one thing I know, it is that the turmoil I felt, wondering what happened to Fallon, was nothing compared to what I saw Von go through when it came to you. Sage, I don't know if you've quite grasped this, but he waited *centuries* for you to reincarnate. Not days. Not months. Not years. *Centuries.* In all honesty, who the fuck does that?"

Ryker had a point.

Which made me feel even more confused.

That night, while I slept, my dreams were as chaotic as the tattoos on Von's body. And although I could not make sense of my tumultuous dreams, there was a string of words that repeated, clear as rain and full of bourbon:

Please do not leave me again, Little Goddess.

And there was something about those words, the desperate way that they were said, that made my heart feel as though it were made of glass and a great mallet had just struck it.

CHAPTER 50

Sage

We had been walking for seven days now, fueled by very little sleep and even less food. Those who could fish, hunt, or had the Earth Curse tried their best to provide the group with some type of sustenance, but we never stayed long enough in one spot for them to be fully able to do so.

Each morning, me, Ryker, and a few others performed the rounds—rousing the people with a gentle touch on their shoulders to wake up so we could continue towards the Cursed Lands. There was one—a man—who did not wake. The fact that I had not saved him—that I had not gotten him safely to the Cursed Lands, bothered me greatly, to the point that my eyes filled with tears. But Graiyson stuck his hand in mine right when I needed it, and told me we needed to continue forward.

And so that's what I did. That's what we all did. We

continued forward.

One foot after another.

Today, I carried a little boy. He weighed no more than a sack of potatoes, but as time went on, he felt a lot heavier than that. His father walked beside me, the man no more than waxen skin and protruding bones. He didn't look well. Just when I started to worry that he might fall over, his weary eyes would drift over to the boy I was carrying, and he'd make it that much further. I realized that the boy in my arms was his reason for pushing ahead—for continuing on. So, despite the ache in my burning muscles, I hoisted the boy higher on my hip and pressed on.

The sound of rushing, turbulent waters caught my attention.

I glanced ahead, past the group which had come to a slow stop.

In the distance, a river wide enough to swallow three Meristones was unfazed by winter's frozen hold. The water rushed in violent currents, tossing and throwing itself, smashing into rocks. It raced towards a waterfall that was shaped like a horseshoe, plunging itself into oblivion below.

From this viewpoint, I couldn't see the bottom of the massive falls.

"Wait here for a moment," I said to the man who was walking beside me. He nodded and nearly collapsed when he sat down. I set the boy beside him, then watched as he wrapped his arms around his father's neck and nuzzled into him. I left them and headed towards the front of the group— finding Ryker and the pugilist brothers, Thadius and Dante, conversing.

"I'm guessing we need to cross somehow," I stated, surveying the snow-covered land on the other side.

"The river bisects the lands for miles," Ryker stated, gesturing ahead. "There is a place further down where the current isn't as strong, and we might be able to pass through there. The only thing is that it's going to add another four days of walking."

"I don't know how many will be able to make it an extra four days," I replied, not liking that idea.

"Agreed," Dante said, his heavy arms crossed over his chest. Thadius nodded.

"If we got enough of the Water Cursed together, do you think you could dam up the one side of the river long enough for the group to pass through?" Ryker asked, looking at me.

"It's possible. I used to manipulate the waters in the lake back home, but that was a small lake. This is a huge river with a strong current, and I don't know how deep it is. If we do manage it, the longer we hold the dam, the more the river will bank up against it, increasing the weight with each passing minute."

"So then, what if we move the group in batches?" Ryker suggested, thoughtfully tipping his head to the side. "Once a group is across, remove the dam and let the water return to normal. When the next group is ready, make another dam."

"That might work," I said, nodding, thinking it over. "The only thing that worries me is that it's going to take a lot to *lift* the water on one side to create the dam. Doing that over and over again is going to deplete our energy stores fairly quickly."

"Okay, so then what if you lift the water from the

riverbed, just enough for people to walk underneath it? That way some water will bank against it, but the rest of it will flow over," Ryker said, tossing out another thought.

Thadius cleared his throat. "That seems rather risky, no? Having everyone pass through together at the same time?"

I nodded in agreement. "If we can't hold it. . ." I trailed off, my mind imagining our powers giving out and the river swallowing . . . everyone. I recoiled at the thought. "It's too risky."

"Then we play it safe and have people go in batches," Ryker cut in. "The first group that goes will be our test group—those who are strong enough to cross to the other side quickly. From there, we'll gauge the exertion on you and the rest of the Water Cursed. If everything goes well, the next group should be those who are weak and struggling. That way if you are unable to lift the water back up, at least they will have a fighting chance at making the rest of the walk to the Cursed Lands. And those who are more able-bodied can take the long way around."

I thought about it for a moment. "I think this is the best plan we have."

"Agreed," Thadius said, scratching his dark beard.

"Now we just need some Water Cursed willing to help," I said, glancing around, my gaze jumping from weary face to weary face. People were exhausted, hungry, and tired. Finding able bodies might be harder than expected.

"We'll start spreading the word," Dante said, gesturing to himself and his brother.

"Alright then," I replied, setting my sights on the wide, angry river thrashing before me.

If we failed?

No—I shoved the thought out.

We would not fail.

We would not fail because there were too many lives depending on us.

CHAPTER 51

Sage

Twenty-three.

That was how many of us there were.

Twenty-three tasked with controlling trillions of gallons of water.

Twenty-three . . . who, if we succeeded, would save the lives of hundreds.

We stood together, shoulder to shoulder, watching the thrashing beast roaring before us.

The river was unfathomably wide, the gradient steep, creating rapids unlike anything I had ever seen before—not even winter's frigid temperature could tame it into submission. It swallowed whatever was in its path. I did not doubt that the rocks that lined the riverbank used to be boulders, but by the might of the violent, ferocious waters, they had been worn down into small stones.

The woman to my left slipped her hand into mine, and even though we were perfect strangers, we were being forged together as sisters in this moment—united by our cause.

I squeezed her hand gently before I looked to my right and placed my hand in the man's beside me. Scared, wide eyes glanced at our joined hands before they rose to my face. He looked ghastly white, his skin slick with sweat even though it was the middle of winter. His hand clamped onto mine and we exchanged silent nods. He turned to his right, placing his hand in the woman's who stood next to him. This small act of unity—*of joining hands*—was repeated, until we all were linked together.

I closed my eyes and took a deep breath, filling my lungs with the icy air. I pictured myself standing on the lake floor, in the calm serenity of my whispering oak trees, allowing it to center me.

When my eyelids snapped open, I shouted for all to hear, "We count down together!"

Twenty-three voices melded together like heated metal forged in a fire.

When we reached the end of the countdown, a warrior's roar tore out of me. Out of *all* of us.

The crowd behind us began to cheer, their voices urging us on.

I threw my power into breaking the water beast. It fought back, testing the bounds of my power—testing *me*.

There had only been one other time I recalled feeling the crushing weight of what I felt now—that time Kaleb had walked out into the blizzard to go find us wood to heat our home. The storm had laughed at me, ridiculed me, and yet, by the end, I shook it to its knees. I told myself I could do that again.

I gritted my teeth and bore down harder.

And harder.

The river would not relent, but neither would I.

Until finally . . . part of it lifted—blasting towards the crisp, blue sky.

The woman beside me grunted as she, too, lifted her section of the river.

And then another raised up. And another. And another.

Until a riverbed of glistening, polished pebbles and dark silt stretched before us. My heart struck a heavy beat when the crowd behind us cried out in triumph, but as much as I wanted to revel in this victory, I knew that I couldn't. Because now came the real test—we had the strength to lift the river, but did we have the endurance to hold it?

We had to. There was no other choice.

The first group—the runners—went first. As they raced their way to the other side, the river continued to throw itself at our wall, banking itself higher and higher—the natural flow of the current was clogged.

"Hold it," I ground out to the others.

"What's that?" shouted a man from the crowd, his voice frantic.

"It's the king's men! They are coming for us!" screamed a woman.

"They are going to kill us!" cried out another.

It took mere seconds for cheers of victory to be drowned out by screams of panic.

"Everyone to the other side now! Fire Cursed with me!"

I heard Ryker command from somewhere behind. Then he was at my side, his voice in my ear. "We'll hold them off. You just focus on the river until everyone crosses through. And then you get yourself to safety."

"Ryker, no," I said between clenched teeth, fighting against the bone-crushing weight of the water.

"You can do this, Sage," he said, and then he was gone—lost in the crowd behind me.

Chaos ensued as the people began to race for the river, away from the king's soldiers.

I thought I heard Ryker yelling commands far behind me, but the roar of the water drowned him out, along with the screams and cries of the people as they ran for their lives. Some helped one another, while others looked after themselves. I couldn't blame the ones that didn't help—they had been reduced to frightened animals, desperate not to be thrown back into the king's horrific cage.

In an instant, heat spread across my back, licking at the beads of sweat pooling on my skin. Winter's freezing temperatures were chased away as a blistering heat emitted from behind me. I wanted to turn, to check on Ryker, but I didn't dare take my attention off the river—not when hundreds of people were currently passing through.

"I can't hold it much longer," the man said beside me. He was barely able to get the words out.

"You must," I said to him, squeezing his hand a bit more.

"I'm sorry," he said, his hand slipping from mine. His legs gave out from underneath him, and he collapsed onto the ground. His section of the river started to come down, but he used whatever morsel was left of his power to just barely keep it up. I was proud of him for doing so—for fighting even when his body had given out. It showed a great deal of strength.

I set my sights on the slowly falling side. Imagining myself holding a potato sack and adding one more, I grunted as I raised his section of the river back up.

Someone ran up beside me, checking on the man. "Leighton, can you hear me?" he asked.

All that came was a groggy response.

"Get him to the other side," I commanded whoever it was.

"Alright," the person replied as helped the man—Leighton—onto his feet. He half carried, half dragged him towards the riverbed path, desperate to get him to safety by any means.

I knew that feeling well.

The fire behind me grew hotter, the heat stretching to my sides. In my peripheral vision, I could see a wall of flame curve on either side of me, stopping at the river. Ryker and the other Fire Cursed had made a protective wall of flame around us—cutting the soldiers off from reaching us.

Ryker was brilliant.

Further down the line, someone else collapsed. This time, that section of the river damn nearly came crashing down. The people crossing that part screamed in terror just before the river swallowed them whole, but another water wielder and I stopped it from doing so. We swore a string of profanities as we hoisted it back up, my bones groaning.

It did not take long for twenty-three to be reduced to eighteen. Then eighteen to twelve. And by the time the crowd had passed the halfway point, there were only six of us left standing.

My limbs felt like silly little twigs attempting to hold up a mountain. I was stuck in a battle of wills against the strong, powerful, current, and I was beginning to fear that I might break.

My clothes were drenched in sweat. My legs trembled beneath me.

My body, *my power*—both on the verge of giving out.

Help me, I pleaded with the goddess within me.

But she didn't respond.

Please. Lend me strength.

Again, no reply.

Ryker's voice came from behind me. "The soldiers are sealed off for now," he panted.

"Take the others," I rasped to him, my tongue like chalk, my throat dry. How ironic, considering I was holding up gallons upon gallons of water.

Three more Water Cursed went down, but the other two and I didn't let the river fall. I screamed internally—it felt like my body was being shredded apart.

And then . . . *I felt her.* I felt the goddess within wake and stir.

I am with you, she said.

Her strength was like a shot of adrenaline in my veins, firming up my wobbling legs.

"I can't—" the woman beside me wheezed before she went down, her hand slipping from mine.

No sooner than she hit the ground, the other woman went down as well, and the entirety of the river was placed on me.

"Sage—"

I cut Ryker off as I roared, "Help the others! Get them to the other side!"

"But what about you?" he asked, his voice urgent, his jaw clenched as he spoke.

"Help the others!" I *commanded* him, my voice cracking like a whip.

That voice I did not recognize, nor the authority that accompanied it.

"Alright," Ryker growled, the word ripe with frustration and torment—the sound of someone who was *being forced* to do something they didn't want to. "I'll get them across. But you do *not* get captured," he demanded of me. "You get out of here as soon as you can."

I nodded—it was all I could do.

Ryker barked orders at the few able-bodied who remained, instructing them to help the Water Cursed who were unconscious—to carry them across. In my peripheral, I could see him bending down to help one, slinging the woman's arm over his shoulder, and then he and the others started across.

I concentrated. Fixated. On this one task.

The strokes of time slowed. The beating of my heart seemed to do the same.

And in that moment, as the last of the prisoners found their way to safety, I alone held the river on my shoulders.

CHAPTER 52

Sage

When Ryker and everyone else had made it to the other side, I withdrew my power.

The river came crashing down, smashing upon the riverbed and bank with such force that the ground trembled beneath my feet. Water misted across my face, mixing with my sweat-wicked skin and clothes.

Creator above, I felt cold—like that internal flame inside me had nearly burned itself out, resulting in little less than a few glowing embers on the verge of combustion. My energy stores were depleted.

Across the way, Ryker yelled something, but whatever he was saying was lost to me. All I could hear hammering in my ears was the slow, rhythmic ticking of my heart.

Ba-dump. Ba-dump. Ba-dump.

Something flashed above me, but when I looked up, all I

saw was the calm, serene azure sky.

"What have you done?" growled a voice from behind me—proud and noble and . . . angry.

My heart picked up its lagging speed, bursting into a full trot, a contradictory reaction to the rest of my body—notably my stomach, which felt like it had been filled with rocks. My shoulders tightened tensely as I turned around.

Aurelius's regal face, framed by sleek white hair, held no hint of a smile.

He wore all white, his richly tailored clothes hugging his lean, muscled body. A thin gold chain slung across his broad chest, tethered to a cape that danced softly in the wind.

But it wasn't his attire that made my mouth fall open—it was his wings.

They replicated the colors of the waking sun, each plume dipped in glistening gold. They were illustrious, spanning out behind him. Ethereal. Powerful. Incredible.

He looked at the bare bones of cloth that once resembled a dress, to my dirty skin and disheveled hair. Blistering golden eyes flicked up to mine. Full of fury.

It was a different type of fury—different from the kind I had seen in Von's eyes, which seemed to be on my behalf.

The fury I was seeing now—it was undoubtedly directed *at me.*

I looked past Aurelius to the curved wall of flame that Ryker and the Fire Cursed had made to keep us safe—to the soldiers that stood behind it.

Understanding nestled deep in my weary, brittle bones.

"You brought an army—" I took a breath, cutting myself short. I choked out the next few words, "—to take them back."

"I have," he said. "As well as you, *wife*." There was not a single ember of love in the way he spoke the word.

Betrayal gutted me where I stood.

"You *knew* about the Well." I felt like vomiting, but the anger filling my veins was far more potent. I clenched my fists together. "How could you let that happen to *innocent* people?"

He rubbed at his jaw as if I had just slapped him across his freshly shaven face. "They are *not* innocent," he said slowly, his voice even and smooth, but the way he held his teeth together as he spoke, told me that he felt nothing of the sort.

Aurelius had known what was happening to the Cursed, and he had done nothing to stop it.

He had . . .

My temple throbbed, a pounding ache reverberating through my head.

Like a spinning top, twisted and left to its own demise, my world began to swirl around and around and around, until the spinning stopped and I fell to my side.

Blackness painted my vision as a memory surfaced . . .

CHAPTER 53

Sage

"Get them off," Aurelius snarled between clenched teeth. He was standing by the large fireplace in our private chambers, the terrible-smelling ooze still clinging to his clothes, to my dress.

After the God of Death left, so did the attendees.

I couldn't blame them—the celebration had been in shambles. The story we had been trying to sell was stripped and laid bare—the lie blatantly spelled out for all to see. The heroes they were celebrating hadn't won the war—the villains had. Naturally, this would shake their beliefs in Aurelius as a ruler, and cause discourse amongst the two realms—a tasty little meal for the heathen God of Chaos, no doubt.

I sighed and pinched the bridge of my nose. Everything was a mess.

"They will not budge, your divineness," sputtered the

red-faced God of Craftsmen who was working—and failing—
at breaking the lock on the shackles. He was a short man,
about as wide as he was tall, his body packed with mountains
of bulky muscle. He even walked like it was a great effort, the
ground shuddering beneath his feet with each heavy step.

Our private chambers were full of people, each one of
them taking a stab at trying to break the unbreakable—the
diamond-like shackles that the God of Death had used to
imprison Aurelius. They had been at it for hours—the early
morning sun which had started peeking its head over the
horizon told me as much. A vibrant red-orange glow shone
through the windows into our room, the light reaching for
Aurelius. As it always did.

Aurelius let out a mighty growl of disgust. "Do none of
you imbeciles know how to get these off?"

"They are trying, my love," I said, walking from my spot
by the window over to him. Gently, I cupped his face as I tried
to bring him comfort. "They will remove them. We will find a
way."

He jerked his head away from my touch. "You do realize
that this is your fault."

His words hit me hard, like a fist sent into my gut. I
sputtered, "My fault? How so?"

"You allowed him into our lives," he grated.

I glanced around, noting just how many eyes had fallen
on me. Normally, Aurelius would never have had this
conversation in front of others, but that leash he kept so
incredibly tight—apparently, he was letting it slacken.

But unlike Aurelius, I didn't particularly care what tea
the court gossips would spill over their morning croissants.

And I wasn't about to let him place the blame all on me. "I did no such thing. You sit on the crown he once had. Everything he did was so he could take it back—"

"You will not speak another word," Aurelius cut me off, his voice raised. He took a step forward, and for the first time, I winced as my husband came towards me—the memory of what happened during our last disagreement edging on the cusp of my mind. "Be careful, wife. You almost sound like you are trying to defend him."

"I am doing no such thing," I said, shaking my head, unable to believe what I was hearing. His words were blasphemous.

"Then why do you tend his orchard, for all to see, with such love and care? Is it because you have fallen for the enemy?"

I couldn't believe what I was hearing. I stated as much.

But it fell on deaf ears because Aurelius continued his verbal attack. "Do you not hear the whispers, goddess? Of what they call you behind your back?" He turned to the God of Craftsmen. "Tell her. I'm sure you've heard the title they have given her." He shifted his gaze, looking around the room. "Go on, someone tell her what they call her."

No one dared to step forward, not for fear of me, but rather the unraveling god before them.

"Very well, if no one has the courage to speak the name you all whisper behind her back, then I will say it." Aurelius turned to me, his golden eyes now imitating the flame he commanded. "They don't refer to you as my wife, or the Goddess of Life. No, they all call you the Goddess of Whores because that is what you have become—"

I slapped him. It was hard enough to knock his head to the side.

I pulled my hand back and cradled my stinging fingers against my chest, shocked at what I had done, and judging by the audible gasps emitted from around the room, everyone else was too.

I regretted it immediately.

"Aurelius, I'm so sorry." My voice cracked, emotion breaking my words apart, like the tide striking a wall of rock.

His nostrils flared. "How dare you strike me." His lowered brow cloaked his eyes in shadow, but I didn't need light to see what lurked in them—

Disgust.

He had never looked at me like that before.

And it was enough to destroy me. This was my king. My love. My husband.

Pain exploded across my chest as if he had wrapped his fist around my heart and was squeezing the very life from it. I felt lightheaded, my limbs suddenly weak.

He turned away from me. "Take her out of my sight. I can no longer stand to look at Death's whore."

"Aurelius, please." I couldn't believe what I was hearing. Tears welled in my eyes.

The guards grabbed hold of my arms, but I was too broken to fight them. They dragged me out of the room and shoved me into the hallway, slamming the door behind them as I ran towards it.

I pounded my fists on the door. "Aurelius!" I shouted, tears wetting my cheeks. That visceral pain continued to grow in my chest until it became so strong, it took the very breath from my lungs.

Sliding down the door, I fell to the ground. I curled into myself, wrapping my arms around my legs. I wept.

Aurelius had been with me since my creation. He was my closest friend. My lover. His arms were all I had ever known. And to feel him shut me out like this? It was like having the sun's warmth stolen from me—leaving me in the cold, bitter darkness.

I was alone.

Completely alone.

I didn't know how long I stayed like that, but it felt like eternity.

I was barely aware of the strong, steady arms that slipped around me and hoisted me from the ground, of the legs that carried me down the hallways, into a private chamber to a room I had frequented many times before. I had come here to play cards, or when I was lonely, or to enjoy the company of the only other friend I had in this castle.

"It's going to be alright," Arkyn said softly as he gently laid me down on the large bed, the fur blanket beneath me chasing the strange numbness from my skin. "He's just . . ." He paused, searching for the right words. "He's frustrated right now."

I shook my head, my fingers weaving into the soft furs. "We've fought before, but he's never looked at me like that."

"He will come around. He adores you, Aurelia. He gave his heart for you." Arkyn sat on the bed beside me, his weight making it dip. He glanced at me, offering me a hint of a smile. *"Don't forget that."*

I wondered if Arkyn was not only trying to convince me, but himself as well.

Aurelius had avoided me for three days, and I'd had enough.

"You can't go in there, princess," said one of the guards as I burst through the double doors leading into the council room.

The council room was oval in shape, the ceiling—made of glass—bathing the room in brilliant sunlight, washing over the marble floors and gold brick walls. At the end of a long stretch of table that housed twenty other gods, two of which were Aurelius's brothers, sat a large throne positioned at the head of the table. In it, sat my husband.

His wrist and ankles were still bound, the matching collar still wound around his neck. His demeanor towards me only seemed to hold even more disdain. I tried not to wince when I felt it fall on me. I tried not to show them the immense pain blooming in my chest—the visceral ache of a heart shattering.

"What are you doing here?" Aurelius said, his regal voice smooth but lacking in warmth.

I ignored the shiver that ratcheted its way down my spine

as I stepped forward, my hands knitting uncomfortably, feeling everyone's eyes on me. "I wish to speak with you."

"And you choose this time to do so?" Aurelius said nonchalantly, turning his gaze to the men seated at the table. Each one of them had grown impossibly still.

"It cannot wait," I offered honestly. Silently, I begged him to look at me, to give me something other than this cold hostility. Even his anger was better than this.

"Then have a seat," he said. His eyes flicked to a younger god sitting to his right, just down from Arkyn. "Theofric, you are excused for the rest of the meeting. Give the princess your chair."

That did not sit well with me. I had never been allowed into the council meetings before. I had hoped by barging in here, Aurelius would see me and wish to speak with me . . . in private. Speaking in public? That was not part of my plan.

"Yes, your divineness," the young god said as he quickly jerked upright. He tried to gather the scrolls set out before him, but he was a bit of a bumbling mess, and in his haste, he dropped one. The wooden ends clattered against the floor, and the scroll rolled under the table.

"Just leave them," Aurelius sighed.

The young god nodded quickly, dropped the scrolls, and then briskly walked past me and out the door. The torrent of air that followed his fast-paced wake brushed across my skin—stirring that ominous feeling once more. My skin prickled.

"Sit, wife," Aurelius commanded, his eyes still not meeting mine.

I did as he asked.

"*Now, what is it that you wish to speak of?*" He didn't look at me.

I lowered my voice. "*Aurelius, not here. Please, can we speak in private?*"

"*This is* my *council, and they are privy to all matters, to* all *threats that might impact my leadership.*" His eyes, cold as the dead of winter, slid to mine. "*So we will discuss the matters between us, right here and right now. The most pressing of them all, my dear wife, is the allegations of your infidelity. You see, before you walked through that door, it was brought to my attention that you danced with the God of Death in front of everyone. And as I've been told, it seemed to be a rather personal affair between the two of you.*"

"*That's not fair,*" I said softly. "*I didn't have a choice in the matter.*"

"*And yet everyone at this table would attest that choice or not, you clearly enjoyed it. That it seemed . . . intimate. Like you had both done it hundreds of times before.*"

"*No, that's ridiculous.*" I looked to Arkyn, my eyes pleading with him to say something, to tell Aurelius that what he had heard simply was not true . . .

But how could he? The God of Truth could not produce a lie. And to say that there was no passion in the way the God of Death had danced with me, the way I had danced with him—well, that would be a lie, wouldn't it?

"*That is what I thought,*" Aurelius said, his eyes fixed on me, reading the redness in my cheeks as I recalled the memory of the God of Death stretching my body before him, of his gaze raking across my skin, stirring the embers within my flesh. "*I have been too lenient with you and the way that I lead. I see that now. I will rectify that. Starting today." His eyes drifted from my face to the pile of scrolls sitting in front of me. "Take a look."*

Dread filled my belly as I reached for one of the scrolls. Slowly, I unraveled it, and read the document.

I gasped and snapped the scroll shut, slamming it back down on the table, horrified at what I had just read. My gaze flickered to Arkyn's, looking for any sign of remorse in his eyes, but I found none. I looked to Aurelius's two brothers, who both looked a great deal like him, but again—nothing. Were they all truly going to allow this genocide to happen?

I turned to Aurelius, my eyes pleading. "You cannot do this."

"Oh, dear wife, how wrong you are. I am king and I can do whatever I want. In case you might have forgotten." Although he did not raise his voice at me, it was impossible not to notice the venom he stitched into each word.

I shook my head, unable to believe that this is what we had come to. "We have lived peacefully with the children of the Old Gods for centuries. You simply cannot just wipe out an entire civilization."

"I can. And I will," Aurelius stated, his mind clearly already made up on the matter. "I listened to you before, and I let them live amongst us. But who took up arms against us in the war? They did."

"Yes, some of them did, but not all of them." I rose from my chair and moved to his side, falling to my knees, my hands held in prayer before me. "Please do not extinguish an entire race because some of them fought against us. Please, Aurelius, it's not right."

His eyes regarded me with little care as I knelt before him. "You have always had such a bleeding heart."

I wished I could take his hand and place it over my chest and remind him that— "It's your heart too," I finished out loud. "Please, don't do this. Some are just children."

And for the briefest of moments, I thought that perhaps my words had gotten through to him, but it was fleeting because his expression turned to stone. "Yes, some of them are children, but they will grow up. And when they do, what will stop them from taking arms against me once more? It is a risk I cannot take—I will not take. As we speak, my sentries are collecting anyone who possesses a droplet of Old God blood from this realm. There are already thousands in my dungeons. I will wipe the board clean of the Old God's descendants—I will cleanse the realms."

"No!" I shot to my feet, rearing away from him. I hardly recognized the male sitting before me.

"No?" he repeated, as if he had never heard the word before. He stood up, shoving the chair back with the backs of his legs—it screeched in protest. He turned towards me, his head cocked to the side. "Tell me, wife, do you know how you kill the descendants of an immortal?"

I shook my head, not because I was answering his question, but because I could not believe what I was hearing.

"Iron and flame. The iron nullifies their powers, and the fire destroys them. I'm sure you are wondering where am I going to get all that wood to create hundreds of pyres?" He nodded to one of the arched windows. "Take a look outside and you will have your answer, dearest."

I didn't need to look to know what was beyond the

window. Tears welled in my eyes. "You wouldn't."

A sadistic smile. "It's already begun."

"No!" I yelled as I rushed over to the window.

Hundreds of workers were scattered throughout my orchard, saws cutting and axes swinging as they took down the trees that I had poured my love, my labor, my life into.

Aurelius was cutting down my orchard—the only thing that was . . . mine.

He stepped beside me, his eyes spanning over the destruction. "Someday, you will understand that this was necessary."

"You're wrong!" I raged as I tore the wedding band from my finger and slammed it down on the windowsill. "I will never forgive you for this."

Aurelius's brows smashed together. "How dare you take my gold off! You think that you have a choice? Do you honestly believe that I would ever let you leave me? Regardless of some ridiculous deal you made with the God of Death. I will never let you leave, Moonbeam. Not now. Not ever."

He let out a mighty roar that shook the castle as he pulled on his wrists with such immeasurable strength, he broke the shackles.

Bits of diamonds rained down on the polished floors.

I reared back.

But his hand struck like a viper. He grabbed my wrist with bruising strength, snatched the ring, and shook it in front of my face. "I will have this welded to your finger." We both grunted as he uncurled my clenched finger—my strength no match for his—and forced the ring back on. "But until then—"

Like a petrified stick being stepped on, he snapped my finger to the side.

I screamed.

A piece of white bone gruesomely shot out, painted in golden ichor—my life's essence marrying with the ring I was being forced to wear.

Aurelius let my wrist go as he tossed me to the side.

Stumbling, I fell to the ground. I cradled my hand against my chest, sobbing.

Arkyn jumped up from his chair, but Aurelius turned to him and snarled, "Sit down."

And like a well-trained dog, that's exactly what Arkyn did. Not that he had any other choice in the matter—the divine command in Aurelius's voice always reigned supreme. Had Aurelius commanded him to go along with this plan of his too? I didn't doubt it.

Aurelius turned back to me, fire in his eyes as he came for me.

I kicked my feet on the floor, rearing back like a frightened animal, away from him.

When he reached for me, I let my light take me before he could.

My tears of pain turned to ones of anger.

Aurelius could break my bones and he could destroy my orchard, but I would not let him take the very thing I had tended with such love and care and use it to kill countless lives—countless families.

But if I was going to save them, I couldn't do it alone.

Which meant . . .

I had a deal to make.

CHAPTER 54

Sage

Black, glittering cinders fell from the amethyst sky like puffs of ash spit out from the mouth of a choking volcano.

I reached out from underneath the cape of my wispy, sheer sleeves, my palm facing upwards, watching with a curiously piqued brow as the ash fell into my hand. The contrast between the small, onyx-colored flecks and my pale skin was as stark as morning to night. Even more curious, the pieces began to melt against the warmth of my hand, just like snow would have. Is that what this was?

Black snow?

My brow raised a bit more.

I had never seen black snow before, but then again, I had never visited the Spirit Realm, and the information surrounding it was . . . limited, at best.

I was surprised I had found my way here so easily, but in truth, I had had a bit of help—the inked markings on my bicep. I used them to track the God of Death here, and although my light walking abilities should have delivered me right to him, something had stopped me from magically approaching any further. It was as if a giant, invisible wall had been placed in front of me, cutting off my path.

When I noticed the ancient wards marked out on a hedge of stones set off to my right and left, I knew what it was—the Blood King had safe-guarded his castle from any unwanted visitors, meaning this was the furthest point I could light walk to. I would physically have to walk the rest of the way.

I glanced ahead.

Nestled in the embrace of the dark, menacing mountains was a grand castle crafted from obsidian. Soaring in structure and grandeur, it stood proudly, dominantly stating its claim over the lands below, overlooking its domain like the king of the jungle surveying its pride. It was ornate and gothic in architecture with cloud-scraping spires.

It was not just a castle—it was an ethereal fortress, and I was spellbound.

A path, winding and treacherous, loomed before me. The sides of it were so steep I could not see the bottom below. Spruce trees painted the sides a lush green, their tops and branches decorated with fresh, fluffy, black snow. It was a wonder they were able to grow there at all in the unforgiving landscape, and yet, they did.

The caw of a raven garnished my attention, my gaze shifting to the moody, purple sky. Its talons held onto an orb— the glass catching the light as it flew over. Wings flapping, it started its ascent towards the castle. It didn't waiver, unbothered by the treacherous, bottomless ground beneath.

Gathering a breath, I continued forward, sticking to the middle of the path.

As I walked, a sound grew behind me—a melodic humming emitting from a deep, male voice. Turning, I peered over my shoulder.

Coming up on my left, sailing on the air, was a boat—long and sleek and as black as the mighty castle up ahead. The bow was chiseled into a serpent's head—its mouth stretched open, revealing sinister, pointed teeth, ready to sink into the world. A head poked out from behind the bow, a male—middle-aged with a great big grin. His fingers gripped the small brim of his hat as he took it off his head. "Ahoy there, miss."

"Hello," I replied, taking in the boat drifting on the current of the air as it pulled up beside me.

Aboard the vessel, people of a variety of ages and ethnicities chatted amongst themselves. Some of them broke off their conversations, turning to look at me. A few of them held wooden oars, their rowing stopped momentarily.

"I take it ye are heading towards the castle." The man propped his hat back on his head and dropped his booted heel against the lip of the boat, a heavy thud sounding. He nodded forward, his stormy-gray eyes shifting back to me. "Would ye like a ride?"

I had two options: climb aboard the peculiar boat or continue the long walk up the treacherous path. I wasn't too keen on either option. I motioned to the space between the path and the boat. "How do I get aboard?"

The man's rough pads stroked his wiry beard as he peered over the edge of his boat, glancing down. He shrugged, a grin curling his lips. *"I suppose ye will have to jump."* He barked out a laugh.

My expression soured, and he cut his laughter short.

He shook his head. *"Apologies, miss. Here."* He waved his hand and a wooden dock appeared, bridging itself between the boat and the path.

"Are you sure it's safe?" I asked, glancing down, down, down. I was not afraid of heights, but I wasn't so sure my magic could save me if I were to fall because of the wards the God of Death had put in place. I'd probably lay there for eternity, broken and shattered, with no hopes of ever being found.

"Safe enough." He nodded once. *"I don't mean to be rude, but I have a few more trips I need to make, so if you could hurry up, that would be swell."*

I weighed my options—deciding the boat was the quickest one.

"Apologies," I said, braving one step onto a wooden board, testing it. It performed an unceremonious groan, causing my gut to churn.

His playful voice shifted to a softer, understanding tone. *"Pardon me, are ye a new soul here?"*

"I suppose I am," I replied after giving it some thought. Carefully, I moved forward—one unsure foot on the strange, hovering structure.

"Ah, well then—" He flopped his hand forward in offering for me to take, *"—allow me to be ye tour guide."*

I placed my good hand in his, keeping the one with the shattered finger held protectively against my chest. His fingers—there was no warmth, no flesh. Just cold, hard bone. I jerked my hand away, my eyes flaring wide. His hand looked like a typical hand—there was skin there, and yet, that's not what I had felt.

"A new soul indeed," he stated more to himself than me. He gestured to a vacant seat. "Please, if you would. And then we can continue forward."

I moved to the seat and sat down, my legs weary from walking over the creaking dock and the proverbial path I was on.

The people began to row, and the boat began to move.

The captain turned his gaze to the castle. "It's really something, isn't it? I've seen it hundreds of times, and yet I'm just as awe-struck as the first time I saw it. Something out of a storybook, wouldn't you agree?"

I nodded, surveying the majestic castle in all of its dark grandeur. "Does it have a name?"

He shook his head. "It was created long before castles were given names. They say that the God of Death used a mixture of lava and rain to create it. He conjured the lava from the underbelly of the mountains—weaving it to his liking. When he was finished, he brought down the rain, quickly cooling it off, thus creating a volcanic glass—the obsidian stone ye now see today. They say the God of Death was the first to use obsidian in the makings of things."

"No, no, Irvine, you have that last part wrong," cackled a woman two rows behind me.

I turned to look at her.

443

Her gray hair, a rat's nest of a mane, was piled on top of her head. She dusted off her dark-green skirt, like one fleck might tarnish her reputation—the action contradicting her appearance. Looks-wise, she reminded me a great deal of the Goddess of Fate and I couldn't help but wonder if the two were related. "The Three Spinners were the first to use obsidian in their makings."

"Oh?" said Irvine. "How do you know that?" he questioned, his forearms crossing over his chest. Inquisitively, he tipped his head to the side, his gruff features doing very little to hide the skepticism written so plainly in the setting of his face.

She smirked, waggling her spindly fingers magically as if she were casting a spell. "Because I do." She looked at me, offering a knowing wink. "Life works in peculiar ways, wouldn't you agree, my dear?" she asked, while letting a gentle wave of her divinity wash over me, telling me what I already suspected—she was a goddess, and I was fairly certain I knew which one.

I nodded in reply, but I didn't say a word, deciding it was best to tread carefully—I was technically in my enemy's territory, after all.

A few moments later, the boat came to a soft stop. My heels clicked against the brick-paved road as I stepped off the boat, along with the other passengers. Alternating on either side of the road was a string of tall, black poles with hanging lanterns. Even though it was daytime, the lanterns were lit—a blue flame flickering inside. The roadway led to a grand entrance to the castle, mountainous in width and topped with a pointed arch. The gateway, reinforced by metal plates, was suspended in the air.

Part of me wanted to turn around and leave, but it wasn't because I was afraid—it was because something about this felt. . . final. Like once I did this, once I made this deal with the God of Death, Aurelius would never forgive me.

But I was past that point, wasn't I?

If losing Aurelius's love was the price I had to pay for saving the lives of many, many, many innocents, then so be it.

"Goodbye, miss!" Irvine called out from the departing boat.

"Goodbye. Thank you for the . . . ride."

"Anytime," he said with a big, warm-hearted smile.

"Come along, my dear," said the goddess with the messy gray hair as she toddled forward.

I sped up to catch her and then dropped my pace to match hers as we walked behind the rest of the group towards the entrance. Under my breath, I whispered for only her to hear, "You are the Goddess of Destiny, aren't you?"

She chuckled. "What makes you think I am her?"

"Because you are," I said confidently. "Also, you look a great deal like your sister, the Goddess of Fate."

"I do," she agreed with a single nod. "To the untrained eye, we are easily mistaken as one another, especially amongst the mortals."

I could see that now.

I had met the Goddess of Fate before, but I had never met the third sister—even though there was once a time that I had searched for her, in hopes of understanding more about my ability to reincarnate.

"I devoted many years to looking for the Goddess of Free Will, but I never found her. She is impossible to find," I said as we walked.

A caw of a cackle sputtered from her thin lips. "She has always been that way, disappearing and reappearing whenever she wishes to. Sometimes I go centuries without seeing her. She's never taken her duties seriously, at least not like she should."

"I suppose that makes sense for someone who is the champion of free will," I answered, my eyes fixing on those walking ahead of me—there had to be close to forty people. "Do you know why all of these people are going to the castle?"

"For the same reason you are—they want to make a deal with the king."

I didn't bother to ask the Goddess of Destiny how she knew—of course the all-knowing goddess knew the reason why I was here. And if she knew that, I wondered. . .

"Am I doing the right thing?" I asked. My regally tilted face and perfectly postured shoulders did very little to hide the uncertainty that slipped through my voice.

She pursed her lips in thought for a moment. "What does your heart say?"

I glanced down at her. "That's hardly an answer."

She looked straight ahead. "Nor was it supposed to be. The answer lies solely within you."

I thought about it for a moment. "My heart hates that I am doing this to Aurelius, but what else can be expected? The heart that beats within has always been his."

Even now, it ached. Viscerally. Even though my mind was made up. And this time, it was my mind I was trusting.

She nodded, her eyes looking ahead. "Maybe it's time you quit answering with his heart and look to your own."

"How? I do not have one that is my own," I exclaimed softly, my brows pinching together.

"No?" she challenged. Her stormy gray-blue eyes shifted to mine. "Then what are you doing here?"

I understood her point, or at least, I thought I did.

And so, I decided, I would trust that voice inside that told me I was doing the right thing. I would listen to it this time, instead of blocking it out like I had done countless times before.

I took a deep breath and followed everyone else inside the castle, Destiny at my side.

CHAPTER 55

Sage

I *could feel him etched into every crevice within this castle—his incredible, dark power, ancient and brutal. It hung on the air, thick and claiming like smoke, but without the lung-choking effect.*

How much of himself had he poured into this castle's creation?

Because it felt like his power had been entombed everywhere—in the ribbed and vaulted ceilings, in the intricate, incredible patterns that were chiseled throughout, in the massive, looming columns that stretched from floor to ceiling.

All of it served to pronounce a claim—this castle and this realm belonged to him.

What it must feel like . . . to belong to him.

I made a face, wondering where the unprecedented

thought had come from.

"How much longer?" I asked the goddess who had been walking beside me for the past half hour, but when I looked down . . . she was gone. I glanced over my shoulder to see if she had fallen behind, but empty, vacant space was all that remained in my wake. And when I looked ahead, the people that had once walked in front of me were suddenly gone too.

I was alone in this sprawling, massive corridor—more grand room than hallway. But I wasn't alone, was I? I didn't need to turn, because like always, I could feel when he was close to me.

"Little Goddess," the darkness purred behind me.

The hairs on the back of my neck stood, but it wasn't out of fear. It was something so much more than that . . . something I'd tried for decades to bury deeply within myself.

"I have come to make a deal with you," I spoke over my shoulder.

"Another one? You have yet to fulfill the last one we made, darling little bride," he said, not bothering to hide the amusement in his voice. I didn't need to see him to know that the left side of his mouth was most likely twisted into a sensually wicked grin. Over the years, I had come to memorize his features and his mannerisms—like a sculptor, I had etched every detail of him into my memory. "By the way, did you like the placement of this tattoo? I thought it was rather . . . cheeky."

I wanted to snap my teeth at him, but I didn't because I knew his ways—his games. Refusing to play them, I said flatly, "I hardly think of it."

"Well, it's not exactly in a spot you can easily see," he

teased. His feet, silent and lethal, made no sound as he closed the distance between us, his shadow falling over me. I could feel the heat of him caressing my back in soft, dark radiance. "Do you know why I picked that spot?" His voice was low. Dangerous. Intoxicating.

Slowly, I turned towards him, my lashes lifting.

Our gazes met, and for a moment, all I could hear was my heartbeat, thundering wildly. Then the sound was gone, swept away and stolen by the storm standing before me.

"Why?" I asked softly, hooked on the allure of the God of Death.

"Because—" he smirked, "—on the night of your creation, when I took you to my mansion in the Living Realm and you dropped the sheet and swatted that plump little bottom of yours, all I could think of was how badly I wanted to sink my teeth into it." His gaze raked over me, eating me up. "That little act of yours had me biting my knuckles for weeks, so tattooing your fine little ass with my mouth's signature seemed to be a fitting way to torment you, just as *you have me."*

I knew it was his *bite that was inked into my flesh.*

Of course, it was his.

I had been mortified when my lady's maid asked what was stuck to my bottom. But that was just it, wasn't it? It wasn't stuck. The bastard had inked his bitemark into my ass. I had sworn up and down that I would get vengeance for it, but now that the divinely tailored god was standing before me, I was curious . . .

"So then . . ." I raised a brow. "Is my bite inked into your flesh, as well?"

"That—" he whispered in my ear, "—I will leave for you to discover on your own."

My traitorous mind flashed with an image of the dark god standing before me—naked. I imagined the heavy muscle in his legs, in those great hips, built for thru—

I shoved the intrusive thought out.

He peered down at me with those never-ending obsidian eyes, and despite how empty I told myself they were, I'd be a damned liar if I didn't admit they were as mesmerizing as the twinkling night sky.

I looked away. This was the male that had tormented me since the day I was born. This was the enemy of my . . .

My what?

Aurelius was no longer my husband, which meant his enemies no longer needed to be mine. It was time I forged my own alliances.

I looked at the first one I was about to make, only to find that the smirk he wore instantly fell flat. His nostrils flared as if he scented something, and his eyes darted to my hand—the one wrapped in white linen.

His gaze jerked back to mine, and he snarled, "Did the mate-fucker do this to you?"

I took a hesitant step back.

Instantly, the fire in his eyes smothered out. He offered me his hand, asking with . . . tenderness, "May I?"

I shook my head, retreating another step. I felt like an injured animal, and the last thing I needed was another predator touching me.

"Goddess, please, I can scent your ichor. It is a fresh wound. Let me see," he said, his voice almost . . . pleading.

"Fine," I said, taking a breath. My brows knitted firmly. "I'll show you, but that is all."

He nodded.

Tenderly, I unwrapped the thin linen, revealing the sorry state of my broken finger, gilded in ichor—jutting unnaturally to the side. The sight of it was grotesque. I could barely stand to look at it.

His lips curled back, but whatever sound he was about to make was suppressed as his eyes met mine. He took a breath—a shaky one. "It needs to be set."

"I know." I was well aware that my body lacked the ability to heal on its own, unlike every other immortal.

He held out his tattooed hand once more. "I promise to be as gentle as I possibly can."

I stared at his offered hand, weighing my options. Eventually, with some hesitation, I placed my hand in his. "Alright."

He stepped into me, gently grasping the broken end of my finger while his free hand steadied my trembling one. "Little Goddess . . ."

"Yes?" I answered nervously as I stared at my finger, so small in comparison to his.

My knees wobbled, alarms ringing. This was a bad idea.

"Look at me," he commanded softly.

My gaze lifted, and that was when the God of Death kissed me—his mouth colliding into mine. The searing kiss struck like a bolt of lightning, entering at my lips, scorching through my body, and leaving through my feet—surely shattering the ground beneath me.

But before my world could cave in, I shoved against him

with my good hand and jerked away from him. "Bastard," I sputtered.

But he did not respond because he was too busy staring at my hand, his brows raised ever so slightly.

I looked down—my finger . . . was healed.

And I hadn't felt a lick of pain.

"How?" I asked.

"I don't know." He shook his head. "It would seem I have the ability to heal you."

I inspected my finger, wiggling it with ease. It was as good as new.

So then . . . it must be true. The God of Death could heal me, and I, the Goddess of life, could wound him fatally. He could bring me life and I could bring him death.

It seemed almost fitting in some strange way, and had our past not been so horrible, I might have found it a bit romantic.

"Thank you," I said, after a brief passing of time. "For healing my finger."

"Of course," he said.

My attention snagged much too long on his lips. I blinked, my eyes meeting his. "Why did you kiss me?"

The left corner of his mouth twisted upwards. "Because I am a bastard."

"Of that, we are of the same mind."

He chuckled. "You mentioned before that you have come to make a deal . . . have you come to make your demands for our wedding, little bride?"

"No," I snarled. "I have come to make a separate deal."

"Pray tell, Kitten, what is it?"

"Aurelius has ordered a mass killing of anyone who has a droplet of Old God blood." Softly, I shook my head, still disbelieving the words coming out of my mouth. "They are innocent people . . ."

"And so, you wish to make a deal to save them." He studied me with as much intensity as a jungle cat tracking an antelope.

"I do." I nodded. "I am willing to trade whatever you want in exchange for letting them come live here, safely in the Spirit Realm."

"As tempting as your offer is, that is something I cannot do."

"Cannot or will not?" I snipped.

He grinned. "I do love lighting that angry fire within you."

I ignored his prodding. "Answer my question."

"Very well. I cannot bring the living to the realm of the dead."

"But then—"

"I wasn't finished," he purred, and like the night of the ball, I found myself transfixed by him—in those starless eyes of his. When he reached for me, I did not deny him. His fingers slid across my cheek, his touch so incredibly gentle. "There is a continent in the Living Realm, cut off from the rest. Edenvale."

I nodded. "I know of it."

"Take them there. I will gift you the ability to create a great barrier that will surround the entire continent. No mortals or New Gods will be able to get in or out unless you allow. Not even your precious king will be able to destroy it."

His thumb grazed my bottom lip—his touch wreaking havoc on my thoughts.

Why was I allowing him to touch me like this? Why . . . did I want him to?

Deep down, I knew the answer.

"He is no longer my king," I replied, peering up at him through the halo of my white lashes. "What do you ask for in exchange?"

His lips thinned.

I almost reached out, almost caught his wrist as he pulled his hand away, but I held firm in my resolve, ignoring those uncharted feelings he stirred within me.

"Nothing," he answered.

"Nothing?"

"That's right," he said, that tenacious smirk returning to his full lips.

"You are supposed to be the maker of deals, are you not? Since when have you done something and asked for nothing in return?"

The smirk grew. "Never."

"So then why now?" I asked, my suspicions growing.

The God of Death tipped my chin upwards, bringing my gaze to his. "Because to the rest of the world, I am the villain, but to you, and you alone, I no longer wish to be."

My heart galloped. "So then . . . what of our last deal? Will you release me from it?"

He leaned in, his lips so close to mine, I tasted his words. "Deal or not, I will never release you from me." His fingers slid from my chin, gliding upwards, caressing my cheek.

"Then you will be a cage to me." My voice was softer

than it should be. I should be angry, and yet, I felt nothing of the sort.

"I will," he agreed in that bourbon tone. "But not of the kind that you are used to. From this day forward, my cage will serve but one purpose—to protect you. Don't you see? You hold the key to this one, and you can leave whenever you wish. And while you are gone, I will wait for you to return, no matter how long it takes for you to come back to me."

"And if it takes forever?" I asked, breathlessly.

"Then it is a good thing my patience springs eternal," he said slowly, so I could feel the weight of his words.

And feel them I did.

The air around us became charged, as if some form of ancient magic was finally awakening.

His voice dropped dangerously low, as if he were pledging a sacred oath. "There will come a day when I will claim you as my bride, and on that day, all Three Realms will address you as queen."

"And when will that day be?" I asked, fighting my damnedest not to kiss him in this moment.

"All that matters is that it is not today, Little Goddess," he purred.

We stayed like that for a while. With his eyes on mine, and mine on his, a silent understanding forming between the two of us.

Between Life and Death.

CHAPTER 56

Sage

The featherlight touch of daylight warmed my left side, but despite its pleasant caress, something was very, very wrong . . .

I couldn't feel my hands. At least, not completely.

Startled, I jerked awake.

Bright light spilling in from a nearby window momentarily blinded me before my pupils adjusted. I was laying on a massive canopy bed—large enough to rival the one in Von's private chambers back at the manor. My arms were hoisted towards the ceiling, causing the blood to drain out, cauterizing the nerves and any feeling with it. Metal cuffs wound around my wrists connected by a heavy, unyielding chain that cantilevered over the wood beam above. The beam, carved with a delicate pattern and meticulously polished, stretched from bedpost to bedpost.

I pulled, testing the iron bonds. When I released the

tension, the chains clanked against the stone wall behind the bed, chattering in laughter at my feeble attempt. Utilizing my feet and my abdomen, I wiggled my way into a sitting position, making it so that my hands were now by my head rather than strung above me. It was a small improvement, but hopefully it would be enough to have some of the blood flow return to them.

Dread pooled low in my belly when I realized that my neck was collared once more, the iron like a well-sharpened knife, cutting me off from my Curse.

"Damn it," I hissed under a frustrated breath before I started to survey my unfamiliar surroundings.

The bedroom chamber boasted of luxurious taste, from the expensive-looking rugs casually tossed over the stone floors to the rich drapery that hung on the windows to the pristine, immaculate furniture, none of which looked to ever have been used—that, or it was brand new. The sitting area was centered around a huge fireplace, framed with a solid slab of white, glittering stone. Off to the side of it, a small private library full of books.

I could handle the unfamiliarity of the room. But the chains that limited my movement? Those I could not. Because the last time my body was tied to something . . .

Flames—scalding-hot flames were lapping at my feet, eagerly chewing up my flesh, my tendons, my nerves. A sound of terror tore through my throat, and I kicked my feet, trying to stop the fire, but the more I fought, the higher it roamed. I pleaded with Arkyn, who was still holding the torch he used to light the pyre, but when he opened his mouth to speak, all I heard was the roar of the flame and the snapping of wood.

It was going to consume me.

It was . . .

It's not real, Sage. It's not real, I told myself. It was enough to break the spell.

Instantly, the flames wicked out.

Gasping in the aftershock of my panic, I inhaled a shaky breath, but it was cut short because the door off to my right swung open.

Aurelius strode in, his golden robe flaring out behind him, caught on his fast-paced current. The look on his face . . . it was unforgiving, and so unlike the charming smile I had come to know in this lifetime.

"You have finally awoken, *dear wife*." He said the last two words in mockery. His lips twisted into the slightest of smiles, one that held no warmth, only callousness and cruelty.

Nausea curdled the contents of my stomach.

I felt like I was seeing *him* for the first time—not the charming Golden Prince, but the *King of the New Gods*.

The memories I had just uncovered, they hadn't just resurfaced—they'd smashed into me with the mighty force of a battering ram. The Cleansings that had claimed so many lives, the destruction of my orchard—all of it . . . it was because of him. Anger spread like venom in my veins, intoxicating my thoughts, filling me to the brim until it all came boiling out. "*You* were the one that *started* the Cleansings."

"I see your memories have finally returned," Aurelius stated. Without a whisper of sound, he walked over to a small bar area that backed one of the settees. His fingers wrapped elegantly around the neck of a glass decanter, half full of red wine. He plucked the diamond top off and poured the wine into a gilded goblet adorned with shimmering rubies.

"Thousands of innocents have lost their lives . . . because of *you*," I hissed, my emotions like a pendulum, swinging between disbelief and anger.

"Innocent?" He laughed sardonically, the sound echoing around me. "I will remind you that when their forefathers raised arms against us in the Immortal War, they sealed their fate for themselves and their future bloodlines. One way or another, all of them will die."

I wondered if my teeth had rattled loose in my head because what Aurelius said was like a blow to the chin. Clearly, he had more memories of our past than he had let on.

Clearly, he had played me like a sap.

"Aurelius, that was centuries ago," I said, watching as he swirled the glass and brought it to his nose, breathing in the scent of fermented fruit. "Forget the past. Forget your anger. Show them mercy," I pleaded with him.

"Show the enemy mercy?" he scoffed, white brows raising in challenge as he walked towards the bed, the belly of the goblet balanced on his two fingers. He let out a sigh, fusing the sound to what he said next. "I don't know where I went wrong with you. Perhaps it was my leniency that allowed you to forget your place. Perhaps . . . I am to blame for your failings." He paused for a moment. It felt like he was speaking more to himself than me. "I was foolish to believe that this time might be different between us."

I sensed the depleted nature of his words—perhaps I could use that to my advantage, to get me out of these chains.

I softened my gaze. "Who says things cannot be different

between us this time?"

He regarded me with a blank expression. "You lie much better than you did before, Moonbeam. Tell me, did the God of Death help you sharpen your serpent's tongue?" He reached for my cheek, but I jerked away from his touch. He blew out a laughing breath of air from his nose, as if to say he had expected as much. "And yet, you do not lie well enough." He slipped his hand into his pocket, while his other one swirled the ruby-decorated goblet, mixing its contents.

"You have my hands in chains and an iron collar around my throat. Excuse me if I am not entirely trusting of your touch," I said honestly, seeing if I could bucket my way out of my quickly sinking plan.

He chuckled. "It has nothing to do with trust, Moonbeam. I know disgust when I see it. You can manufacture all the lies you want, but those ice-cold eyes of yours reveal the truth." He raised the goblet to his lips.

"Aurelius, I—"

He cut me off. "Save your lies, I couldn't care less to hear them." He tipped the goblet back and drank a few swallows. After, his golden eyes shifted back to mine. They were *glowing*.

The air turned ominous.

"You've been walking for days, with little food or water. Tell me—" he flashed his perfect teeth, tinged with red, "—are you thirsty, Aurelia?"

"No," I answered, a horn of warning sounding in my head.

"Are you sure?" his regal voice teased. "This one—" he tapped the side of the goblet, "—is a divine little concoction."

The way he said it . . .

My gaze darted over to the decanter, to the deep-crimson liquid inside of it, and my skin began to crawl. Panic wrapped its fists around my lungs, and I sputtered for air. "It's my blood, isn't it?" I choked out.

"Partly, yes," he answered as he sat down on the bed, one leg crossing over the other.

Suddenly, I became aware of a tingling sensation on the side of my neck. A cloudy memory aired, no more than a flash of teeth and a piercing of pain and a swirl of unconsciousness. My expression soured.

Aurelius sucked a tooth, before he admonished, "Oh, come now, don't make such an awful face." He paused for a moment, his tone becoming more conversational. "That night in the bathing pool, I debated draining you completely dry, just so I could watch you suffer for a month or two while your feeble body tried to regenerate your blood. It took everything within me not to."

Debating and doing were two very different things, which begged the question . . . "So then, why didn't you?" I asked.

"I have a couple of reasons. The first is, as I stated before, I foolishly thought we could make a go of things this time around. When Arkyn told me you were without your memories, I thought that if I showed you the version of myself that you first met all those years ago, the one who charmed you, then perhaps things would be different. But alas, that version of me truly died a long time ago." He tipped his head ever so slightly to the side in that dignified way of his, but the words he said next were nothing of the sort. "And the second was because I wanted to feel what it was like for you to welcome me between your legs once more." He bit his bottom lip before he let it spring free, his lips twisting into a malevolent smile. "And true to your whorish nature, welcome me you did."

Asshole, I screamed internally.

But instead of saying that out loud, I took a good hard look at my losing hand and kept my tongue tucked firmly between my teeth. Something I just barely managed to do.

And I mean *barely*.

I thought back to that dreadful night in the bathing pool. That had been *the true* Aurelius. The version I saw after—*the Golden Prince*—was just as he said . . . that one had died a very long time ago. He had been playing a part, and I had willfully fallen for it.

I had never felt such anger towards myself, such frustration. I hung my head.

Aurelius spoke in a soft voice, as if he were taking pity on me. "Come now, it's not all that bad. Today should be a day of victory for you."

"What does that mean?" Wearily, I looked up at him.

"It means that you finally got what you wanted, Aurelia." He flicked a piece of lint off of his pant leg as he said flatly, "The mortal king is dead."

CHAPTER 57

Sage

I could feel it, deep down. What Aurelius said was true. He had no reason to lie about the king's death. At least, none that I could think of.

The king was . . . *dead*.

And not by own my hand, as Ezra had once predicted, but by Aurelius's—a turn of events I had not seen coming.

"Are you not pleased?" he asked, a white brow raising in question.

I . . . I didn't know *what* I was. Shocked. Confused. I felt an assortment of things. Curiosity included.

I shook my head. "How did you know that I—"

He cut me off, finishing my question. "Planned to kill the king? It is as I told you before, I have exceptional hearing."

Which meant . . . "You listened in on my *private* conversation with Kaleb."

"I did," he answered nonchalantly.

It was a violating truth—one I did not like. And yet, I wasn't surprised by it either. He had listened in on my conversation with the healer as well. And he drank my blood when I was unconscious. What else had he done that I was not aware of? I paled at the thought.

"Mortal blood has never held much appeal to me," he mused.

I glanced up, finding him peering down at his goblet, or rather, what was in it.

"But the blood of a royal mortal? Well, it has a different taste to it. The longer their ancestors have ruled, the more power is sewn into it. Mix it with a bit of immortal blood, and it's quite palatable." He raised his glass in cheers to me, and then he took a drink.

That's when I realized it. He had mixed *my* blood with the *dead king's*.

It made my stomach roll, to the point that I thought I was going to be sick—

No, that was a lie—I was *definitely* going to be sick.

I lurched to the side, as far as my chains would allow and I dry-heaved.

"You are not going to vomit," Aurelius commanded, his voice conjuring my attention. I just barely caught the flash of light as it passed over his glowing eyes. As if he had snapped his fingers and performed some type of magic trick, my stomach instantly settled.

The feel of my body bowing to his will . . . it was not unfamiliar.

How many times had he done that to me before?

"That's better," he sighed. "I wouldn't want you to ruin my furs."

I glanced down at the furs, but my thoughts were nowhere near them. "Why did you do it?"

"Do what?"

"Kill the king."

"Ah," he said. "When I returned and found out that the king had thrown you into the Well even though I had instructed the stupid mortal not to touch a pretty white hair on your head, I decided his usefulness had come to an end." He paused for a moment. "That is the problem with mortal kings, is it not? When they are given too much power, they forget their place is beneath us immortals, not above. It is a testament of their small, feeble minds." Aurelius sighed. "I do not know why the Creator gave me the ability to command the actions of Gods and Demi Gods, but not the lowly mortals. Alas, it has come in handy, especially with you—many times over." He raised the goblet and drank, his throat bobbing.

I made a face, but the unease in my stomach did not return, which meant that Aurelius's command was still holding. I had broken free from it once before—that night in the pool when he told me not to move. But what I felt back then was different from now—the weight his words carried. They seemed heavier now, like an anchor holding me down. Which meant that Aurelius was stronger than before. Was his power returning to him, or had that been a lie too? Just another part of the show? It made me wonder how much of what he'd told me was untrue.

"You said that you wanted to do something beneficial for the people of Edenvale. Was that true? Or was that a lie?"

"Of that, I meant every word," he answered in his poised, regal tone. "This mortal continent has been plagued with the children of the Old Gods ever since *you* stole them from my dungeons and brought them here. Instead of being rid of the infection, your defiance has allowed it to spread." White lashes lowered, sweeping over high cheekbones as he glanced down at the goblet. "It would seem you are doomed to repeat yourself, Moonbeam. Nonetheless, I will rectify your mistakes and do what the mortal kings of Edenvale have failed to do—I will wipe the Cursed from these lands. And then I will Cleanse them from the Living and Immortal Realms too." He finished off the goblet and set it down on the bedstand, a metallic *thunk* sounding. His gaze returned to mine. "And now, I have *the means* to do it."

I gasped as I realized what *means* he was referring to . . .

The unresponsive soldiers. That was how he was going to do it.

It also explained why they didn't move. They were not made of mortal bone and flesh—they were *Demi Gods*—under his control, *commanded* to stand there like that.

"How are there so many?" I asked, shaking my head when I recalled the silent army, standing row by never-ending row. There had been so many of them . . .

"Must I explain to you how children are made, Aurelia? We attempted many, many, many times in the past." His lips curled coyly.

But his words were lost to me. My mind was racing, clicking a thousand pieces together at an unfathomable speed. The women who were being conscripted, the healers, the sudden increase in female souls that were being collected—it all made sense now.

When I had dinner with Aurelius, the man next to him had inquired about his brother. Aurelius not only remembered the man's brother, but he immediately asked *how* the brother's wife was doing. When he found out that she was ill and pregnant with child, he *requested* her to be brought here immediately.

"You are using women to *make* Demi Gods for you?" I snapped, cinching the chain taut as I surged forward. The chains rattled, giving me less than a few inches. Anger pumped into my veins, filling them up, until they felt ready to burst through my skin.

"I use the humans as breeding stock, yes. Despite what your mortal-sympathizing mind believes, they are truly no different than cattle." His shoulders performed a careless shrug, so small I nearly missed it. "I did it in our past life, as well, unbeknownst to you."

Betrayal pressed down on my shoulders, my heart—but it was nothing compared to the wrath I felt. I turned molten hot, screaming, "They are *dying* because of you!"

The chains groaned as I pulled against them. The cuffs bit into my wrists, sinking like teeth, biting into my flesh.

I didn't care—I was feral and filled with rage.

"Calm yourself," he commanded, a wave of light passing over his glowing eyes.

Instantly, the fire in my veins was doused out. My body went slack, bowing to his will, as if I were nothing more than a child's useless doll, forgotten in the street.

He continued, "Many of them die, yes. Their too-small bodies were never intended to carry immortals. However, my divinity makes the children incredibly strong. We found that by feeding them a semi-solid tissue found in the bones of the Cursed, it accelerates their ability to grow at an unfathomable speed. Within a year, they are adults. Miraculous, really. Although I will admit, it's a bit of a bloody affair to get the marrow out, and it must be extracted when the Cursed are alive, but it's a small trouble considering the end result."

I was transported back to the Well, covering my ears and trying to block out the screaming of the prisoners that were dragged to the floor above us. There had been blood—*so much blood* that it rained down in some parts. I'd thought they were being tortured, but now . . .

"That's what they are doing with the Cursed from the Well."

"It is," he confirmed, and I realized I had spoken my thoughts out loud. Aurelius inspected his nails—flawless and pristine, just like the rest of him. If only that shiny, golden, charming exterior wasn't the exact opposite of what lurked beneath—a rotting, infested corpse that served only himself.

I wanted to scream.

I wanted to fight.

I wanted to do something—*anything*.

But I couldn't do a damn thing because like my heart, my body had betrayed me.

His lips thinned. "Don't look at me like that, Aurelia. I am not the monster I can see you making me out to be."

"You are raping and killing women. I fail to see how that doesn't make you a monster," I said, my voice too calm—just as he had commanded me to be.

He laughed at that. "Although I am immortal, I do not

possess the stamina to breed so many. For some, all that is necessary for them to conceive is my touch over their abdomen. I am the God of Life after all."

"And for the ones that do not conceive that way?" I said, the anger behind my words lost to my soft tone.

"You forget that I am the King of the New Gods, and that the vast majority of Edenvale praises my name." He leveled my gaze. "You'd be hard-pressed to find a female that isn't willing to go to bed with me once they learn who I am. Your lady's maid, the strawberry blonde, included."

No . . .

The morning Aurelius left for the countryside was the same morning Cataline had left to go home—or so Brunhilde had led me to believe. I thought of the never-ending line up of carriages. There had been so many.

Cataline would have been in one of those carriages—possibly scared and afraid.

If I could have vomited, I would have.

"You are disgusting," I said, much too monotone.

Aurelius chuckled. "You didn't seem to think so that morning before my departure."

Once again, I regretted sleeping with another male.

And once again, Von had been right. His words sounded in my head—*you have horrible taste in men.* Truly. Truly, I did. The bastard was right.

Aurelius rose from the bed, took the goblet from the bedstand, and walked over to the bar area. He left the goblet there, a smear of blood dried on the rim, for one of the housemaids to clean up.

"The dressmaker . . . Why didn't you take her with the

other women?" I asked.

His eyes, as luminescent as the glow of the morning sun before it emerged above the horizon, shifted to mine. "Because, just like you, she was cursed to be barren. Once I learned that, I lost interest in her."

A cacophony of bells rang out, severing our conversation instantly. The ringing was so loud, the castle trembled. But Aurelius's expression was unperplexed. If the loudness of the bells bothered his immortal hearing, he didn't let on.

The chiming bells lasted thrice as long as it did for morning praise.

After they stopped, I asked, "What's going on?"

"Those are coronation bells, princess." He smiled an ethereally handsome smile, the architecture of his features . . . breathtaking. Not that I could say the same for what was on the inside. "Edenvale looks forward to welcoming its new king. In precisely one hour's time."

"And I suppose that would be you." My tone still sounded like the morning waters of a lake—flat and calm.

"You are correct," he said proudly, not a single strand of silky-white hair moving out of place as he walked to the side of the bed. He carried perfect posture, his broad shoulders set back. White lashes flickered, his gaze falling to mine. "A new dawn is upon us. As Edenvale's king, I will make good on my word. I will march my army to the east, to the Cursed Lands, and there, I will wipe the slate clean."

Ezra, Harper, Ryker, Lyra, and Graiyson—their smiling faces flashed through my mind. The prisoners and everyone who occupied the Cursed Lands . . .

They would all be gone.

"Please do not do this, Aurelius," I pleaded far too softly. I turned to the only bargaining chip I had. "If you unchain me, I will figure out a way to bring the Endless Mist down. Think of it, you could go back to the Immortal Realm then."

"If I were to allow you to do that, the Cursed would scatter across the Living Realm like mice, which would make it much harder for me to get rid of them. For once, your troublesome mist will be of benefit to me, by keeping them all locked here." Theatrically, his brows crinkled in false concern, but the twinkle in his eyes stated the opposite. "But do not worry. After I have finished Cleansing Edenvale, *then* you will bring the Mist down and we will leave this cesspit. Then I will build an even larger army, and I will destroy the Old Gods, once and for all."

"I would rather die than go with you," I snarled.

He chuckled. "And yet, you will, regardless of your wants, because you still possess something that belongs to me."

A chill spider-walked the length of my spine.

He leaned over top of me, his fingers pressing on my left breast. "And one day, I shall find a way to take it back, even if that means ripping it out with my bare hands." He curled his fingers and snatched them away.

My heart leapt—not in the way of fear or sadness, but rather as if it *liked* that thought.

It wanted—*wanted*—to be reunited with him.

I felt dumbfounded—this heart was not mine. It never was. It had *always* belonged to him. My body was just its keeper.

How much of having Aurelius's heart beating within me

factored into my feelings for him? Had *any* of my feelings ever been genuine?

I thought back to when I first met him in this lifetime, of the intense feelings I had felt so quickly for him. I had warred with myself to the extent that I felt as though I was being split in two—my mind cheering for Von, while my heart wanted Aurelius.

But what I didn't understand then, I understood now—the heart beating within my chest loved Aurelius. But I never had.

. . . *I never had.*

This epiphany hit me like a landslide, but instead of falling into a pit of sorrow as I realized how much of my past life had been a complete lie, all I felt was . . .

Free.

It was as if the door to a cage that I had lived in since the day I drew my first breath had finally sprung open, and now, I could finally stretch my wings and find my independence.

Deep down, I felt that part of me—the goddess part that I was often cut off from—was smiling.

And when she shared it with me, thousands of forgotten memories instantly bloomed.

Memories of a goddess walking the lonely palace halls, wondering when her husband would finally have time for her.

Memories of a goddess who was never allowed into the council meetings because her word wasn't considered to be worthwhile.

Memories of a goddess who was always greeted as *princess*, never *queen*, because her husband, the king, would never allow it.

But the most prevalent of all the memories was the one of the goddess who *stood* beside her husband's throne—day after day, year after year, decade after decade, century after century.

And despite her loyalty, she was never granted one of her own.

Not even so much as a measly stool beside his.

"Did you hear what I said, Aurelia?" Aurelius asked, his kingly voice the pick and the command it bore the hammer, chiseling me from my thoughts.

Aurelia.

That *name* . . . he had given it to me before I had one, naming me after *himself*. Because to him, I was never my own person. I was always just an extension of him, of what he'd created me to be. A trickle of fire warmed my cooled-off veins—the hold his compel held over me was beginning to fade.

I felt my divinity radiating within. The feel of it—*of her*—it was the same feeling that day at the training barracks when I melted the cuffs from the wrists of the conscripted men. I had thought that a goddess had come to my aid.

But now I realized that it had all been *me*.

"That—" I grated between clenched teeth, "—is not my name."

"Oh, no? Then do tell, what *is* your name?" His eyes narrowed into slits as they swiped towards mine. "Perhaps you would prefer Death's Whore?"

"My name is Sage!" I roared, my words like a battering ram—smashing through my mortality, *unleashing me*. Filled with strength, unlike anything I had ever felt before, I surged forward, pulling on the chains that imprisoned me. The wood post above me groaned once before my might—the might of a goddess—snapped the ten-by-ten-inch post in half. I leapt out of the way as the wood pillar came crashing down, narrowly escaping it as it smashed into the bed.

I was just about past the foot of the bed—just about to leap off—when the chain dragging behind me snapped taut. Panic-ridden, I looked back, briefly catching view of what was anchoring the chain, or rather, who—Aurelius. He snarled at me as he yanked it backwards with his godly strength, sending me flying towards him, my right arm twisting at an unnatural angle.

A grotesque *pop* sounded in my ear, followed by white-hot pain that scorched its way into my shoulder. At the same time, a scream shredded through my throat as I tried to make sense of what had happened, but my thoughts were scattered, blinded by my agony.

He used the chain to pull me off the bed and onto the floor. I landed with a thud, the side of my hip taking the brunt of my fall, but I heeded it little mind because the pain in my left shoulder was so much worse.

Blackness licked at the rim of my vision, trying to conquer it completely.

Stay with it. Stay with it, Sage, a voice—my voice—said. Whether I spoke the words in my head or out loud, I didn't know.

Aurelius stood over top of me, the iron chain groaning under his relentless grasp as he pulled on it. "Quit your incessant screaming and do not struggle against me," he said in his commanding, noble voice, a flash of light passing over his eyes.

My mouth snapped shut so fast my teeth rattled. My body went lax.

No! This couldn't be. I thought I had broken free from his command.

"That's better," he sighed softly. "Contrary to the adorable little thoughts you conceive in your mind about escaping my control, the divine blood within you was built to serve its superior. I am your king, and whether you like it or not, your body was built to serve my order—to *appease* me." He bent forward and his fingers hooked my collar. Using it, he hauled me and my lifeless left arm—which I was certain had been torn from its socket—to my feet.

Pain lacerated through me, nearly taking my vision, but I held my ground, refusing to hand myself over to the land of unconsciousness. I clenched my teeth together, my right hand tucking under my elbow, propping my sagging left arm up where it naturally should have been. In doing so, I was granted a sliver of relief.

"Do you know how I kept you compliant for all those years, Moonbeam?" he asked, his face mere inches from mine. "At first, my words alone were enough to compel you for days at a time, but as you grew older and stronger, my verbal commands lasted less and less. That's why you are able to go against my command after a short passing of time—just as you did that night in the bathing pool. Just as you do now."

Oh yes, I remembered that night, of the immense, horrific pain that ravaged my body as he drank from me—the sound of my life's essence being slurped into his mouth, and with each heavy, torturous pull, eventually, I had passed out.

"But do you know what is stronger than my word?" He

raised his wrist to his mouth as his top lip pulled back, his canines lengthening. "My ichor." He bit into his wrist, his teeth plunging beneath his pristine skin as he filled his mouth with ichor.

Still locked under his most recent command, there was nothing I could do but watch.

He brought his mouth crushing down against mine at the same time his thumb and his forefinger drilled into my jaw, triggering it to open for him. Warm liquid filled my mouth and the taste of rich honey washed over my tongue.

His hand immediately replaced his mouth as he pulled away. He covered my face, making it impossible to open my mouth and expel the contents he had forced within it. "Swallow," he commanded.

I tried to shake my head, tried to tell him *no*, but I couldn't do any of that, and the muscle within my throat did as it was told.

The tears that had formed in my eyes began to dry up as I felt that familiar feeling of bliss and rapture creep over me.

It numbed the pain in my shoulder, while it made me feel an insatiable hunger.

Until all I craved was . . . him.

Golden eyes met mine as he removed his hand from my mouth. "Do you want more?"

I hated myself as I nodded. "Please."

"Then drink." He lowered his wrist to my mouth.

My tongue traced a droplet of ichor as it ran down the length of his muscled forearm and my body shivered in response. His ichor was divine. Powerful. Nourishing. And the way it made me feel—like I could do anything.

Be anything.

My hand, which had been supporting my dislocated arm, slipped free, and when my arm fell, I felt no pain. I clasped his wrist as I brought it to my lips, and then I started to drink.

My body became rapturous, starving for more of him—in every possible way.

And as if they had a mind of their own, my hips began to move—communicating with him what else my aching body now needed.

A rich, deep chuckle rolled through him as he swept me into his arms. He whispered into my ear, "This is how things will be for you now, Moonbeam."

As I drank from him, he carried me bridal-style to the bed, the chains dragging on the floor behind us. There, he laid me down with gentle tenderness. The bed dipped under his weight as he moved between my legs. Using his knees, he shifted them apart while I drank from his arm.

I wasn't aware that I was naked until I felt his fingers brush between the swell of my breasts—the feel of his warm skin luxurious against my own. My eyes flared open, meeting his incredible gold eyes.

Reassurance was all that I found in them, and happily, so incredibly happily, I handed myself over to him.

"Welcome back—" his hand drifted down my stomach, trailing lower and lower, "—Aurelia."

I peeled away from my broken shell and escaped into the forest of my mind.

There, I found refuge under the protective canopy of a powerful, swaying oak tree.

In its shade, the sun couldn't find me.

CHAPTER 58

Sage

Hundreds of eyes were watching us, but I didn't care.

I was too busy admiring the stained-glass windows of the temple. They twinkled with colors I had never seen before— who knew there could be so many shades of oranges and reds and yellows? Certainly not me.

I sat on the floor, slumped against the gilded throne with the sun carved into the top. The thrones that belonged to the old king and queen had been removed and now only one remained. Whatever became of the queen and her children, I didn't know. Nor did I really care about her or her ridiculous wigs.

I giggled softly and a hand brushed my cheek.

I looked up and golden eyes met mine. Creator above, how I—

"You feel divine, Moonbeam." Aurelius's voice was in

my ear, his body on mine—

No!

I jerked away from the thought but not his hand. *Never* his hand. I could hear his beautiful ichor thrumming powerfully inside, waiting for me.

My mouth watered. "Please," I whispered.

He chuckled before he softly scolded me. "Later, Aurelia, when the coronation is over."

I blew out a dissatisfied breath and watched as the priestess who conducted morning praise and a young woman approached us. Just like everything else in this room, the gilded robes the priestess wore were so incredibly beautiful— the way they shimmered reminded me of the kiss of sunlight upon glittering waters. The young woman beside her carried a red pillow with a ruby and gold crown sitting proudly on top. Tall spires raised from the crown, matching the ones on the top of the throne. Carefully, the priestess raised the crown for all to see before she placed it on Aurelius's head.

"I pronounce thee King Aurelius, lord and protector of Edenvale," she said, taking a step back.

The people cheered, their clapping like thunder in my ears.

A string quartet started to play, and the applause wicked out. The combination of the violin, cello, and viola were lovely, and if my wobbly legs would allow me, I would have danced.

I looked to the vast crowd, finding a familiar face.

Arkyn was sitting in the front row, his eyes fixed on me.

His expression—I had never *seen* him look so sad.

And for the life of me, I couldn't understand why.

CHAPTER 59

Sage

Metal scraped against my teeth as something was shoved down my throat, triggering my gag reflex. I choked and my stomach clenched, seconds away from squeezing its contents up my esophagus and launching them out.

Whatever it was slid from my mouth, and I was jerked upright and onto my side, my eyelids flaring wide open. Hands held my hair back as I vomited copious amounts of gold liquid all over the fur blanket that reminded me of a lion's hide.

Tears pricked my burning eyes. The vile smell of the acidic contents stung my nostrils, giving my stomach another violent churn.

I vomited again.

And again.

And when I was done, hands tugged me back into a

warm torso. Something wiped at my mouth—a cloth of some sort. A hand slid tenderly over my cheek, a desperate voice asking, "Sage, can you hear me?"

The voice was familiar, but my mind was cloudy, and whoever it was, I couldn't quite place them.

"What's wrong with her?" the troubled voice shouted in another direction, no longer directed at me. I followed the sound, as if I could see the notes dancing in the air. They landed on—

"A demon of a man," I whispered, the familiar words triggering something within me. My heart began to quicken in my chest. My voice cracked as I asked the towering darkness leaning against the stone wall, "Von?"

"Not quite, little dove," a deep baritone rumbled, the sound playful and teasing—and gods, it sounded so much like *him*. "The prickling's ichor has twice the potency levels of opium. It's going to take her a while to come down from it," he said, directing his voice to whoever was holding me.

Sloppily, I rubbed my eyes, trying to wipe the clouds from my vision. I didn't believe the bourbon voice who said he wasn't Von, but since when had he ever called me *little dove*?

"Can you do anything else to help her?" the voice behind me asked, his tone painted with concern.

"Shoving my fingers down her throat was the best I could do. I'll shadow walk her to the Cursed Lands. There, she'll recover," he said, pressing off from his shoulder blades as he strode towards me.

"Take me to the Cursed Lands?" I asked, my weary mind like a toddler's, holding up two pieces to a four-piece puzzle and unable to connect which piece went where.

"Yes, Sage. Ezra will be there. She'll help fix your arm," said the voice directly above my head.

I craned my neck and looked up, meeting familiar gray-blue eyes. An excited squeal left my lips—*I knew those eyes.* "Kaleb," I cooed. I reached up and patted him on the head, but I miscalculated and nearly poked him in the eye. Sticking my tongue out, I concentrated and tried again.

Gently, his hand encompassed my wrist. He smiled down at me, his shaggy blond hair falling forward, framing his masculine features. "I'm here," he reassured me.

His words were like a warm blanket—so warm, I tugged them closer.

Kaleb's head shifted back up. From this view, I could see the day's growth of stubble, a few shades darker than his dirty-blond hair, beginning to poke out. I brushed my fingers along the cropped, coarse pieces, curious if they would make a sound.

"What about the king's advisor?" Kaleb asked, his throat bobbing. I was tempted to poke his Adam's apple, it's sudden appeal equivalent to the nose of a dogs—oh so boop-able.

I tried but failed miserably.

Kaleb sighed and caught my hand, gently lowering it back to my chest.

"Whatever repercussions he faces for betraying his father—" the Von look-alike rumbled, "—well, that's on him."

Kaleb ran his fingers through his hair and his long locks took on a wavy look. "He told us where to find her. It wouldn't sit right with me . . . leaving him here."

The king's advisor? A few rusty cogs turned—

"Arkyn?" I asked, my blurry hand that looked like it had one too many fingers falling to Kaleb's wrist.

Kaleb sighed, "See? She's drugged out of her mind and she's *still* piecing things together. You and I both know that when she sobers up, and I tell her that he helped us and we left him to suffer the consequences, she's going to trot her stubborn ass back here to try to help him. And then you will have to rescue her all over again."

"He has a point," I exclaimed profoundly as I raised one finger in the air, wagging it around for all to see.

The male grumbled—the sound born from the depths of his chest. "Fine, I'll help the king's turd. But on one condition."

Kaleb nodded. "Alright. What is it?"

"I want your firstborn," the male conceded with a wicked smile.

My brow crinkled. *That hardly seemed fair.*

Kaleb sputtered, "My firstborn?"

I nodded somberly, slurring out, "That's what he said."

"Yup," the male chuckled, the sound of it not rich and playful like Von's, but rather, a bit . . . chaotic, like he wasn't quite running on all four wheels. "That's what I want."

"But—"

The man's laughter cut Kaleb off. "Relax, I'm just fucking with you. Besides, the firstborn deal is more my sister's thing."

My head flopped over to the male I'd originally thought of as Von. I understood now that although they were very much cut from the same proverbial cloth, there was a world of difference between the two.

When he disappeared before my very eyes, there were no shadows that slithered around him. No, there was only a wild darkness and a billow of smoke.

"Where's he going?" I whispered to Kaleb, suddenly afraid the walls might sprout ears and listen to me. I eyed them wearily.

"He's going to find Arkyn, and then he'll come back for us." Kaleb let out a sigh, his weary gaze meeting mine. "I think."

"That's nice," I said with a yawn.

I curled into Kaleb and shut my eyes—the sweet allure of sleep calling my name.

CHAPTER 60

Sage

Hints of rosemary, mint, lavender, and some other herb I couldn't quite detect bloomed around me, filling my sense of smell with the scent of healing.

My eyelids fluttered open as I slowly stepped into my consciousness.

There was a fuzzy-looking boy sitting on my bed. His head lolled forward as if he were fighting sleep, and just when I was certain he was about to head-bob into the bed, he startled himself and jerked upright.

His eyes snapped to mine and a massive grin burst across his face.

My eyesight cleared and—

"You're awake!" Graiyson yelled at the top of his lungs, his body vibrating with excitement.

"I am," I rasped, my heart strumming happily. It was

good to see him.

"How are you feeling? You've been sleeping forever, like some fairy-tale princess. Although, your hair tells another story. It looks like one of the rats from the Well decided to make a nest out of it." He giggled, the sound joyful.

A whisper of a crackling chuckle rolled free from my lips.

I glanced around. A massive tent surrounded me, warm and clean and filled with the scents of many, many, many herbs. The room hosted twelve single beds, six on each side. All of them were empty—well, except for the one I was in.

My brows furrowed. "Where am I?"

"You're in the infirmary," chirped Graiyson, as giddy as ever.

"I gathered as much, but where specifically?" I asked, the sound of heavy fabric flapping to my right garnished my attention.

"You are in the Cursed Lands," Ezra said as she bustled through the tent's entrance, a wicker basket in one hand and her cane in the other. Her milky-white eyes peered in my direction, but they stared blankly past me.

"Ezra?" I whimpered, tears brimming.

"Hello, my child," she spoke through her smile, bobbing her cane from side to side as she wobbled her way over to my bedside, her shoulders ticking rhythmically from side to side as she approached. She knocked her cane against the bed stand, a knowing smirk on her lips. She plopped the basket down with a mighty thud. I peered skeptically over my shoulder, banking on the basket being full of rocks. One look confirmed as much. Scattered on top were a few blackberries—where she found them this time of year was a mystery to me.

Ezra plopped onto the bed, dropping like a sack of potatoes, her legs kicking out in front of her. "That's better," she said on a loud exhale. She laid the cane across her lap and then reached out her hand—just as a mother would do when she wanted her child to take it.

I slipped my hand into hers and her smile instantly bloomed. Her warm fingers coiled gently around mine, giving them a delicate squeeze. She directed her voice to Graiyson, "Would you give us a moment?"

Graiyson nodded as he shoved off the bed. "I'll go tell the others that she's awake," he said excitedly.

"You do that," Ezra replied with a smile, the skin around her eyes and mouth crinkling—her wrinkles a testament to a life well lived.

Once Graiyson had left the tent, Ezra gave a satisfied nod at his departure. Her voice grew soft as her other hand fell over mine. "Tell me everything," she said, those three little words warming my heart—which, I reminded myself, did not quite belong to me.

It was his.

. . . *his.*

Memories of his body over mine, his lips kissing mine and his—*No!*

I shoved off from the memory and focused on telling Ezra everything that had happened—everything but *that.*

That . . . I would never tell a soul.

When I was nearly finished going over what had happened over the past few months, Ezra's hand never leaving mine throughout the entirety of it, the tent flaps flipped open and in walked a male who made my inflated lungs falter on their exhale.

Obsidian eyes locked with mine.

But that connection—the one that felt like there was a vine or a string or something tethered between us—it wasn't there. I took in the rest of his face, realizing that although he had the same eyes as Von, he was not him.

Shadows didn't linger at his fingertips or curl around his feet like some faithful house cat, not like they did with Von. In their place, a scentless smoke drifted from him—as if he were a smoldering fire, one windy breath away from erupting into destructive flames.

Onyx leather that could easily pass as light armor wound tightly around his mountainous body, from his booted heel to his trim, narrow waist to his broad—*broad*—shoulders. So broad, they looked as if he swam the entirety of the Selenian Sea each morning before breakfast.

My gaze flitted back up to his smirking face. His features were a bit finer than Von's, but Creator above did they look alike, so much so they could pass as twins. Speaking of twins, he had two identical piercings beneath his bottom lip, their placement reminding me of a snake's fangs. Above them, a nose ring. A scar ran down the left side of his handsome face from forehead to diamond-carved jaw—a crack in the perfect canvas.

Was *he* the brother Von spoke of?

That would certainly make sense. When we were in Belamour, Von had said his brother was in the Spirit Realm, and I had thought that meant he was dead. But no, looking at the dark, ethereal male before me, he was *very* much alive. And if he was Von's brother, that made him—

"You're a god," I stated bluntly as he strode towards me, his long legs chewing up the distance.

"I'm well aware." A toying grin grew on his full lips. "Females tend to scream those exact same words when I'm between their legs." His voice tasted like luxurious chocolate on my tongue—rich and dark and dangerous, like once you had a taste, you couldn't stop with just one.

Ezra clicked her tongue. "Folkoln."

He chuckled—a smooth, velvety laugh. "What's the problem, Ezra?" He gave her a wink. "The offer I made you all those centuries ago still stands."

Ezra sucked a tooth. "I'd rather not get a disease."

That only made him laugh more, the smoke at his sides growing ever so slightly—like they had been fed with oxygen. He raised one lone black brow, the twist of his smirking lips exuding a cocky arrogance that might even surpass Von's. "Oh, come on, *old girl*. You know I'm clean."

"As clean as the bottom of my shoe," she muttered admonishingly, finishing her statement with a shake of her head. "And quit feeding off me, you energy-sucking leech. I know what you're doing."

He licked his lips, something demonic flashing over his

fiery black irises. "But you taste so good, Ezravaynia. You always have."

. . . quit feeding off her? An offer from all those years ago?

Ezravaynia?!

My head swiveled, shifting back and forth from Ezra and Folkoln.

"What exactly am I looking at here?" I asked them both.

"A conversation between two old friends," Folkoln answered first, his gaze shifting to mine.

I looked to Ezra. "How *old*?" I wasn't *just* asking about age.

"Old," she said with a crooked smile, her blind eyes staring at nothing. She took a breath before she said, "I am immortal, although I've never accepted the title of goddess, because in truth, I'm not one. I come from something much older than the divine—much older than the changing languages passed down by the human tongue. You see, child, the word for what I am no longer exists."

"I don't understand," I stated with a great deal of confusion. "I've watched you age over the years. I've watched you lose your eyesight too." The space between my brows crinkled like a scrunched-up piece of paper. "How is that possible?"

She held my hand tightly, her words spoken directly to me. "Because I choose to live as a mortal—to experience life as they would."

And I don't know where, but somewhere, deep inside, her words plucked at a familiar string—a feeling—because once upon a time, I had wanted to do the same thing. "Is that why my body acts more mortal than immortal?" I asked her. "Did I choose this for myself?"

She nodded.

"So what does that make me?"

She gave my hand another squeeze. "It makes you free."

And although that wasn't what I was asking, her answer could not have been more meaningful. In my last life, for so much of it, I had never known freedom. My life revolved around serving my husband and being a good, doting wife, even though he'd never honored me, not in the same way I honored him—not even close. And I had turned a blind eye to it all.

Back then, I had been no more than a ghost of the person I was meant to be.

A ghost who wished to live in color—just as the mortals did.

Just so I could *feel*.

And when I was born anew in this life, that was exactly what I had done.

My childhood had been painted in the shades of laughter, of Kaleb and I running barefoot through the trees, screaming "you can't catch me!" while the other tried to do exactly that. My teen years had been forged from sweat and frustration, of training with Ezra and learning how to hone my Curse, how to fight for a battle she'd never told me was coming. And when I reached adulthood, the bonds of friendship had carried me through the roughest parts of this short life—of when my brother was taken from me.

All of it—the good, the bad, the heartbreak—had all pointed to one thing—*I had lived.*

And there was one person who had been by my side throughout it all . . .

I turned to Ezra, emotion crackling my voice. "Thank you."

"It is not my sacrifice that made this life possible for you," she said.

My brow furrowed. If it wasn't her . . . "Then who?"

But it was Folkoln who answered. "It was my brother's. He traded his happiness so that you could find yours."

CHAPTER 61

Sage

"Sage!" Harper exclaimed as she breezed into the tent, a swipe of red painted across her smiling lips. Her voice brought me out of my conflicted thoughts surrounding Von— a topic I had no idea where I stood on. Everything about us was confusing. But I was more than happy to brush those thoughts aside as I was reunited with my best friend.

Harper rushed over and flung her arms around my neck. "It's so damn good to see you."

I hugged her back, surprised to find that my arm, which had been dislocated before, was now in good working order— I imagined Ezra had something to do with that. I bet if I looked to my side, my arrow wound would be healed, too, although it might have sprouted the odd skin-like hair. Ezra's concoctions and tonics and salves were never without a few strange side effects.

I would be a complete liar if I said being reunited with Harper didn't coax a few tears to brim. When she pulled back, she quickly wiped a few of her own away. We took one good look at each other and broke out into grins.

Ryker walked in with a big cocky smile saddled on his lips. "Hey there, sleeping beauty." The twins exchanged spots and he gave me a tight hug—the kind I felt deep down in my soul.

"Don't crowd her," Harper scolded Ryker as she shooed him away, the beads hanging beneath the hem of her cropped top chattering as she moved. She wore a pair of tight leather pants, slung low to her hips, exposing her chiseled abdomen.

The tent flapped open once more. This time, it was Kaleb. His eyes went wide when he saw me, his shoulders falling with relief. In mere seconds, he was at my side, taking me in his arms. He hugged me tightly. "I'm so glad you're alright," he said, burying his face into my neck.

"I'm alright," I reassured him, hugging him just as tightly back.

We stayed like that for a short while—Kaleb's hug revitalizing my depleted soul.

"Thank you for finding me," I whisper-spoke.

He pulled back and his gray-blue eyes met mine. Bags had formed underneath—telling me he hadn't slept in a while. He thumbed over his shoulder to Folkoln, who had plopped onto the empty bed across from mine. His ridiculously large boots—clearly, he had the same massive flipper feet as Von— were kicked up and his hands were tucked behind his head.

"Folkoln and I didn't do it alone," Kaleb said.

"What do you mean?" I asked, confusion weighing my

brows.

He shook his head slightly as he shrugged one shoulder, as if he were still in disbelief about it. "The king's advisor—Arkyn—showed Folkoln and me where Aurelius was keeping you. It was in a part of the castle that no one knew existed. And it was heavily guarded. Arkyn told the guards they were needed elsewhere, giving us a chance to get to you."

I sat with that information for a moment. Arkyn had . . . helped me? But that would have meant that he went against his father. Once Aurelius found out what he did—which he would, because Arkyn couldn't tell a lie—that would mean only one thing . . .

"Aurelius will kill Arkyn for it," I blurted out, my voice etched in urgency. "We can't let that happen."

Kaleb spoke over his shoulder, "Told you."

"So you did," Folkoln mused.

"He's safe for now. Folkoln gave him a place to lie low for the time being," Kaleb reassured me.

I glanced at Folkoln, noting the wicked twist to his lips, and decided I did not feel reassured one bit. But at least Arkyn would be safe—*ish*. Heavy emphasis on the *ish* part.

I heard more movement coming from the tent's entrance and looked to see who it was. Lyra stood there, her hand holding onto . . . Graiyson's.

I blinked, my gaze bouncing between the two. Although they didn't share a lot of physical traits, the big doe eyes were a dead giveaway now that I was seeing them side by side. So *that's* why his eyes seemed familiar. Graiyson and Lyra were most definitely brother and sister.

Kaleb backed away as the two siblings came to the side

of the bed. With her free hand, she pulled a folded piece of paper from the pocket of her petal-pink skirt hemmed with a delicate white lace and handed it to me.

I opened it, reading the flowery script.

Thank you for giving me my brother back. I owe you everything.

And when I looked back up, Lyra was sobbing, her tiny shoulders shaking as she wept. It was the first time I had ever heard her make any sort of sound. She dropped to her knees, scooped up my hand, and pressed it to her forehead.

Graiyson wrapped his arms around his sister, pinning her auburn hair to her neck as he hugged her trembling frame.

My eyes went misty. Softly, I shook my head. "But it wasn't just me." I looked at Ryker. "You got them the rest of the way."

"No, Sage, I won't take any credit for this." Ryker shook his head. "You were the one that gave them hope . . . You were the one who saved them."

Graiyson poked his head up. "We'd still be down there if it wasn't for you." He threw a hand to the tent's entrance. "Everyone out there knows it."

My brows furrowed in confusion.

"This isn't the only family you've reunited, Sage," Harper spoke softly as she stepped behind Lyra, her hand falling to her shoulder.

"They are waiting for you," Graiyson exclaimed. His face brightened with a big smile, exposing that one broken tooth. "You should go outside and see."

"Graiyson, she just woke up," Harper scolded him. "She needs bedrest."

"She's rested enough," Ezra said. Her hand clasped the handle of her cane as she slid off the bed and began to walk towards the entrance. "Come, child. Come see what you have done."

I looked to Harper for answers.

"I guess if Ezra is giving you the all clear, you must be good to go." She sighed and shook her head, the ends of her long ponytail falling from its perch on her shoulder. She extended an arm to me. "Come on, I'll help you up."

Nodding, I took her arm. Ryker moved to my other side, and together, the fire twins helped me onto my feet.

It was a bit embarrassing how wobbly my legs were—no better than a newborn fawn—but I took my time and slowly, I was able to walk half decently again.

Graiyson held the tent flap to the side as I passed through it.

Wearily, my eyes shifted to the sky. I drew a relieved breath when I saw nothing but clouds blocking out the sun. A cool, wintery breeze played with the tips of my hair, and although it reminded me of Von, I could not deny that I took comfort in it.

I looked forward. My gaze dropped and my heart stumbled.

Standing before me, in a labyrinth of freshly fallen snow, were dozens of people. Many wore faces I recognized from the Well. Some grew the biggest of smiles when they saw me, while others began to weep. But the common factor among them all?

Not one of them stood alone. They all stood next to someone—a loved one, their reason for fighting, their hope.

Hand in hand, Lyra and Graiyson walked out into the gathering, joining them. When they turned towards me, their eyes pooled with tears.

And I'd be a liar if I said mine didn't fill with them as well.

Life had a funny way of coming full circle, and this was one of those incredible moments. When I'd left the cottage, I'd had one mission—to save Kaleb and reunite my family. Although I had failed Kaleb, that journey had led me here, standing before the people that I had not failed. Standing among the families I had reunited.

Kaleb wrapped his arm around my shoulders. He sniffed back the tears he was trying not to let fall, although he was doing a rather poor job of it.

We all were.

I felt the magic of the fire twins as they stood behind me, their hands on my shoulders confirming how close they were. Ryker stood behind Kaleb and me, and Harper to the right.

Then the missing piece stepped to my side.

"There is a thin line between success and failure," Ezra's voice crackled as she slid her arm across my lower back, locking her side to mine. "With this victory, you have shown a great deal of self-discipline. And for that, my child, you have made me proud."

CHAPTER 62

Sage

Chaos.

Complete and utter chaos had broken out in the cavernous tent that was dedicated for meetings such as this one—if it could even be called a meeting. The makings of a riot seemed more fitting. A slew of voices shouted over one another, trying to get a word in, but only adding to the disorderly nature instead. Even Harper and Ryker, who stood beside me, had joined in.

If I didn't know any better, I would think Folkoln, the God of Chaos, was playing a role in the colossal downfall of this urgently called meeting, but he and Kaleb had returned to the Spirit Realm the day after I woke in the infirmary tent.

That was a week ago now.

Since then, I had started lightly training with Ryker and Harper—nothing too strenuous, as my body was out of shape due to castle life. It felt good to be out in the crisp, wintery air, though, feeling that familiar burning in my muscles and the satisfactory ache that came after. Being able to move without a python-inspired squeeze-the-life-out-of-you corset was a freedom I'd never take for granted again. Not to mention being able to use my powers and feel the water swell from my fingertips. On the downside, my nightmares had returned. *Those* I had not missed, but Ezra was working with me to try to control them. I hadn't done much with my Fire Curse, as I didn't feel comfortable using it around the villagers—safety and all. But Ryker said once my stamina was back to normal, he'd take me to a clearing up in the mountains where I could practice safely without putting anyone in danger.

Apart from training, Ezra had been teaching me about the Cursed Lands. They stretched a couple thousand miles from their east to west borders. The east border backed the Selenian Sea, which was accessible in some places where the Endless Mist didn't weave so closely to the coast. There, the fishing industry thrived, as well as those with the Water Curse. Further inland, the Earth Cursed enjoyed the expanse of the sprawling prairies, where they could grow various foods in the abundant, fertile soil. Much of the Air Cursed preferred to live up near Orion's Peak, in the embrace of the Stonehelm Mountains, where they could teach their young how to command the winds.

Although the Cursed tended to gravitate towards specific locations within the Cursed Lands, there were no set rules about where one was supposed to live. If someone with the Curse of Water decided mountain life suited them better, then that's where they moved.

A good portion of where Edenvale and the Cursed Lands connected was cut off by the unpassable Stonehelm Mountains. North of the mountains, the land was flat—flat enough for troops to travel through. That was where the fighting took place. Ezra said it was like a continuous game of tug-of-war, where one side would win and gain ground, and then during the next round, the other side would win and take it back.

It had been like that for decades.

The fighting wasn't constant, but because the Cursed did not know when they would be attacked, warriors had to stay close to the border. Over time, towns and villages began to spring up along it—this was so families could be with their loved ones who were serving in the war. Originally, the Cursed had hoped that the crown would call off its pursuit to eradicate them, and so the homes in the villages were tents at first, as the common belief was that they would be temporary. As time went on, the usage of tents never changed—and it just became a way of life. However, there were some houses that had cropped up.

The largest of the towns along the border, Valenthia, served as the central hub for war meetings. That was where I was now, listening to a plethora of loudly voiced concerns for the news Ryker and I had shared less than a few hours ago.

We had stood before the room of nearly fifty men and women—some Elders and some warriors—and told them what we had learned: that the God of Life was now king, and he was making an army of Demi Gods.

Upon hearing this, they erupted into chaos.

So while they all bickered and tried to figure out how they were going to fight an army of Demi Gods, I stared at the massive table positioned directly in the middle of the tent. It was a polished slab of marbled wood, and although the wood was beautiful, it was the legs that grabbed my attention. On each leg, an animal was chiseled—a bear, a wolf, a fish, and a cougar.

"Enough!" Ezra shouted, her cane cracking like thunder against the wooden table.

Unsurprisingly, the room fell quiet—it was not often that Ezra raised her voice.

"Bickering like a bunch of hyenas isn't going to solve the problem," she said with a shake of her head. She pulled her cane back from the table and lowered the bottom to the ground, her arthritic hands falling neatly over top of its handle.

"Then what do you suggest we do?" rasped an older man whose voice sounded like gravel. He stroked his long, white beard with one hand while his other held the underbelly of the bowl of a long-stemmed pipe.

"I'm getting to that," Ezra said, her hand diving into a coat pocket—fishing for something.

Everyone watched, wondering what it might be.

When she retrieved a rock and slapped it down on the table, I nearly fell over.

And by the looks of the rest of the people in the tent, they nearly did too.

"We're going to need more than a rock to save us, Ezra," said the older man as he sipped on his pipe, puffs of white smoke rolling from his mouth. He glanced at the smoke and it instantly dispersed.

"Well, of course this rock isn't going to help, Sedric. I just wanted to get it out of my pocket," she chuckled, followed by a satisfactory sigh. She patted her side. "That's much better. These old bones feel lighter already."

For the second time, everyone almost fell over.

"As you were saying, Ezra?" the older man—Sedric—inquired.

She thought it over for a moment, and then she said, "I'd suggest you all begin preparations for battle."

A chestnut-haired warrior stepped forward. Like so many of the people in this tent, his clothing was made of deerskin, which made sense, as Ryker had told me that deer were in abundance in these lands. Despite the stern setting of the warrior's face, he was handsome. If I were back at the Broken Mare in Meristone, I would have taken a liking to him.

But that lifetime was, well, a lifetime away.

And as it stood, I had *more* than enough problems with men.

The warrior spoke to Ezra. "How exactly do we prepare to face an army of Demi Gods? No matter what we do, they will slaughter us. And even if we did manage to defeat them, the God of Life will just make more."

"Koa has a point," Harper sighed, her arms crossing over her chest.

A few people muttered in agreement.

"So, then what? Are you suggesting we don't even *try* to fight?" Ryker's voice came from beside me.

This droplet of a thought was carried out in ripples. A light chatter filled the tent, the conversation spreading from mouth to mouth as more and more people chipped in their own thoughts. Some said they also wanted to know the answer to what Ryker had asked, while others suggested different ideas.

I glanced up at Ryker, noting the firm setting of his jaw and the muscle ticking in it. I rarely saw Ryker so . . . intense, and I had a feeling it wasn't just because of what was being discussed. Something was telling me it was more than that.

Koa narrowed in on Ryker. "Don't put words in my mouth," he warned.

"Nah." A cocky smile, one straight out of Von's book of grand fuckery, saddled up on Ryker's lips. "Unlike your family, that's not really my style."

"Ryker!" Harper scolded.

At the same time, Koa spat out, "You son of a bitch."

Before Koa could charge, Ezra cut in. "If you two are going to behave like dogs, then you can go outside. Or you can nip your tongues and listen." She waited, giving them a chance to decide. When neither of them said anything, she gave a satisfactory nod. "There is one god that will help you."

Those eight little words were enough to send the tent spiraling back into chaos. The light chatter turned into shouting and words of dismissal, like a smoldering fire fed with a mass amount of oxygen and dry kindling.

Eight little words—that was all it took to make the room ignite.

I sighed, the sound lost amongst the shouting. I couldn't help but wonder if choosing to have a meeting with so many people was a bad decision on the Elders' behalf. They would have been better off having a smaller meeting—something might actually have come of it because—at this point, no one was getting anywhere.

Ezra whacked her cane against the table once more, instantly leashing the rabid beast she had created.

The tent went silent.

Pulling her cane from the table, she turned around, her movement as nimble as a teenaged girl. "Behold, your savior." She pointed her cane at . . . me.

Eyes—*too many*—shifted to me.

"Me?" I sputtered.

Ezra gave me a toothy grin. I had a feeling this was about to get a whole lot worse. Then, with her tongue gilded in splendor, she exclaimed grandly, "Behold, the reincarnation of the Goddess of Life, Lady Light."

I braced myself, waiting for them all to burst into laughter. I knew how I looked with my clearly mundane appearance—no sunshine-y radiance or shadowy aura here. There was nothing grand about me, nothing that boasted of any type of greatness. Nothing that made me—

People started to kneel.

One after another.

My face turned ten shades of awkward—*Creator above, I was a shit goddess.*

"Please don't do that," I said to one younger male that stood just off to my left as he bended his knee.

"Lady Light," a woman cried softly, as she also lowered to the ground.

"Uhh, you don't have to," I said to her, my hands held up, gesturing for her to stop, but my plea fell on deaf ears as she lowered to the ground and dipped her head in respect.

Ryker chuckled beside me, the deep, rumbly sound snagging my attention. He winked at me, and then to my complete mortification, he started to bend the knee.

"Oh gods, not you too," I groaned, my hand shading my eyes, as if shielding my view would make this whole awkward experience more palatable . . .

It didn't.

"I don't want to be the only one left out," he whisper-spoke to me in his swaggering drawl.

The only one left out?

My head swiveled like a top as I took around the rest of the tent. Everyone—including Koa, Harper, and Sedric—was kneeling. Well, everyone but Ezra.

Ezra was sitting on the table, her feet ticking rhythmically underneath her patched, faded skirts, the hem worn and coated in the essence of the earth. Courtesy of a lifetime of wandering.

She looked . . . pleased with herself.

"Two centuries ago, you saved the children of the Old Gods from being Cleansed from both the Immortal and Living Realms. Although that was many generations ago, this has never been forgotten. The people before you—" she gestured to them all with skyward-facing palms, "—may worship the Gods of Old, but they praise your name as well. For if you had not gone against the God of Life, not one of these people would be here today . . . Not one of them would have been born into existence."

I swept my arms around my torso, uncertainty filling my voice, "But I . . . Ezra, I barely know who that person was—that part of me."

Ezra chuckled. "You took many years to find her in your last life as well. But on your journey to self-discovery, you did not walk alone. There was one who walked that path with you."

I didn't need to ask who she meant. I just knew.

Her eyes sparkled with mischief. "Perhaps it is time the two of you be reunited at last."

CHAPTER 63

Sage

"So you mean to tell me that all of this time, you've known where the Blade of Moram is, but you didn't breathe a word to any of us about it?" Ryker groaned in disbelief. He had one heavily muscled arm tossed over the back of the settee he occupied, which sat directly across from the one I was sitting on. In his free hand, he balanced a glass on his leg, three fingers' worth of freshly poured spirits inside.

"The timing wasn't right," Ezra said as she bumbled around the tiny kitchen, her hands patting the worn, wooden countertop in search of the spoon she'd set down. Harper, who was also standing in the kitchen, supervising whatever concoction Ezra was working on, slid the spoon closer to Ezra's hand. When she felt it, she grinned in triumph and snatched it up faster than a poor man finding a coin on the streets.

Ryker's deep-brown eyes slid to mine. "What does that mean?"

"Spirit Realm if I know." I shrugged, glancing at Lyra, who had been one busy little bee. She sat cross-legged on the floor, leaning over top of the coffee table as she worked on drawing a picture of the Blade of Moram based on Ezra's description. Lyra's fingers were stained black from the stick of charcoal she was using to draw. Somehow, she had managed to get a bit on her cheek. Graiyson sat beside her, his brows raised in wonder as he watched his sister work.

After the meeting ended, the five of us had returned to Ezra's small but comfortable home, where I had been staying since the day I awoke in the infirmary. Harper, Lyra, and Graiyson lived here as well, but Ryker lived on his own. Judging from the way the girls in this town batted their eyelashes at him, I had a good idea why he preferred his own space.

It was safe to say that some of the blood of the immortals thrummed powerfully in the fire twins' bodies. Harper's lithe frame stretched to six feet, while Ryker had a solid six to seven inches on her. Both of them possessed rich, brown eyes and skin—lit from within with an orange-red undertone. And both of them were damned good looking, and well aware of it too.

"It means . . ." Ezra started as she lowered her face over a pot of boiling herbs and used her hand to waft it towards her, taking a deep inhale. When her curved shoulders sagged from her exhale, she continued, "I could have told you, Ryker, but it wouldn't have done a droplet of good, because the decision to save Von lies solely with Sage."

"Me?" I blurted out, confusion drawing my brows together. "I thought you said the Blade of Moram was going to save Von? What do you mean by *me*?"

"And it will, child, but you are the only one who can get it." Ezra tapped the wooden handle on the lip of the pot, knocking a few droplets off, before she rested it on the counter. "It's done," she said to Harper.

Harper glanced at the small flame that danced beneath the pot, instantly smothering it out. "We sort of need to know *where* it is, if we're going to get it."

"I'm getting to that," Ezra said, her hand sliding along the counter as she walked over to a row of open shelves that lined the kitchen walls—much like back at the cottage. Ezra rose to the tips of her toes as she reached for an empty jar, her arm not quite long enough to reach.

"So then where is it?" Harper asked as she reached over top of Ezra, grabbed the jar, and handed it to her.

Ezra sniffed the jar and then she grinned. "Thermes de Luxe."

"The bathhouse?" Harper and I sputtered at the exact time.

Ezra nodded as she bustled her way back over to the pot. "That's where the Blade of Moram is, in the hands of a vengeance-seeking soul."

What did the bathhouse have to do with a vengeance-seeking soul?

One nasty Goddess of War—that's what.

"She'll never give it to me," I exclaimed to Ezra. The last time I saw Von's sister, things had gone south in a hurry—to the point where she tried to strangle me.

"Well, of course she won't *give* it to you," Ezra said as she walked back over to the pot. "But she will make a deal with you."

"A *deal?* With *me?"* I shook my head. "What could *I* possibly have that the Goddess of War would want?"

Ezra began to spoon some of the contents of the pot into the empty jar, and despite her blindness, she didn't spill so much as a drop. She chuckled. "How should I know?"

I had a feeling she did, the sneaky old bird. Sometimes, conversing with Ezra was like having a conversation with, well, rocks. She'd been like that for as long as I had known her—giving out just enough information, but never all of it.

I let out an aggravated sigh.

Harper walked towards us, two steaming cups of tea in her hands. She placed one on the table in front of Lyra, and then offered the other one to Graiyson. He shook his head. She raised it towards me, silently asking if I wanted it.

Softly, I said, "No, thank you."

She looked at Ryker, but when she spotted the cup of spirits in his hand, she didn't bother to offer him any. She maneuvered gracefully around the coffee table and sat down beside me.

"So when are we going?" Ryker asked, turning his body enough so that he could peer over the back of the settee at Ezra. "I can have the horses ready to leave within an hour."

"You are needed here," Ezra replied as she placed the filled jar down on the counter with a heavy *thunk.* Steam swirled from the top.

"Lyra and Graiyson have only just been reunited," Harper stated before she glanced to me. "Looks like it will be just me and you then."

"No," Ezra cut in. "You will stay too."

"You can't be serious. Surely, you're not expecting her to travel on her own? Immortal or not, it's still dangerous for her out there. Not to mention she doesn't even know the way." Harper's head swiveled to mine, an apologetic smile dressing her lips. "Sorry, I hope that didn't sound rude."

I gave a soft shake of my head.

"She won't be going alone," Ezra answered as she started her way towards the living room, about ten paces from the kitchen.

"Then who will she be traveling with?" Ryker asked, his brown eyes watching Ezra as she sat down beside him.

"He will," Ezra said.

Tendrils of black smoke whispered into existence, not far from the coffee table. They snaked their way to the floor, forming boots first, then legs and a torso. Lastly, they formed a face—one very handsome, snarling face.

Obsidian eyes, full of wrath, shot like daggers towards Ezra. "You'd better have one fucking good reason why you didn't tell me you knew Saphira has the Blade of Moram." Folkoln threw one hand to the side, slicing the air. "Do you have any idea how long I've been looking for it?"

"Not as long as your sister, I would imagine. And I have two reasons," Ezra said with a chuckle. "Neither of which I will divulge to you. Now, are you going to continue to act like a toddler or are you going to help her get the blade?" Ezra flicked her head my way, gesturing to me.

"Of course, I will help her," Folkoln growled before his onyx eyes shifted to mine. "Let's go."

"Now?" I sputtered.

"Now," he confirmed as he appeared in front of me. Without a word of warning, he grabbed my wrist and pulled me into his mountainous frame, then shadow walked us to Belamour.

CHAPTER 64

Sage

Of all the places I expected to see again, the bathhouse was not one of them. Yet here I was, standing in the back alley, peering at the same back door I had walked through dozens of times before.

Moments ago, I had been in the Cursed Lands, watching Lyra draw the Blade of Moram. Now, thanks to Folkoln's shadow walking abilities, we were here in Belamour—the ten-day ride via horseback reduced to seconds.

Folkoln stood beside me, his muscular, tattooed arms threaded loosely over his chest. His eyelashes dipped and his gaze slid towards me. "Are you ready to go in?"

"Just one minute," I said, my eyes going back to the door.

My hesitancy wasn't because I feared Saphira—no, she might have a serpent's tongue and a viper's strike, but it wasn't that. It was much deeper.

Once I went into the bathhouse and faced the Goddess of War, if I was successful and got the Blade of Moram back, that meant Von would be free of his deal. And whether I was ready for him or not, he would come like a hurricane, back into my life, and he would suck me up into his storm.

. . . What if he hurt me again?

Because learning the truth of our twisted past, of what he had done to me—learning that had shattered me. And I was *just* barely picking up the pieces.

"As much as I'm enjoying the little feast your mixed emotions are serving, I'm growing tired of waiting," Folkoln said testily.

I turned, my gaze meeting his all-too-familiar eyes. "Is he worth it?"

Folkoln quirked one brow in question. "He's your bonded, you dumbass. Of course he's worth it."

Bonded.

And there it was again. That word that Von had used over and over again.

Safe and secure. Steady and strong. The exact opposite of what I felt for Von right now.

"What does it mean?"

The one raised brow dropped, knitting with its dark twin. "Are you serious?"

"Yes, I'm serious," I snipped back.

"Do you know how our souls are made?"

I shook my head. "Not really."

"Our souls are forged from the stars." Small bits of smoke seeped from his upraised palm, and like a sweep of paint upon a blank canvas, they began to paint a black, starry sky. To my complete surprise, the stars, which were made of smoke—*they twinkled.* A hand, also made of smoke, reached across, plucking one of the stars—the brightest of them all. "On the day of our creation, the Creator looks for the brightest star. They take it and place it on their mighty anvil." The hand did just as he said, placing the star on the flattened top of a smoke-crafted anvil. "Then they take their hammer and strike the star—only once— splitting it in two." As he said that, the hammer raised and then swung back down, cracking the star right down the middle. The two halves fell to the side, and like a coal that had cooled, the star's brilliant light burned out. Folkoln rolled his wrist and the smoke disappeared. "The Creator then takes those two halves and places them beneath our flesh, giving us life. But pairs are not always born in the same era, meaning some never find one another. That is why most mortals don't believe in the bond, nor do they really know much about it—they simply don't live long enough to experience it. But when it comes to us immortals, due to our long expanse of life, we are well aware that the bond exists." Although it was small, I caught the tiniest crack of emotion in his perfect, ethereal mask—telling me that Folkoln had yet to find his. "When two halves of the same soul forge together, the star inside will shine again, its light so bright that it will permanently weld them back together—forging the bond. After that, the covenant made between them can not be broken."

Despite it being a lot of information, it did not feel overwhelming. If anything, it felt like an old memory being dusted off, but the picture itself was faded and hard to make out.

Folkoln continued, "Once the bond welds them back together, the couple is referred to as bonded or fated mates.

They are territorial over one another. Protective and committed. To the point that they are willing to give their life for one another."

Just as Von had done for me, a small voice whispered inside.

And yet, he took away your ability to create, and made you live for decades in pure misery! shouted another.

I ignored them both. "How do two halves forge together?"

Folkoln smirked. "Well, sex of course."

Well, that answered that.

"What if I—" My eyes flicked back and forth between two gravel stones, larger than the rest. "What if I don't want the bond between us?"

"It's a bit late for that, goddess. You two have already forged as one. And even though Von hasn't touched you in weeks, all I smell is his scent on you. You are his bonded, his fated mate—through and through."

"But I never had sex with him," I tossed in Folkoln's face. Immediately, I regretted my bluntness.

"Are you sure about that?" He raised an insinuating brow.

Of course, I was sure. Yes, Von had given me a few orgasms, but it was from his tongue, not his—

Wait.

"Von and I had sex in my past life?"

"You are not the fastest goddess, are you?"

I shot him a look, my brain firing thoughts at a mile a minute. "So then if we're already bonded, why does it feel . . . weak?"

"Because you died, Sage!" Folkoln exclaimed, his voice not loud enough to be a shout, but not quiet enough to be conversational either. There was an urgency to it. "You died in his arms, and it nearly destroyed him. When you returned in this life, without any memories, the bond for you isn't as strong as it should be. Von believed that if you two were to join again, it would weld the bond back into place, reawakening those feelings in you whether you were ready for them or not."

I shook my head, thinking back. That day in the woods, I'd wanted Von with such intense need that I had practically begged him. But he had all but turned me down. Was that so the bond wouldn't be forged back into place? I sucked in a breath—understanding hitting me square on the chin. I had been searching for a reason to believe Von hadn't just been using me, and there it was.

If he really wanted to get back at Aurelius, if that was his master plan, he could have forged the bond between us back then, and yet . . . he hadn't. All because he wanted me to have . . .

Choice, my voice and Von's said together.

Something Aurelius had never given me.

And yes, once upon a time, Von had taken my choice to create. And that was fucking brutal of him. But I could not ignore the fact that even though he did that, eventually, the past version of me had chosen to welcome him into my bed, to bond myself to him. And although I didn't understand past me's reason for doing so . . . I wanted to.

I wanted to know our story.

I looked to the bathhouse—I knew what I needed to do.

CHAPTER 65

Sage

Saphira wasn't in her room.

But if the breathy moans and heavy panting coming from the next room over were any indication, I figured I knew where she was. The scent of sex clung to the damp, warm air, and I bit back a gag. That was the last thing I wanted to be smelling, especially considering *who* it belonged to.

While I tried not to upchuck my supper, Folkoln swaggered around the room, lazily inspecting where his sister had been living, a hint of intrigue written plainly on his features. Unlike Von, Folkoln's footsteps were not silent—if anything, they were intentionally loud. The hard soles of his leather boots struck against the ground with each step, like the rhythmic ticking of a clock, counting down the seconds.

The sounds from the other room came to an abrupt stop. There was a splash of water, a loud bang—like a two hundred-pound potato sack had fallen onto the floor—and then—

"What are you doing here?" snarled a feminine voice from the doorway.

Standing there was Von's sister, her sharp, long canines bared. A luxurious black robe adorned her trim torso, the subtle sheen of the material reflecting the candlelight. She tied it loosely at her waist. It covered her sex, but not enough to cover the swell of her breasts. Beads of water slid down her skin, soaking her robe and the spot where she was standing. Her hair, the color of a raven's feathers, was drenched, the tendrils clinging to her slender neck and shoulders.

"Sister," Folkoln said in flat greeting, his back turned to her as he plucked the lid off of a bone-carved dish and inspected what was inside.

But she didn't reply, because by that time, her hateful gaze had landed on me.

A shiver spider-walked the length of my spine.

"You," Saphira spat, her snarl turning feral. She took one threatening step towards me.

Did she recognize me from before? Von had placed some sort of magical veil over me, blurring my features from those who might do me harm. It had worked on Arkyn for quite some time before he figured out who I was, but now, without Von, I wondered if the veil was gone—which meant Saphira was seeing me for who I was—the Goddess of Life.

I reached down for my power, feeling that familiar swell of water stir in my fingertips like a faithful old pet coming for a good scratch. I wasn't about to let her strangle me again. No, this time, I'd fight back.

But there was no need, because Folkoln flashed in front

of her, his hands shoved into his pockets, his broad back facing me. He tipped his head to the side, ever so slightly. "Aww, come on now, sis, is that really how you want to play it right now?"

"*She* is the reason we *lost* the realms," Saphira growled with such disgust that saliva sprayed out of her mouth.

"That's not entirely true. It was Von's choice to make, not ours," Folkoln replied, his voice calm. "Besides, if it were *your* bonded, you would have done the same. And you know it."

"Don't you dare speak of *my* bonded!" Saphira screamed at him with such ferocity, it was a wonder the roof didn't blow off the ceiling.

Folkoln merely stood there, soaking in her wrath. The smoke that hovered around his body writhed in pleasure, like it had just been fed more air. Despite this, his voice was somber. "The Creator is cruel."

There was a silent acknowledgment between the two—one I didn't quite understand. Had Saphira's bonded died? That would certainly explain her abrasive personality.

Saphira dropped her loosely crossed arms and strode around Folkoln, over to a private bar that sat kitty-corner in her room. "So then, are you going to tell me why you shadow walked the enemy into my room?" she asked, shedding the layers of her anger and donning something much calmer—I didn't know which was more frightening.

"We have come to make a deal with you," Folkoln said, turning towards her.

"Continue," she said as she took three empty decanters from the bar top, popped the tops off, and then waved her hand above them. Instantly, they began to fill with a deep, red liquid.

I stepped forward. "We know you have the Blade of Moram. We wish to make an exchange with you."

Saphira turned from the bar top, that peaceful nature snapping when she set her hawk-like eyes upon me. "And what could *you* possibly have that *I* would want in return?"

Folkoln cut in. "Your wings, Saph. If you give us the Blade of Moram, I will return your wings to you."

Return her wings to her?

What did that mean?

I remembered the vicious scar slit vertically down her back, the peculiar way they angled closer to one another the further they went. *Wings.* Like Von, Saphira must have had wings at one point. And if Folkoln was offering them back—had he been the one to take them from her?

Questions swirled abound, until a memory flickered free. It was of a pair of beautiful, feminine, black wings encased in molten glass. Ivory flesh, dappled with ichor, clung around the bones which had once been attached to its owner's back. The God of Death stood beside me, telling me the story of when he had taken his sister's wings, and throughout it all, never once did my hand leave his.

Saphira's response pulled me from my memory. "I would rather light my wings aflame than release Draevon from his suffering. For all I care, he can spend the rest of eternity like this. He deserves as much."

Now I understood her anger towards him—he had taken her wings.

Yet, still, in that memory, I supported him for doing so.

"If you give me the blade, I'll talk to Von about having your exile removed," Folkoln stated, striding over to the bar area beside her.

"I've grown rather fond of living with the mortals." She gestured to the door. "Unlike immortals, when you end their pitiful lives, they do not return to annoy you."

That answered what the loud bang had been in the other room.

Folkoln grabbed one of the decanters, raised it up, and eyed the contents. "You've come a long way, sister. I didn't think you were the type to sip on peasant blood."

"He wasn't a peasant," Saphira growled as she snatched the glass container from Folkoln and set it back down.

Folkoln chuckled as he said, "By the looks of that watery trash, he definitely was."

"*You*, of *all* immortals, have no right to tell me who I should be drinking," she growled. "And as I won't be giving you the Blade of Moram, you might as well take Von's little pet and leave."

Von's little pet? It took a grand amount of willpower not to wrap a water bubble around her head and drown her for calling me that.

"There has to be something you want, Saph," Folkoln said.

"I can promise you, there is nothing," she snipped.

Folkoln's expression clouded over. Sighing deeply, he said, "She gets his feathers."

The goblet Saphira had just picked up fell from her hands. The empty metal cup sounded in protest as it struck the marble floor.

Saphira swirled towards me. "How many do you have?"

Something protective coiled within me. "I don't know," I

replied honestly. I had never taken the time to count them, although I had a rough idea how many there were. An instinctual part of me didn't want to divulge just how many I had.

When the feathers had first started coming to me, Ezra gave me a chest that was nearly half full of the same onyx-colored silken plumes. She never explained where those feathers had come from, but because they matched, she suggested I put the other feathers with their kin. Now, that chest was nearly full. I had a good feeling that the feathers in the chest were ones I had collected in my past life, the first being the one left in Von's wake that day he ended the war.

Saphira looked to Folkoln. "Does Draevon know?"

"He does," Folkoln answered, offering me an apologetic glance as he fought some sort of internal war with himself.

"It would seem you do have something that I want." Saphira smiled wickedly. Her tongue snaked over her lips— painted the color of dried blood. "I want the feathers your mate has given you. And in return, I will give you the Blade of Moram."

The space between my brows crinkled. "Why would you possibly want those?"

"I have my reasons," she said, offering no more.

I glanced at Folkoln, but his expression was unreadable.

I knew there was no use in prying. I'd spent enough time around Von to know he could be rather tight-lipped when it came to specific things—his sister was probably no different. And I knew bartering with something I didn't understand was probably not the smartest idea, but what other choices did I have?

"I don't have them in my possession right now," I said to her.

"That's fine. When the time comes for them to be assembled, that is when I will take them," she replied.

Assembled? I was tempted to ask, but again realized any questions were most likely futile.

"Well, do we have a deal or not?" Saphira asked as she loosely threaded her arms over her chest. Her knitted brows and thinned lips made her look stern, but her lush, emerald eyes sparkled with intrigue.

Folkoln cut in with his deep rumbly voice. "Give her a minute, Saph."

But I didn't need a minute, because my mind had already been made up the moment I stepped into the bathhouse. And I realized it was a foolish deal to make, but again, my options were limited.

"Fine," I said. "You have yourself a deal."

"Excellent." Saphira's eyes sparkled with malevolence. She waved her hand, and in it appeared an onyx-colored blade that looked like smoked glass. Ancient power radiated from it. "It can be used as a dagger or—" the blade began to lengthen, transitioning into a beautiful sword, the tip so sharp, it glinted in the candlelight, "—it can be used as a sword. Whatever it's wielder chooses. Oh, and a small warning, the blade tends to have a mind of its own. Don't be surprised if it turns up at convenient or . . . inconvenient times."

She handed it to me. Wearily, I took it.

"The Blade of Moram is yours now. Use it wisely, *dear sister*," she cackled and Folkoln sneered.

CHAPTER 66

Sage

After we left the bathhouse, in the early hours of the morning, Folkoln shadow walked us back to Valenthia, but just before we returned to Ezra's house, I felt it—

Scalding heat.

It licked hungrily at my flesh as if it would like a taste, coaxing pearls of sweat to pool on the surface of my skin, dampening my brow and slickening my neck.

"What's going on?" I asked Folkoln, his arm wound around my waist, mine looped around his neck. In my free hand, I held the Blade of Moram, cradling it against my chest.

"We're going to find out," he replied determinedly.

Blinding light flashed and then—

We were *flying*.

Folkoln's massive, black wings were spread out above us, gliding on the current as he flew us through the air. Each feather was rimmed in twinkling silver. The sight of them . . . it snatched the oxygen from my lungs.

They were *incredible*.

Beautiful.

And apart from the glimmer of brilliant silver, they reminded me of Von's.

I looked at Folkoln's face, reminding myself that he was not Von, but what I saw in his eyes snapped me out of my spell. Reflected upon a canvas of black were colors that had no place being there—oranges, reds, and yellows.

Panic launched its mighty fist into my stomach as I turned my head.

Valenthia was on fire.

The once proud town that served as the central hub for the resistance had been reduced to flames and ash. The tents, the houses. Their strong frames that had borne the brunt of years of war had caved in on themselves. And the ones that hadn't, the ones that were still burning, resembled little more than toothpicks. Smoke billowed into the air, signaling to the world the destruction that had taken place here. It was thick and heavy and it clogged up my lungs and irritated my eyes.

When we reached a spot where the dense smoke parted, that was when I saw them . . .

The charred corpses. Both big and small.

I screamed, tears brimming.

Devastation painted the ground before me.

And ravens—*so many* soul-collecting ravens.

"Let me down!" I cried out.

"They have passed from this realm, Sage."

"That . . . that can't be."

"I'm afraid it is," he said, his voice surprisingly gentle. "By the looks of it, the army is tracking east."

The army.

Realization dawned as sure as the morning sun I had grown to despise.

Aurelius. He had done this. He had brought his army here and caused this destruction, just as he'd said he would. But his soldiers were nowhere in sight, which meant they were on the move, sweeping across the Cursed Lands. Were my friends out there as well? Fighting or trying to help get the Cursed to safety?

I glanced down, scanning the ground below, the loss of life.

What if they were among them—

No!

I refused to believe that. *They are alive*, I told myself. *And I need to get to them.*

I looked eastward. The army had left one massive, scorched footprint behind. Urgency filled my voice. "We must follow them, Folkoln."

"We will." His wings flexed, shooting up and slamming back down with such tremendous strength that we catapulted forward at an incomprehensible speed. The grounds below became a blur of ash and despair, the same horrific message repeated over and over again.

Until it wasn't. Until the world slowed.

My body went rigid.

War had come. And it had stained the world in blood and gore and sadness.

Cursed and Demi Gods collided, fighting with

everything they had—magic, weapons, and fists. The ground, which should be blanketed in snow, had turned to mud from the heat of battle—of fire fighting fire.

I scanned the grounds as we flew overhead, frantically searching.

A lethal shot of panic injected my heart, because caught in the middle, surrounded by Demi Gods who were quickly closing in, was—

"Harper!" I shouted, turning to Folkoln. "Help her."

Black eyes met mine. "I will not fight a war for the living." His voice was firm.

"Then let me down," I said, growling.

"Fine." Sleekly, he tucked his wings in, and we dove towards the ground.

As soon as my feet touched the burning, bloody earth, I shoved the Blade of Moram into Folkoln's hands. "Get Von."

"Wait!" Folkoln barked, but his words were lost to me, the muscles in my legs firing up as I ran towards Harper, a silent prayer on repeat . . .

Creator above, let me get to her, I pleaded desperately.

For a moment, I could see her. Still standing, but just barely.

She was holding her side, a flame sword in her free hand as she slashed wearily at the Demi God closest to her. Her hair tie had reached the ends of her hair, nearly falling out. She roared, her sword biting into him, blood spraying onto her already battle-painted face.

But he didn't fall.

He grabbed the blade, and twisted the sword from her hands, leaving her weaponless. But not for long—she threw her palm towards him, a tornado of flame blasting in his direction. It sent him back, flying into the soldiers behind him.

Another soldier moved behind Harper, his fingers clenching as he slowly raised his fist.

Harper screamed, her hands flying to her head as he plucked at her mental strings.

I roared, conjured a water spear, took aim, and hurtled it. It soared through the air, straight and true, burrowing into his head.

Harper swirled towards me, eyes flaring when she spotted me through the tidal wave of soldiers that separated us. "Sage!" she shouted, her voice nearly swallowed up by the sounds of clanking swords and shields, merciless cries, and desperate yelling.

She blasted another soldier with her flame, just before his whirlwind nearly found purchase. But just barely. Whatever was wrong with her side was affecting her movement. And by the looks of her weary, pain-stricken face, her wound was serious.

Twin blades formed in my hands as I started fighting my way to her. And she to me.

My heartbeat hammered in my ears, drumming so loudly I heard nothing else—just that quick, heavy, steady beat, the same sound I had heard when Kaleb died in my arms. The same sound I heard when I believed my forest was burning. The same sound I heard when Von shattered my heart.

That sound had played in the darkest moments of my life.

And here it was, playing again.

But this time, it was for Harper.

It was a countdown.

The seconds I had left to get to her.

The earth shot up, the ground turning into deadly spikes beneath my feet. Just before they impaled me, I blasted the ground with water, the force of it projecting me up into the air—out of their reach. Midair, I twisted, eyes fixing on the Demi God that had set her sights on me. Before I landed, I hurtled one of my twin blades at her. The ground shot up in front of her and she blocked my attack, at the same time I landed.

She stepped out from behind her barrier, smirking—her teeth razor sharp. Like they had been filed down to look that way.

. . . What had Aurelius done to them?

Her wrists touched, one hand pointed skyward while the other pointed down. She thrust them towards me, and the ground heaved, like a giant snake had burrowed underneath it, and it was headed right for me, tossing anyone in its path, ally or foe, out of the way.

I held my ground, knowing I couldn't outrun it. And just when it was a blink away from reaching me, I gave a mighty roar and plunged my sword into the ground. Her attack smashed into my sword with such force I wondered if my teeth had rattled loose in my head. But my blade held—I held—and it was enough to block her attack.

I tore my blade from the ground—a strength, unlike anything I had ever known, pumped through my veins.

"How dare you," she seethed, her voice so twisted and monstrous, it made my blood run cold. She screamed in anger, striding towards me as she raised bits of ground behind her—shaping them into arrows.

Two could play that game.

I glanced to my left, conjuring a handful of daggers to float behind me.

At the same moment, we released them.

Earthen arrows collided into azure daggers—obliterating each other upon impact.

But one of mine slipped past her defenses, embedding itself in her torso. She stumbled backwards, sputtering, but I did not see her fall because—

"Sage!" Harper cried out to my left, weakly stumbling towards me.

"Harper." I raced to her side, and I slung her arm over my shoulder. "Where are the others?"

"Those who could not fight fled further east—Lyra, Ezra, and Graiyson included. They should be safe for now. But Ryker—" She winced, her hand, covered in fresh blood, clutched desperately at her side.

"What about Ryker?" I asked, my hand brushing over hers, a silent plea to let me look.

Gasping for breath, she answered, "He should be here fighting, somewhere, but I haven't seen him in a while." She grimaced as she removed her hand.

I steeled my features. The wound in Harper's side . . .

"It's bad, isn't it?" she asked.

It was. It was hard to decipher the torn leather of her armor from her shredded skin, but I could easily make out the jagged bone beneath and the way it unnaturally jutted out. Whatever had hit her had not just taken a fist-sized chunk of flesh out of her side, it had broken her ribs.

"It is. But you are strong, and you are going to make it

through this." I took her hand and placed it back onto the wound. How Harper had managed to fight with such an injury—it was a testament to her incredible strength. Her incredible will.

I meant what I'd said—Harper was going to live, but that was contingent on me getting her out of here. There was a narrow path that led to the outer rim of the battlegrounds—if I could make it there.

No. I *would* make it there.

"We need to move," I told her.

She nodded wearily.

We waded through a sea of dead and injured soldiers, Harper's weight increasing on me with each passing moment.

Again, my heartbeat thrummed in my ears—ticking down the seconds I had.

Each time a soldier attacked, we worked together to defend—either her hand shooting out a burst of flame or mine throwing a glass-like water dagger. And although that worked for a short while, her reaction time was becoming slower, her eyelids fighting a battle of their own.

"Come on, Harper." I forged steel in my voice, hoping it would do the same for her. "We're going to make it. Think of Lyra. Ryker. Graiyson. Ezra." I repeated that same message to her over and over, hoping she would latch on to it.

And for a time, she did.

But then I felt her arm slip from my neck, and her legs gave out. I caught her, but just barely. Her torso slumped against mine. I shifted her weight, putting more of it on my good arm. Gently, I tapped her face, trying to rouse her as I said her name.

But Harper wouldn't wake.

I tried again and again, but nothing.

My heart ticked loudly in my ears as my shaking hand moved to her neck. I checked for a pulse. At first, I couldn't find it. But after another attempt, I did. I exhaled a small breath of relief. "You are not going to die here," I promised her, tears brimming. "I'm going to get you help."

Harper needed her twin. He knew these lands better than I did, and he would know where to find a healer to help her. But I needed to find him first. My head whipped around, searching for him, but there were too many soldiers.

Call for him, said an ethereal voice inside of me.

And so, I did.

I tilted my head to the sky and roared, "Ryker!" My voice was like an ax, severing the cries of war. It was so loud, it was like the mighty face of a mountain sliding off and smashing upon the ground. I did it again, channeling that same divine strength.

And again. And again. Until I was certain that my mind was playing tricks on me, because in the distance, I heard—

"Sage!"

My heart plucked a heavy chord—*Ryker*.

I twirled in the direction I heard his voice, doing my best to support Harper's weight, her body collapsed into mine.

I yelled for him once more.

His answer came back quicker this time. Quickly, I shouted back.

And then I saw him—he was running straight for us, his fire bow in hand as he took down anyone who dared step on the path between us.

"Harper!" Ryker cried out, his bow and arrow wicking out as he took her from me. He picked his twin up, her head falling against his chest. His eyes darted to her injury, growing wide.

"It's bad, Ryker," I told him, my voice cracking with emotion. "You need to get her to a healer as fast as you can."

Before he could respond, Ryker swirled around me, supporting Harper with one arm as he used his free hand to blast an approaching soldier with his white flame. The soldier screamed, but just before he went down, he sent a burst of flaming throwing stars straight for us. I conjured a dome-like shield of frozen water and the throwing stars lodged into the side. Their flames fizzled out. I removed the shield and it turned into a pool of water at our feet. The throwing stars fell to the ground and then they disappeared, like ash on the wind.

Ryker turned to me. "Are you not coming with us then?"

I shook my head. "I need to stay here and fight."

Ryker's features twisted for a moment, before he leveled my gaze. "I understand, and I won't cheapen your noble intentions by demanding you come with us. But the one thing I do demand is that you fight until you can no longer fight, and then you get out of here in one piece."

I nodded. "I will." I touched Harper's hand, my eyes going to Ryker's. "Take care of her."

"I will," he promised, and then he left, disappearing into the sea of blood and weapons and soldiers. The makings of war.

Time granted me no mercy as a Demi God set his sights on me. He was taller than most and had a nasty gash on his left cheek. The skin dangled grotesquely. He raised his hand, white-knuckled fingers clenching at air, and heaved from the war-torn soil a flaming beast that I had no name for. It was all snapping, vicious teeth, and blazing fur. It had the body of a bear, but the head of a wolf—forged from both earth and fire.

And it was bloody huge.

It charged straight for me, its flaming hide rippling like long grass being swayed by the wind. Although the beast was big, its size affected its speed.

I would use that to my advantage.

I rolled my wrist, my empty palm filling with the handle of my water blade, the densely packed molecules rendering it as strong as a diamond.

Holding my ground, like a matador with a bull charging for them, I waited until the last moment. Just when the beast's dagger-like teeth were a snap away, I dodged to the side, running my blade along its side as it ran by—its heat singeing the hairs on my arm.

The beast roared in pain, but not defeat.

Snarling and rabid, it turned and looked to me, its nostrils flaring. It pawed at the ground and then it charged again.

Something whirred to my left. I turned, swung my blade, and deflected the arrow that was on course for my head—not a moment too soon and not a moment too late. The conjurer of the fire beast grinned at me, a bow in his hands.

It was the last thing I saw before the beast hurtled into me, scooping me up with its forehead and throwing me into the air. Wind knocked out of me, clothes on fire, I flailed as I came back down, its massive mouth waiting for me—waiting to snap me in two. I tucked my arms in, grasped the handle of my blade with both hands, and plunged it straight into its waiting mouth, taking it to the ground with me.

With the earthen fire beast defeated, I blasted my burning clothes with water, dousing the flames. My skin groaned in discomfort, but I'd caught it quick enough it had just barely started to burn. I might suffer a few blisters, but that—

Another arrow whizzed by.

My spine arched, the muscles in my legs firing as I bent backwards. The arrow sailed over my chest, missing me by nary an inch. I leapt upright, conjured another sword, and turned to the Demi God.

He sneered, his face so much like Aurelius's, I paused. He raised his bow, nocking another arrow. But he didn't get the chance to fire it because a Cursed, one I recognized from the Well, swung a battle ax made of earth and stone at him. The razor-sharp blade bit into the Demi God's side.

I didn't see what happened next because a wave of Cursed and Demi Gods descended upon us. They were all running in the same direction . . .

But *what* were they running *from*?

I swirled to my right and fought the powerful tide of warriors threatening to sweep me away as I tried to see what was coming for us. Tried to see what had sent both enemy and ally scattering like a spooked herd of antelope . . .

My eyes widened.

Golden wings ate up the horizon, their vast expanse etched with flame.

Aurelius.

And he was coming straight for me.

CHAPTER 67

Von

For weeks, I had lain on this cement slab like a useless meatsuit as my healers conducted their tests. And not once had I felt a thing.

But now . . . I could feel.

I could feel the ice-cold metal as it pressed against my skin. At the same time, Folkoln's hand wrapped around my wrist.

"This might hurt," he acknowledged, his tone flat.

Then the blade slit into my forearm. Skin and sinew snapped as the blade severed off a chunk of flesh about the size of my clenched fist.

"Fuck sakes!" I roared as I jerked upright, my eyelids flaring open.

Folkoln's ugly mug was the first thing to greet me. The Blade of Moram, in his hand, was the next. It had blood on it. Not mine.

"Good morning, sleeping beauty," he said sarcastically, smirking to himself. "How nice for you to join us again in the land of the dead."

I pushed him away. "You are the last thing any soul should see upon first waking."

"You really shouldn't talk," Folkoln chuckled as he tossed something on my lap. "You are free from your deal, brother."

I glanced down, finding two slabs of severed, tattooed skin. One was bloody and the other was not. The skin color was different, but they both had one linking factor—both were inked with a skull wearing the Crown of Thorns. The one belonged to me, which meant that the other one was from the royal ass licker.

I waved my hand over top the slabs of flesh and they disappeared, swallowed up by shadows and erased from existence.

My deal with Arkyn was done.

I looked at my forearm, peering at the bloodless wound. Threads of skin wove overtop of one another, slowly stitching themselves back together. I flexed my hand and rotated my arm. Creator above, it felt good to be able to move again.

"How did you find the Blade of Moram?" I asked, glancing to the injury in my stomach made from Sage's blade. It was starting to heal, but at a much slower rate.

When Folkoln didn't answer right away, I looked at him. "What is it?" I demanded.

"Saphira had it."

Adrenaline pumped into my veins. Saphira's hatred towards me was deeper than the Da'Nu. She would not have parted with the Blade of Moram easily. Unless she got something out of it.

"What did you trade her?"

"I didn't trade her anything." Folkoln's onyx eyes met mine. "Sage did."

It felt like a massive stone had been dropped into the well of my stomach, heavily striking the bottom.

"Fuck!" I yelled as I leapt off the table, my shadows slithering around me, nearly breaking off into their actual forms. "What did Sage trade her?" I grabbed his tunic, balled it into my fist.

He exhaled a breath. "Your feathers."

"And where would she get the idea to trade them?" I snarled at him. Although I already knew the answer.

A vein kicked in Folkoln's jaw. "I told her."

I bared my teeth at him as I snarled, "Then you have betrayed me."

Folkoln stood his ground. "I *did* what was necessary to save you."

I roared at him, the sound animalistic, as I shoved him away from me.

Folkoln started, "Brother—"

"Where is *my mate?*" I demanded, cutting him off. He could save his empty apology for another day. Right now, all that mattered was *her*.

He clenched his jaw, released it, and said, "She is in the Cursed Lands . . . fighting Aurelius's army."

At that moment, the Blade of Moram disappeared from Folkoln's hand.

"What did you do with the blade?" I asked, urgently.

Frantically.

Folkoln shook his head as he peered at his empty hand. "I didn't do anything with it."

Which meant . . . "It's gone to her."

Terror. Sheer, horrific terror—the kind in which I had only felt once before in my long life—seeped under my skin, lighting every nerve ending, every fiber aflame.

I needed to get to her.

CHAPTER 68

Sage

Aurelius landed with such force that the ground trembled beneath my feet, startling the stubbornest of birds from the trees in the distance—something hundreds of soldiers couldn't even manage.

"After all that I have done for you, and this is how you repay me?" Aurelius growled, his regal voice infiltrated with disgust.

"All that you have *done* for me?" I mocked. "You have done nothing but bring me and others pain, Aurelius. You do not deserve to be king of anything."

"I am the sun!" he roared at me, the sound as loud as a blacksnake whip splitting flesh. "I am a God. The King of Kings. How dare you insult me. You, the worthless daughter of the moon. Good *for nothing*."

The goddess in me roared to life.

Yes, he had been born of the sun, and it was his light that sustained life, from the plants to the trees to all living things. But I was born of the moon. It was *my* gravity that held the realms in place. *My* caress that kept the tides moving.

And for him to rise, I had to bow.

Not anymore.

I was done bowing.

I raised my hand to the azure sky, conjuring a sword, but instead of water and ice, obsidian and glass answered—

The Blade of Moram.

"So this is how it will be then," Aurelius snarled as he tossed his hands to the sides, flame swords appearing in each one. One had a curved blade and the other one was straight. If he were to put the pommels side by side, they would form a sun. He dragged the tips on the ground as he began to walk towards me. His massive, golden wings spread out behind him, dominating the horizon.

"You made it so," I hissed as I stepped forward, crossing my feet, one over the other, swinging the blade—testing it. The weight. The length. It was a perfect combination—perfect for me. As if it was made for me.

Aurelius picked up his speed and I charged.

Our swords collided in a blur of black and red, arcing off one another in a clash of sparks.

I swung again, my blade clipping his, but gaining no ground.

I tried again, looking for any weakness in his swordsmanship, just as Ezra had taught me. But time after time, I found none. He moved with such precision and ease. His skill far surpassed my own. And I knew it.

My blade became locked between his crossed ones, placed in the shape of an "*X*."

"Impressive," Aurelius said just before he sent his boot into my abdomen, kicking me back with his immortal strength.

I flew backwards, my body sliding along the unforgiving ground. I grunted as I came to a rolling, skittering stop, but the potent adrenaline thrumming in my veins made me blind to the pain my body surely felt.

"But not impressive enough," he stated.

Quickly, I jerked up.

Aurelius summoned his flame and sent it straight for me.

I shot to my feet, conjuring my Water Curse, but this time, my fire answered instead.

Luna answered instead.

And she exploded—*I* exploded.

My mighty shout rang out and my power shuddered, not out of fear or weakness, but because of the hunger it felt. The hunger to destroy *him*—the male who had taken so much from me, from everyone.

My flame, colored in the lilac-blue glow of the moon, shot out in front of me, smashing into his flame of orange and red. Our powers roared, two mighty dragons—one made of the sun, and the other of the moon—battling for dominance, thrashing and snarling and snapping at one another.

The heat produced from our flames chewed into the war-torn grounds, melting it, as if it were made of ice, not dirt and stone.

My friends' smiling faces flickered in my mind—Harper, Ryker, Lyra, Graiyson . . .

I could not lose this battle, which meant I needed to do more. Fight harder.

Grunting, I raised my foot as I tried to take a step forward. It felt as though someone had their hand pressed against my shin, trying to push it back.

I roared as I focused, bottling every bit of energy and strength I could and pouring it into that one task. And it was enough. Enough to push Aurelius's flame one step back.

I took another. And another. Until I was running—my flame obliterating his.

But when I was an arm's reach away from him, I was met with his laughter. "You truly think you have an advantage over me?"

My jaw slackened—me thinking I was gaining ground? That I was beating him? It had *all* been a ploy—I wasn't winning, but he let me think I was.

He disappeared, my flame shooting past, blasting into the distance. I snatched my power back before it could hurt anyone or anything.

A wall of steel pressed into my back. An arm banded around my torso while a hand snaked around my throat—crushing my windpipe. Aurelius's mighty wings slapped once, and my feet lifted from the ground as he flew us into the sky.

"I will enjoy snapping your neck this time, and while your pitiful body tries to recover, I'll send every mortal you have ever loved to the Spirit Realm," he promised.

No! I wouldn't let that happen. I wouldn't let him take any more lives. But what could I do? I'd thought that I could fight him, but I realized now that I had been a fool. His powers were well beyond my own. So what could I—

Just then, light reflected on the sharp edge of the obsidian blade. That was where I found my answer.

Von had once told me that the Blade of Moram would bring his salvation, but if it fell into the wrong hands, it could mean my demise. And although it wasn't my weakness, in the same sense that the Crown of Thorns was, it was a weakness nonetheless because of who I was linked to . . .

Sage, no! Do not do this. Von's voice carved its way into my mind, wild and frantic. And . . . afraid. So very, very afraid.

Von? I asked, feeling *his* shadows reaching for me. As if they, too, were trying to get to me.

Yes, it's me. Just hold on. I'm coming for you, he pleaded. And it was like a knife had burrowed its way into my soul. And by the sounds of it, his as well.

But Aurelius's hand tightened around my neck. He lowered his head, and he breathed into my ear, "Sweet dreams, *wife.*"

There isn't enough time, I whispered through our bond, tears clouding my vision.

Because I knew what I needed to do, the sacrifice that I needed to make so that all of this would end here. Today. No more lives would be lost because of one man's hate. No more. No more pain. And no more suffering. And no more families destroyed.

Sage, please, don't do it.

I'm sorry, Von.

His desperate roar was the last thing I heard before I turned the Blade of Moram, now in dagger form, and plunged it into my heart—into *our* heart. The blade lengthened back into a sword and shot into Aurelius's body, tearing through him.

"You stupid, little bi—" he choked, his ichor spraying against the back of my head.

At the same time, blood bubbled on my lips—warm and thick and . . . *how strange*. It did not taste of copper anymore. It tasted as sweet as honey.

Wincing, I dabbed my mouth with the back of my shaky hand. Lowering it, I inspected the smear of thick liquid.

But instead of crimson mortal blood, I found silver.

The ichor of the gods.

Weakly, I laughed. Aurelius had been wrong. I did not bleed gold after all.

His hand slipped from my throat, the other one falling from my waist. The sword that pinned us together was now the only thing that supported my weight, keeping me locked to him and suspended in the air. I cried out at the horrific pain—it's claws like razor blades splicing apart my body. Feebly, his wings flapped, jerking us up and down in the air as he fought to keep from falling. All the while, I fought to remain conscious, the pain I felt was insurmountable.

Crack. Crack. Crack.

It sounded like someone stepping on too thin ice, moments from falling in. And the sound was coming from within us. Weakly, I looked down at the obsidian handle— hairline cracks were forming throughout it. The Blade of Moram was *shattering*. Shattering into hundreds of tiny pieces. They shot off like cannon fire—obliterating our organs, piercing through our flesh, breaking our bones.

But the greatest blessing of all?

It *freed* us from each other.

I fell, the ground swirling towards me—coming faster and faster.

But I never struck the ground because *Death* caught me.

You came for me, I whispered weakly through our bond.

I will always come for you, he sobbed, pulling me into him.

Cool droplets of rain struck my face.

Please, do not leave me again, Little Goddess.

It was a plea.

A guttural one. A desperate one. A familiar one.

Yes, that was right. I had heard it before. A long, long, time ago. But when or where was lost to me because my body shuddered once and then . . .

Nothing.

CHAPTER 69

Von

She was shattered in so many places and stained with so much ichor that my trembling hands did not know where to touch and my blurry eyes did not know where to look. And no matter how hard I tried to heal her, her body would not respond to mine.

Her deflated lungs ceased, her veins shattered, her bones broken.

Don't leave me! I roared through our bond.

But she did not respond.

I clutched her to me, weeping into her broken body, my wings curling protectively around her. I should have done more to protect her from him—from *this*.

I should have done more . . .

And I never should have listened to Ezra. I should have stolen her from this place, from this realm, and taken her to mine to keep her safe, locked away from anything that could harm her, just as my instincts had been screaming at me to do.

Let her live, Ezra had told me when Sage was reincarnated. *Don't tell her what she is. Just let her memories return on their own. She wanted to live like a mortal in her past life, now she can finally do that. Do not rob her of it. If you truly love your mate, you will sacrifice your happiness for hers and you will let her live.*

And so, for Sage, that's what I did.

It had destroyed me to be away from her, but I'd let her live out the life she had once wished for, and *this* was the result. But I refused to let this be the end.

"You will not take her from me!" I roared at the sky—at the Creator, at anyone who would listen.

There was *one* thing I could do to help her.

I gathered her in my arms and stole her away into my shadows, taking her to those who had made that fucking blade.

I took her to Mount Kilangor—to the home of the Three Spinners.

I thundered into the throne room with Sage's lifeless body in my arms. The Goddess of Fate sat at her spinning wheel, forging threads of green. The Goddess of Destiny stood behind her sister, inspecting the freshly spun thread.

"Weave her another fate!" I demanded of them.

Their heads jerked in my direction, assessing Sage.

Fate spoke first. "I do not need to read her spool to see that her story is finished."

My voice turned pleading. "Please. I will give you anything."

And then I did something I had never done before . . .

I dropped to my knees.

Looking at Sage, I said, "I will relinquish my throne. My title. My powers. Whatever you want. I will pay whatever cost in exchange for her life." I tore my unwilling gaze away from Sage, looking to the Spinners in search of an answer.

"None of that interests us," Fate said, canting her head to the side.

"We have everything we need." Destiny gestured to the room around us.

"There must be something. Name your price and I will pay it. I refuse to go another span of centuries without her."

They exchanged looks with one another, and it told me all that I needed to know.

"She will not reincarnate again," I sputtered, choking on my bitter words.

"The heart, which was necessary in her creation, has been destroyed, so no, she will not reincarnate again," Destiny replied, her hand waving. A spool of white emerged from the wall of shelves they kept them on. She grasped it and began to unwind it—going to the very end of it, reading. A confirming nod. "She has reached the end of her journey in these realms."

No. That couldn't be.

"Her heart was tethered to her body, not her soul," I growled desperately.

"It does not matter. It was still a part of her," Destiny replied. She snapped her fingers and Sage's spool disappeared.

"What if I gave her my own?" I snarled at them, my temper flaring.

"That will not work," they both said.

"And why not?" I growled.

Fate answered, "Because, God of Death, you do not possess a heart to give. The reason you do not bleed is because the Creator did not give you a heart upon your creation. " She looked at Sage. "They waited until she was made. *She* is your heart. That is why you bleed for her. And the reason she cannot heal herself, but you can, is because she is not whole either. You see, her heart was forged as you."

It was a truth I had felt for centuries now. Whenever I looked at her. Whenever I heard her laughter. She was my heart, my mate, the other half of my soul. I was willing to give anything for her. Sacrifice anything for her.

Do anything for her.

I rose from the ground, cradling her shattered body against my chest. "Weave her another fate."

"We told you, we cannot," Destiny snipped.

"I don't think you understand—I was not asking. I am telling you. You will weave her another fate, because if you don't, if Sage does not live . . . then no one else will," I snarled as I opened the cage, unleashing the beast within.

A horrific sound shredded through my throat—the sound more monster than man as *he* took the helm. My bones hissed and popped as they grew, my body stretching to mountainous proportions. Piercing horns emerged from my head, lengthening back and tipping up at the ends. The rounded tops of my ears burst into points, shooting out like two sharp blades. Although I could not physically see myself, I could feel the ink pouring into my vision—tingeing my orbs completely black. My wings flared out behind me, my adrenaline coursing through them—through my bulging veins.

"Nockrythiam," Destiny cried out.

I peered down at her. She looked no bigger than a cat.

"The Ender of Realms!" Fate screamed, taking a protective step back.

I glanced at my bonded, her lifeless body stretched across my tattooed forearm. Seeing her like that, it only reconfirmed what I needed to do—

My power, amplified beyond my own understanding, cleaved through their ancient wards like a mighty ax, releasing my monstrous shadows. They shot towards the Wall of Weavings, wrapping around the shelves.

"God of Death, you mustn't—"

But my roar cut Destiny off as I heaved with everything I had, prying the shelves free from the wall—hosting the spools of all the living and all the dead—and held it over the pit of boiling-hot, ravenous lava.

For her, I would bring everything to an end.

Because I was not a hero. I was the villain.

The Spinners screamed, caving in on each other, begging me not to, but their pleas fell on deaf ears, just as mine had fallen on theirs.

A cane struck the ground, the sound echoing around the mountain's walls.

"Silence, sisters! The God of Death has come to bargain with us for the life of his mate. He has made his side of the deal very clear. One life in exchange for all the living. Perhaps . . . we ought to listen," rang out a mighty, familiar voice.

The voice of the Goddess of Free Will—

Ezra.

ACKNOWLEDGEMENTS

I'll be honest, I don't even know where to begin with this one. At the time of writing this, I've been a published author for ten months, but over those months I have met so many incredible people, and to narrow down who to thank, well, it just feels impossible, but I'm going to try my best! I cannot express enough gratitude and love to:

To my beta readers, thank you so much for reading *Between Sun and Moon* in all of its unedited glory. You all made me feel so much better about my rough little story and helped to shape it for the better. Without you, BSAM wouldn't be what it is today.

To my ARC readers, I'm so thankful for *all of you*! Thank you for applying, for supporting and reading *Between Sun and Moon*. Thank you for the reviews—to a small fry like me, you have made a world of difference.

To my street team, I am *so* grateful for you amazing

souls. You guys have quickly become the highlight of my day. You bring so much energy to the team, and so much support my way, I honestly don't know how I'll ever be able to thank you all enough. I adore you all. <3

To my editor, Jessica McKelden, you have become one of the most vital parts of my team and it has been so wonderful getting the chance to work with you again. You bring so much experience, patience, and knowledge with you. Thank you, thank you, thank you!

To my proofreaders, Whitney at New Ink Editing and Vanessa Barbas at Veerie Edits. Whitney, we connected over our love of books, and look where that love has brought us— to here! Your wisdom and editing skills truly made BSAM shine. Thank you for making me look "smart" with this one. Vanessa, my darling, it has been such a dream come true getting to work with you on this project. Thank you for being a part of my editing team and making sure my book baby was ready to be shown to the world! I will never be able to thank you enough for *all of the things* you do for me and this series.

To my formatter, Amy Kessler at Imagine Ink Designs, it has been so wonderful to work with you on this series. Without you, BSAM wouldn't look nearly as pretty as it does. Thank you for being part of my team.

To my cover designer, Keylin Rivers at Fantasy Cover Design, you worked your butt off to make this cover what it is. I don't even know how many hours you poured into it, but I am eternally grateful you did. I didn't think we'd be able to top BLAD's cover, but I think we just might have pulled it off.

To my bestie, my soul twin, Helyn, the woman whose

strength I am in awe of. Sage, too. I know the past year was not an easy one for you, and yet, you continued forward. If there is one thing I do know it is that dreams come true. I'm living proof of that. Yours will too. <3

To my mama and papa, who were tasked with raising an independent, creative, wild, Gemini, thank you for not stifling my growth or forcing me into a box that I did not belong in. Thank you for encouraging me to think for myself and be who I needed to be. Thank you for cheering me on as I climb this huge mountain, my goal well above the clouds. Thank you, mom and dad. Your support means everything. <3

To my mother-in-law, Kathy, thank you for being my unofficial official *book dealer* and pushing my books to all your friends. Haha! And thank you for raising my wonderful husband, for teaching him how to be a good man. Vanessa, Chelsey, and Brooke, I know you played a role as well. Thank you all.

To my brothers, Josh and Justin, thank you for raising me as your *third brother*. If you didn't instill a whole lot of tomboy in me, I doubt Von would be half the man he is. Michelle and Kristen, thank you for teaching me about the power of femininity and getting me back in touch with that side of myself. Thank you all for raising me as your little sister/brother, for your endless support, and love.

To my family and friends, bits and pieces of you have gone into the creation of this story, and even into some of the characters. This story wouldn't be what it is without each and every one of you.

A special thank you to Alisa Sonnenberg, Sara Flanagan,

Vanessa Rasanen, Angela Van Liempt, Kyleigh Cuico, Ris Schindler, Nikki Grey, Julie Doliszny, Merrit Townsend, Candice van Staveren, Shayla Smith, Siara Saylor, Lauren Clark, Megan Yerg, and *so many others* that I know I'll remember after writing this and will wish I had included. You all have supported me in one way or another and I cannot thank you enough. <3

To my husband, my soulmate, my love, Tanner. Thank you for your constant support and eternal patience. You constantly show me what it is to be loved by a good man, and I could not imagine doing this thing with anyone but you. Through and through, you are my *bonded*. And I'm so thankful for you and this beautiful life we are building together.

To my readers, my TikTok and Instagram family, without you this dream of mine couldn't live on. Your passion for this series is what gets me through the tough times of being an author.

Thank you *all* for giving me the opportunity to tell Sage and Von's story.

<3 Jaclyn

About the Author

Jaclyn Kot is a prairie girl, an avid reader, occasional Netflix binger and a total foodie. She is a proud mama of many chickens, two fabulous kitties and a good doggo. She lives on a farm in Saskatchewan, Canada with her husband.

She writes high fantasy fiction and likes her fantasy served with plot twists, a side of spice and morally grey males with a palate for strong-willed females.

It is her hope that readers will fall in love with Sage and Von's story just as much as she has.

Looking for the latest information on the Between Life and Death Series or wanting to connect with Jaclyn? You can here:

www.instagram.com/jaclyn.kot/

www.tiktok.com/@jaclyn.kot

www.jaclynkotbooks.com

Printed in Great Britain
by Amazon